WHO KILLED GOLDIE WITH HIS SOLID GOLD OSCAR?

If Toby Challis didn't find out, he'd spend the rest of his life behind bars.

WAS IT . . .

Solomon Roth—who devoted his life to keeping his movie studio spotless in a dirty world?

Aaron Roth—Sol's prodigal son, Goldie's father, whom she hated for reasons still unclear?

Jack Donovan—the publisher who knew enough to blackmail the wrong people but not enough to know when to stop?

Morgan Dyer—the beautiful woman who was Toby's only ally and who still hadn't forgotten how the Hollywood system destroyed her father?

Vito Laggiardi—the mobster who wanted a piece of a Hollywood studio—and would stop at nothing to get it?

They all had something to hide or gain by seeing Goldie dead—and having Toby Challis take the rap.

HOLLYWOOD GOTHIC

By

THOMAS GIFFORD

BALLANTINE BOOKS • NEW YORK

Library of Congress Catalog Card Number: 79-15618

ISBN 0-345-29009-7

This edition published by arrangement with
G. P. Putnam's Sons

Manufactured in the United States of America

First Ballantine Books Edition: July 1980

for Camille

I am not I;
he is not he;
they are not they.

It ain't a business. It's a racket . . .
                    —Harry Cohn

[1]

TOBY CHALLIS lit a cigarette and tried to remember his lines. He'd been trying to remember his lines ever since that night in Malibu, and it was a hell of a job. But now was definitely the moment for a cigarette, eyes squinting against the smoke, jaw firm in a grim, heroic, existential smile. . . . It was a little cheap as actors' tricks went, but that was the point. Cheap and easy, and it almost always worked. Not always: he was no actor and he felt like a hybrid, a cloddish miscalculation, half Humphrey Bogart and half Danny Kaye as Walter Mitty. He tried to think of a tough little joke for the guards, something to dribble philosophically from the corner of the grim little smile, but that was where he ran into trouble. His script needed a damn good polish, maybe even a rewrite. Sure, a rewrite . . . beaucoup bucks, but worth it, a damned good rewrite by the best in the business. But he was the best in the business, Toby Challis was money in the bank, and he couldn't think of anything funny to say to the guard. Shit, the main guy always had a wisecrack for the cop-at-the-end . . .

He looked around at the dark, empty hangar: oil-spotted concrete floor, the smell of small planes, jet fuel, and lubricant and grease, the peculiar nastiness laid across the scene by the pervasive cold, dampness. The lights of the main terminal glowed far across the runways. The rain diffused the luminescence, gave the structure the look of a UFO settling down to swallow them all up and take them to a better place where the music was playing and the lights were bright and gay . . . . a place where Mickey and Judy had come up the pathway past the great oak tree and found the barn of their dreams . . . *What a place for a show! We can do it, I know we can. . . .*

He shook his head, forced the unreality away. It was

1

happening more frequently in recent days. He would be sitting in his cell, reading a novel or a magazine, and somehow he would find himself fitted neatly into a movie, never one that he'd written, but always someone else's. One day he drifted off into *Mr. Lucky* and he'd have sworn it was all solid reality: the gambling boat, the fog on the pier, and Cary Grant spotting Laraine Day. . . . Another time, the mountain village in *Out of the Past* had taken the place of his cell, and he'd walked with young Bob Mitchum from the filling station to the café with the nosy waitress, and sat down, ordered pie and coffee. . . . While these interludes were wonderfully enjoyable, they worried him. He had enough sense left to know that madness lay that way, good-bye and into the bin, Toby old fruit. Yet, the years ahead, destined to be passed in a cell with a lidless toilet and a bed hinged to the goddamn wall, those years were psychically unacceptable. He wondered when he'd start screaming and not be able to stop.

The rain had slackened somewhat from the morning's feverish downpour, hung now like a fragile Japanese screen rippling in the breezes. The sky was a dirty, smudged gray and the big jets whined and howled like a riot at the zoo. The newspapers said the two-year drought was over, in its place a series of God's little jokes, watery disasters, village swept away, graveyards excavated, vast meandering homes dumped down canyon walls and disappearing beneath thousands of tons of mud and shale. Malibu was hammered day and night by the storms off the Pacific . . . that made him remember the beach house where he had once worked so well, gotten drunk far too often on fine Laphraoig, and discovered just what sort of woman Goldie was. . . . And he inevitably remembered her lying there, still warm, her blond hair clotted with blood and matter, and his Oscar with its special marble base on the floor not far away. The marble was sticky. There were a few strands of long blond hair glued to the stickiness, and he recognized the scene, when it came sweeping toward him like a runaway meat wagon, recognized it without hesitation because he had been there before, a hundred times. At the movies.

"Won't be long now." One of the guards stood at his

shoulder, a man of fifty or so who was friendly and matter-of-fact about Challis' predicament. His name was Daniels and he had a brother-in-law who lived in Newport Beach and was a cutter at Twentieth, nominated for an Oscar once. He enjoyed chatting about the show business with Challis, ignored the fact that Goldie's head had been caved in with an Oscar. "Lousy weather, either you got your drought and your Santa Anas, or you got your flood." He lit a cigarette and frowned at the rain. "But we've got a clearance to go." He blew smoke into the wind and coughed. "I want you to know, if it was up to me you wouldn't have to wear the bracelets. Stupid. Where the hell they think you're gonna go? Wouldn't get far with that famous face—trial made you a star, y'know." Challis smiled, nodded, could think of nothing to say. What was there to say? He was afraid, quite desperately afraid. Prison society: he'd seen enough television shows devoted to the inhumanity of life inside, the brutality, the bestiality. And now Toby Challis, a screenwriter with impressive connections and an Oscar, convicted of beating his wife's brains into the rug, was sentenced to life imprisonment, open and shut. Toby Challis, forty-two-year-old white American male, sheltered until recently from life's harsher side, was going to find out what was true about life on the inside and what was worse than the stuff you heard.

The pilot was chatting with the other guard and the copilot. Unexpectedly he broke into a hearty, rumbling laugh and shook his head. The guard and the copilot nodded appreciatively. For an instant the pilot looked across the width of the hangar's sliding door, caught Challis' eye, looked away, his face suddenly sober.

"Being inside—you'll get used to it," Daniels said. "Fifteen years, you'll be out, a new man. . . . They got lots of books inside, movies, all that stuff. . . ." He sucked at the cigarette. Challis wondered how many times he'd said the same thing to other poor unfortunates, ax murderers, slashers, stranglers, trash-bag killers . . . the whole cast.

"I'll be nearly sixty," Challis said. "Not so new . . . a *different* man, though, I'll buy that."

Daniels nodded philosophically. "Well, if you don't mind my saying so, I hope it was worth it to you. There's

3

always the damned bill to pay at the end. My father, bless his soul, used to tell me about the free lunches he'd get at the saloon . . . how he used to lament that free lunch, no free lunch anymore, he'd say. Always got the tab waiting for you."

Challis shrugged. What was there to say?

"It's not quite the middle age I'd seen for myself," he said at last.

Daniels flipped his cigarette butt into a puddle and ground it out beneath a heavy heel. He began whistling tunelessly, looked at his watch, clasped his hands behind his back. Challis leaned against the doorway—the huge sliding doors—and stared out at the rain.

There was, in fact, a middle age he'd seen for himself. Not a middle age exactly, but a sort of time he'd thought of as an Indefinite Future, a time when he'd gotten through the clutter of problems and difficulties which always seemed to be littering the path, everyone's paths. There was always a piece of work to be gotten past: a screenplay which inevitably went wrong and required a fifth version, a sixth, to meet the approval of a banker or an executive's wife or girlfriend . . . or even an offer to do a piece of junk for money he couldn't quite refuse, or a trip to Australia or Romania or some other place he knew he'd never visit on his own. There was always something. There was Goldie and how she was going to be resolved: how the problems she created would finally have to be sorted out. But up ahead, somewhere, was that Indefinite Future he wanted, intended to have.

It had always appeared to him the same way. A man wearing an immaculate white suit, a pale blue shirt, a white tie with a touch of cream in it, stood above a beach, leaning on a stone wall. The breakers frothed against the pale, smooth sand, and sunshine exploded like a rain of diamonds on the shifting surfaces of the water. Tanning bodies lay motionless on beach towels, and the soft wind kept the man dry, though the day was hot. He wore dark glasses. He leaned against the wall, watching the people on the beach, who never moved a muscle; then he walked away through the crowds surging along the pavement by the wall. The only sound in this faintly surreal vision of his own private promised land

4

came from the furling surf, like the little white box that reproduced the swishing sound and which he plugged in and kept by his bed when he ventured away from Malibu. That, and from somewhere came the sound of a Django Reinhardt-kind of guitar and a song at once familiar yet not quite identifiable. When he thought about it, which was often enough to keep the scene fresh in his mind, he assumed that he was the man in the white suit who seemed to enjoy his surroundings but was somehow untouched by them: a calm, serene, uninvolved observer who was there, but wasn't there, all at the same stray moment. He remembered an inscription he'd once seen on a sundial. *Horas non numero nisi serenas.* I count only the hours that are serene.

Now, of course, the future looked quite different, and in a way it was all Goldie's fault. Simple-mindedly, worn down by the trial and the blur of what had happened since he'd found himself staring down at her remains, he wondered how it could all have turned out the way it did. It was so remarkably unfair, and it made such a mess of the pretty, ambiguous, enigmatic picture in his head. The man on the quai in his white suit. . . .

When the small plane was ready, they wheeled it around in front of the hangar door, where it sat impudently crouched forward on the fragile, spindly wheel assembly protruding from its nose. Rain beaded on the silver fuselage, dripped off the back edge of the insubstantial-looking wings. A flying cell. No escape. Challis longed to slap his arms and get the blood circulating, but they were pinned in front of him by the handcuffs: he felt the scream of frustration building inside him and swallowed hard against it, pushing it back down his gullet toward the unpleasantness in his stomach. He'd have given his Mercedes for a drink.

"This is it, Mr. Challis." A hand rested on his shoulder, gave him a gentle shove, and off he went across the rain-spattered tarmac like a small boy's boat on a park pond. "Steps are slippery, Mr. Challis. Watch your head there. . . ." He climbed into the tight little cabin and settled in a rudimentary seat, where a guard buckled him snugly in. Daniels waved at him from the hangar doorway, flipped him the thumbs-up sign, and Challis

5

tried to produce a confident smile. He didn't want to worry Daniels. The cabin hatchway filled with the leathery-faced pilot, the copilot, one other prisoner who had been given an injection to calm him down, and the guard already on board slammed the hatch and locked it.

They began to taxi at once. The turboprops whirred loudly and everything shook and they were hurtling down the runway, climbing away, with the crosswinds buffeting them as they gained altitude. A hole in the weather, someone had called it back in the hangar. Some goddamn hole, he thought. Rain smeared greasily across the oval glass beside his head. He had never flown in a tiny plane before: for some reason he'd thought the state would provide a smarter aircraft for transport to what he always thought of as the Big House. . . .

He closed his eyes and fought a new surge of claustrophobia, tightening first between his knees, gritting his teeth. Better to drift off into the anesthesia of a movie playing inside his head—hey, you guys, what's playing at the Brain tonight?—better than this intolerable, choking frustration. Could he cope? He forced his eyes open. Play Bogart. . . . He would have to look at the world and stifle the urge to shriek and ignore the handcuffs and the doors always locking him in and pull up his socks and cope. . . . But he had never imagined in his life what it would be like to be deprived of his freedom, the opportunity to get the hell up and leave. As the tiny aircraft pushed on through the shifting, changing clouds, he realized he faced a future of nothing but restraint. He supposed he would eventually go mad. Or go dumb, vegetable like, which would be even worse, though if it came to that, he supposed there wouldn't be enough left of his brain to know it. . . .

From the beginning, the flight had seemed like such a bad idea, had been so tentative, so full of jumps and swerves and little ups and downs, that he'd grown accustomed to it. The cloud layer had gone from light to dark to light and back again. The winds had swiped at the plane often enough to have become an almost unremarkable aspect of the flight. And his mind had been operating in such a pit of depression that he was, in any case, too far gone to worry about the weather. He re-

6

membered a very amusing novel he'd read in which a character beset by a gastric upset had spent his infrequent moments of lucidity praying for death. Challis appreciated the man's state of mind.

Which was when things began to go wrong.

The clouds were suddenly empurpled, rich and dark like overripe blueberries, and the tiny aircraft seemed in his mind's eye to have become a shaft launched at the tightly stretched membrane covering the fruit. The darkness grew deeper in seconds, and then they had penetrated the membrane, been absorbed into the pulp of the dense clouds, and Challis realized that it was snow swirling from the cavernous blackness all around them. The gale increased at the same time and the metal of the fuselage and wings cried out, pulling at the rivets to get free and go with the wind. The other prisoner slumped sideways, dangling forward from the seat belt, his head blocking the narrow aisle. He hiccuped wetly and moaned as the bottom dropped away again and then slid steeply for several seconds: the descent ended abruptly as if ropes had yanked them to, and with a gagging sound the man emptied his stomach onto the floor. Challis looked away. The stench broke across him like a filthy wave, and he turned back to the window.

Without warning his forehead was slammed against the edging of the window as the plane skidded wildly to one side. Pain ricocheted down through his eyeballs. He was pitched hard against his seat belt, felt it dig into his belly. The guard in the seat across the aisle said, "Holy shit!" and with a cracking sound his seat belt gave way. He came flying sideways and slammed into Challis, pinning him against the curving bulkhead. Challis smelled the Tic Tacs on the man's breath, feebly tried to push him away, thanking God the handcuffs had been taken off once they were in the air. For a moment they struggled to right themselves; then a swift bank to the left sent the guard sprawling backward into the aisle, where the edge of a seat back caught him in the ribs and knocked him to all fours.

The copilot burst into the passenger compartment, his face white, his eyes swinging wildly from the doped prisoner dribbling a fresh geyser of vomit to the groggy guard who was swearing and grabbing at his back and trying to avoid the mess in the aisle. "Everybody all right back here?"

"Sure, man," Challis said, "this is great, just great, y'know?" He touched his forehead, saw blood on his fingers.

The guard looked up, pushing himself to his feet. "Hey, what the hell's going on?" There was no time for an answer as the plane dropped abruptly again and the copilot was flung back through the doorway and out of sight into the cockpit. The sound of static erupted from the radio beyond the doorway, then stopped entirely. The door slammed shut, flew back open, and the copilot reappeared. "Hang on," he yelled over the storm and the creaking metal and the groans of the sick and wounded. "Little trouble, nothing to worry about . . . wind's got us off course." He pointed at the sick prisoner. "He's okay, is he?" The pilot's voice came from the cockpit, loud, unintelligible, angry, and the pale copilot disappeared again. The guard lurched forward, tugging at the deadweight of the doped man, trying to get him back to his seat. Challis strained to see beyond the blowing snow, but it was useless. How far had they dropped? It was impossible to guess. He leaned back, feeling nauseated. He tried to swallow, but he was too dry: his throat opened, closed, and he began to cough.

"Goddamn toy airplane," the guard growled, wedging himself back into the seat. "Can you believe it? They never should of let us off the ground in this thing . . . you all right? Your head?"

"Scared," Challis said.

"Bet your ass, scared—"

The plane plummeted again, more severe than the drops that had come before. Challis' breath left him; he looked out the window again and felt his eyes widen. They had fallen beneath the clouds and through the thick blowing snow which mixed with drifting bubbles of vapor hanging between the mountaintops, and he saw that they were flying in a valley with densely forested slopes on either side of them. His view wobbled as the winds whacked at the stubborn little plane. Off to the side he saw a blue-gray flatness of lake, murky behind the snowstorm. The thick fir trees seemed almost black, and he couldn't see the tops of the mountains: just the blackish menace of the cliff walls. The engines throbbed and the plane struggled upward, desperately trying to vault whatever lay ahead. They slid off sideways and turned slowly, back toward the lake and crosswise against the wind, which was trapped and capricious in the valley. The guard stared out the window, knuckles whitened against the back of the seat ahead of him. Challis was frightened, couldn't speak. A downdraft swept them at the lake, a great paw of wind swiping at them, and he closed his eyes again. When he opened them they seemed to be skimming across the water, fighting for altitude against the great hand pressing them down, pushing them into the lake. Whitecaps rose like a bed of sawblades, whirring.

Finally the pressure relaxed and they were pushed upward, flung ahead, speed increasing as they swung toward the hillside. Challis couldn't estimate air speed, but the tops of the fir trees were flickering darkly thirty feet below as they grabbed for enough height to keep them alive. It took forever. Where, where was the top of the mountain? At the next glance the treetops seemed closer, and then he heard a cry from the cockpit: "We ain't gonna make it, Charlie . . . *we ain't gonna make it.*"

The last thing he saw before turning himself into a huddled ball wedged as tightly as possible between the seats was the guard's gray face, turned toward him, mouth open in a soundless scream, eyes round like black pinpoints of terror.

The sound of the engines cut out.

The weight of the plane whisked them through the first few treetops, but in a matter of three or four seconds they began plowing into heavy branchwork and thicker trunks, and the wings flickered away like large silver birds and the fuselage tipped sideways, seemed to roll glidingly down the dense green boughs slowly, bouncing almost softly. Perhaps the feeling of gentleness was entirely in Challis' head: the evidence, which included the decapitation of the leathery-skinned pilot by the sheared glass of the windshield, the breaking of the copilot's neck, the fatal concussing of the guard, who bounced around the cabin's interior like a puppet whose master was suffering a conniption fit, and the

9

strangulation of the doped prisoner, who somehow slid down through his seat belt until it caught him under the chin and wrung his neck—the evidence gave no indication of gentleness.

When the rolling had stopped, Challis was cramped, upside down, and his own blood was running out of his nose. One leg had been bent unnaturally against the metal seat back, his trouser leg was torn, there was blood smeared across his kneecap, and the knuckles of both hands were scraped raw against metal which might otherwise have done even more damage to his head. Without really considering what had just happened, he used all his strength to lever himself out of the upside-down awkwardness. He saw the corpses of the guard and the other prisoner, smelled the flight fuel, which was undoubtedly leaking from ruptured lines, and reached out to steady himself. He missed whatever he had been reaching for and fell, lightheaded and in shock, forward onto what had been the ceiling of the cabin and was now the floor. Face to face with the strangled prisoner, whose tongue and eyeballs were ruptured and bleeding and protruding, he fainted.

[2]

GOLDIE ROTH had never really grown up, which was both good and bad. Good, because she remembered her childhood in remarkably acute detail, due in large part, Challis had always presumed, to the fact that she had never entirely left it. She remembered the parties at which her famous mother and powerful father had presided, with an eye and ear for literal recall which is common among the young. For instance, her grandfather, Solomon Roth, came more fully to life in her wicked little recollections than he ever quite seemed in real life; and she had a sure hand at literary caricature when it came to describing Solomon Roth's famous employees.

When she finally put together a novel—which was widely held to be a public exorcising of her own private demons—it dealt with her coming of age at "Bella Donna," the unfortunate name of the Bel Air mansion where they all lived and which was destroyed in a famous fire. It was not exactly a loving portrait of those years, and one rather good review was headlined, "Slow Poison by Tincture of Bella Donna." It sold very well on the West Coast and appeared fleetingly on *The New York Times*'s best-seller list. The paperback edition eventually brought in nearly a million dollars, and that was as far as her literary career went. But she was finally independent of the family—that is, her father, Aaron Roth—which was just as well, because her welcome in Bel Air, Holmby Hills, and the other prominent outposts of the film community, while never very warm, was effectively worn out. A lot of people were put out about what she had written, particularly those individuals making appearances in the novel's pages under funny names but always with the right initials. Those most irritated were sometimes heard to gloat that

11

Goldie never appeared at the Bel Air Country Club following the book's publication, a minor triumph, however, since she had never appeared there before the book's publication, either. But, still, she was a kind of outcast in her own country. She was no longer welcome at many private homes where she had once been a regular decoration, and for a time Seraglio, the new postfire mansion, was off-limits, as well. Solomon Roth had fought to rescind her banishment and, as always, had finally prevailed. But it had all been quite an ordeal, though vastly amusing to Goldie, who was in her mid-twenties and really didn't give a shit.

So maybe it wasn't good that she remembered everything. It depended on your point of view, which, Challis reasoned, made it just like everything else in life. From his point of view, at least when he first met her, it was good. Her unfettered life-style, her irreverence and wit —however childish and rude—at the expense of the show-business Establishment turned him on: he was introduced to her at Aaron and Kay's annual Fourth of July holocaust shortly before the storm accompanying publication broke. He had won his Oscar a couple of years before for a film Aaron Roth had personally produced. When he tore himself away from his typewriter on the Fourth of July, he was working on an adaptation of Kipling's *The Light That Failed,* for which Aaron and Maximus were paying him $250,000. It was never produced but he got into Goldie's pants that first night, a turn of events which reinforced his belief that life is composed of a little of this and a little of that.

In addition to her natural sense of the absurd and a wonderfully dirty mouth, there was something else very good about Goldie—the way she looked. Challis was reminiscent in those days of a charming character from a George Axelrod comedy, vaguely mid-thirtyish, polished loafers and baggy cashmere sweaters, a tendency to drink too much and to be rather funny when he did; Goldie was in the full flush of her yellow-and-brown California-girl look then, and it hadn't begun to go stale and come apart like aging hollandaise, the way that particularly delectable look so frequently, so horribly did. Seeing her for the first time, coming off the tennis court with her legs and arms and hair all honey-colored and her mouth jutting in a pout that was going to become awfully familiar, he was a dead duck. It was her manner, too: childish, spoiled, capricious, given an attractive texture by extremes of enthusiasm, high spirits, and anger. You didn't fall in love with a creature like Goldie Roth. You wanted her as a trophy. There was one immutable truth about the prototype; it was the key to their allure, the cause of their undoing, and it never seemed to change: they liked being trophies. What they wanted was a man feeling lucky and proud to have somehow reached the pinnacle and gotten one of these rare and wonderful and doomed birds of passage for himself. But when the trophy developed a patch of tarnish here and some wine-and-cigarette breath there, when every six months or so brought a deposit of cellulite or some goddamn thing that required hugely expensive treatments by the latest European seer, when suddenly the trophy sat awhile on the shelf . . . why, then they wondered what it was about them that had become so unlovable. They forgot that they had defined the rules. The process never seemed to change. Challis had seen it happen a hundred times among people he knew. But watching this particular girl, with all the unimaginable tarnish and rust and nastiness just out of sight over the Beverly Hills, all Challis knew was that this blond, tan, tennis-playing trophy was exactly the trophy he'd been looking for.

Later, when they had been married awhile, he looked up from his typewriter and saw her lying naked in the sun on the deck of their beach house. She had white plastic globes where her eyes should have been and her belly kept tensing, then relaxing, tensing, relaxing. She was doing vaginal isometrics, which were all the rage that year, or so she informed him, and that was when it was getting on toward the bad part. Staying a child was becoming very hard work and the returns were diminishing. It wasn't enough for her that she looked fine, tawny, lean: she knew by then that being a child of nature and impulse was wearisome, for Challis, for herself, for anybody who knew her. Yet she was lost

13

looking for what role she was going to play next, now that she was over thirty.

Challis sipped his gin and tonic, listened to the crashing surf, squinted at the sunshine hitting the Malibu stretch of ocean and glaring nervously off a million waves and eddies. You could go blind watching the sunlight on the water, reflecting like an infinity of mirrors. Somebody famous ran past on the beach and waved at him, a sheepdog floundering happily behind, getting his feet wet in the surf. Goldie was listening to a rock radio station, her naked stomach and fingers jerking to the beat. At one time, a time he could barely remember, he'd have gone crazy at the sight of that expanse of brown flesh and curly hair. Beside her on the wooden deck a can of diet soda lay on its side where she'd knocked it over, the liquid staining the towel. He had a habit of looking at such scenes, any scenes really, and thinking about where the camera should be placed. Sometimes it made him angry because it removed him from reality; other times it kept him from cracking up.

Challis looked at his typewriter and the half-filled sheet of yellow foolscap. He looked at the television set, where the Dodgers were beating the Cardinals and Vin Scully was quoting Aeschylus and Euripides. His glass of gin and tonic—the sixth in this series, by actual count—was sweating like a fat umpire in the St. Louis sun. Goldie turned over, lay on her belly, spread her legs, and began flexing her ass. Challis frowned. He wondered who was sleeping with her these days. One of his friends? Maybe somebody right here in the Colony . . . it would be a nice humiliating touch at parties, and she rather liked humiliating touches. The thing was, did he care anymore? He didn't think so. And he wouldn't care until the last liquor store had sold its last bottle of gin, to paraphrase Margo Channing à la Joe Mankiewicz. And the next thing was, so far as he was concerned, what exactly did he care about anymore?

He stared at the Oscar, which was at the moment using its great marble base to hold down a ratty, slowly growing, marked-up stack of yellow paper.

"Well," he said to the Oscar. "What?"

Oscar didn't give a fig, as they used to say in olden

days when Cornell Wilde and Tony Curtis and Donald Crisp had kept the surly barons in order.

Five years further on, the body of Goldie was at his feet. She wore a heavy sweater with a thick rolled turtleneck. No pants. A tank watch with the sapphire on the winding stem: was he crazy? Why else catalog these details while his wife cashed in her chips, bought the farm, shuffled off this—ah, let's see, on the floor a Vuitton address book swept off the desk as she had clawed the air, grabbed at the last strands of life. All the Rodeo Drive loot scattered across the remains of poor, bitchy old Goldie. . . . The honey-streaked hair with undiminished thickness and sheen and heft: blood caked; her skull battered in, a fury of hatred and frustration; and the Oscar smeared with her blood and hair. . . . The statuette replaced on the desk, gazing down sightlessly at the murdered woman. A trophy used to kill another trophy.

Challis saw the flash of the Oscar reflecting the firelight, slicing through the air again and again as it must have done, Goldie going down, the base of the statuette smashing through the skull's shell, spraying blood and the brains, pounding bits of bone into the slippery gray matter. He saw it, he heard the awful wet sound, and he woke up screaming. . . .

He opened his eyes, winced as a coughing fit racked his stiff, snow-covered body. Somehow he'd gotten out of the wreckage. Unlike the movies, there had been no fire, no exploding fuel tanks, despite the odor he recognized, and he was alive, in one piece. He lay in the mud and snow, the afternoon sky effectively blotted out by the dark trees and mist. He looked at his watch. Only an hour before, he'd been standing in the hangar, waiting.

Moving gingerly, he got up and walked back to the battered fuselage, which had acquired the sad look of a broken toy under a gigantic Christmas tree. He looked in past the broken glass of the windshield. Snow had blown in. The two bodies were white with it. He wasn't quite sure of what he was seeing, then realized he was staring into the raw stump where the pilot's head had been. Gagging, he staggered back, slipped in the icy

15

mud, and fell down. He shook his head, clearing the image away. A clump of wet, heavy snow fell off the boughs above him, slid down, and glanced off his shoulder. He stood up, stumbled away into the trees.

He woke up again lying against a tree trunk. The cold was eating at him. He was so stiff that he assumed for a moment that he was freezing. His leg pained him, and his head, where it had struck the side window glass, was tender to the touch, throbbed mightily. The sky was finally visible, a dirty late-afternoon gray with snow blowing steadily from every direction at once. He wondered, almost objectively, how he was going to keep from freezing to death during the night. Leaning back against the tree, he swept his eyes out across the valley. The snow obscured details, but he saw far below him the ribbon of black road, which seemed flat from his perspective but which was in fact working its way up the mountainside. Nothing moved anywhere in his field of vision, nothing but the ceaseless shifting snow. He closed his eyes, but what he saw frightened him: the Oscar, gleaming brightly, flashing through the air, chopping again and again, growing a dripping coat of blood on its base. . . .

He came to again. Darkness was lowering across the valley like the final curtain on a bad play, and he knew he was going to die. He was alone on the side of the mountain and the snow was deepening all around him. When he opened his mouth to take a deep breath, he heard his snow-caked beard crack like breaking glass. His brain was still ticking over . . . Warren Beatty dying in the snow at the end of *McCabe and Mrs. Miller.* Challis decided he was going to die wishing he'd written a movie that fine. Christ, he knew it was the end for sure—he heard voices. High, piping voices getting closer, the heavenly choir. So, this was it, they came piping and they led you away, just like Frank Capra had always sort of hinted they would. . . .

'Twas brillig and the slithy toves
Did gyre and gimble in the wabe
All mimsy were the borogroves,
And the momeraths outgrabe . . .

16

The voices were coming closer. Challis smiled, felt his beard crack again. The subconscious was such a peculiar place, he mused quite calmly. He would never have guessed that his dying hallucination would have been of "Jabberwocky." My God, his life could have flashed before his eyes, but instead, from a burying place deep in the heaped-over mounds of childhood, the Lewis Carroll poem had worked its way back to the surface. Then, much to his own surprise, he began to wonder, when would the processional of his life, the long march past, the final review, begin? Come to think of it, he'd always counted on that final view of who and what he'd been, the last chance to wave a cheery farewell to the young man, and before that the boy that he'd once been. As the sound of the voices came closer, he decided that the least he could do was stand up and meet his fate while foursquare, a beamish boy on his own two feet. Well, he could have used a drink, but . . . He slid up the tree trunk, the snow drifting off his shoulders. His eyelashes were stuck together with snow and his mustache was frozen solid like a brush made of ice, weighing ten pounds. Spooky business, dying, but his spirits had actually lightened a good deal. He was beginning to feel rather silly. And he began walking toward the piping, chanting voices. Which was when he stepped over the edge of a small cliff and tumbled through the bracken and snow and brambles onto a frozen, muddy pathway edging narrowly along the mountainside.

Beware the Jabberwock, my son!
The Jaws that bite, the claws that catch!

By God, they were getting closer still. He peered out from inside his head, through the bars of his eyelashes. He rubbed at the snot dripping from his nose, laughed, and felt his beard crack again. Ice cut into his face, and he stopped laughing. He stood up slowly, feeling a sharp pain in his side. His leg hurt and his head hurt. As long as he had the symptoms, he wished he were drunk. When was all the hurting going to stop?

17

Beware the Jubjub bird and shun
The frumious Bandersnatch!

He took a few faltering steps and caught his breath.

Good Lord, but they were small!

Somehow—aside from all that dancing-on-the-head-of-a-pin bullshit—he'd always assumed that angels were, well, *big*. Majestic, magnificent, terrific wingspread and all . . . of course, Capra had seen them as sort of cuddly old men, chummy and good-natured and hesitant. Anyway, it didn't matter, because that had been the movies and this was something else and he'd have to break that habit—this was real life, dying and angel visitation, hallucinatory or not. But they were so small, these funny looking little creatures, brightly colored, puffy parkas where there should have been those long creamy robes, and they weren't flying or floating . . . they were staggering along and looking down at the path, and the lead angel couldn't have been more than four feet high!

Challis drew himself up to his full six feet and began to say something. "Hey there!"

The first angel's eyes widened. The mouth fell open. Snow blew thickly between Challis and the angel.

"Bandersnatch!" the angel shrieked. "The Bandersnatch!" Then he turned tail and ran smack into the following angels.

Challis scowled and fell face forward in the mud and snow, dead to the world and feeling no pain.

[3]

CHALLIS HAD TAKEN a somewhat earlier flight than he'd planned. Being summoned to an Australian location to doctor somebody else's screenplay had taken its toll both physically and mentally. For a week he'd tried to put some life into the stoic, stalwart characters drawn from a wooden best-selling novel: he'd given them verbal habits, physical twitches, taken a tuck here and there, restructured the second half of the story. He turned a solemn, boring sermon into a rather base caricature and picked up fifty thousand in the process. Somebody from the studio had suggested that he might want screen credit. A bad joke? No, the man had been well-intentioned, and Challis had politely declined. The director, a mature hell-raiser of seventy, had insisted on getting drunk every night in Challis' hotel room. "Challis," he kept saying, "they don't understand me, they never have. First, I was, I still am, a writer . . . don't ask me how I got into the goddamn director's chair—I don't know. Any asshole from a sheep station in the outback can *direct* a picture. But they've forgotten I'm a writer. Now, let me tell you how this piece of shit should play, never forgetting we've got a couple of talking bogies for actors." The week had taken a considerable toll, all right, and Challis had stopped off in Fiji for a couple of days to dry out. But he'd wanted to get home. He'd wanted to see Goldie, and he'd wanted to be sober.

So he'd gotten in earlier than planned; the standard gold 450SL had started after the week's rest, and he headed up the Pacific Coast Highway from LAX with the morning sun glowing brightly behind the fog crouching over the city. The ocean was calm and peaceful and white sails slid across the surface like enormous shark's fins. What traffic there was as he

19

reached Malibu was coming the other way, and he drove fast with the top down, letting the moist breeze wake him up. He turned left and went through the Colony's gates. It was a beautiful morning, clean and wet and the sun glowing brighter every minute. Christmas was only a week away, and he'd survived a week with the temperature hitting 120 every day and he was glad to be home.

He was surprised to smell coffee in the kitchen. The container had dripped halfway full. A radio was playing softly somewhere. He heard the surf in the particular way that meant the sliding glass door onto the long deck was open. There was wet sand on the kitchen floor.

Still carrying his bag, he walked into the living room and stood quietly by the desk that looked out at the water. A fire had burned down in the grate and the wind coming up off the beach fluttered papers on the desk. It was cool, dim, fresh in the room.

Goldie was screwing some guy on the rug. They were naked and there was wet sand ground into the rug, and her hair was wet. As far as Challis knew, this was the first time, but then, it would be, wouldn't it? He felt the sickness in his stomach and went back into the kitchen. They hadn't noticed him. He mechanically got a cup and poured himself coffee, put cream in it, added brown-sugar crystals because in California everybody said brown-sugar crystals wouldn't give you cancer and if you couldn't believe everybody, who the hell could you believe? With his bag in one hand, the hot coffee in the other, he went back to the living room.

Goldie's eyes were tightly closed and her jaw was clenched and she was shaking. They were just getting there, and the conversation was about par for the particular course they were playing. In times of crisis, Challis habitually fell back on composing dialogue in his mind and then saying it, thereby removing himself slightly from the unpleasant reality of the moment. He put the suitcase down softly, walked across the room, stood looking down at them.

"When you two are done," he said, "I'd like just a moment of your time."

The effect was all that he could have hoped for. The

sexual act, the ardor itself, was dampened with a pathetic suddenness. He looked past the steaming coffee into four terrified glazed eyes and two flushed faces. The scene became one from a very amateurish porno movie or one's worst private nightmares. Naked bodies were rolling in all directions, limbs flailing, voices crying out. He was surprised that they didn't handle it with rather more aplomb. In his gut, he probably felt a good deal worse than they did. But, of course, he made his living writing words for people to say in equally unlikely and melodramatic situations. He watched them struggling to their feet. There were no robes or shirts or towels in the room. In a movie the scene might just conceivably have been played for laughs.

"Look at the bright side," he said. "I'm not carrying a gun."

"Oh, shit!" the man said. His chest was hairless, and sprinkled with red splotches, decorated with the standard terrace of awful gold chains. He looked terribly ordinary: middle-aged, tanned down to his neck, gray hair, splay-footed. Goldie didn't look so hot either. Her mouth looked sort of raw and smudged.

Challis walked past them and went out on the deck. He sipped the coffee, scratched his beard, leaned on the railing looking out at the water. What in the world were his next lines? He couldn't seem to get a grip on the scene, and he loathed the idea of crying, which was what he felt like doing. Goldie had frequently accused him of being buttoned-up, buttoned-down, but never unbuttoned. Inhibitions were his "bag," as she was fond of saying; he was afraid of his emotions. He blinked back the tears and waited while he heard the sounds of the unidentified chap packing it up. Eventually he heard Goldie's voice: "Toby . . ." He turned around. She was standing in the doorway, leaning against the rough wood of the siding. She wore Levi's and a sweater, and her face, expressionless, was impossible to read.

"Toby," she said with surprising softness, "don't be sorry you came home too soon." The surf rushed in his ears. "This was bound to happen . . . it's a miracle it hasn't happened before. Oh, Toby, don't look like such an idiot. You're so dense, so stupid, so wrapped up in

21

that goddamn typewriter . . ." She threw her head, the hair clinging wetly. She grabbed a towel from the back of a chair and began angrily drying the darkly streaked hair. "This jerk you saw," she called, walking away, "just the latest in a long line, Toby."

He followed her into the kitchen. She was pouring coffee.

"Don't take it personally, okay?" She grinned sourly at him.

He swiped at the coffee mug, watched the hot liquid spray upward in a wave, staining the camel-hair sweater. He heard her shriek as the coffee burned through to her big golden breasts. The shrieking stopped when the flat of his right hand connected with the side of her face. She fell forward, caught herself against the sink. She blinked at him. He realized with considerable satisfaction that she was terribly frightened. There was blood in the corner of her mouth. He felt his adrenaline rushing, his senses bared. The smell of coffee was overwhelming.

"Don't take it personally," he said. "Okay?"

It must have been the smell of the coffee that brought on the memory of that remarkable morning at Malibu. When he opened his eyes, the memory of Goldie's terrified eyes and her cheek flaring red as she fell sideways was gone, but the smell of the strong coffee remained, assailed him, cleared his head. He'd forgotten that he was supposed to be dead. So far as he could tell at first glance, he was at the center of a semicircle of squatting fellow mortals. Small fellow mortals.

Somewhere a disc jockey was babbling

A morning disc jockey. Challis recognized the voice. He squinted at the morning's bright grayness. Clouds hung low in the valley. He was sitting in a shallow cave, a depression cupped out of the rocky hillside, and it was morning and he wasn't quite dead. He was beginning to get the picture.

"Bandersnatch!" cried a high, squeaky voice. "He moved . . . look, he moved. Ralph, come here, Bandersnatch just moved."

"Relax," Challis croaked. "Don't talk so loud, little boy."

22

A bulky figure appeared in the corner of Challis' vision, clumped in out of the blowing cold. He was as wide as he was tall and looked to be about thirteen. He paused, looked down at the small blond boy whose piercing cry had just stopped rocketing off the stony, icy walls. "Stevie, for God's sake, be quiet. You'll start an avalanche. Don't you know nothin'?"

"No, Ralph, I don't," Stevie replied solemnly.

"God, you can say that again," Ralph muttered. He looked down at Challis. His face was swarthy, his hair thick and black, his eyes a lustrous dark brown. He wore a blue down-filled jacket which made him look like a large beach ball with arms and legs. "You awake? You feel all right?" Ralph's eyelid jumped, a tic.

"Coffee?" Challis tried to swallow. He didn't understand what was going on, but coffee would probably help.

There was a fire crackling nearby, on the ground beside it a camper's collapsible pan with a longish handle. Ralph poured coffee powder into a tin telescoping cup, heated the snow in the pan over the fire, and made coffee. A heavy-looking backpack leaned against the wall of the cave. Ralph handed over the cup and watched while Challis sipped. Six other boys, ranging in age from maybe ten to twelve, watched quietly. One was cross-eyed; another's mouth hung slightly ajar, a trail of saliva working its way down his chin. The tin cup was hot as hell. Challis grinned at them over the cup's rim.

"That's good," he said. "Thanks . . . ah, what the hell is going on? What happened to last night? Who are you guys, anyway?"

All the faces turned toward Ralph, who was busy tearing pictures of naked girls out of a *Penthouse* and putting them on the fire. He scooped another hand full of snow from the cave's lip, dropped it into the pan, swilled it around over the fire.

"We are campers," Ralph said, smiling faintly. He put coffee powder in another cup. The other campers were munching candy bars. Ralph reached into his backpack, withdrew a Mars bar, and handed it to Challis. "Our leader wandered away and we couldn't find

23

him, so now we're on our own . . . it's no big deal because Ralph Halliday is always prepared." He brewed his own cup of coffee and sat down across from Challis. Music played on the radio, a small Sony propped against the backpack. "That's who we are, and I know who you are." His eyes caught Challis for a second, and the faint smile reappeared. His eyelid began to dance nervously. He looked away.

"You're Bandersnatch," one of the smaller boys said.

"Frumious Bandersnatch," another said, slurring the words. There was something off-center in the scene, but Challis couldn't pin it down.

"Listen, you guys," Ralph said calmly, as if lecturing a group of kindergarten children. "Go police the area. We need twigs and sticks for the fire. And snow . . . here, take the pan, collect snow in it. And put your candy wrappers in your pocket. No littering, or I'll bury you at the back of this cave. You got that? Okay, get going." He waited, taking little swallows of coffee, while the boys jumbled quietly out into the cold. Ralph was the top kick, and the rest of the kids acted like boot-camp recruits. When he and Challis were alone, he waved some smoke away and said, "You want a cigar?" He reached for the backpack. "My dad smuggles these things in from Cuba—"

Challis began to chortle, felt the roar of laughter growing. He remembered suddenly that he'd believed at first that they were angels. And now he'd met them and he still didn't know what they were, but, my God, there was coffee and a warm fire and *Penthouse* and candy bars, and now, beyond all the boundaries of imagination, a Cuban cigar. Maybe he *was* dead. Maybe heaven was just a bit more primitive than he'd expected.

"We saw the plane go down, see? So we were heading that way, thinking somebody might've got out, see? Some of my men, well, you seen 'em—little gimpy there, some of 'em, right? So I keep what passes for their minds—just a joke, heh, heh—occupied with a little singing, a little . . . well, you know, what they say. A little laugh, a little dance, a little seltzer down your pants . . . just a joke, heh, heh."

Ralph got a cigar for himself, lit it, and looked at

it appreciatively. "Yeah, I been smoking these things since I was eleven. I'm thirteen and a half now, see?"

"There's something funny here . . ."

Ralph smiled slowly.

"I know," Challis said. "You're doing Eddie Robinson—"

"Key Largo," Ralph said, nodding. "Been working on it since I was ten. I used to do Benny and Cagney, and my Kirk Douglas wasn't bad, 'cause he's got a kind of high voice. That's why my Peck is so bad . . . you gotta get the deep voice. Anyway, my Robinson is so good it's all I do anymore."

"How's your Ralph Halliday?"

"Very funny. I haven't done Ralph Halliday in a long time, see? I've forgotten how. Nobody any good does Ralph Halliday . . . it's like Benjamin Franklin, nobody does him. Ralph Halliday! A nothing, a kid, and I don't do kids." He blew an arrow of smoke toward the entrance to the cave where the brightness had already given way to dark clouds and the beginnings of either snow or sleet.

In the silence, with only the wind whirring outside, they heard the eight-o'clock newscast from Los Angeles.

"And the record rainstorms show no signs of lessening in the next few days, which is bad news for all you residents of Malibu and the canyons all the way from Bel Air and Beverly Glen to Laurel. Foothill Drive is blocked with mud as of the moment, and Pacific Coast Highway, opened at noon yesterday, is already blocked again with overnight mudslides.

"In the mountains the rain has turned to snow again, and in the Arrowhead–Puma Point area we've got a couple of human-interest stories in the news this morning. Rick Wallace was on his way up the mountain last night but didn't make it. The roads are completely snow-blocked, not open to any traffic, so all we can tell you is that both the plane carrying convicted wife-killer Toby Challis and the camping party of retarded children from St. Christopher's School are up on the mountain and out of contact with the rest of the world. The small aircraft carrying Challis and four other passengers and crew radioed that it was going down in

25

the storm yesterday afternoon, and nothing has been heard since . . . the little lost campers have not been heard from since the day before yesterday, when they left Arrowhead on an overnight trip with a counselor from the school.

"On the Hollywood scene, the latest on the David Begelman affair, which has got a lot of folks white-knuckling it in Bel Air and at the Polo Lounge—"

"Little lost campers!" He snorted. "Makes me wanna puke." He glared at the ash on his cigar. Challis munched thoughtfully on his Mars bar, wondering where the conversation was about to go. His head was clearing and he was beginning to remember the reality of his situation. The radio announcer had it right on the button: he was convicted wife-killer Toby Challis, and from out of nowhere, in the most unexpected way possible, he had become a free man. But the brand of freedom was . . . well, it reminded him of Dudley Moore getting his wishes realized in *Bedazzled:* the letter of the wish was granted but not the spirit. Stuck on a mountainside in a snowstorm with a bunch of retarded kids and the reincarnation of Edward G. Robinson. On the other hand, he could be sitting in the remains of the airplane with his head on the seat behind him.

But what was he going to do now?

Wait to be found? Try to go for help? Leave the kids? Take them with him if he left?

Or try—he had no idea how—to escape?

The thought of escape tantalized him. He felt a rush of life: his senses seemed to sharpen.

Ralph made no further comment about the radio report.

"You wanta stand up? Move around. . . ."

Challis nodded, reached for Ralph's shoulder, and slowly got to his feet. His head brushed the roof. Ice grew like moss, smelled cold. For an instant his head swam, his vision became pinpoints of light at the distant ends of twin dark tunnels. He steadied himself against Ralph's stocky frame, waited for everything to come back. He was stiff, but not as bad as he thought he'd be: the warmth of the campfire must have taken the chill out of his bones.

26

"You okay?"

Challis nodded. "Let's go outside."

They met the returning twig party, each of the boys carrying clumps of sticks and leaves. Ralph told them to fuel the fire and stay inside the cave, get warm, and don't fight. His authority was absolute. Together, going slowly on the slippery snow and ice, Challis and Ralph set off. The snow was thicker than Challis remembered yesterday's had been; stinging in a strong, gusty wind, and colder, too. The trees looked black, dark; foggy clouds dipped down into the valley, giving them a sense of eerie isolation. It was utterly quiet but for the wind and the snow pattering all around them, their breathing and footsteps. The small sounds which accentuate the quiet. . . .

They found the footpath where they'd encountered one another. Five minutes further on, around the bend, they stopped. The wind pushed a bank of gray vapor away from the mountainside, and far below them they saw the rope of blacktopped road snaking its way painfully, slowly upward. From above, it looked flat and seemed almost to be alive, squirming as snow skittered across it.

"Look," Ralph said, pointing. "You see that? There, see?"

"Christ. . . ."

Two vehicles were edging along at the lead end of the black road. Ahead of them there was no road.

"Snowplow," Ralph said. "They've both got red lights on top."

"Can you see that?"

"I got good eyes, see. Snowplow and a cop car, maybe . . . or an ambulance. They're looking for us, see, *all* of us."

"It's pretty slow going," Challis said. "It'll take them a couple of hours to get up this high."

"I don't know. Looks like they're making pretty good time to me." It was true: already the black ribbon had taken the two vehicles out of sight behind an outgrowth of treetops.

"You're right," Challis said. He licked snow from his mustache, wiped caked snow from his eyebrows. "An hour at the most." He looked around him, analyzing the topography. He had to figure out a way to stay free. He saw an outcropping of rock, ice, and snow twenty feet above them. It reminded him of a scene he'd once written. "Come on, Ralph, grab the other end of this log. . . ."

They hauled, tugged, and yanked the fifteen-foot length of rough, barky wood up onto the ledge. Panting hard, Challis inspected the boulder, the accompanying smaller rocks, the few small trees attached to the basic mass, and the covering of ice and snow. He kicked at the perimeters, wedging his boot into a moist, unfrozen opening between the rim of the rock and the earth. He pushed his foot in as far as his ankle allowed. He hoped it was a deep hole burrowed by an animal.

"This is all from a movie I once wrote," he said, regarding the scene and getting his breath. "Never got produced, of course, but I stole it from a hundred other movies anyway. The pioneer family, pursued by I forget who, decide to make their stand up on a mountainside. Dad—say, Jimmy Stewart—has been shot in the leg and can't really do anything . . . but he can tell the others, the sons and daughters and the perky little wife, she was supposed to be Debbie Reynolds, as I recall—anyway, Jimmy lies there holding his bloodstained leg and explains the use of leverage, how even weak human beings can move mountains if they've only a mind to. Well, you get the idea."

"So we're gonna move the mountain. . . ."

"Well, just a smidgen of it. . . ."

"And block the road!" Ralph's dark eyes flashed at the prospect.

They fitted the log into the hole, pushing it until it stuck firmly, nestled under the boulder. The log projected back at a considerable angle. Challis could get a grip around it about five feet from the end. "This may," he said, "take a little time." He began to hoist himself up, bringing his full weight to bear on the log. He bounced. At first he thought that nothing was happening, merely a nasty twanging along the length of the wood, like a bat cracking in your hand against a heavy fastball. Ralph watched for a moment, then bounded off, came back with a short, thick stick, and inserted it five feet from the log and began digging at

28

the ice and snow bonding the boulder to the mountainside. Challis kept bouncing. Ralph moved along, digging, scraping. After ten minutes they were sweating, but Challis thought he'd felt a bit of give.

Below them the snowplow had pushed on almost out of sight, unreeling the road behind it like a slug might leave a wet trail.

"Let's try again," Ralph said. He grabbed his lever and with a stone jammed it into what seemed a promising spot. Challis shifted the log. The angle had declined somewhat, so he could apply his weight nearer the end. With the first mighty surge, he felt more give, heard what must have been the tearing away of roots and mud and ice. Again he leaped, pulling down, and again, and again. When it finally came loose, it hung, tottering for a moment: they rushed forward, stepping half into the crater from which it had been dislodged, and pushed, their shoulders against the dirt and mud, and then it went, crashing through the snow, taking trees with it, rolling slowly, implacably, like a medieval juggernaut, smashing and grinding, growing larger gradually. It smashed against a tree, swayed in the low web of fir boughs, then slid off, gathered speed again, now nearly twice the size it had been at birth, and with a swoosh of sound which carried up the hill like an airplane taking off, it hit a stand of medium-sized leafless trees growing on the facing of rock perhaps ten feet above the road. Like grasping fingers the trees seemed to cling, and for a shred of time the roaring sound stopped, the huge ball of snow, trees, mud, ice, branches, hung suspended above the road: then, almost gently, the trees gave way and let the juggernaut drop with a soft thud directly onto the road.

Ralph raised a fist, and Challis hugged him, lifting him off the ground.

"It must have weighed tons by the time it landed," Challis said. "Took a lot of snow with it . . . damn near an avalanche."

On the walk back to the cave, Ralph grew serious. "Why was it we did that? Really."

"Good question. So they wouldn't catch us—"

"But they're trying to *rescue* us, not catch. . . ."

29

"Ah, Ralph." Challis sighed.

"Look, let's level, see. Did you knock off your wife?" Ralph trudged along, head down, hands in his jacket pockets.

"Nope," Challis said.

Ralph nodded.

[4]

BACK AT THE CAVE, Challis sipped at another cup of coffee while Ralph supervised the cleaning up of the campsite. The demeanor of the children under Ralph's instructions was amazing; his energy and intelligence were unmistakable. Obviously the boys considered him much the same as an adult leader, yet the fact was he was one of them. It was strange, though Challis would never have called Ralph "normal," whatever *that* meant, not with Edward G. Robinson always unmistakably close at hand. Normal . . . Challis reflected on his own state: he hardly saw himself at home among any group of convicted murderers. Perhaps that was the bond between them: neither one was quite what the world believed him to be.

Shortly before noon they were ready to set out. Challis led the way, with Ralph behind him, moving in and out among the boys, helping those who slipped and fell on the ice and snow or who suddenly just got cold and frightened and lonely. Having no idea where they were going, at least not in terms of a destination, Challis moved off up the mountainside. They moved at angles, back and forth among the firs, climbing steadily. Alone, hearing his own labored breathing and from a great distance the occasional chatter of the children, Challis began to think seriously, for the first time since he'd come to in the wreckage, about his own perilous circumstances.

Did he have any real chance to get away? And what did getting away really mean: getting away from the police, but to what? What could he do even if he escaped? How could he get money? Who could he contact for help? How could he get hold of a fake passport if he wanted to leave the country? It wasn't a movie, and he wasn't a hero. He was utterly unexcep-

31

tional in terms of helpful abilities or inside knowledge, in terms of bravery or stealth or cunning or contacts. . . . Solomon Roth? Could he go to Sol? And how much did the matter of a conviction make to a friend? And who were his friends, really—the kind of friends who would risk aiding a convicted murderer?

The quality of his freedom was pretty poor. He was loose, like an animal escaped from a zoo, but he was hardly free. A real escapee—says Humphrey Bogart in *Dark Passage*—had a better chance. Lauren Bacall had picked him up, intentionally, because she sympathized and understood his plight. He shook his head, trying to erase all the images which flooded his mind the more he thought: they were fiction. The people in the images shut down for the day and left the Warner lot, or Columbia, or RKO, and went the hell back to Holmby Hills or the terraced hillsides of Bel Air to sip their martinis and thumb through the next day's pages. He was Toby Challis, out of breath and frightened, undoubtedly lost, with only a fat kid with a backpack to see him through another night, and nobody was going home at five o'clock.

They reached the top of the mountain in the early afternoon. Unexpectedly, there they were, having labored upward through a low-slung cloud. Ahead of them, surrounded by the stubby wooded peaks, was a gray circle of water, a small lake. Snow seemed to hang above it, and foggy clouds slid past on the wind. He couldn't imagine how far away it was: a mile or three or ten, he had no experience in such matters. Together they sat down on dead limbs and snowy rocks, stared out at the lake. The snow rattled on their parkas. Challis squinted hard at the lake and the shoreline. He shook his head, feeling the snow cake crack on his beard. His teeth were chattering. He tugged his raincoat tighter. It was a mess.

"Ralph, take a close look out there."

"What am I looking for?"

"Some sign of life," he said. "I can't see anything . . . are there any lodges over there, near the lake? There ought to be, houses or lodges, and they ought to be empty in this kind of weather. If we're going to go in that direction, we might as well find a house. It'll take the rest of the daylight to get there."

It was pathetic. That was the only plan he had, simply finding shelter, getting in out of the storm. Maybe then he could settle down and do some thinking. Maybe. . . .

"There's a place over there," Ralph said. "At the end of the lake . . . the right end. Unstrap the pocket side of my backpack—there's Zeiss field glasses in there, little collapsible ones." He grinned. "My folks worry so much that I'm crazy maybe, they get me all sorts of stuff. There's a bright side to everything, see?"

Challis found the binoculars, peered at the right end of the lake. Half-hidden among the trees there was a weather-beaten grayish building. He couldn't make out any more about it, wondered at Ralph's being able to see it at all. He looked around the rest of visible shoreline, saw nothing that looked like a dwelling to him, and put the binoculars back in Ralph's pack.

"Okay, I guess that's it," he said. He gathered the group around him and told them where they were headed, how long it might take. "It's not going to be easy, men," he said. "But it's our only hope." He was sure he'd written those lines for a television show a long time ago. "Are you with me?" He looked down at Stevie, the youngest, or at least the smallest. "Are you with me, pal?"

"Sure, Bandersnatch," Stevie said. "All the way."

The afternoon was endless. The glow behind the snow and clouds dropped past the mountaintops about three o'clock, and it kept getting darker and colder. The snow came and went, the wind never let up. They pushed on, sinking through frozen snowcrust at one point, slogging through wet muddiness at another. The children trudged along without complaint. For a time they got Ralph to recite the Lewis Carroll poem, which they chimed in on at crucial moments. Ralph passed out the last of his candy bars. Challis developed a headache, and his cut, bruised leg began to give him some trouble. He got tired. The sky began to go dark, but even after dark they could see: the clouds were thinning. The snow still was driven on the wind, but more and more it was blowing off the ground, whip-

33

ping at their legs and guts and faces, but not coming from above.

By seven o'clock, having rested frequently as they went, they were close enough to see the building in the moonlight. Close enough to reach the flat road tracing its way around the lake. By seven-thirty they were standing outside the house, which was a timbered affair, two stories at one end, a single story at the other. A long balcony/deck faced out toward the lake, and the branches of the firs scraped the roof sides here and there. The wind whistled across the lake, blowing snow like ghosts sliding over the thin ice.

The house was dark, curtains drawn.

Leaning away from the wind, they went along the side of what must have been the garage and then along the back, where they were out of the gale and the moon made the snow sparkle icily. Challis tried the door that gave onto the patio. To his considerable surprise, the door opened. He peered inside, saw nothing in the darkness. "We're in luck," he said. "Now, be very quiet, come in, and just stand still." He waited while they went inside. He was now guilty, quite possibly, of obstructing officers in the pursuit of their duty, causing a landslide, kidnapping the children, and trespassing, if not actually committing forcible entry. It had been a full day.

Breathless, they stood in the kitchen, waiting. Challis eased the door shut. Once the shuffling and sniffling and panting had died down, he thought he heard something—music, soft and turned low, but it was music. Or was it inside his head? The wind whined outside, scraped at the windows. He led the procession toward the kitchen doorway, down a hallway, then suddenly around a corner into a high, two-storied room with vaulted ceiling and a living room sunken three steps. In the far wall, a gigantic, walk-in-sized fireplace dwarfed a small, flickering log fire. Two squat table lamps cast a dim glow over a topography of low, soft-looking gray couches and darkly shining butcher block coffee tables. The music was indeed coming from speakers artfully concealed among the plants and dark wood. He looked at Ralph, who shrugged. "Somebody's home," Ralph said. "Where are they?" Challis tried to think, his mind and body worn out. He looked at the kids. They stood quietly, wiping their noses, yawning, waiting.

"Whoever you are"—the woman's voice came from above, low and sarcastic, a deep, almost hoarse voice —"I've never seen a drearier bunch."

A balcony ran around three walls, and she was standing against the glow from a doorway behind her. She wore a long white terrycloth robe, a towel wrapped around her hair, and was leaning forward, both hands on the railing, looking down at them, watching calmly.

"Ah," Challis said, nodding. "We are that. Dreary, tired, hungry, orphans of the storm . . . lost campers." He concluded his remarks lamely.

"Not, perhaps, the best possible day for camping out," she said. "Still, here you are. Turn on some lights, get out of your coats, and get warm by the fire. I'll be down in a minute."

Challis couldn't make out her features, and then she was gone. The deep voice, the taint of sarcasm, made him feel safe. A calm, laid-back lady, thank God. He wished he knew what to say to her. He wished he knew what the hell he was doing. He wondered if she'd been listening to the radio. What a time for a cute meet. . . .

The boys clustered around the fire. Stevie was already half-asleep. Someone else was trying vainly to recite "Jabberwocky," and the group generally had had the starch taken out of them. Challis pitched another log onto the fire and dropped onto a couch. Exhaustion hit him like a mailed fist. "I'm hungry," Stevie said, his eyes heavy, barely open. "Me, too," someone said from the floor. Challis nodded. "Just hang on."

She came down eventually, still in the robe, her darkish blond hair dried, hanging straight to her jawline, bare feet flickering beneath the terry cloth. She stood at the top of the three stairs, looking at them, shaking her head. "My god," she groaned. "Are you all right? Hungry. But, first, is anybody hurt? Banged up? Anything?"

"Just hungry, see," Ralph said. "Tired and hungry, see."

"Meet Edward G. Robinson," Challis said.

"Johnnie Rocco," the woman corrected him.

35

"Right on," Ralph said, grinning.

"Okay," she said. "Food first, and we'll get to know each other later." She turned to Challis: "Can you make it up the steps, Soldier?" He nodded. "Why don't you herd the lads upstairs. There are two bathrooms, a shower in each one, lots of great big towels, get everybody cleaned up . . . they'll sleep better clean." She smiled at him, them. She had pale green eyes, even white teeth that had been capped. An actress? But her face meant nothing to him. Tall, in those indeterminate late thirties. Her face was tan for somebody with her hair color, faint lines around her mouth and the corners of her eyes. She regarded him levelly: "Earth to scoutmaster . . . still with us?" The kids, somewhat recovered, were staggering loudly up the stairs, reverting to kid's racket now that they were safe.

"Barely," he said.

"I'll get going in the kitchen." She watched him. "Go on," she coaxed, "the first step's always the hardest."

Cute meet, he reflected again, as he got the showers going. The steam felt good and it was a relief to hear the exuberant sounds, smell the soap. He dumped all the dirty clothes into a wicker clothes hamper. In the mirror he regarded his own face, reddened across the cheekbones, his beard matted, hair blown and sweaty, lips cracked from the cold and wind. The cut on his knee was scabbed over and the knee was stiffening. His nose was windburned, peeling. His back ached, his neck was stiff, his left arm was bruised, all reminders of the plane crash. Drenched in self-pity, he decided to postpone his shower until the boys were fed and asleep. A little while longer couldn't make any difference.

Gathered around the kitchen table, they ate peanut-butter sandwiches and bowls of tomato soup. The woman kept the toast coming for the sandwiches, kept the soup bowls full. Challis felt like one of the towel-wrapped kids. While they slacked off, their bellies filling comfortably, she sorted the dirty clothing and started the first washer load. He finished his soup, watched her.

"Time for bed," she said. "Rinse your dishes and just stack them on the counter." They did as they were told. Then she led them into a room with a bar,

36

a television set, three more couches arranged around an empty fireplace, bookcases, and a pool table. She showed them how the couches opened out into beds and let them finish the job. She handed around several blankets, showed them where the bathroom was, and told them it was okay to leave a table lamp burning if they wanted to. Ralph was the last one in bed. He looked up at Challis. " 'Night, Bandersnatch." He winked.

" 'Night, Bandersnatch," the rest of them chorused.

"Sleep tight, men," he said, waving from the doorway.

"Leave the door open," Stevie called frantically.

"Of course," the woman said. "Wouldn't dream of closing it."

In the hallway she said, "Go take a shower, you're a mess. I'll fix us a toddy, and then you can tell your amazing story."

"Prepare to be amazed."

He stood under the shower letting the heat sink bone-deep. The thing was, he didn't feel like an escaped convict; instead, he felt simply as if he had returned to real life from an extended absence. This was the way life was supposed to be. The rest of it was totally crazy. Drying off, he discovered that she had hung a large blue terrycloth robe over the door while he'd been in the shower stall. He put it on and went downstairs.

She was sitting by the fire. The room smelled of hot wine and lemon and cinnamon. He recognized the Sidney Bechet recording of "Laura," the knifelike horn floating the melody across the room. The logs burned with considerable enthusiasm, warming him as he collapsed on the couch facing hers. She poured him a mug of the mulled wine and he sipped, ignoring the pain as it bit at his split lip. She watched him, leaned back with her legs tucked up on the couch, and gave him a slow ironic smile. Wide mouth, the cool green eyes, strong features, tall, broad-shouldered.

"You're tired," she said, "so let me save you some trouble. There's no need to go through all the bullshit about being the leader of the camping expedition. That's all rubbish and you're much too worn out to make a convincing lie of it anyway."

He frowned, blinked at her. "I suppose that's just as well. Why aren't you afraid?"

"My name is Morgan Dyer, this is my house. I came up here for a long weekend and got snowed in. Without the storm, you'd have had the place to yourself . . . but without the storm your plane wouldn't have crashed and you'd be getting acquainted with the inside of a state prison. Six of one, half a dozen of another, Mr. Challis."

Challis nodded. "The radio."

"And I followed the trial," she said. "It was rather like a forties movie."

"The similarity occurred to me. I felt like John Garfield getting railroaded. *Dust Be My Destiny,* but you're too young to remember that." He squeezed his forehead tiredly. "It happens more and more now. I'm retreating into fantasy, I suppose . . . this, the plane crash, these kids, this is the first time I've felt alive in weeks. Maybe it's a fantasy, too, only I've gotten deeper into it this time."

"Rubbish," she said softly. "You're tired, but it's real . . . you really are here."

"But if it were real," he said, "wouldn't you be taking some kind of precautions? I'm a convicted murderer—"

"Don't forget, I followed the trial. You may have beaned your wife with an Oscar, or maybe you didn't, but you're not a criminal. From what I've heard, you could have had good cause . . . which is not exactly the same as saying she deserved it, but not entirely different, either."

"What do you mean, you've heard?" He couldn't get a handle on any of it. She was being elliptical, and he was so tired.

"I've been in and around the movie business all my life, grew up with it. I used to go to bed with the sounds of screenings down the hall in the projection room. I still know people who knew your wife . . . her mother and father, too, and I sat on her grandfather's knee once when I was about three years old." She got up and turned the Sidney Bechet tape over. He watched her, not quite getting it. While the tapedeck worked its way toward the beginning of the music, she said, "I dated Jack Donovan a couple of times, too. Not long before he began seeing your wife—"

"Ex-wife," he said, staring into the fire, listening to her deep voice and the hiss of the burning logs.

"Yes, presumably she's as ex as anyone can get."

"You're not overwhelmed by respect for the dead."

"It's a phoney attitude. Very prevalent out here, of course. All you've got to do out here to get some respect, my father used to say, was get the picture in the can on time and under budget and quietly drop dead. Presto, everybody agrees you should have gotten the Thalberg award. You know what they said about Louis B. Mayer's funeral—half the people there wanted to be sure he was dead." She came back and sat down, smiling and pulling the robe tight. "Respect for the dead should be born out of respect for the same guys living. From what I've heard, I didn't have a great deal of respect for your wife."

"It sounds to me like you kept your ear to the ground."

"Not really. She got herself talked about." Sidney Bechet soared off into "Sweet Lorraine," and he felt her eyes boring into him. "And then she got herself killed." She shrugged. "You knew her best. How much respect did you have for her?"

"I'm sorry she's dead."

"Did you kill her?"

"No."

"What are you going to do? I may be relatively sympathetic to your predicament, but I can't hide you in the fruit cellar until they stop looking for you."

"I don't know . . . I don't want to go to prison. I don't belong in prison." He sighed, shook his head. "I guess I'll try to escape. I don't know how, though. I mean, who the hell knows how to do a thing like that? Escape from some goddamn dragnet."

"I don't think they call them dragnets anymore—APB's, I think. There'll be an APB on you."

"Well, all right. I still don't know what to do. And stop staring at me. What you see is someone with little bits of white bone poking out through the nerve ends." Impatiently, trying to shake off her eyes, he grabbed at a stack of books on the table at his elbow. *The Black*

Gardenia, The Little Sister, The Murder of Roger Ack-royd, The Cavanaugh Quest, Frequent Hearses, The Barbarous Coast, The Maltese Falcon. "What the hell is all this? Murders, murders, murders . . . You must be crazy."

"Murder is my business," she said. "I own a bookstore, nothing but mysteries. The Murder, He Says, Bookshop. We carry both of the novels you wrote back in the sixties, the *early* sixties—"

"Does anybody ever buy them?"

"Sure. Trivia collectors."

"Thank you very much."

"There is a steady demand for any mysteries with a Hollywood background. You wrote two. I've even got an autographed first of *The Final Cut.* Your trial and conviction, you'll be glad to know, has driven the value sky-high."

"How nice for you."

"Last week a collector in La Jolla offered me a thousand dollars for that particular volume. I'm thinking it over."

"Only in America," he moaned.

"Only in Hollywood," she said.

[5]

HE WOKE with a chisel of bright, glaring sunlight prying his eyes open. From the window he could see out across the lake, where the morning light flowed down the mountainside in a thick wave, as if the Disney people had already been hard at it. His trousers, shirt, sweater, and underwear were laid out on a chair, clean. The torn knee had been stitched up. While he dressed his aching body, he breathed deeply at the window. The night in a warm bed seemed to have softened him, made him feel the aches and pains more intensely. The snow was melting and leaving wet spots on the driveway. It dropped from the eaves like a metronome, and fir trees that had been white and heavy-laden the day before were now dark green, wet. He was admiring the view and trying to ignore the realities which were groping their way toward the center of his consciousness when he heard the soft rapping on the bedroom door.

"Good morning," Morgan Dyer said, sliding swiftly into the room and closing the door behind her. She was wearing faded Levi's, a heavy cardigan sweater with a belt and with shoulders halfway down her arms, tennis sneakers. "Sleep well?"

"Fine. But I feel like sasquatch has been using me for a soccer ball. I've led a sheltered and sedentary life until the day before yesterday—is that right? Day before yesterday? Whenever . . ." He pulled up the covers, straightened the pillows. "I really appreciate all this, washing these things . . . a place to sleep, no policemen in the middle of the night. I . . . well, I'm not quite sure how I can repay you—"

"Don't be silly, you're talking rubbish again—what could you do in your position, put in a good word for me with the warden?" She went to the other side of the bed and got the tangled blankets smoothed. "But we do

41

have to decide what we're going to do with you. Unless you're planning to just wander off into the mountains, sort of mystically, in which case something will probably eat you tonight and your problems will be over. Otherwise your problems are just beginning. First, there are all these children who have seen you. The first time they see a picture of you, they're going to start talking about good old Bandersnatch."

Challis stroked his beard, smoothing the unkempt, wild patches back toward his ears. "I think I can fix that one. Are they up yet?"

"Having breakfast. The plump one is really something—Edward G. Robinson—he just took over the kitchen, scrambled eggs, fried bacon. Funny, though, when he came out of the bathroom, he was smoking a cigar." Her green eyes flickered. "I asked him what he wanted for breakfast, and he pointed his cigar at me and said, *'More, yeah, that's what I want, more.'* Unnerving, first thing in the morning." She regarded him quizzically across the bed. "What do you suggest?"

"Send Edward G. up to see me, and do it privately, not in front of the rest of them."

He brushed his teeth with a brush dangling from a rack in the bathroom connecting to the bedroom. In the mirror he saw that his flat blue eyes were clear and bright for the first time in months; staring at the face, it occurred to him for the first time just how famous the trial had made it, and what the papers and television were going to do with it once they realized he had survived the plane crash. The trial coverage had only been a starter. The manhunt would be carried out on another scale altogether, and his face would be everywhere. . . . He spit out the toothpaste, wiped his mouth, and went back to lie down on the bed, scrunching pillows behind him. He glanced at the bedside table. *Death of a Ghost, Smallbone Deceased, The Locked Room, The Schirmer Inheritance, Death Under Sail.* He shook his head.

Ralph came in, minus his cigar. He came with the confidence of a natural take-charge guy, dark, bouncing, hyperactive.

"Sit down, stop jiggling, and listen to me." Challis waited while Ralph calmed down, with only one foot still nervously tapping the floor. "Now, look, Ralph, you've saved my life—if you hadn't found me out there, I'd have gone into shock, either frozen to death or gotten pneumonia and died from that . . . I owe you a lot, I owe you everything, Ralph." He watched Ralph stir uncomfortably, half-smiling, eyes downcast. "Now, you know who I am and you know I know you know . . ." Challis chuckled. "Right? Okay. I'm going to try to escape, because I didn't do what they say I did. And I'm going to depend on you to keep the kids from talking about me to anyone. *Anyone*. Can you do that? Can you keep them from talking about Bandersnatch? No matter who asks them?"

"Sure, they'll do whatever I tell 'em. They're not the brightest kids in the world, see, but they know me, the guy who takes care of them when things are going against them. And if I tell 'em they dreamed there was a Bandersnatch, then it was a dream, see."

"Shake on it," Challis said, taking the boy's hand.

"If I don't see you again . . ."

"You'll see me again."

"Yeah, but if I don't . . . well, good luck, okay?"

"Okay, Ralph."

Without a backward glance, Ralph jumped off the bed and bolted. Morgan reappeared in the doorway with a huge mug of coffee. "Is everything all right?" Challis nodded. "You never existed at all, is that it? Edward G. does seem to have a slightly hypnotic effect on them." Challis nodded again. She put the mug down on the table. He smelled the coffee, remembered the cave and the warmth of that fire, the pages of *Penthouse* curling as the flames licked at the naked girls. He didn't think about that other coffee smell, the day he got back to Malibu ahead of schedule.

An hour later he watched from behind the bedroom curtains as the sheriff from the tiny mountain resort town of Cresta Vista arrived in a light blue police van with the departmental crest on the doors. The sheriff was a tall man wearing a blue fur-collared jacket and a fur hat and aviator shades. He stretched to something near six and a half feet once he was properly unfolded, and he walked with a slight limp, as if he'd long ago gotten used to a football knee. There were damp spots

43

all over the driveway where snow had melted. For a while the sheriff stood looking at the lake, then the house, which was when Challis caught sight of the disaster in the snow.

From where he stood, the footprints in the snow made perfect, unmistakable sense. Strung out in a ramshackle row were the small footprints of the children, just spread out enough to be identifiable. Beside them, deeper and larger, were the tracks of a man. The sheriff reached back into the car and brought out a two-way radio's microphone. Cupping it in his hand, he began talking, his eyes raking the house, the snow-covered lawn, the lake, which glared feverishly in the sunlight. How could he miss the footprints? They were so obvious. . . . The windows in the village of Puma Point glared in the sun at the far end of the lake.

Below, Morgan opened the front door. "Jeff," she called, "what are you waiting for?" Challis saw her step outside, hugging herself in the cold. "I've got a house full of people who need rescuing. Come on in—I'm so glad you were in the office when I called. . . ." The sheriff's hard face broke into a broad grin, taking ten years off his age. He turned his back on the footprints in the snow and called:

"Where are those little devils, Morg? Let's get 'em out here . . ." She beckoned him toward the house, and Challis tiptoed to the bedroom door. The kids were banging around, getting ready to go.

"Everybody's fine," Morgan was saying, "cleaned up, rested, fed . . . This is Ralph, who sort of runs the show."

"How's it goin', Ralph?" The voice was hearty.

"Fine, see, it's goin' fine."

"Wha—" The sheriff was taken off guard by Edward G.

"Have you got time for a cup of coffee, Jeff?"

Challis thought: For God's sake, don't overdo it.

"I'd love one, Morg, you know me, I run on the stuff . . . but we got a bunch of parents waiting down at the bottom of the mountain to see these kids. Give me a rain check."

"You got it."

"You know, it's amazing," the sheriff said, "the way

these kids got through alone. Their leader, poor bastard, wandered into town last night, half-frozen . . . he's in the hospital right now." He shook his head. The bedroom door was ajar and Challis saw them standing at the foot of the stairs. The kids began piling out of the house. The sheriff watched them go, lingered. "You know, Morg, they could have run across that plane crash, the same general area . . . I don't suppose they mentioned anything about it?"

"Are you kidding? I'd have noticed anything like that—have they found the crash site yet? Good God, talk about irony—going to prison for life and you get killed in a plane crash. Makes you wonder."

"They haven't found it yet, but they will. Roads are still blocked, but now while it's clear they'll get the choppers in there, they'll find it."

"How are the roads from here on down? I'd like to get back to civilization today or tomorrow."

"Now, that's what I can't understand, what's so all-fired wonderful about civilization? And what's so civilized about LA, anyway?"

"Jeffrey . . ." she said in a warning tone.

"Right. Well, there are some snow and mud slides, but tomorrow it ought to be smooth sailing. Unless we get more storms. Terrible weather—Malibu's really catching it. Keep your radio on. Or give us a ring in Cresta, just to make sure . . ."

They went outside, and Challis went back to the window. So no one was looking for him yet. And even when the wreckage was found, there would be time spent searching through the mountain forests for him, or his body. The sheriff stood by the van chatting for another moment, then made sure all the kids were accounted for, and squeezed himself in. Ralph was sitting by the window in front, waving to Morgan as they drove away. Challis watched the receding automobile, its red light flashing cheerily on top, until it was gone around the distant curve of trees.

After a late-morning brunch of eggs scrambled with shrimp, tomatoes, celery, and curry powder, they settled down in the sunken living room. The wind had risen, and even the whipsawing sound of it made him cold. He built a fire and she put a tape on the Tandberg deck. Frank Sinatra was singing "I Cover the Waterfront" and Challis thought of the first time he'd heard the recording, a long time ago, a college boy who could never have dreamed what lay ahead.

"Tell me the whole story," she said, sitting down cross-legged on the floor before the fire, leaning against the couch. "Maybe we'll think of what you should be doing . . . and maybe not." Her face seemed to say that she'd already given it some thought and drawn a blank.

"The day Goldie was murdered," he said, as if giving the title of his oral report. The sound of his voice was familiar, going over the same ground.

"I had an apartment in West Los Angeles where I'd been living since moving out of the Malibu house. I'm not complaining, it was a nice apartment, big palm trees outside the window of the room I wrote in. I could see Century City, and Westwood and Beverly Hills were two minutes away. . . . I was sitting at my desk, it was just before noon, and the fog hadn't burned off yet. I was looking out the window, waiting for those triangular Century City towers to take shape through the fog, and the telephone rang. I was expecting a call from my agent about a screenplay deal that had been perking for about three months, fifty grand up front, and it was important to me. I'd already had three calls from other guys, an actor and a writer, and all they wanted to talk about was Joe Namath's knees, could he take the Rams to the Super Bowl. . . . I couldn't think of anything to say about Joe Namath's knees. Another guy called to ask me if I'd heard about the fella who was half-black and half-Japanese. I said no. He said every December seventh the fella attacks Pearl Bailey. That was the kind of morning it had been, the phone rings, and I pick it up thinking about the fifty grand . . .

"Well, it was Goldie. She was sitting on the deck at Malibu, I could hear the surf in the background. She was kind of up, you knew the adrenaline was going, pumping hard. She wouldn't just chat, she was too high, she couldn't slow things down and get her attention span under control, but the point was, she wanted me to come out and have dinner with her that evening."

"Was that usual?" Morgan asked. "Did you still see much of her."

"That's just it, it wasn't usual at all. We tended to be pretty self-conscious with each other . . . things had gotten pretty bad between us. So I hadn't been back out to the beach house since I'd left. I asked her why, what was the big deal. She said—and this is a quote, so far as I can trust my memory—'I need your advice, Toby. This time I'm going to fix the bastard once and for all.' Unquote. I didn't even ask her who she meant, because I assumed she was referring to her father, Aaron Roth. She always called him 'the bastard' in the same tone of voice, pure venom out of an old Spider Woman movie. She always spoke of or to him in the snottiest possible way . . . so that was it, she was finally going to fix Aaron once and for all."

Morgan said, "But could you tell what the fixing of Aaron Roth was going to involve? How do you really *fix* somebody?"

"I don't know."

"Why did she hate her father? I mean, you make it sound like more than a daughter's spite."

"Oh, it's always been more than spite. The thing about Goldie was that she always identified strongly with her mother, Kay—"

"Kay Flanders. More or less America's Sweetheart. Did you know her well?"

"Sure, I knew her. Kay was a star back on the Maximus lot in the days when Sol Roth, Goldie's grandfather, was still personally running the show, down to every last detail. The *whole* show. Kay wasn't quite as big as Garland and Rooney, but she was the closest thing Maximus had—she could pretty well do it all, dance and cry on cue and belt out the big numbers and push her chubby little fingers into her dimples and coo the love songs, and she was pert, perky, prettier than Garland, and came across as happier. But she was always in Judy's shadow. Because Kay wasn't a genius, and Judy was . . . but she was second only to Judy, and I think Sol was perfectly content with that. . . .

"Anyway, she was a star when Sol put Aaron to

47

work on the lot, the old let-my-son-work-his-way-up routine that puts the kid in the executive-office block in six months. Aaron apparently fell hard for Kay, and Kay must have eventually taken a liking to him . . . she was a sweet, wide-eyed innocent, virginal and pure and all that stuff on film, but of course she was a real person, older than people thought, and she was very near the top of a very big heap, and it must have occurred to her that marrying Aaron Roth was a hell of a career move. So one summer, there was a hell of a wedding at the Bel Air mansion."

"The Seraglio," Morgan said.

"No, Seraglio came later, after the fire. They were married at Bella Donna, the one Goldie wrote the book about. Bella Donna dated back to the twenties, sort of an Italian villa Sol built for his one and only wife, Rebecca, long since departed. . . . Aaron and Kay had a very big, *big* wedding, from what I've heard. Sol actually had Fritz Heimrich, who was under contract, come out to the house and direct the ceremony for close-ups and inserts—this was the day before the actual wedding took place. They filmed the real thing, too, and the reels still exist. Credits, cast, everything. People used to say they were surprised that Sol didn't shoot the wedding-night fuck itself. The irony was that Sol is such a puritanical old guy . . . he really is, always has been, a maniac about doing things the right way.

"When Goldie was born, the works—Maximus publicity . . . Simon Karr made sure Kay, America's little favorite, became America's favorite mother—whoopee! Kay went on making pictures, Maximus did their best to keep her changing with the times. When I met Goldie, let's see, Kay was probably forty-five. She wasn't well then, but I wasn't told very much about her problems—hell, it was a very dark secret. She was making a mystery at the time, and they were shooting her close-ups through gauze, all that stuff. Freddie Nugent, the cameraman, said they were putting more Vaseline on the lens than he was using on his hemorrhoids. . . . I was on the lot writing a thing for Jimmy Stewart and Ralph Bellamy, it never got made, which is lucky for all of us, and I used to see the rushes of Kay, and you could see the decay, it was well past the beginning of the end . . . she was coming apart. The mystery only got release outside the States, and the difference between the Kay in the movie and the Kay I saw over dinner occasionally was scary . . . she looked like something had gone wrong inside of her and was eating its way out toward the light, like an awful plant. She did some television specials, the one with Danny Kaye was pretty good . . . but she just had that look, she was used up.

"And Goldie was completely devoted to her, all the more so as Kay began slipping. Her health really went. Goldie became a nurse, practically, and Aaron never slowed down a step, just kept working harder and harder, staying on the lot sixteen, eighteen hours a day. And she never forgave her father. Goldie's the one who started the story that Aaron carried on a script conference with Tony Flyshaecker all the way through the funeral—the truth was he interrupted a conference with Flyshaecker, went to the funeral, and back to the conference afterward.

"Goldie started a lot of talk about Aaron. He made himself an easy target, not the warmest guy in the world, but I never saw him treat Goldie with anything but courtesy. Aaron can be the worst kind of shit heel, but some of Sol's class rubbed off on him, had to, I suppose."

"It's a sad story," Morgan reflected. "Typical though. Typical of California, of the movie families, they could call it the Bel Air disease. Families screwed up with power and money, and then people go away or die or something. . . ."

The wind whistled in the fireplace chimney, sparks flew up, and a draft of cold air slithered across the hearth. The light coming through the closed draperies was dull, bleak.

"So I went out to the beach house. Got there about a quarter past eight, said hello to Artie at the Colony gate. Artie said it was good to see me, said he missed me . . . 'Miss your smiling face' was exactly what he said. Anyway, he waved me on through, and I parked behind the garage. I still had a key, which I wasn't supposed to have, but I'd just forgotten to give it back to her. I had it out to unlock the door connecting

49

the chain-link fence and the garage itself, but the door was unlocked—nothing unusual about that. That's one of the things about the Colony, you don't have to spend all your time worrying about locking doors.

"I went up the walk, around to the side door. The sky was dark except for a bloodred line at the horizon, and the surf was maybe three feet—I remember, because it was so damned good to see and smell it all again . . . in my mind it was still home, where I belonged. I stood there maybe thirty seconds just watching that deep red turn to midnight blue, it moves that fast as it's going down below the horizon, then I went in the house. I called her name a couple of times, walked down the hallway toward a glow, a lamplight, coming from the main room—it's just a small house, you know—I can't recall if I thought there was anything wrong, I was coming down the hall and I suppose I thought she was out on the deck or making drinks . . . then I came into the familiar room where I'd done so much work and, shit, here it starts to get all blurry. The whole thing traumatized me, put me in some weird shock-corridor, nightmare-alley kind of thing . . . there she was on the floor, lying on her side, the arm on the floor flung up above her head—I wasn't thinking straight at all—okay, I'd had several drinks before I left my place, getting up the guts to see her again, it's true, she still meant something to me. . . . Christ, you're getting the whole gruesome story, aren't you?"

"I asked for it."

"I remember looking down at her, thinking heart attack, a fainting spell, an accident. I bent down beside her, and I was repeating her name, and then I saw my Oscar on the floor just around the corner of my desk. It had blood and her blond hair stuck to the base, and it scared me, made my skin crawl. I grabbed Goldie's face, pulled it around, and then I saw her eyes, wide open, staring at me, dry, staring, and I got something sticky on my hand and I knew it was blood and stuff. . . . It was perfectly obvious that she'd been struck on the head and was now dead.

"Then I think I heard something, some noise, a footstep, inside or outside, I didn't know, and I grabbed the Oscar without thinking, it was the only thing close at hand resembling a weapon. My brain was climbing the walls, I felt dazed and crazy, but I know damned well what I was thinking at that point—I figured the murderer was still there, that I'd caught him in the act, and then the door came busting open and there were four cops all over me, guns drawn, and it wasn't too terribly surprising that they voted me most likely murderer.

"If you recall the trial, it turned out that they had been tipped off that Goldie had been murdered, that she was newly dead, and they'd gotten to the house in about twenty minutes, and there stood I with my piccolo."

"Your bloody piccolo," Morgan amended, her wide mouth turning up just fractionally at the corners. Challis found this change of expression peculiarly reassuring. "Would you like a drink? Or coffee?"

"A Scotch and soda would keep me talking," he said. "It's past noon."

"Good. I want to know what it was like inside the trial, with all the machinery whirring . . ."

"Bloody boring, actually."

She got up, went to the sideboard, and came back with a bottle of Glenlivet, a pot of ice cubes, two heavy squat glasses, and a siphon bottle made of thick green glass with some long-ago brand name almost worn away. She poured two sturdy drinks. The soda hissed across the ice.

"Hilary Durant was your attorney. How could that have been boring?"

"Hilary Durant didn't exactly bust a gut. He was civilized, he had a big fee coming from Solomon Roth, and he thought I'd simply gotten a bellyful of Goldie, gone crazy at her latest excess, and beaten her to death. So far as I could tell, I didn't have a motive, and I figured that once they got digging into their investigation, they'd turn up somebody else, somebody with a motive and opportunity, and he'd be the killer."

"Circumstantial evidence is usually enough to do the trick," Morgan said. "I don't know how many explanations of that I've read in my mysteries . . . failing an eyewitness or being caught red-handed, but then, you

51

were caught more or less red-handed, weren't you? I mean, so it obviously seemed." She poked the embers and laid two more logs on the fire. Her blond Mary Travers hair caught the flaring flames' reflection.

"Well, Arnie Pryce prosecuted; figured he had me, open and shut. Murder weapon in my hand . . . and he and his people set about building a motive for me, which is just what I thought they wouldn't be able to do—not a believable motive, anyway. Which is exactly where I was wrong. Obviously Pryce knew juries, knew this jury, and knew what they wanted to hear. So he went to town on the nature of my relationship with Goldie, which, God knows, was a stormy, lurid business regularly punctuated by public screaming matches, Goldie slapping and scratching me, me occasionally taking a halfhearted swing at her. Pryce painted me as eaten up by jealousy and Goldie as a nymphomaniac, screwing and carrying on with anybody who chanced by and then flaunting it in my face. And there was any army of people willing to testify to our mutual nastiness and her sluttishness . . . so the point was that Goldie had been a bitch and I had been driven to kill her, never mind about the call tipping off the cops, which they said was obviously someone in the Colony who had heard the last argument before I killed her . . . never mind that the caller said she was dead, not getting killed—all that was immaterial. Well, Durant kept pushing on the telephone call, to no avail whatsoever." As he talked, he was recalling the bitterness he'd felt throughout the trial, watching it all go against him, watching the evidence in his favor, which seemed so crucial, so telling, continually shunted aside. He heard his voice cracking.

Morgan said, "We can stop—"

"So Durant said that the police had taken the Oscar and clumsily smeared my prints and anyone else's, including possibly the murderer's—talk about pathetic! He got better when he tried to prove that I'd have spattered myself with blood from her scalp, yet there was no blood on my clothing . . . he kept telling the jury that all they had to see was a reasonable doubt, but the spattered-blood routine didn't do it, either. Then he began the not inconsiderable task of trying

52

to whiten Goldie's reputation—what a joke! It was all rigged, of course. Sol provided the character witnesses for us, I swear to God half the out-of-work character actors in Los Angeles swore to high heaven that they'd seen us in a hundred different settings doing the lovebird tango—I mean, these poor clucks perjured themselves as a favor to Sol Roth. Of course, the jury could barely contain its mirth at this fool's parade. The point was, the jury wasn't any dumber than anybody else, they didn't believe our people, who were lying, and they did believe Pryce's people, who were telling the truth. Then Durant called Jack Donovan to testify for us—Donovan, for Chrissakes, her *boyfriend,* who actually said that they were just good friends, that we were planning a reconciliation, all kinds of pure bullshit. Don't ask me how Sol got him to do it. . . . Well, Donovan was a big mistake for our side. Pryce chopped him into coleslaw in cross-examination."

"It wasn't much of a defense," she said. Challis was staring into the fire. He was sweating from the memories.

"But what else was there? I didn't have an alibi. I was there, I was holding the fucking Oscar, she was still warm. . . . Her behavior really had driven me nuts—I really said the things those witnesses said they'd heard me say about her . . . In my fantasies I'd bludgeoned her to death a hundred times. Hell, I'd have voted to convict—"

"Except you didn't do it."

He shrugged helplessly.

"Then somebody else did. Your only hope is to find out who did it. The system has worked its way with you, found you guilty of murder, and now by a whacko quirk of fate, you're loose. You can't go to anyone, because the case is closed, you're a fugitive, and anyone who helps you is in big trouble. . . . Is that accurate, Soldier? And if you give yourself up, the case stays closed, you go to prison, and there's nobody out here to do anything about it. So, hadn't you better do it yourself? So what have you got to lose?"

"I don't know," he said. He was exhausted. The Scotch was hitting him like Merlin Olsen in his prime.

"Well, I know," she said, standing up and beginning

53

to pace. "You haven't got anything to lose but your life sentence. What more can they do to you?"

"But I don't have any idea how to go about it."

"Listen, you've got me, and I've read all the books and seen all the movies. . . . Now, there are two key elements in all that you just told me—no, three. First" —she ticked them off on her fingers—"there's the unknown stuff Goldie was going to tell you that would fix somebody, presumably Aaron Roth. What was it? Second, you say there never was any real investigation, which means that there could still be one . . . and third, who was trying to frame you?"

"Frame me?"

"The call to the police. Obviously someone knew you were coming, killed Goldie, tipped off the cops, and let nature take its course."

"Christ . . ."

"You've got to conduct your own investigation, Toby."

"Sure, with my face on every front page in California."

Slowly she came and stood in front of him. "Think. There's always an angle, a way to do things in Hollywood. Never forget that."

[6]

SHE LEFT HIM alone in the late afternoon while she went into Cresta Vista. He sat by the fire with a cup of coffee cooling beside him and tried to read. That didn't work. He thought about turning on the radio, decided he wasn't quite ready for reality. It was snowing again, and as darkness slid down from the mountaintops, he lost sight of the towering pines, the lake, the road. He tried very hard to remember how the innocent man tracked down the killer in books and movies. He thought about his own books and screenplays, but that was all completely different: it was all planned in notebooks and stacks of filing cards, and nothing was going to go wrong you couldn't fix. You had a plan, you stuck to it. *And now for something completely different— real life!*

When she came back, her face was flushed from the cold and there was snow in her hair and she was carrying a bag from the Rexall store. She hung up her coat and pushed him down into a chair at the round butcher-block kitchen table.

"Now, we're going to work a small order of miracle here," she said, smiling brightly. "You're going to walk out of here a new man."

The guard in the hangar had said something like that to him. He saw the man's face, the apologetic eyes, smelled the oily hangar. The tiny plane was being wheeled around before him. . . . She was turning the hot-water tap on full blast, dropping towels into the steaming sink. She threw an apron over his shoulders and cinched it up tight around his neck. She put a scissors on the kitchen table. He started to stand up.

"Come on," she said. "Give me a break, okay? While you were talking, I was thinking. I've got a plan that

55

makes perfect sense, assuming you want to go ahead and see what we can turn up about the real killer."

"We?"

She ignored his curiosity. "It's your old face that's going to be all over every front page in California . . . not your new one. Trust me."

"I hate people who say 'trust me' and 'have a nice day.' I want to kill them——"

"You really shouldn't say things about wanting to kill people, Toby. Coming from you, it's not too terribly funny. Now, sit still and look up here." She took the measure of his face, a comb in one hand, the scissors in the other. He shuddered. "You're not going to be funny-looking under all the hair, are you? I mean, you're not an ugly person? No chin, buck teeth . . ."

"The cheaper the crook, the gaudier the patter."

She made an initial swipe with the scissors, and he heard the grinding of the blades in his beard. A clump of beard fell onto the apron. Challis closed his eyes.

"You're the barber, so talk, barbers are supposed to talk," he said.

The sound and the tug of the scissors stopped for a moment, but she said nothing. He wanted to know more about her.

"What did you mean about going to sleep as a kid with the sound from the projection room coming down the hall? How did you know Jack Donovan, and what was that about sitting on Solomon Roth's knee when you were a little girl?" He jerked suddenly. "That was my ear . . . stick to the beard." He turned to look at her. "You're suspiciously involved in all this, now I come to think of it. I'm serious." He frowned into her smile: she wouldn't meet his eyes, kept her own gaze tied to the scissors, the comb, the falling bits of beard. "Out of all the people in the world, you come to my rescue——"

"Don't be paranoid. There's nothing to be suspicious about. Turn your head straight, lift your chin. I didn't mean to be secretive certainly, but it was your story that was so interesting. . . . I've never been convicted of anything."

"Maybe they just never caught you."

"Anyway, I've always been close to the movie business. My father was Harry Dyer, the director . . . he worked at Maximus for a while, I visited the lot one day when Solomon Roth was on the set where Dad was working—that's when I sat on his knee. I was very little. . . ."

"Harry Dyer," Challis mused. "He had a very nice touch with mysteries. Jacques Tourneur learned a lot from your father, Preminger learned how to make *Laura* watching your dad's pictures. . . . That must be where you got hooked on mysteries. Your father—I think of him with Dick Powell, George Macready, Tom Conway. And Milland did a couple with Dyer . . . I seem to remember that Harry Dyer ran into some trouble, something funny, in the fifties." Should he have said it? That was what happened when you let down your guard and thought out loud. The scissors made their steady, monotonous clipping sound.

"Yes, he ran into some trouble. My father was no innocent. He knew the business and he understood the kind of price you had to pay to make movies at all, let alone good ones, but he kept on. He'd been a writer doing scenarios for the silents, he'd been a cameraman, he even did some stunts, second-unit direction, then he got to direct. . . . I don't mean to sound corny, but he really paralleled the growth, the changes in the industry. And he did make some good movies, *West of Dodge* and *Hellcat Battalion* and *Pearl* and *The Man in the Fog*. But in the end, he ran into some trouble. . . .

"The problem with Harry was that he was a good listener, people were always unburdening themselves to him, and he'd sit patiently with them and listen to their confessions and buy the drinks. Well, in time, he came to know too much, and some people at the top decided something had to be done. I don't think it ever really occurred to them that he'd tell anything, but he had to be put in his place. So they took him off a couple of pictures in a row, they let it be known that he drank too much, wasn't reliable, none of which was true. Then, when no one else would hire him, these big wheels took him back, saying we'll stick by you even if no one else will, gave him some crummy little stinkers to direct. But that wasn't enough for them . . . this was at Paragon, of course. *Peeper* was in its heyday back then, and they really had the low and dirty on Freddie Hatfield, who was Paragon's biggest star—I mean, it was bad. Not just dope and hookers, but chains and whips and boys and girls ten or eleven years old, and a kid found dead in Hatfield's goldfish pond. It was the story of the decade, and the problem was, it was true. To avoid lawsuits, Manny Froelich at Paragon suggested a compromise. You give us back Freddie, and in return we'll give you the accumulated dirt on somebody else in our employ. It wasn't that uncommon—they threw Harry Dyer to the vultures. Freddie Hatfield, as it turned out, went on molesting and killing little children until he made the mistake of accepting Manny Froelich's invitation to go fishing on Manny's yacht. That day Freddie had his terrible accident, went overboard and was never seen again—sobbing and breastbeating at Paragon, super-duper funeral with an empty casket, the works. While Freddie is wearing cement galoshes and feeding the fishes out west of Catalina. . . . The lies about my father ran to the standard booze-and-broads stuff, and they kept him on a little salary, but he didn't get any more pictures. He played out the string, going to the beach near the Santa Monica pier every day . . . he'd sit there and shoot at seagulls with a Red Ryder Daisy Air Rifle. And then one day they found him lying on his side in the sand, dead as a dodo, a big smile on his face."

She stood back and regarded the last stubble of beard.

"Hooray for Hollywood," he said.

"Well, that's the show business," she said, leaning in and gauging the shape of his face. "I don't believe I can get it much closer with the scissors." She took the hot towels out of the sink, squeezed them out, and applied them softly, wetly to his face. "How long have you had the beard?"

"Twelve years," he said through the steam and towels. "Did you ever work in the business?"

"After what they did to my father? No, thanks. I spent a lot of time worrying about trying to revenge my father, but that was a waste of time. Or I thought so. I vacillate on the question of revenge. It's part of my fantasy life." She was shaking a can of shaving cream. Slowly she took away the hot towels and threw them into the sink. She stroked his beard's remains with the back of her hand; then the whoosh of the lather and her fingers massaging it in. He smelled the lime aroma, closed his eyes, and relaxed again.

"Come on, talk to me," he said.

"Dad left me some money, so I got a master's and most of a doctorate in English at UCLA and Stanford and married Charlie Sharpe who was a bright 'Hollywood' lawyer. We lived in Brentwood, and I really did the housewife thing, a life of incredible privilege and no real responsibilities other than listening to Charlie and fixing Sunday brunch by the pool for him, his clients, their wives and 'chickies,' as they used to be called. Ugh. Bloody Marys, eggs Benedict, crap. This was before the Perrier period, just my luck, so I had drunks falling into the pool, writers, directors, producers, New York sharpies of every stripe and variety. This is how weird it got—I played so much tennis that my sneakers actually got bloody, like toe shoes . . . like ballet—can you actually believe that? Somehow, looking back at my bloody footprints on the patio, I realized that tennis didn't mean all that much." The razor slid through his beard without a tug.

"I don't mean to sound snotty," she said. "I had friends. My friends . . . everybody hoped when we grew up we'd turn out to be Dinah Shore. Everybody thought about Dinah and Burt Reynolds. It got to the point where I wasn't even disgusted by thinking about other people's lives. Bob Evans and the football announcer, Steve and Ali, Rod and Britt . . . Who was your gynecologist, your hairdresser, your tennis pro, your gardener, your pool man, your stockbroker? Did you see Cher at the Right Bank Tea Room? Matthau and Marty Ritt at the races? Who was taking a crack at writing the new dirty novel? I began to care what Joyce Haber and Jody Jacobs were writing about.

"And I decided to get out. All Charlie Sharpe would talk about was putting a project in turn-around, three-picture deals with development money on the front end and points at the back end, above the line and below the line, investors from Oklahoma City, negative costs, payoffs, and payouts and child-molestation charges

. . . so I got out and Charlie Sharpe didn't really notice because he was in Hamburg raising German shelter financing, but when he got home he found all the plants were dead. I just closed up the joint and forgot to tell the fucking plant man . . . he really was a *fucking* plant man, he was fucking Patsy Bloom and Cheryl Tomkins among my friends, in fact. . . . I also forgot to tell the tree man, the crushed-rock-and-gravel man, the lily-pond man, the tennis-net man, the bird-feeder man, who was a hummingbird expert of note, and the ant man, who was supposed to rid Charlie's game room of a particularly hardy breed of ants who seemed to me to have joined us directly from the pages of S. J. Perelman—anyway, maybe killing the ants could be a new game for Charlie Sharpe. It's all right with me."

She carefully finished shaving his neck, and he felt naked. She wiped his face with another damp cloth and patted the pale skin dry. She leaned back and looked at him, lips pursed. "Do you feel tough? Can we risk a mirror?" Her pale green eyes flared with her smile. She handed him a mirror. He peeked through squinting eyes.

"Hmmm," he said, slowly opening them. "Hmmm. I've never seen this face before . . . I was a helluva lot younger when I went undercover, hid my face. I suppose it looks thinner than it did twelve years ago. And I lost weight during the trial." He moved the mirror farther away. "Christ, have you ever seen a more gruesome color? My face looks like I'm wearing a diaper for a mask. Take it away," he said, handing her the mirror.

"Yes, diaperlike is a remarkably accurate description." She bustled around him, brushing against him; he smelled her perfume, her hair, saw the tiny diamonds in her ear lobes, admired the way her checked cotton blouse drew snugly across her small bosom. "However, we have this little white bottle of Coppertone QT lotion, which I'm going to apply very carefully to that dingy gray face and which will turn you into something resembling a Zuma Beach lifeguard. From the neck up."

For fifteen minutes she massaged the lotion into his

face, forehead, ears, neck, wiped it all away, massaged another layer in. "Somehow, you've got to come out basically the same color everywhere."

"You sound doubtful."

"I am doubtful, pardner. Stand up, follow me to the bathroom."

"I feel like a naked Frankenstein's monster."

"You're being born again. Just don't dawdle."

He followed her, stood leaning against the bathroom door, watching while she prepared several packets of potions on the tiled countertop. He seemed to remember Goldie doing roughly the same thing.

"Shampoo time," she said.

She was arranging a bath towel around his shoulders when he asked her what he really wanted to know.

"Stop bouncing around for a second," he said, putting his hands on her shoulders, looking down at her restless, flickering eyes. Her mouth had a natural characteristic jut to it, the lips slightly thick and sculptured: he kept noticing these little things, and he'd seen enough movies to know that was a bad sign. Bad, that is, if you were on the lam and needed to walk down those mean streets by yourself and make like a tough existential antihero. "Just answer this—why are you going to all this trouble and danger to help me escape? Or whatever the hell I'm doing. You're becoming an accessory of some kind, and dammit, I've got to know why."

"Are you done shaking me?"

"I'm sorry—"

"Bend over the sink."

He bent over, and she began to pour water from a pitcher over his head.

"I've always been bookish. My mother and father always read a lot, books, screenplays, magazines, encyclopedias. I grew up seeing movies and reading. My father had the most amazing collection of pulp mystery magazines, hundreds of them, and I just sat down and systematically read them. And the people who used to hang around our house—Frank Gruber, Harry Kurnitz, Raymond Chandler, Elliot Paul, a bunch of other mystery writers—they all used to talk with Harry about plots and characters and atmosphere, to Lorraine, too, my mother, and I listened and I'd read their books and tried to understand how they wrote them." She was working shampoo into his hair as she talked. "Then I went off to college, and one day I decided I was ready to write a mystery novel of my own. So I tried and tried, and it never worked out right, but I never quite gave up. I've been making notes ever since, cutting gruesome stories out of the newspapers, filling one folder after another. In the back of my mind I've got this terrible fear—that I can read 'em, but I can't write 'em. Close your eyes tight, I'm going to rinse. But I do keep trying, one notebook after another. It's the plots that usually go haywire. I don't know how many times I've done a hundred pages and I begin to think something's not quite right, I read it all again, and it hits me that I'm writing a book that Ellery Queen or Bret Halliday or Ngaio Marsh or George Harmon Coxe wrote thirty years ago and I read lying in a hammock twenty years ago."

She was squeezing water out of his hair, and his back hurt from bending over. He took a deep breath, figured that a man who survived a plane crash could survive a shampoo at the hands of Morgan Dyer.

"Keep your head down, eyes closed. We're just getting to the key step. Now, to continue my justification for breaking the law . . . and, of course, you're not going to believe it. But this—your predicament—is a ready-made plot. You're a mystery novel that's come to life, and at the very least I can recognize one staring me in the face. So this is my chance to be a participant, even if I can't write a novel. Is that pretty weak motivation in your eyes? I mean, you're the writer."

"I don't know," he muttered into the washbasin. "How do I know? . . . No, I don't think that's why you're doing it. Not really. But it's probably more fun for you to pretend it's the reason, and it's your business. It's all right with me—"

"But what is the reason if it isn't my frustration as a mystery writer?"

"Revenge. You were talking about revenge . . ."

"Hmmm. You're not as dumb as you look."

She pulled his head up by the hair, and he faced himself in the mirror.

"And I look pretty dumb."

"Put your head back down."

Two hours after that she finished cutting his hair, combed it, gave it a whiff of holding spray, and led him back to the mirror.

With the beard gone, his face and skull had developed an entirely new shape, leaner, more sharply hollowed and defined. The tanning lotion had given his face a California-copper look, which he could see was going to blend with his nose and forehead, given a few more careful applications. His hair had grown from a dark brown to a sandier tone and by subtly shaping the hairline at the temples, ears, and the nape of his neck, she had completely altered not merely the color of his hair and eyebrows, but the framing of his face.

"Be honest . . . would you recognize yourself?" She bounced around him, primping him, attacking stray hairs with a comb. "Be honest."

"No, I honestly don't think I would recognize myself. I am a new man. I even feel different." He was having difficulty controlling a budding sense of wonder.

"Don't forget, you don't have any papers to show you're a different man. So you've got to be careful. No speeding tickets, for instance, no getting into any trouble . . . but I'd say you're in the clear as far as being recognized. We've got to get you some clothing —you can't go tracking down a murderer in what you're wearing."

"Oh, shit! I'd forgotten about all that." He smiled grumpily at her.

"Well, you need some tutoring. Let me tell you how to do it."

[7]

HE WOKE UP in the early morning with the night winds still ripping across the lake, tearing at the windows of his bedroom. He'd been dreaming hard, and when he woke he was sure the cops were hot on his tail for the murder of his wife—only he was tight-lipped, grim-eyed Alan Ladd in *The Blue Dahlia,* worried about the metal plate in William Bendix's head, wishing he didn't have to say good-bye to Veronica Lake. It took several scary minutes to get it all straightened out, and while he worked at it he clung to his blanket, holding it tight to his chin. The return of the lapses bothered him, intensified the unreality of the truth of his situation. But then, maybe that was the key to getting through what lay ahead: accept the unreality and play it like a movie. That was essentially what Morgan had told him the night before; she'd stressed that all you could go by in a situation such as his was what she'd learned from the mystery novels she'd spent her lifetime reading. *Look,* she'd said, *this is the way they do it.* He relaxed his grip on the covers and felt his heartbeat slowing down. He felt suspended uneasily between reality and illusion.

He had a hell of a time recognizing himself in the bathroom mirror, and over coffee and toast Morgan emphatically assured him that he looked like he'd just come back from lying in the Acapulco sunshine and bore very little resemblance to Toby Challis. "The eyes," she said, "we can't do much about the eyes . . ." She shrugged; as far as the eyes went, he'd have to trust to luck. Finally she stood up. "It's time."

She called the sheriff in Cresta Vista while Challis listened on the extension.

"Jeff, I thought I'd take your advice and check on

the roads. I'd like to drive into Los Angeles this morning . . ."

"The sooner the better, Morg," he said. "The snow's supposed to start again this afternoon, but right now I'd say it's okay."

"I guess everything went all right with the kids," she said.

"Sure, sure." The sheriff sounded tired, harried. "Honest to God, Morg, I've never seen anything like the past few days. We've been going crazy since yesterday afternoon . . . the choppers got a break in the weather, went in, and found that downed plane . . . the prison plane, y'know? They found it just before nightfall, and we had a helluva snowslide between us and it about midnight. Worked all night on the snow, and this morning the wind's too bad for the choppers, so we're still trying to get there on the road. I'm telling you, I'm bushed."

"Can they tell if there are any survivors?"

"Pretty hard to see in among the trees. It's amazing they found it at all, really, with the weather and all . . . but they didn't report any movement." He sighed heavily and made a slurping noise. Challis could see the paper cup and smell the coffee in his mind. "All we can do is get there as soon as we can. Well, anyway, they're honking the horn for me. So drive careful-like, and take your time."

"I will, Jeff. And good luck."

"We'll be all right. It's those guys in the plane, that Challis fella and the rest of 'em, they're the ones need luck."

In the garage, Challis opened the rear door of the green Mercedes sedan. The backseat was covered with cardboard boxes of books addressed to Murder, He Says, Bookshop. Morgan stood beside him, holding three wool plaid blankets and an old raincoat. It was cold and damp in the garage. He could see their breath.

"Take your pick—the trunk or the floor. We can't run the risk of your being seen. The mountain's a small world, and everybody knows me. I didn't bring anybody up the mountain, and I'd better not bring anybody extra back down."

65

"I'll get on the floor in back," he said. "Cover me with the blankets, tilt some of the boxes out over me."

It was a tight fit, brought a reminder of the aches and pains of the past few days. She drove with the radio on. His body seemed to absorb each bump and turn.

In a little while she said, "Hang on. We're just entering Cresta Vista."

When she stopped for a traffic light, irrational fear took over: he felt eyes boring into him. He held his breath. It took forever; then they were pushing forward. "The town's full," she said. "Everybody doing their stocking up while there's a break in the storm. We'll be out of it in a couple of minutes."

The winding, slippery drive curling down the side of the mountain left him clawing at the floor, his foot braced against the door. Every few minutes claustrophobia would set in, he'd begin gagging in the heat and the wool of the blankets; then a sudden swerve and he'd see the Mercedes hurtling off into the abyss, plummeting down to disappear among the pines, and he'd forget the heat and the wool and pray for survival.

Finally, in the outskirts of San Bernardino, she pulled off onto a side road and stopped.

"Okay, can you get out?"

"I can't reach the door handle." He heard her get out and open the back door. He pushed forward, struggling like an inchworm, until he'd worked his way out onto the gravel roadbed. He staggered to his feet and smiled, followed her into the front seat.

They drove through the cool, soft fog with a promise of more rain in the air. He smelled the Pacific. Morgan stuck the tape of Sidney Bechet into the underdash deck, and "Sweet Lorraine" filled the car. He looked at her as she drove. He was connecting the song and the woman, her level sandy eyebrows, long nose, and what now struck him as the key to her face: the wide mouth with the little steeple point in the center, the built-in impishness to the hint of smile which remained even when she was intently watching the road unwind.

She hooked off to the south and slid on into the Fox Hills shopping center. Rain had begun to speckle the windshield. The red monolith of the May Company building loomed over them.

"Give me your sizes," she said, turning off the headlamps. It was dark, though it was just past noon. "I've got to get you some clothes so you'll look like everybody else. A sport coat, a couple of shirts, a pair of slacks, underwear, socks, shoes, a sweater, a raincoat . . ."

He gave her all the sizes, said, "I haven't got any money—"

"Don't worry. I'm going to get you some cash, and I'll charge all this stuff. You just sit here and think about what you're going to do when I get back."

"Morgan," he began, "I don't know what to say. . . . You're nuts to be doing this—"

"Look upon yourself as research. Don't forget my book."

He listened to the radio news and heard that the rescue crews from Cresta Vista and the California Highway Patrol were trying to reach the sighted wreckage of the light plane carrying blah-blah-blah . . . He knew the story. But they still didn't know he was missing: as far as anyone knew, everyone in the plane was dead and accounted for. He inspected his face in the mirror on the back of the sun visor. It was quite incredible: the dark tanned face, the sandy hair and eyebrows that appeared to be sun-bleached. It was Toby Challis' face and it wasn't: he felt anonymous, but he also felt as if everyone passing the car was staring at him.

She'd been gone an hour, and came back heavy-laden. He saw her coming and got out to help. She was laughing: it was a game. Rain dampened her face; he wanted to kiss her, knew he had no business entertaining such a thought. There wasn't really time for being human: he *wasn't* quite human, anyway. He was a convict. And he was newly back from the dead.

She pulled into a gas station on Sepulveda and he changed clothes in the men's room. A gray-herringbone tweed jacket, a blue cotton shirt, tan straight-legged slacks, brown-and-black saddle shoes, black socks, a plain leather belt, a Burberry raincoat. He put a blue V-neck sweater, another shirt, another pair of identical slacks, some toilet articles, extra underwear and socks into one sack and ran through the pelting rain back to the car. The neon lights of the station reflected on the wet paving, in the windshield.

She handed him a bank envelope, thick. "Here's some mad money."

He opened it. "My God, this is too—"

"Toby! Don't be an idiot. It's five hundred dollars in tens and twenties. It's all you've got, all you can get, and you can't use any credit cards—we went through this last night. Take it, shut up about it, and tell me where we're going." She pulled back onto Sepulveda, heading north.

"The Beverly Hills Hotel," he said.

"And what are we going to do there? Maybe they'll page you in the Polo Lounge." She stopped at a red light, and an LAPD black-and-white drew alongside. The driver glanced over at Toby, who froze. The cop smiled faintly, nodded. Toby nodded back, feeling weak: he was going to have to get the hell over that. The light changed, and they moved away together.

"Look, *we* are not going to do anything. You are going to drop me off and I'm going to . . . well, begin. Alone."

"I'm going to come with you. I want to help—"

"Listen to me, Morgan. I don't want to sound corny, but there are some things a man has to do alone."

"You're right. You don't want to sound corny, but you do anyway."

"I'm not kidding. I've got to be alone and try to figure this out. It's my life we're playing around with. I can't drag you in any further. They catch me now, you're still clear. . . . I can't let you risk your own welfare—"

"You know, Toby, you actually talk like one of your screenplays."

"Please don't make this any harder for me than it is, Morgan. Please. Just leave me at the hotel—"

"Oh, God, all right," she said peevishly. "But I'm going to give you my address and telephone number. You never know. You might want to buy a book— you could stop by the store. Or come to the house and borrow one." She turned right on Olympic, left on Beverly Glen, and was headed north toward Sunset. The rain swept past them, muddy in the gutters. She'd started the cassette again, and the piercing wail of Bechet's "Laura" filled the car. Ahead of them the Bel Air gates loomed out of the rain. A light glowed in the guardhouse. Bel Air looked like a rain forest. Three Rolls-Royces stood in a row at the traffic light, waiting to make their sorties out into the real world. The first one was turquoise, and he'd never seen a turquoise Rolls-Royce before. All the Roth family drove Rolls-Royces, but none of them were turquoise. Dumb color for a Rolls.

She maneuvered the sharp left from Sunset into the hotel driveway. Above them the rain seemed to weigh the towering palm trees down, and the pink hotel looked crummy, water-soaked. It was meant to bake in the sunshine, welcoming Elizabeth Taylor back to her customary bungalow. Looking crummy and damp, it welcomed the convicted murderer.

She stopped at the crest of the glistening black driveway and waved the parking attendant away. She took a notepad from her purse and jotted down the address and the telephone number. Watching her, he already felt lonely. Left behind on an island full of ungodly dangers.

"Call me," she said. "And give me a kiss."

He leaned over and kissed her. Her mouth was like ice.

"For God's sake, be careful," she said. She was looking straight ahead, down the driveway. He opened the door, retrieved his sack from the seat, and shut the door. He watched as the Mercedes slid off down the driveway, back toward the traffic on Sunset.

One parking attendant was on the telephone. There were no waiting guests, no arriving cars. Another attendant was standing under the long marquee up the steps by the entrance to the lobby. Challis walked toward him, trying to catch his eye. He stopped beside him. In the lobby, logs roared in the fireplace.

"Eddie," Challis said. The attendant, his face blank, eyes helpful but unrecognizing, looked him head-on. Challis had never seen the place so deserted. The only sound was the rain drumming on the marquee and running off the sides. "Eddie . . ."

"Can I help you, sir?"

"You don't know me?" Challis whispered. "Come over here," he said, tugging at his sleeve, drawing him into the wall.

"Ah, what can I do . . . ? Hey, wait a—"

"Eddie, my boy, compose yourself, prepare yourself, and don't scream or anything . . . it's me, Challis." He held Eddie's arm tightly. "Come on, don't give me any shit, Eddie. Look, it's me."

Eddie's face went peculiarly gray. "Who's shitting who . . . whom, I mean. It is you, isn't it?" He looked off at the driveway, doing a take. "I mean, it is, you are, aren't you?" He looked away, looked back again. "Where the hell's your beard?" He was whispering, too, but he was having understandable difficulty grasping what was in fact the evidence of his eyes and ears. "Anyway, you're supposed to be in jail . . . holy shit, man," awe creeping into his voice, "You're supposed to be dead in that plane crash!" He was a tall, skinny kid who'd always made Challis think of the way Henry Aldrich should have looked on the old radio show. Maybe it was the way Eddie's high voice kept losing hold of itself. Eddie was twenty-five, and Challis had gotten to know him simply because he had recognized Challis, an unusual experience for a writer. Eddie wanted to write screenplays; everyone parking cars or pumping gas or waiting tables wanted to get into the show business, and played every card dealt them. Fate had dealt Challis to Eddie, and Eddie had pursued it. One Sunday Challis had even asked Eddie and his girlfriend to stop by the place in Malibu for brunch, and the day had turned out well. The kid's work showed some talent, and Challis' agent, Ollie Kreisler, had said he might be willing to represent Eddie on a one-shot movie-of-the-week deal. It hadn't panned out, but Eddie was grateful. And so, in need of transportation, it was to Eddie at the Beverly Hills Hotel that Challis had come.

"I didn't die," Challis said, holding Eddie in place. "I got out of the plane. I'm here and . . . Stop looking at me like that, damn it, I'm a customer talking to you about my car. I'm here, and nobody knows it yet. I've got to do what I can to find out who killed Goldie . . . it's my only hope, Eddie."

"Jesus, in your shoes, man, I'd try to escape, Mr. Challis. Ship out on a freighter to the Far East, y'know, or head for Mexico . . . you'd have a better chance, y'know what I mean?" He'd accepted Challis' presence, just another oddball turn of events in Movieland. Nobody back in Dubuque would believe it.

"Eddie, look, I need a car . . ."

A faintly crafty expression lit Eddie's long, permanently adolescent face: freckles, blue eyes, wide all-American mouth. "Listen, I'll make you a deal. If, say *if*, you somehow beat the frame they hung on you, you have to promise, I mean *swear,* man, you'll get this thing I'm working on to Maximus . . . to Aaron Roth himself. Promise me, and you got yourself a set of wheels. Deal?"

"I promise, for God's sake." A black Stutz pulled up, but the other attendant got it. "Where's the car?"

"Show you the kind of pal I am, I'll let you have mine . . . '65 Mustang ragtop, dark green, needs a little work on the chrome, but—"

"Eddie, does it have a wheel at each corner? Fine. The chrome doesn't worry me."

"No, but the puke might."

"Puke? What puke? This is no time to play games with me."

"No, I'm serious, man. You know Matilda, the girl I brought out to your place? Well, we were out at Catalina around Christmas, see, and on the way back, on the seaplane, y'know? Well, Matilda got to feelin' a little queasy . . ."

"Really, it's okay, Eddie."

"And she kept it down until we landed, but about five minutes after we got in the car, I had to stop for this asshole runnin' a red light, and poor Matilda let fly with about a quart of dago red. I told her to do it out the window, but then this guy has to run the light . . . anyway, the dago red went straight ahead, hit the window and the dashboard and ran down inside the heating ducts on the dash. So the car can get to smell like puke, but otherwise—"

71

"Eddie, for God's sake!"

"Come on, we'll go get it."

They walked through the rain to the lot where the Mustang squatted next to a couple of sleek Mark V's.

"The keys are in it," Eddie said, opening the door. "Top's manual."

Challis slid in behind the wheel. Eddie was peering down at him, as if making a final identification check. "So you think it was a frame?"

"Shit yes. Mr. Kreisler was in here during the trial —well, he's in here all the time, of course, but he said hello, remembered me from that time you took me to his office, and we shot the breeze for a minute, he said he figured the fix was in . . . called it a half-assed investigation, said Hilary Durant still needed help to tie his shoes and wipe his bottom, and said it all went back to Goldie . . . that it was all Goldie's fault, whatever the hell that meant." Eddie shrugged. "So, if I can help, lemme know. But I still think you should hop a freighter to somewhere a hell of a long way from here."

Challis nodded. "Thanks, Eddie."

"Anyway, that Oscar meant too much to you. I remember how you handled it when you showed it to Matilda and me. You wouldn't have killed her with that Oscar, no way."

Challis smiled. "*I* never even thought of that, but I hated to see it introduced as evidence. Maybe you're right . . ."

"I'm really sorry about the puke, Mr. Challis. And . . . shit, man, good luck. As far as I'm concerned, you're up on the mountain dead." He tapped on the fabric top, Challis rolled up the window, and as he swung around to leave the lot, Challis saw the gangly figure standing in the rain, watching him, shaking his head. Huck Finn wondering at the passing parade.

Challis was hungry.

[8]

OLLIE KREISLER'S OFFICE was on the top floor of a tall building at Sunset and Doheny, which was the sort of place a smart talent would want for his agent. As Ollie occasionally remarked in suitable company, you didn't get to the penthouse by fucking up, and fucking up was something that if Ollie had ever done at all was now buried in the distant past, beneath a mountain of successful deals. Ollie was calm in an intense, dour way, a kind of immaculate calm which bespoke his Pasadena upbringing and Princeton education. He had things so carefully under control that you hated to run the risk of disturbing any part of it: there was the fear that it was the one utterly unforgivable transgression you might commit insofar as Ollie Kreisler was concerned.

Consequently, Challis parked in the underground ramp and paved the way with a call from the lobby. He told the secretary that he was Ned Tannen, Ned Tannen *personally,* calling from Universal, and that if Mr. Kreisler couldn't take his call immediately, he, Mr. Kreisler, would surely regret it for the rest of his life. Ten seconds passed, and then the familiar soothing voice came on: "Ned, old-timer, what in the world can I do for you? You have my undivided attention."

"What's green and red and goes sixty miles an hour?"

"I don't understand that actually—Ned, is this a joke?"

"A frog in a Waring blender. You're not laughing, Ollie. You're supposed to laugh when I use my best material."

"Ned, you baffle me. My secretary just said . . . Ned, are you all right? You sound as if you might have a cold. Say something, Ned, please say something."

"Listen, Ollie, I'm not Ned Tannen. Just don't hang up . . . it's Toby."

"I see. Well, now we're getting somewhere, though a ruse of this kind is not in the best of professional taste. Toby who?"

"How many Tobys have you got on your client list, Ollie?"

Without missing a beat, Ollie Kreisler said, "Only one, but I would have bet rather a lot that my Toby was dead. Up until ten seconds ago."

"Well, you'd have lost. I'm downstairs in the lobby."

"Will I recognize you?"

"I hope not."

"I see. Well, then, Margo won't recognize you either. So why not come up."

"I'm hungry."

"I'm sure you are, old boy. I'll do what I can. Tell Margo you're Mr. Benson."

"Okay. I'm on my way."

"Toby?"

"What?"

"You do amaze me."

Margo was a very classy girl from an Eastern school. She looked like Phyllis Thaxter, pale and well-bred, and was a perfect representative of the Kreisler Office, as it was known, though there were three other partners. She looked at him calmly, with a remote smile that said he should be ashamed of himself. "You weren't Mr. Tannen at all, were you? You're Mr. Benson." She shook her small head. Her glasses hung on a chain around her neck and rested on a flat Eastern chest. She was very pretty. Challis had known her for three years. He watched her eyes linger on his face for a fraction of a second longer than seemed necessary. "Please, follow me, Mr. Benson."

None of the other secretaries or assistants looked up as she led him back to the corner office. Before she knocked on the door, she said in a perfectly modulated voice, "Would turkey on whole wheat be all right?"

"Wonderful. And a beer. Any kind of beer."

She nodded, opened the door, and said that Mr. Benson was here. As she passed him, she caught his eye, shook her head gravely, and muttered, "Ned Tannen." Then she astonished him with a wink and closed the door behind her.

"My God, she smells good."

"She is a top-drawer girl," Ollie said, half-sitting on the slab of glass which rested on two pink-veined marble columns and served as his desk. "Very good Park Avenue firm . . . family, I mean. And now," he said, forcing himself to remain in characteristic repose, "what the fuck is going on here?" His voice rose an octave but was immediately yanked back to the lower register where it belonged. "It goes without saying that I'm glad to see you. At least, I think I am."

Challis began the recitation with the plane crash, the storm raging outside. As he talked, he paced the immense room with its Calder mobile and bank of windows beyond which Beverly Hills looked gray-green in the steady downpour. The trees in the office swayed gracefully in the breeze of the air changer, and Challis saw himself reflected in the steel-framed movie posters filling any wall space not already covered with dull, oiled bookcases. Kreisler's foot, encased in a highly polished black penny loafer, swung in the space between the pink marble columns. He wore a pale gray sweater and brown gabardine slacks, and he listened without flickering a muscle.

Challis heard himself dwelling on the woman who had come to his aid on the mountain. He didn't want to mention her name to anyone, but he did want to make clear what a creature she was, how she'd thrown herself unequivocally into the battle. Just talking about her gave him a lift, made him think that there could be a way out.

Finally Ollie interrupted: "Cut to the chase, cut to the chase."

Challis finished up quickly, describing his parting with Morgan and the acquisition of Eddie's car. Ollie clicked a cough drop around in his mouth and stared at him. "I don't know whether you're lucky or not. But, on balance, I'm persuaded that you probably are. Certainly lucky to have survived the crash, to have found this Wonder Woman type. But the rest of it is going to take some thought. Did you have anything in mind that I might do to help?" He stood up and yawned as if this sort of problem came his way with boring regularity. His telephone buzzed, and he answered it, listened, sighting down the barrel of a gold fountain pen. "I won't say I'm insulted by that figure, Leon, but I'm sure Jerry would be insulted, so I'm insulted for him. You've offended me by proxy. So let me tell you . . . no, please, Leon, may I continue? Thank you. It's Jerry's third original for a major, and given what those pictures are doing I think it's only fair to advance by hundred-thousand-dollar increments. We both want to be fair, don't we, Leon? So the tab on this one is three hundred thousand, with the normal consideration on points which—shall we be open and frank, Leon?—which we both know doesn't amount to what Jerry calls diddley-squat. So tell your krauts that's how it stands and save us both some time. . . . Yes, thank you, Leon. And *hasta la vista* to you, too." He leaned back against a bookcase and said, "Well?"

"No, I haven't any suggestions for ways you can help. . . . That poster, Ollie, I never noticed that poster before. *The Man in the Fog*. Why do you have that up in here?"

"It's a very handsome poster, for one thing, and rarer even than *Laura* posters. And the director, Harry Dyer—you remember Harry Dyer, don't you, Toby?"

"He died on the beach at Santa Monica. He went there to plink at the gulls with an air rifle . . ."

"You don't say? That has an apocryphal ring to it, doesn't it? Anyway, Harry Dyer was a client here when Maxie Trautwein founded the agency. Maxie had this poster in his office for years, and when Maxie died, I made off with it. . . . See, down here in this billow of fog, you can see where Dyer signed it. 'For Max, who resents giving me ninety percent of his earnings, Harry Dyer.' But what this bit of trivia has to do with your problems . . ." Ollie Kreisler sat down on a cream-colored couch of nubby fabric and put his feet up on a coffee table.

"It's a coincidence," Challis blurted out. "It was Harry Dyer's daughter, Morgan—she was the woman on the mountain."

76

"Look, you know how tiny this world is. Nothing ever surprises me here, the same faces keep going by. It's like a shooting gallery." When Ollie spoke, Challis smelled the wild-cherry cough drops. "Her husband, or former husband, Sharpe, was involved in a couple of deals we put together out of this office . . . lawyer, Charlie Sharpe, that's it. I had some meetings with him, somehow it came out that Harry Dyer would have been his father-in-law. He said he'd never seen a Dyer picture. Well, that pretty well fixed him in my mind—that and the fact that I once saw him at the Bistro with a white-belt-and-shoe combination. God! I fear for our industry sometimes. Anyway, so she's the one who did the facial, the hair job. It's a small world."

"The funny thing, Ollie, is that she followed the trial very closely."

"I hope you know I did my best for you when I testified, Toby. I had to admit that you and Goldie had a fiery marriage in the grand old Hollywood tradition. I mean, everybody admitted that, but think of the stuff I left out—the time you threw that Waterford rose bowl of Connie's at her, for instance. Connie always said she wished you'd hit her, because then the rose bowl wouldn't have broken. I did my best, Toby—"

"She not only followed the trial," Challis went on, nodding away the glittering shard of Ollie Kreisler's guilt, "but she said she'd actually met Goldie . . . and had dated Jack Donovan."

There was a knock at the door, and Margo entered with a tray of sandwiches and four bottles of Olympia Gold. She wore an enigmatic smile which revealed a glimmer of white tooth. Ollie thanked her; when she was gone, he leaned toward Challis, said, "I'd throw you to the cops in exchange for one night with Margo. I think you should know where you stand, Toby. Have a sandwich and don't worry. She's from the old school. She would never fuck a Jew. Which is why I hired her. Margo keeps me humble." He poured a glass of beer and pushed it across the coffee table. "Please sit down, Toby. You've seen Beverly Hills in the rain before."

Challis sat down. Sinking into the couch, he had to fight the weariness, the tension. "Has your house slid down the side of the canyon yet?"

"Terribly amusing, old fellow. On a par, I'd say, with your remarks about Manson doing his night work in my neighborhood." He took a small bite of turkey sandwich and watched while Challis crammed his mouth full. "It surprises me about Ms. Dyer and Jack Donovan. Don't try to talk with your mouth full—the disguise is brilliant, but your eating habits will give you away. Now, if Jack Donovan had been found murdered—not such an awful idea, either—Morgan Dyer would have gotten my vote as suspect number one." He sipped some beer.

"What are you talking about?" Challis moved his hand to brush crumbs from his mustache, realized he had no mustache.

"Well, Max Trautwein told me the story," Ollie said, making a sudden face. "Good Lord, I forgot to take my cough drop out of my mouth. I've eaten it." He seemed to be accusing Challis, then went on: "And Max was right on the spot when it happened, and he was close to Harry Dyer, naturally. You see, Toby, it was Jack Donovan who wrote the last big piece on Dyer, the one that accused him of all sorts of unsavory misbehavior. The story Max told me was that the studio fed Dyer to Donovan to get somebody else off the hook, not an uncommon practice in those days. I'm not sure actually if Donovan wrote the piece or if he was the leg man for the bone-picker who did, but the point remains the same. A dead Donovan would have led, I'm afraid, to Morgan Dyer, which illustrates my point—namely, that life out here is like a big movie with a single cast, a closely monitored, tightly contained world with its own laws, natural and otherwise." He sipped the foam off his beer and bit another small edge from his sandwich.

"She didn't say anything about Donovan and her father," Challis said, remembering her comment about wanting to revenge her father.

"Well, you'd hardly expect her to, would you? Though it is odd that she'd date the man . . . but then, I'm rather old-fashioned. I've always had an unwavering belief in the restorative powers of a feud, real honest-to-God bad blood, as long as you get even in the end. Donovan is the sort of man who can inspire bad blood, I suppose, though I personally don't mind him all that much." Ollie stroked his finely sculptured chin and looked through his gold aviator glasses at the poster from *The Man in the Fog*. "A certain kind of Irishman, a street fighter with an overlay of civilized manners. But he's got the soul of a bomb-throwing gunrunner operating out of a Belfast alley. He's always having parties out on his yacht, raising money for the orphans of the 'troubles' . . . you know damn well the money goes to buy *plastique* or gelignite or automatic weapons, you just *know* it. It's his nature . . . he's just the sort of Errol Flynn type who would appeal to your late wife."

Challis swallowed a dry cud of turkey and said, "You do think I was framed, don't you, Ollie? They tell me you think the fix was in—"

"Is that what they say? My, my." He finished the last of his sandwich and patted his mouth with the linen napkin Margo had provided.

"Well, is that what you think? Don't be shy."

"It's my gut feeling, Toby," he said after a moment's thought. "But I hesitate to say it, because a man in your position can hardly be blamed for grasping at any straw he can find. And my opinion is a particularly insubstantial straw . . . there's no real hope inherent in my gut feelings. Do you understand what I'm saying?"

"For God's sake, Oliver, now *you* cut to the fucking chase."

"I think it—the trial, the getting rid of one expendable screenwriter—was the best possible solution to the fix that the industry, and particularly Maximus, found themselves in. Figuratively, you'd shit on the rug. That's the way it *looks* to me, that's the way it *feels, smells*. But the point is, I have no evidence to support my belief. Maybe I'm just harking back to the old days, when the fix was in on everything. . . . If the cover is ever removed from all the movie-industry suicides and accidental deaths, let alone murders, something far worse than the creature from the Black Lagoon is going to come waltzing out—that's probably what I'm thinking of and why I'm thinking you were a convenient patsy. Am I living in the past, my boy? Or do things never change, after all? I hear about some murders in the rock business these days—Jesus, the rock business! Talk about getting your hopes dashed and your hair curled! And nobody ever seems to get caught . . . or it gets hung on poor Juan, the gardener, who did it all while zapped out of his poncho on angel dust. Well, shit, old sock, one leaps to the conclusion that the fix is in. I have been told in the dark and murky depths of the Bel Air Hotel's jungle garden, late at night, who murdered Marilyn Monroe, and damned if I don't believe it, but there ain't gonna be no trial, trust me. In your case, who the hell was going to make waves over dinky little Toby Challis?"

Challis was on his feet, pacing, catching the odd glimpse of his strange new self in the windows. "But the Roths made waves," he said. "What more could they have done? Sol paid for my defense, pulled out all the stops—"

"Hilary Durant? Land sakes! Forsake your innocence and let me tell you that Hilary Durant is not a prime example of pulling out all the stops—Hilary has been at a full stop for years. And whatever you're up to now, stay away from dear old Hilary. I grew up with the little creep . . . as a child he always wanted to play doctor with the other little boys." He plucked another cough drop from a tiny enameled box and placed it on his tongue, made it disappear. "You haven't insisted on my advice, but let me tell you the way my mind is working. Start with the presumption that you didn't kill Goldie, that we don't know who did, and that you were set up as the natural patsy to take the heat off somebody else. If you didn't kill her, somebody else obviously had a motive . . . but since they had your nuts in a hammerlock, they—the cops —didn't try to figure out who else might have wanted the lady dead. That's what you've got to do, pin down the other fellow's motive. . . . Toby, I'm betting that Jack Donovan's up to his keester in all this."

"Are you saying you think Donovan killed her?"

"Jesus, Toby! Of course not! How the hell do I know who killed her?" He sucked the cough drop and glared at Challis. "I'm merely saying that you might probe the idea of Donovan."

Traffic was thickening down on Sunset. Challis could see the house Shirley Temple had bought for her parents. The gray stone Getty mansion brooded glumly in the rain like a sluggish pet wondering where its master had gone.

"I saw Donovan and Aaron Roth at Ma Maison a couple of weeks ago—'closeted' is the appropriate expression. The room was full of people trying to figure out if David Begelman had ever had his fingers in their bank accounts, and Roth and Donovan were deep in conversation, enraptured with one another. Then Marcel Onions—the French director who has his black little heart set on doing the Billy the Kid spectacle—Marcel came over and they looked as if they'd been caught smooching in the men's room at the Sports and Health Club . . . and I had assumed that Aaron didn't approve of his daughter consorting with an operator like Donovan. Maybe her death brought them together like *Love Story*, who knows? In any case, Onions joined them for coffee, and now I hear that he's a cover subject for Donovan's magazine, *The Coast*. A cover . . . Onions? I say that that makes no sense, he's nothing like a big-enough deal, if you get my drift. How do I hear this tidbit? From a staffer at the magazine—I mean, little itty-bitty Marcel is a client of ours and the cover is happening and I don't know about it . . . which gives me pause —imagine my surprise, if you will. Of course, my only real concern re Marcel is keeping him away from ten-year-old boys and seeing that Roth lives up to the points deal on the Billy the Kid thing, which he keeps threatening to put into turnaround . . . now Aaron wants to set up one of those phoney development deals, pay Marcel a million dollars to develop two projects, only not really develop them, then write the million off as a loss and have Marcel kick back half a million, which he can sink into oil and natural gas. Marcel can put his half-million into the harem of small boys he's always wanted, and nobody's lifted a finger for the money." Ollie clicked his cough drop

81

against several thousand dollars' worth of bridgework. "But who knows how it will all turn out . . . still, my contention is that there's something a little brown around the edges of the Donovan/Roth rapprochement."

Challis said, "Is Aaron headed for trouble?"

"Name me a big producer who isn't—at least potentially. They're all a little scared, what with the feds looking under this bush and that. Begelman and his funny checks are just the tip of the iceberg, as they say, and they're right, obviously. So everybody's a little edgy . . . in Aaron's case, one independent producer leased him a ski lodge at Aspen for peanuts, a buck or something, and gave him a forty-thousand-dollar rec-vee as a Christmas present . . . well, the idiot writes it off as a business expense and Aaron doesn't declare it as income, you know how it always worked. Well, the tax chummies are watching, or so we're told—"

"But Aaron, is he into this stuff deeply? Is he headed for real trouble?"

"Look, Sol is a bigger danger for Aaron than mere G-men, if that's what you mean. If Sol doesn't catch him on the fiddle, he'll be all right, I suppose. Unless something happens to put him in the spotlight . . . to the G-men he's just another guy in Gucci shoes and Ralph Lauren duds, one of many. As far as I'm concerned with Marcel the Frog, I only know what's on paper—his little private deals are really no concern of mine. I am merely saying that morally I fear the worst . . . it's just that Oliver Kreisler can smell this stuff a mile away. Just remember what Harry Cohn said—It ain't a business, it's a racket."

"What you're saying," Challis mused somewhat numbly, "is that since I didn't have an ironclad three-picture deal, it was less trouble to have me take the rap—"

"In light of the fact that, A, you were holding the murder weapon in your hand when the police arrived, more or less, and, B, you did seem to have a motive . . . I'm not saying they would have made something out of whole cloth. You were cut to fit, you must admit." Ollie stopped sucking, pushed his glasses up his nose, and waited for Challis to come to rest. "You know how serious your situation is, don't you? Get rid of the soft focus, this is not a movie."

"I know, I know. But the trial is over. I was convicted. We're not talking about heroics at the last minute to sway the jury. The jury is back home, having a TV dinner, watching *Laverne and Shirley* and wondering why Kareem doesn't run to the other end of the court half the time . . . they were out two hours to reach a verdict, I was lucky they didn't come over the railing and fucking lynch me . . . you're telling me the fix was in but I shouldn't reach for straws . . . well, with all respect to your better judgment, maybe I can bust it, find out who really did it."

"And maybe not, Toby." Ollie looked at the flat gold wristwatch and shook his head. "I've got a meeting at Paramount I cannot miss. But let me tell you what's been percolating in the back of my mind while we've been getting the lay of the land here. The fact is, I've got a better idea, better than trying to buck the system we're not only up against but are part of, as well. Realistically, you and I know you can beat anything in this business. There's *always* a way out of any trouble. I've got a client shooting a picture on an island out in the Pacific . . . I mean it is *out* in the Pacific, a soft sandy rock with a couple of rusty Japanese bayonets lying on the beach. Nobody but six guys wearing dried leaves for pants and running a tavern for two hundred people making the movie. They'll easily be there another six months, maybe longer. And it could easily be two hundred and one people making the movie. . . . We can put you in a box of ham sandwiches and you'll go right onto the plane we're using. N-o-t-h-i-n-g to it and you're a technical adviser all of a sudden. Then we fix some papers and a cover story, and you spend a couple of years in Singapore or Hong Kong working on your tan. Then you come back as somebody else. Write a screenplay or two in Hong Kong, hell, you can come back, go live in Klosters or Florence. . . . It could be done, Toby. Let's put it this way, old-timer, I'd do it if I were you

—this is no bullshit artist talking to you, Toby. Listen to Ollie Kreisler—I'm telling you he can make you safe, and Ollie Kreisler does not bandy words."

Challis picked up his new raincoat. "I'll have to get back to you, Ollie. I appreciate it—"

"The offer stands. We're brothers, Toby. We ride together." Ollie's eyes almost glistened with emotion. Challis wondered if he was done.

"I've never resented the ten percent," Challis said. "I want you to know that if . . . if I don't see you again. Brother." Challis grinned.

"Sometimes I wonder what you have where your soul should be."

"It's probably off somewhere with your sense of humor."

"Possibly. In any case, I want you to know that I've never resented the ninety."

"But, Ollie, I've got to have a crack at making somebody believe I'm innocent."

"I believe it. Be satisfied with me. Go to my island, help make a movie."

"You know what I mean. But thanks for the information."

"You heard none of it from me."

"One last thing—would you have recognized me?"

"No. You're perilously close to becoming the invisible man, and there are dangers in that, too, old man. So be careful." He walked Challis to the door.

"So long, Ollie."

On his way out, Margo stopped him at her desk. "Mr. Benson, let me validate your parking ticket." He handed it to her. She licked several little stamps and stuck them on the back of the pasteboard. She looked up at him primly, handed it back. "You remind me of someone . . . around the eyes."

"It's Errol, everybody says that. Errol . . ."

"Flynn?"

"Leon."

"Oh, Mr. Benson . . ."

"You know, Margo, you smell wonderful. Don't ever change that."

"Why, thank you."

84

"But Mr. Benson has got to keep moving."

"Even your voice." She put her glasses on. "It's funny . . ."

"It's a small world," he said, closing the door behind him.

[9]

CHALLIS WALKED across Sunset to the Hamburger Hamlet next to Schwab's. It was chilly, and the rain surged in the gutters, coming down out of the hills above Sunset. From the look of things, there would be no joy in Trousdale Estates tonight. It was that odd, depressing hour of the late afternoon, and the constant rain was blowing as the wind picked up, curling around the collar of his spotless raincoat and wetting his neck. He bought the late edition of the *Times* and sat in the outdoor section facing the street, the heating elements overhead glowing red, and ordered coffee. He kept his raincoat on, watched the traffic, and wondered what Ollie had meant when he said being an invisible man had its own dangers, too, old man. Invisibility struck him as the one crucial advantage in doing what he had to do—a requirement, actually. But some antecedent of Kreisler's remark echoed in the back of his mind, just out of reach. . . .

His thoughts were wandering when he noticed Margo, wearing a chic belted trench coat and a matching rain hat, bending into the storm and coming across the street toward him. She swept the sidewalk café with her eyes and passed out of his vision when she entered the restaurant. He hunched over his coffee and studied the front-page stories about the continuing storm damage. Had she seen him? Had she somehow recognized him? The way she had looked at him . . . What the hell was she doing in a Hamburger Hamlet, anyway? From the corner of his eye he saw her being ushered into the outdoor section. Linda Ronstadt's home was in danger of being washed into the Pacific, but she said she wasn't leaving, she was going to fight it out. Game girl. She was a neighbor of his; she had, in fact, provided him with some of his nicest impure

86

reveries. Margo was seated against the wall, where she could watch him; he had to contort himself to keep her at the edge of his vision. Butterflies were turning into killer bees in his stomach, and the fear of recognition made him sweat. Why didn't she say something? What was the silent surveillance in aid of? His coffee was cold and growing a provocative white scum; he stirred it, turning the scum to chunks. She was still watching him. He wanted to leave but felt paralyzed. A waitress brought her a Bloody Mary. He waited. *He* was buried deep in the paper, the story simply noting that searchers were still seeking the wreckage of the plane. No picture, and his name mentioned only once. Tomorrow morning it would be different, and he shrank at the thought. She was still watching him.

Fog was blowing down out of the hills. The traffic lights on Sunset were blurring, growing larger, like balloons inflating. A tall man strode briskly up to the railing and waved vigorously. "Margo, it's me . . . Margo, over here." He was laughing. "For God's sake, honey, put on your glasses." He shook his head and made for the entrance. Challis sighed, stood up, folded his newspaper, and looked directly at Margo, who was fumbling with her purse, retrieving her glasses. Then he walked past her, made way for her date at the door, and went back to the pay telephone.

"Good afternoon, the *Times*," the lady said.

"Editorial, please."

"Editorial," another voice said.

"Pete Schaeffer," he said. The restaurant was dark, purveyed a burnished oxblood look that jarred with its name. The tables were filling, and the business at the bar looked good; he wondered if he'd see anyone he knew. He almost looked forward to the next test, but the tension in his stomach wouldn't go away.

"Schaeffer here."

Challis took a deep breath that turned out to be a shallow breath because nerves were constricting his chest, making him feel and sound like a man who pants into the telephone. "Pete, you're not going to believe this . . ."

Ten minutes later Pete Schaeffer acknowledged that

he was convinced. "Jesus, Toby," he whispered, "we just sent another guy to Cresta Vista to look for you. The betting down here is that you wandered away in a daze and probably drowned in Little Fawn Lake. The last stiff they found in Little Fawn Lake was Muriel Chess . . . or was it Derace Kingsley's wife? I forget. That was back in the forties—anyway, you're not in the lake. Look, I'm going to go put a couple hundred on your surviving, okay?"

"Make it four hundred," Challis said. "I deserve a piece of the action."

"Shit yes—hey, when are you going to give yourself up?"

"Don't be an idiot."

"I was afraid you'd say that. Anybody but the mountain lady know you're alive?"

"Kreisler."

"Don't tell me—he said he'd get you top dollar at Universal for your story and *National Inquirer* serialization rights?"

"He was very nice about everything, nothing like that."

"Then call Lazar . . . call Scott Meredith. This could be the break you've been waiting for."

"Pete, this situation has its serious side . . ."

"I know, I know, but you mustn't be such a sobersides. What do you want from me, anyway?" Schaeffer's high voice almost got lost somewhere behind his forehead when he whispered.

"I've got some questions. I need some advice. Meet me somewhere . . ."

"Listen, I told you when you married Goldie, what did I say? I'll tell you, I said don't come crying to me if it doesn't work out, and it didn't work out, and here you are, crying to me. Meet me at Pink's, we'll have a chili dog, and I promise not to bring the cops. I can't get away for a while—say, eight o'clock. What do you look like?"

"Clean raincoat and a half-assed tan. No beard."

"Ugh."

He walked back to the parking garage. The fog was thicker, and traffic was crawling, blocking the intersection each time the light changed. He nearly ran over a man who loomed unexpectedly out of the fog, stepped obliviously into the path of the Mustang. Until the final, almost fatal moment, the man in the fog had been invisible.

And it occurred to him what Ollie Kreisler had meant. It was something from Harry Dyer's old movie about the man in the fog. Somebody, Zachary Scott maybe, had said that a man in the fog was invisible, and somebody else, probably Geraldine Fitzgerald, had said that an invisible man, a man who was believed dead, was the easiest man in the world to murder. No one can die twice. Challis was surprised that it had taken him so long to remember it. "Sweet Lorraine" had been the song from that picture: Lorraine had been the killer and also Harry Dyer's wife. A tidy little in joke for the family and friends. And now Morgan Dyer played the theme song on tape, at home, in the Mercedes. Challis smiled to himself. Life was a movie. Out here, anyway, he thought, if no place else.

He worked the Mustang onto Sunset and headed east along the rain-blunted, sadly gaudy Strip. Pat Collins the Hip Hypnotist still turning people into chickens in front of their families, still at it after all these years, babbling along underneath the blond beehive . . . Filthy McNasty's . . . the Dirty Grunts live at the Roxy, one week only . . . Dino's, the restaurant that grew famous on the old television show *77 Sunset Strip* . . . used cars, a thousand restaurants . . . Cyrano's, where Goldie had thought the waiter faking French was so cute . . . Roy's for six-hundred-year-old chicken, and Butterfield's, where you ate quiche and fruit salad in the sunshine. Up in the hills, all the houses clung to the rain-soaked mud, trying not to begin the long sorry slide into their neighbors' backyards, the houses on stilts with rain running anxiously across the patios and making tiny, destructive little rivers weakening the underpinning of the Hollywood Hills . . . in the houses you could hear the occasional creak as the timbers pulled and the rain beat incessantly on the rooftops. Somewhere up there, Morgan Dyer was listening to Sidney Bechet's "Sweet Lorraine."

Eddie's ragtop had a small tear that let the rain draw a bead on the back of the seat just behind Challis' head. The rain bounced in a steady drumbeat off the hood, and the wipers made it almost impossible to see. He drove slowly: an accident on Sunset Boulevard was not on the agenda. Finally he pulled off and drove a couple of blocks to Santa Monica, drove back west, and parked in the Tropicana Motel parking lot. Inevitably he saw Tom Waits standing in the doorway of the office, watching the rain slam angrily into the lot. He was wearing a cap, a plaid shirt, and a black suit from the Salvation Army. Challis could almost smell the booze on the suit.

He turned the radio on. The Lakers were playing in New York at the Garden, and Chick Hearn sounded pissed off. Chick Hearn always sounded pissed off, though, and the Lakers were winning. At the half there was a news broadcast that brought it all up-to-date.

"The wreckage of a State of California light plane carrying convicted murderer Toby Challis to prison, lost in the mountain storms of four days ago, has been found in an uninhabited area about fifteen miles from Little Fawn Lake and the village of Cresta Vista. The crew of two, a guard, and another prisoner on board have all been found dead in the wreckage, and names are being withheld pending notification of next of kin. However, the search party, headed by Sheriff Jeff Billings, reports that the body of Challis has not—repeat, has not—been found. Sheriff Billings had this to say . . ." There was a slight wait, followed by a transmission full of static: "Challis' body is not in the plane or in the immediate area. It's snowing up here now, but we've got twenty-five men and we're going to be searching all night. He's probably injured and somewhere in the vicinity. No, there are no weapons missing from the plane, but we have to consider the man dangerous. We figure to have him in custody by tomorrow morning sometime. Or at least we hope to have found his body . . . it would be mighty tough trying to survive up here in the cold, without food, for this long a time." The static ended and the announcer said: "Stay tuned for fast-breaking news on this, your Los Angeles Laker radio station." They went to a commercial, and Challis switched to another frequency.

". . . and Sheriff Billings has warned all the residents

of Puma Point and Cresta Vista and the Little Fawn area to lock up for the night, not let anyone in, and notify the Cresta Vista sheriff's office if they spot anyone who might be Toby Challis. He is tall, bearded, with dark hair, and may be injured and disoriented. Stay at this spot on the dial for any further developments." Challis tuned in another station, heard a much clearer broadcast of Sheriff Billings' voice as he was interviewed.

"Well, Bob, one thing we can be thankful for is that we found those kids who were lost up there. Who knows what might have happened if Challis and the children had run into one another?" He turned back to the second half of the Lakers game and dozed off and on until it was over, his brain partially conscious and worrying about what was going to happen. The rain seemed to calm him.

At ten minutes before eight he drove to Pink's hot-dog stand near the corner of Melrose and LaBrea. He parked behind the shoe store next door. There were six people waiting in line, half-unconscious from the smell of the chili and onions. The rain dripped over them, and behind the open counter the regulars were dishing up the victuals, pouring the frozen blocks of chili into the stainless-steel vats, tweezing the paper-wrapped tamales from the steamer, inserting the thick red wieners into the buns and ladling the dense chili over them.

Pete Schaeffer had just arrived, stood towering over the end of the line like an exclamation point. He was six and a half feet tall with huge feet like the pieces of flat, flapping cardboard that kept balloon men from tipping over. He'd once been a collegiate basketball player, and he had the typical round shoulders; beneath his crumpled, stained rain hat was a high dome of freckled forehead, thinning red wisps of hair that filled out beneath the tops of his ears and shambled off disconsolately over his shirt collar. He wore a terrible cheap plaid shirt, crummy old corduroy pants, and muddy sneakers as he stood in the rain. His small blue eyes had the faded, worried tint of a middle-aged man who wore his years uncomfortably, like a cheap suit that was too small. The sleeves of his shirts, in fact,

91

were always too short, giving him the look of a man who had just been tacked up on a wall by the label in the collar. Like every writer in Greater Los Angeles, he was working on a TV pilot; what made him different was that he'd sold two, one of which had run four years and made him quite a lot of money. On Pete Schaeffer, however, the money didn't show. "Hey, man," he said in his high nasal tone, "I'd have known you anywhere."

"Don't say that," Challis said. "How's Joyce?" In the line waiting, small talk gurgled like the rain in the gutters.

"Well, she's into M and G now," Schaeffer said. His ears stood out like jug handles beneath the brim of the spotted rain hat. "Still living in, if that's what you mean."

"What's M and G?"

"Moans and groans, asshole. She does voice-overs for porn movies . . . you know, ooh, aah, ugh, grunt, squeal, all that stuff. Take that away from those pieces of crap, and what have you got?"

"Movies of people fucking and sucking."

"Well, sure, but the voice-over is important. This morning she had a real crisis, the guy she was working with had an accident on the Harbor Freeway and didn't show . . . so Joyce had to do both the man and the woman. I mean, that's a strain, baby cakes." He had reached the long counter. "Two chili dogs and an orange drink for me, a chili dog and a chili tamale with orange for my procurer here." He paid, and they carried the food indoors and found a corner table. Incredibly, Challis was hungry again.

Schaeffer took an anxious, enormous bite, and chili began the long, slow descent down the bulge of his small, round chin. "Now, what's the scoop?" he mumbled with his mouth full. "I know about the plane crash, the kids, the broad on the mountain, all that shit, but what now? You're not gonna make some goddamn grandstand fuckin' play—don't tell me that, Tobe, we're too old for that crap."

"I'm too old to go to prison is what I'm too old for," Challis said. "I've gotta find out who killed Goldie . . ."

Schaeffer groaned. "Man, you're one slow study. No,

I mean it, Tobe, one helluva slow study . . . you just don't *get* it, do you? Whoever snuffed Goldie is a back issue, forgotten." He stared at Challis like a scientist with a cellular slide that just wasn't matching up, took another huge bite. "Remember the case of Public Enemy Number One, the Big D, John the Dillinger? The lady in red got him out front of the Biograph in Chi town and the G-men put it to him . . . they buried old John under about a million tons of scrap iron, said they didn't want his grave to become a shrine of some kind. Well, bullshit, Tobe, that was all crapperino, because the guy under the scrap iron could be your uncle Mike for all I know, but it sure ain't John Dillinger, just like it wasn't Dillinger in front of the Biograph. The thing was, the G-men had to get Dillinger or the Senate was gonna cut off the dough, kill Hoover's Bureau. So they got a guy, called him Dillinger, and made a deal with the real Dillinger to be a good boy, keep quiet, and disappear—keep the dough, we'll never prosecute you, just don't spill the beans. So Dillinger lived the rest of his life in sunny Cal and the FBI is still with us—you get the picture? Okay, now, there's a lesson there, like if the juice is big enough, there's nobody who can stand up to it, which is where you come in. Whoever put paid to Goldie is in deep out here, and I can figure, conservatively, a thousand scenarios . . . say, the mob, or somebody somewhere holding some paper on the Roths, or on anybody big at Maximus, wants to pull off a bit of an object lesson, just to show what they can get away with. So they kill Goldie in a particularly gaudy way and frame the husband, somebody the Roths know to be innocent—well, the point is made, and you are the man in the middle . . . you take the fall, and everybody learns a lesson." He sighed, still whispering, and swiping at his mouth with a fragile, soaked paper napkin. He had chili all over his fingers. "What was that last thing Goldie said to you? When she asked you to come out for dinner?"

"She said she had something on Aaron, she was going to fix that bastard once and for all."

"Aha, see, that's wrong!" He was waving his second chili dog at Challis. Outside, the rain drove straight downward, hammering at the parking lot. "She didn't say anything to you about *Aaron* . . . she just said she was going to fix that *bastard*. In court nobody believed she said it at all—it was the desperate attempt of a murderer to throw up a mystery suspect, a straw man. Well, I figure you're telling the truth, okay, but that still doesn't mean it's Aaron Roth. Jeez, look at the meatballs she runs around with. Half the coke sniffers and bondage freaks in Los Angeles . . . she hangs out at the Whisky and the Roxy and works out a week at a time down at La Costa, I'm telling you this lady is up to her ass in guys who qualify for the role of bastard . . . and murderer. And there's Donovan, too, for God's sake . . . a surfeit of bastards, and she could have been talking about any one of them. Come eat, eat."

The chili tamale went away and he ate half the chili dog, drank half the orange. Nobody was paying any attention to them. He felt almost normal, but for the constant doubt making a home in his belly. Finally he said, "Don't you know anything about anything that you should tell me? Any specifics? You and Ollie are full of all this other stuff, but how about a quick look at the real story? I *know* I'm in a mess."

"Okay, all I hear is that there's something going on between Donovan and Aaron Roth—don't ask me what, because I don't know. Except it's got to do with money, probably dirty money of some kind. Vegas? Blackmail? I've got no names . . . just the connection. The thing is, what would bring them together? Jack was in Goldie's camp, and that meant he wasn't going to see much of Aaron—so Goldie's dead, and suddenly Donovan and Aaron are an item."

"It would help to know who Goldie was talking about when she last talked to me."

"You are so quick, Tobe!" Schaeffer grinned crookedly across the mess on the table. "But so dumb. You're not going to find out what they hid under their little pile of scrap iron, never. You've got to forget the whole thing, get lost. Your case is closed, baby. Permanently. You have got to locate the underground railway, the Big Escape Route—that's where I can help. I know some cops who think you got greased but good, they'd fix your way out of it just for spite."

"Ollie Kreisler said he could do it. He halfway convinced me," Challis said. "Now you tell me you know a way—cops yet."

"Shit, Tobe, nobody who counts ever has to pay up out here, you know that. Now, you are not exactly heavy on the clout scale, but you've got friends. Ollie can get you out, I might even be able to do it, and you haven't even dropped your little bone of difficulty at the feet of Aaron Roth, who might be persuaded to roll you up in a rug and ship you somewhere just to get the whole thing over with. But there's one small catch, of course. Go to the wrong guys for help—say, the guys who used Goldie to prove a point, if that's the scenario—and you'll find yourself at the beach in about six weeks, a leg wedged against a piling under the Santa Monica pier and your head up at Zuma."

"That's a catch, Pete."

"So stop now, stay at my place, I'll have a chat with my LAPD pals . . . or go tell Kreisler, yes, Ollie, anything you say, Ollie."

Schaeffer followed him outside, walked him to the Mustang.

"What are you going to do, Tobe?"

"I think I might go poke around the beach house. Maybe there's something there . . . from what happened in court, it didn't seem to me that anybody even looked at Goldie's stuff, her . . . stuff. If I know Aaron, he hasn't gotten around to having anything done with it."

"You mean you're going looking for a clue," Schaeffer said. "Shit, Tobe, that's crazy. Where do you think they're gonna go look for you?"

"They think I'm still up on the mountain. Half-dead."

"Bullshit. They know you could be anywhere . . . it's been days since the fuckin' plane crashed. And you tell me you're returning to the scene of your crime! Jeez, Tobe . . ."

Challis slid down into the front seat and turned the ignition.

[10]

CHALLIS FELT the force of the rainwater that had
rushed down out of the hills and was shoving crosswise
at the Mustang as he headed west on Sunset Boulevard.
The low spot halfway between the Beverly Hills Hotel
and the East Gates of Bel Air was hubcap-deep in
mud-thickened slush, and traffic was backed up in
both directions. He waited it out and left the radio off,
listened to the rain chewing at the raggedy top and the
constant drip where it had gnawed through. Traffic
opened up as he passed on through Pacific Palisades.
Everybody was staying home. Theater marquees blurred in forlorn brilliance; the odd nightwalker sheltered
in a doorway here and there. The smell of mud hung
ominously in the air as he headed down the long, sloping highway which finally brought him to the sea and
the Pacific Coast Highway.

Heading north was an ordeal. The bluffs overlooking the highway and ocean were collapsing in huge
slabs, working their way steadily toward the expensive
hilltop homes like a swarm of gnashing, unstoppable
monsters. On the other side, over the sound of rain,
the earth seemed to shake as the Pacific delivered one
immensely heavy blow after another. Three times
everything on the road stopped entirely where mud
and stones and flower gardens and fencing had broken
loose and crashed down across the north-bound lane.
Dump trucks and bulldozers with twirling red lights
on the cabs pushed and tugged and were loaded down
under the rampaging tons of earth. Highway-patrol cars
clustered on the outskirts of each mudslide and fed
traffic past. Nobody here was going to waste time
looking for Toby Challis. Compared to several thousand tons of mud, Toby Challis could be somebody
else's problem. Ahead of him, in the spinning red

96

light, he saw a spoke of white picket fence protruding from a pile of mud like a scrawny human arm.

The lights in the shopping center on the far edge of Malibu across from the Colony flung that lonely, weary glow at the storm. A squash of cars, trucks, patrol cars, and TV panel trucks was clotted off to the left, trying to funnel on through into the private reserve. The trucks were loaded with sandbags and volunteers; the tires sank deep into the moist gravel and grassy mud. Challis worked his way into the mess behind a bulldozer being towed on a flatbed by a heavy cab. Looking out the window, the rain blowing in his face, he spotted old Artie Daniels at the Colony's gatehouse. His bald bullet dome was covered by a yellow rubber rain hat, his body by a matching yellow slicker. The bulldozer edged on through. He pulled the Mustang even with Artie, who had too much on his mind to concern himself with checking the list. "Hi," Challis called, looking directly into the familiar face. "Bob Roper, Asylum Records. Linda said she'd notify you— I'm gonna help her secure things, you know."

"Next thing it'll be Jerry Brown," Artie growled. "Go on, go on." He had barely looked at Challis, had kept looking on down the line of cars to assess the night's work still ahead. Challis goosed the Mustang ahead, wormed his way through the other cars, trucks, and swarming bodies. Bodies in raincoats, sweatshirts, jogging outfits, blue jeans, swimming trunks, bodies soaked through, caked with sand and mud, hair plastered to skulls, hands holding shovels, rakes, and plastic pitchers of Bloody Marys. There were people he knew, others he recognized, dozens of strangers pressed into service, even some gawkers looking for the chance to help a star bail out the dining room.

He drove past the back of his beach house and parked about fifty yards farther on, against Bernie Provo's hedge and out of the way. He stood under the overhang from Bernie's garage and watched the manic swirl of activity. Lights were on everywhere, glowing through the rain, making it look like smoke. Fog blew in, filled the areas between the houses, swirled in the rain. No one paid any attention to him.

The beach house was both familiar and frightening.

The place where Goldie, who didn't deserve her fate, whatever she was, whatever she had done, had been beaten until she was dead. He felt the unmistakable flutter of the willies in his belly and chest, the tightening; he walked numbly, slowly, in the general flurry of activity, bumped and jostled by the crowds of sandbaggers. A movie star he'd known for years walked past in Levi's cutoffs and a poncho, sipping from a can of Coors: no flicker of recognition.

He pushed the gate in the white fence open and walked along the side of the garage. At the end of the garage he reached for the key on the ledge above the door frame. It was still there, untouched all these months. Rounding the side of the house, flat-roofed and soaked and dark, he caught the full force of the wind and spray from the exploding white surf, mixing with the hard rain. The beach seethed with activity. There was a coffee depot beneath one cottage built out over the beach on stilts. Hundreds of people dealt with the sandbags in long lines, passing them along. A couple of spotlights threw the beach into long shadows, turning the scene strangely ominous. Shadows moved across his face, thrashed against the glass doors on the deck. He took a deep breath, fitted the key in the side door, and went inside.

The air trapped inside the house was stale, smelled of the ocean, and sand gritted beneath his feet. Pete had been right: he felt like the killer returning to the scene of his crime. It was here he had lost his freedom, last seen Goldie, whom he had once loved, whatever else had passed between them, here where his life had come apart. He stood in the hallway listening. Wind whistled down the fireplace chimney. From a great distance he heard the shouts on the beach. He was sweating hard and his breath hurt in his chest. Now that he was back, the psychic shock rippled through him, malevolent, mocking his puny grip on sanity. In his mind he heard things from other times, Goldie's voice lashing him raw, "Eh, Pancho, meet Mr. Challis," and her laughter and the dark, grinning, heavily muscled beach bum flashing huge white teeth at him. He saw the desk he wrote on covered with her cocaine paraphernalia, the electric melt point tester, the tray

98

of glass slides, the safety razor blade, the beveled triangular glass flake plate, the mound of snowy white coke, the fourteen-karat-gold bottles and spoons and straws, the scales and pestles, the Honduras mahogany stash box—it all came back to him as he stood in the dark, as if the candles were flickering and Goldie was laughing, her head back and hair falling through the air like a rope, and Pancho staring, mouth open, teeth white as the cocaine, wondering what was going to happen next.

For half an hour he puttered about the house, looking for a clue of any kind to what Goldie had wanted to tell him: a pointer, the hint of a relationship or a fact, a crack in the wall of silence that sealed her off from his questions.

Rummaging through a cavernous lower drawer in the big desk, he came across a disheveled pile of Goldie's old astrological charts. There had been so little order in Goldie's life, yet she had been receiving the monthly charts without interruption for years. And typically she'd torn open each new envelope, glanced briefly at the contents, and left it on the kitchen counter for weeks at a stretch, or pitched it under her deck chair, or she'd drop it into the drawer as she passed the desk. The charts were like all the other California trendiness, and like a toy, once you'd laid out the dough and gotten your hands on it, it was okay to kind of forget about it. But it was in this drawer that Challis found, dropped among the charts, the thick red leather date-book for the past year.

Tiredly he sat down and spread the book open in the soft pool of light from the architect's lamp clamped to the edge of the desk. For an hour he paged through the year, jotting down his own notes, copying entries that tended to recur or which seemed to relate to Donovan, or simply seemed to appear adjacent to notations regarding luncheon dates or conversations with Donovan. He didn't know what he was looking for, he was just sniffing it out, hoping. When he was done —when he'd reached the last day of Goldie's life and quickly slammed the red leather cover shut—he sat staring at his own sheet of foolscap, sitting in the familiar chair where he'd assumed he'd never find himself again.

Call Jack—no damned mercy!

Jack: What's going on? Cut the bullshit.

Jack: Whose side are you on?

Jack: Why no action? This appeared four times.

Give J.D. swift kick!

M re K? Huge capital letters, traced, retraced, appearing twice.

Max. TV=V.L.?

Why V.L.?

LV=VL?

And on the final day of her life Goldie had made the final cryptic comment, underlining it several times.

TOBY—THE TRUTH.

He sat staring at the jottings, not quite noticing them after a while. The beach house was not a good place for him to be, it was too full of the past, and you didn't have to be a genius or a shrink to figure that one out. He heard someone on the beach singing the Yale fight song, "Bulldog, bulldog, bow-wow-wow." He didn't know any Yale men in the Colony. Why would a Yale man want to live in the Colony? It made more sense that David Begelman thought it was important that people thought he was a Yale man. Aaron Roth actually was a Yale man. He lived in Bel Air, which made more sense if you dealt in stereotypes, and that was the only way to deal, God knew. The singer came closer, had a coughing fit, fell silent. Challis turned out the light on the desk after dropping the datebook back into the drawer of charts. He closed the sliding door onto the deck and made sure everything was the way it had been when he came in. He gave the room a final look, took a deep breath, and eased himself out the door onto the redwood-planked short side of the L-shaped deck. He locked the door. Below on the beach the work went on. The rain was blowing across the deck harder than ever. He was turning to go down the few steps to the path when he heard a sound—a cough or a hiccup—coming from around the corner. He went back instead of running, a decision utterly beyond his powers of explanation. As he reached the corner, he heard the sound again.

A large wet figure hurtled out of the darkness, knocking him sideways, back against the wooden railing, which caught him across the kidneys. He sank to his knees, reached desperately for the pain in his lower back. The figure, a heavyset man in a raincoat and stocking cap and pajama bottoms, smelling of martinis, rushed toward him. "Fuckin' goddamn fuckin' burglar pervert ghoul bastard." His hands were balled into heavy fists and his feet were bare, caked with sand. Rain streamed down his face, plastered his thinning hair to a massive skull. "Get up and fight, ya fuckin' fuckface coward!" He staggered.

Challis levered himself up, using the railing, the agony in his back easing and his brain focusing on what seemed, against all odds, to be happening. He turned to do what he should have done to begin with, run away, but one of the huge paws caught his collar and pulled him back down onto the slippery redwood. "A fine woman bashed to death here," the man panted, tiptoeing at the edge of incoherence, concluding with, "fuckin' asshole ghoul." Challis pushed him back ineffectively and caught the tail end of a right cross on the temple. "Help!" the man croaked. "Help!" Challis' hand fought for balance, found a red clay pot full of wet earth, yanked it up and swiped at the man's head, cutting him off in mid-cry. "Shit!" the man gurgled. "Oh, shit . . . my head." Challis leaped forward again, struck again, the flowerpot glancing off the great head and hitting the shoulder. The stocking cap was draped over a large jugged ear, and the nose seemed to be leaking from the first blow, but the light was almost nonexistent, ninety percent shadow. The man weaved on his knees, muttering to himself, struggled to his feet; they had changed positions, and he now blocked Challis' exit. "Look out behind you," Challis said, pointing. When the man had slowly managed the turn, Challis drove a fist into the midsection, doubling the man over, then straightened him forward over the railing and heaved mightily, with the strength of pure desperation, and dumped the gangly, loose-limbed body over the edge into the shrubbery bordering the stairway leading down to the sand.

Challis stood holding onto the railing, his legs shaking, his eyes wandering furtively across the comings and goings on the beach. No one noticed what had happened above on the deck. He gulped air, felt the cold rain on his face, fought the tide of fear and nausea. He felt as if he'd become a savage, the frightened killer the court had told him he was.

[11]

THEY NEVER STOPPED, the memories never stopped: Goldie would be with him forever, her face at once beautiful, taunting, seductive, remote, laughing, snarling, and distorted and frozen in terror. The dreams were always the same in the end, regardless of how they began: the sunlight fading to salt-smelling evening, the booze or the dope in the air, Goldie yelling to a pickup to come out and meet her husband. This time there had been somebody moving on the deck, a sound, heavy breathing and running, faces with frightened eyes. Then he woke up in a hot, sticky sweat, cold air coming in at an unfamiliar screen window. The sound of the rain was gone, and as his head and eyes cleared, he saw clouds of fog billowing beyond the gray rectangle of tattered screening. Slowly it all came back to him, and he got out of bed. Out the window, he stared at the motel's courtyard with its gravel and scrub grass and shuffleboard courts.

The night before, he had checked the drunken man's body to make sure he wasn't dead, then had wormed his way back out through the Colony's gates. He'd driven around the rain-slick streets until well past midnight, until the shaking in his hands and legs had quieted and his heartbeat was back to normal. He had tracked down a hamburger and a cup of coffee at Ship's on Wilshire in Westwood, had sat in the window watching the rain until he caught himself, head down, mostly asleep. From there he'd headed down to Little Santa Monica and driven along beside the high muddy inclines shoring up the railroad tracks until he saw the Easy Rest Motel's blotchy neon sign through the rain. It was a dripping white frame affair, an exhausted palm tree, twenty units in a sad courtyard built on the wrong side of 1940. An old geezer with a round pink

103

face, smooth as a beach ball, and one eye gone milky with cataract was sitting behind the counter. He was reading a tattered paperback copy of *Anthony Adverse* while a pop psychiatrist on an all-night talk show babbled about premature ejaculation from inside an old cathedral-style Philco. My kind of place, Challis thought, registering with Eddie's name.

Now it was almost ten o'clock, and there was another crazy day to face. Twenty-four hours before, he'd been lying on the floor in the back of Morgan Dyer's Mercedes. It had been a very long twenty-four hours, and he wished he knew how much he'd learned. He took a shower and thought about it. Ollie Kreisler and Pete Schaeffer had separately offered him ways out of town, and the rest of what he'd learned kept pointing at Jack Donovan.

Dressed, he sat on the edge of the bed and looked at the list of items he'd copied from Goldie's datebook. Those clearly relating to Jack Donovan obviously reflected her impatience, the cause of which was utterly mysterious. *Whose side are you on?* put Donovan in the middle of something, between Goldie and someone else, a maneuver she frequently employed in her personal relationships and which made her less than universally loved.

But the rest of the notations had the look of an unbreakable code. *M re K? Max. TV=V.L. Why V.L.? LV=VL?* None of it meant anything to him. Nothing at all.

He paid his bill and drove east on Little Santa Monica, edging his way carefully through the thickness of the fog, turned right on the Avenue of the Stars, and parked in the huge lot wedged in behind the Century Plaza Hotel and Twentieth Century-Fox. In only a couple of years the studio had gone from being an ulcer ranch to the top of the industry with *The Omen, Silent Movie, Silver Streak,* and *Star Wars.* It was a miracle, of course, and that was what the business was all about. The miracles, few and far between, helped to make up for all the unbelievably tacky shit infesting the fabric of everyday life. He had breakfast in the Century Plaza coffee shop, smack between a pair of miracles, Twentieth and ABC-TV. And people still asked where they'd hidden the American Dream.

He opened the Los Angeles *Times* to page three and lost his appetite. The bearded face stared back at its disguised owner and the headline said: "CHALLIS STILL MISSING." In smaller type: "Mountain Search Intensifies." And in the story itself mention was made of the possibility that he had somehow eluded the search teams and gotten off the mountain, storms or not. He forced himself to turn back to the front page, which was devoted almost entirely to the effects of the continuing rains. He chewed a forkful of scrambled eggs and glanced around the large room, which lay in a rather somnolent valley between breakfast and lunch. There were maybe twenty customers working their way through sweet rolls and bagels and lox and coffee, and every damn one of them was reading the Los Angeles *Times*. He touched the side of his face, just to make sure his beard hadn't suddenly reappeared.

Outside on the promenade that tunnels beneath the Avenue of the Stars like something from the twenty-first century, a landscape of concrete with the Shubert Theater and *Beatlemania* on the left and *Star Wars* still holding at the Plitt on the other, he nearly bumped into an ABC-TV executive he knew and a PR guy from Twentieth he'd always known had coveted Goldie's round, tight little ass. He watched them from the corners of his eyes as they ricocheted off in different directions looking worried about their fading suntans. They hadn't even noticed his existence, let alone his identity, but it didn't make any difference. He felt terribly obvious and exposed and jittery.

The offices of *The Coast* magazine took up a lot of high-priced territory in the ABC Entertainment Center, a sea of chamois-colored carpet on which floated a fleet of Corbusier chairs, tables with glass tops an inch thick, Boston ferns and elegant, swaying little date palms, and something Challis thought might just possibly be hibiscus. Working himself up to a frontal assault, calling on the shades of Raymond Chandler and Marlowe and all the other private eyes who had trekked across all the carpets toward all the snotty receptionists in pursuit of all the villains, Challis plunged toward the gimlet-eyed blond. She had frizzed hair like a Boston fern that was not yet big enough to develop a beautiful droop; her fingernails were as long as piano keys, painted dark brown, and on the middle finger of her right hand someone had implanted a gold star in the nail. She looked up with the kind of blank, arrogant face perfected by girls of twenty-five.

"I'd like to see Mr. Donovan."

"The line forms on the right," she said.

"Tell him it's—"

"I'm sorry," she said, trying to show she wasn't, "but Mr. Donovan is in a meeting and he really cannot possibly be disturbed. I'll have to wait until he's free. Take a seat, please, Mr. . . . ."

"Claude Smith, Maximus Productions." He smiled at her. "I won't take up much of his time." He headed for one of the leather-and-chrome chairs, sat down.

"He *is* all booked up for the rest of the day, you know."

"I'll take my chances."

Now that he was in the office, he began to wonder what the hell he thought he was doing, what he expected to pry out of Donovan. To begin with, he would have to tell Donovan who he was, and once he was revealed, what was Donovan likely to do in response? What if he called the cops? What if he had a gun in his desk? Challis squirmed in the chair. But everything in Goldie's datebook seemed to point to her relationship with Donovan: she must have confided in him . . . he must have some clue to what she was doing, what she wanted to tell Toby. So, what was there to do but risk it? He looked at his watch.

The magazine was only a few years old, and he'd heard that the beginnings had been hangnail and threadbare. Donovan had come west with a background in publishing, or so the story went, but he hadn't acted as if he had heavy money behind him. In a way it was his second tour of duty on the coast, but also, in a way, he'd never really left after making his first stop as an ad salesman for a local TV station, then as a columnist's leg man and small-time publicity agent, then as an agent at one of the big shops that eventually merged and became bigger yet. Back in Jersey and

New York City he'd worked the business end of several magazines and newspapers, made a reputation for propping up incipient DOA's. And then it had been back to Los Angeles, blowing his own horn for all it was worth. *The Coast* would be the magazine for the entertainment industry, for politics, for social investigation, the magazine that would tell Californians what their state—Donovan had taken to calling it "the lead-edge state, the place where everything happens first, the place the world makes a habit of watching"—really amounted to. It all sounded wonderful, but *The Coast* had been a sickly baby the few times Challis had read it—and then his life had blown up in his face and he didn't see much of *The Coast.* Now, sickly infant or not, prosperity had come to Jack Donovan.

On the wall facing him, spread from floor to ceiling, was a color blow-up of *The Coast*'s first cover, an aerial shot of the entire Los Angeles area all the way to the sea, which was a masterpiece of matching and joining dozens of individual photographs. Challis sat quietly staring at the various landmarks of his adult life, wondering what enabled the magazine to project such an image. Perhaps it was just the Los Angeles syndrome, the belief that a false front was as good as the real thing.

Half an hour later the door opened and a bizarre-looking elderly woman dressed in a voluminous black caftan swept toward the receptionist trailing an overwhelming aroma of verbena. She clanked beneath lots of gypsy jewelry, bracelets and rings and several necklaces dangling a variety of amulets. Her nails were bright orange, not quite matching her henna-rinsed hair, which looked like the fuzzy halo of a dead dandelion. She clutched an ancient, cracked black leather satchel overflowing with papers and folders, the whole package bound together with a colossal rubber band. She shuffled back and forth in front of the receptionist.

"I must insist, young lady, I must." She sounded like Eleanor Roosevelt. "This is of the greatest possible importance to Mr. Donovan. I was up all night working it out, it's terribly, terribly important." Her voice dropped dramatically and the jewelry set up a cry as she drew a conjurer's line in the air, the orange nails almost leaving a trail behind them. "Danger," she crooned, "danger all around him . . . he's off center, you know that . . . terrible danger. . . . It was all there last night, plain as day." She turned to Challis. "You there, young man, can't you feel it? Even here in this very room?" Her round eyes had a pinhead of light at their dark centers, pierced him, a flickering bird's eyes, blinking like two camera shutters. "Honestly, don't you feel it, sir? Ominous . . . oppressive forces working against our dear Mr. Donovan." Challis began to stammer a non sequitur, but she rescued him by turning back to the girl. "He'll want to know, this I assure you, Marguerite."

"My name isn't Marguerite," the girl said, surprised.

"You *seem* to me to be a Marguerite. I knew a Marguerite once . . ." She interrupted herself: "Well, what does it matter? What does it signify? I must see Mr. Donovan, poor Mr. Donovan." She marched, jangling, to a chair on the other side of the glass-and-chrome table next to Challis. Once her eyes clicked up at him, as if she were recording his presence, putting his picture in her files. "You have a weak face, young man. Prey to temptation, a wounded character —what's your sign? I can help you—"

"With all due respect," Challis said, "I sincerely doubt that—"

She had raised one clawlike, beringed hand, bracelets banging down toward her elbow, was about to say something, then stopped with her eyes refocusing above his head.

A tall man wearing a dark blue pinstripe suit had moved quietly around the corner, presumably coming from the important meeting. His face was deeply tanned, fans of squint lines at the corners of his eyes; his nose was long and Hamitic, curved like an inward-pointing scimitar, and his small ears were tight to his skull and the tops were hidden by a fringe of gray hair cut short to look long. He looked like a Borgia prince waiting for the poison to work on his dinner companion. He was followed by a fat young man with skin the color of typing bond and a mustache that resembled a scruffy mouse at rest. The fat man stopped at the desk.

"Mr. Laggiardi has a meeting in the valley," he said. He checked his digital watch. He set his briefcase on her desk, since the watch required a free hand to depress a button. In his dark brown gabardine suit he resembled a large mound of earth slowly drying on a sunny day. "Please alert our driver." He lowered his voice, whispered moistly, "Mr. Laggiardi does not wait on curbs for limos." The girl nodded at the sheer enormity of such a prospect. "Your Mr. Donovan will be joining us later. After we've had lunch . . . and if Mr. Roth should call, tell him we ran over a bit here and are on our way." He picked up his briefcase and sighed heavily. There was an angry-looking boil on the back of his broad white neck where his collar rubbed at it. "Oh, yes, if New York should call us at this number, tell them to reach us at Maximus this afternoon—now, that should do it."

Then, without a word to each other, the two men left the office, the fat man holding the door for Laggiardi. Challis had the impression that he was witnessing the comings and goings of a group of actors. He reflected that Laggiardi bore all the trademarks of a New York clout-*meister* venturing inside the enemy camp, probably with an eye toward carrying out some mischief along the lines of looting, sacking, and plundering.

A few minutes later a man roughly the size of a telephone booth appeared from the recessed corridor. He stood about six-feet-four, and Challis would have guessed his weight at 240. He was balding, with what hair he had graying and combed straight back from his massive sunlamp-pink forehead. He wore a Brooks Brothers gray herringbone suit with a blue Oxford-cloth button-down shirt and a striped regimental silk tie, black wingtip shoes, as if he had made this most recent trip west with a firmly held refusal to give up his New York uniform. He wore his round-faced gold watch on the underside of his wrist, secured by a blue-and-red wristband. He consulted the watch as the receptionist said, "Mr. Donovan, there are some people . . ." He looked across the room, his broad pink Irish face smiling, his small blue eyes twinkling like stars that had burned out millennia ago. "Aha," he cried as he spotted the lady with the orange hair and the caftan, "my dear madame!" He enclosed her shoulders in the arc of his immense right arm, hugged her, and began walking her back toward the receptionist. "A thousand pardons, madame." He grinned. "May the sun and the wind always be at your back, may you be in heaven half an hour before the devil knows you're dead, so forth and so forth, my dear lady, but I shall have to see you on the morrow. . . . Dear girl," he said to the receptionist, "will you promise to fit madame into the schedule tomorrow? There's a good girl!"

The old lady began fumbling with the cracked satchel, catching papers in the rubber band, half-spilling them. "But you are in danger," she dithered, "dire, terrible danger."

"You're telling me, dear lady, you're telling me!" He took her by the shoulders, met her round bird's eyes with his cold twinkling blue ones. "At the moment, I am late for a couple of very important dates and then a party . . . but tomorrow we shall share a biscuit and a dram and you will tell me the worst." He caught sight of Challis, nodded abruptly with a quick, phony, fading grin as if he had just noticed one of Laggiardi's gunned-up hopsels left behind to enforce some odd, brutal demand. Donovan's gaze passed quickly on, back to the receptionist, and the bantering, bullshit tone was replaced by coldness. "And, Jill, Buller has an hour to clean out his desk. Sixty minutes and not a minute more. . . . Ah, Hal"—he turned to see yet another body appearing from the corridor—"I was just telling Jill to start the timer on you, old fellow. You've got an hour to become a part of my past—is that crystal clear?"

Hal Buller was middle-aged, portly, and sweating. His face was flabby and looked newly pale. He held a balled-up white handkerchief in his hand and his eyes were red. He said hoarsely, "Fuck the sixty minutes, Jack. You can have the crap in my desk. And may the wind always blow in your red face, you stupid mick bastard!" Buller pushed past. When he slammed the door, the room reverberated with the ensuing silence. Donovan beamed from face to face.

[12]

BACK DOWN on the floor of the concrete wind tunnel beneath the Avenue of the Stars, Challis felt more invisible than ever. The whole business in Donovan's office had been a farce: how the hell was he going to get to see the guy? Kidnap him? He couldn't give his name and he couldn't explain why Donovan should spend any time on him. He was an invisible man, no doubt of it, and the problems of getting anywhere with his investigation seemed overwhelming. He decided to drop in at the Hong Kong Bar for a drink and some serious thought.

The heavy wooden door opened off the sad deserted patio. Immediately he was in a world of darkness and bamboo and wicker. It was a large tiered room where he'd spent several harmless evenings with funny-looking drinks, people who looked better in the dark, and some great jazz men and ladies. The long bar ran almost the width of the room on the right, and it was sparsely populated, looked like a set for an old Dick Powell tough-guy picture.

Challis climbed onto a stool and asked for one of the funny drinks, which he knew ahead of time would be sweet and girlish and sickening. When it came it was wearing a little paper parasol and a gardenia and reminded him of a movie whore pining away in Singapore waiting for Fred MacMurray to shoot his way in and rescue her. It was that kind of day. Challis' spirits were veering back toward a pronounced preference for life as it was lived on the screen of the revival houses, or the screen in his head.

Down on the small square stage, a guy in a sweatshirt was checking microphone sound levels while Zoot Sims blew into a slender golden soprano sax. "Moonlight in Vermont." His pianist wandered out, made a passing remark to Sims, who nodded without missing even the slightest, most sublime inflection. The piano player sat down and eased his way into the melody. Sims swayed slightly and Challis remembered seeing him in the mid-fifties, was intrigued by how little he had changed. Still the same massive head with the wiry, tight sandy hair, the chesty build, the bent knees when he began to blow, the prominent nose, and the overhang of his brow. He was playing "Sweet Lorraine" now, and Challis thought about Morgan Dyer and wished to God that his life was simpler, the way it had been right up to the night Goldie died, he wished he could call Morgan and tell her how Zoot Sims played the saxophone and maybe she'd like to go to the Hong Kong Bar and have some funny-looking drinks and maybe she'd find herself liking Toby Challis quite a lot. . . .

A deep, thick, resonant voice steeped in cigarette smoke and rich bourbon growled at his shoulder: "You know why Irishmen never have hemorrhoids? 'Cause they're such perfect assholes!" A laugh rumbled deep, stirring the gravel in Hal Buller's throat. "Name's Hal Buller, Mount Vernon, Texas, by birth." He rested his elbow on the bar, hand extended, and Challis shook it, giving his name as Bob Roper—the name he'd used at the Colony. He'd known Bob Roper in grade school; he'd died as a graduate student in Italy. "Well, Bob, it's been a turkey shoot all day long, and you're looking at the turkey. You saw me get canned up there. . . . What the hell is that you're drinking? Looks like a fairy drink—shit, I feel like a fairy. Bartender, one of these silly damn things for me, and another for my friend Bob. No offense, if you're a fairy, Bob, no offense. Fairies are taking over out here. Well, shit, I got nothin' against fairies, not a thing." He nodded heavily, settling in comfortably against the bar. "I sell ads, Bob. Space, time, any kind of ads you want sold, Hal Buller's your man. And I'm at liberty, as you know." He lit a Lucky Strike and sucked the first smoke down to his toes. He coughed, sounded like a bullfrog at the bottom of a well. He held the cigarette between thick fingers, rubbed his chin noisily with the palm of his other hand. He wore a Masonic ring, diamond insignia on black. "You ever been fired, Bob?"

"Sure," Challis said. "Everybody's been fired."

"Mmm." He nodded. "But at fifty-four, to get dropped in the crapper at fifty-four, it's gotta make you think. Texas . . . maybe I should head back to Texas. Christ, I can sell anything, not just ads—any-goddamn-thing, y'know?"

"Sure, I know."

"Jesus Christ, you could put your eye out with a drink like this—little piece of wood in this umbrella thing." He broke the parasol between two fingers and placed the gardenia carefully on the bar. "You a pal of Fast Jack Donovan? What's your racket, anyway?"

"I'm an investigator," he said, betting a long shot.

"Private?"

"Right."

"Well, no shit. I knew a shamus once, poor bastard, couldn't make a go of it, now he's selling used cars in St. Joe, Missouri. Funny world. He was a shamus in Philly and then in Miami Beach. Damn near starved to death. Funny thing," he mused, "old Clyde was a fairy. Nicest guy in the world, too. You starvin'? How's business?"

"It's good if you don't mind getting your hands dirty." Challis had written that line for a movie that never got produced. No wonder.

"Well, you touch Fast Jack and you'll get dirty, and that's no lie." He puffed hard, ground out the butt, finished the drink, signaled for another, and lit a second Lucky. He wasn't even out of breath. "You workin' for him? Or on him? Just like to know my footing, y'know."

"On him. Client back in New York needs a check on current activities. I'm starting from scratch." Challis shrugged, the question implied: what can you tell me, Hal, old buddy?

Buller's new drink arrived and he took a quick sip. He broke the parasol, placed the gardenia beside the first. The bar looked like it was staring up at Hal Buller. "What do you want to know about Fast Jack? I've known him, what? Twenty years, I reckon. Twenty years . . . the middle of my fuckin' life and I spent it

114

with that miserable sumbitch." He coughed, squinting at Challis through the smoke. He cupped a hand and drew the cigarette off his lower lip. "He fires me and then comes running down the hall asking if I need some money, says he could come up with five grand severance if I needed it—shit, I told him fuckin' A I needed it, just send me a check. He will, too. Christ, I hope he burns forever in a fiery pit!" He let a laugh loose in his chest again, let it rattle around. "Fast Jack . . . you know what I mean, *fast?*" Challis nodded. "Well, he's fast . . . he could throw a lamb chop past a wolf! Like old Bob Feller, the old Van Meter, Iowa, fireballer. You remember old Bob Feller, don't you?" Challis nodded, remembering old Bob Feller just fine. "Well, he finally got the fast one past Hal Buller, and it took him twenty years to do it. I lasted twenty years, and now, pffft, the last fastball and he catches me flatfooted, pickin' my nose, lookin' at the third goddamn strike. And for what? The mick has to get rid of me because I went out on calls one day in a fuckin' leisure suit! The mick hates polyester, coordinated shirts, white shoes and belts, but I had to wear that shit—my wife, goddamn pinhead, bought it for me, for Chrissakes. And anyway, I was down in Orange County calling on car dealers—man, they swear by those fuckin' leisure suits down there, you're an asshole if you don't wear one." He sighed and shook another Lucky out of the flattened pack. "So prickface mick bastard tells me it's the straw that broke the camel's back, that I'm out of touch with the times, says—and I quote—he slaps me on the back, says, 'It's time to hit the trail, podner, it's the last roundup.' And him spending the morning kissing the Mafia's ass."

Zoot Sims had strapped on a big horn now, was rocking on the balls of his feet, the bottom of the sax cradled in his groin, blowing around the edges of "These Foolish Things."

"The Mafia," Challis repeated. "Everybody talks about the Mafia, sure, but talk and seventy-five cents will get you a cup of coffee. Right, Hal? My New York client is after something solid."

"Come on, what's solid? Where you been, man?

There ain't no such thing as solid in this town, you, me, Fast Jack—we all cover our tracks all the time. It's the way the business works, publishing, movies, TV, it's the same everywhere, you know that. I can give you some of the shit on Donovan—no charge, believe me, just give me your word, Bob, you're gonna make it hot for the miserable shit heel—but forget solid, forget proving it." He poured half of the funny drink down his gullet and gave Challis a big, sour, mean Texas grin. "You want the shit for your client, Bob, or you gonna turn it down?"

"I'm listening, Hal."

"He's listening. Way to go, Bob, way to go." He disappeared in a cloud of smoke, and the cough hacked away, scraping the bottom of something.

"Is that office just a front? Cosmetic? Or is he really doing that well?"

Buller lit another Lucky and took a long look at Zoot Sims. "Go back a ways. Last year Jack's girlfriend gets herself murdered—her ex-husband got it hung on him, that guy that's in the papers now, poor dumb sumbitch. Well, Jack's girlfriend was the only daughter of Maximus Pictures, so I figure Jack was in pretty tight with Aaron Roth—you follow me? Okay. With the daughter dead and her old husband going over for it, Roth was suddenly all alone—now people said he and the daughter didn't get along worth shit, but who knows? I ask you. And Roth and the old husband were supposed to have been pretty good friends, the guy was a screenwriter, worked for Roth at Maximus, the usual incestuous Hollywood number, right? So with one of 'em dead and the other in the klink, Donovan moves in on Roth . . . brought together by their grief, you might say. Christ!" He frowned at the remains of his drink and flapped his hand at the bartender, pointed at the mug. Challis shook his head, indicating he had plenty left. Zoot Sims had moved on to "The Moon Was Yellow." Glenn Ford and Rita Hayworth in *Gilda* flickered in Challis's head.

"Donovan's got about as much emotion as a rattle-snake," Buller continued. "No grief, no nothing, but it was his chance to close in on his girlfriend's father. What if Roth and his daughter hadn't gotten along?

Death heals all wounds, y'know, Bob, old fella, old shamus? Sure you do, you been around. You got a face that's, y'know, been around. So Fast Jack sucks up to the Roths, Aaron falls for it, being a silly-ass movie tycoon with no sense at all, and I figure Maximus is now financing Donovan's rag. An alliance of the grief-stricken, but Jack's got 'em hypnotized—they haven't caught on to him yet. Christ, Donovan hasn't got a pot to piss in that's not leased . . . the 450SL, the penthouse on Sunset, that goddamn yacht he spends most of his time on. Shit! It could all disappear tomorrow." He tied into his new drink. The bar had sprouted a third eye. "Whattaya think of that? Make your client happy?"

"Who knows what will make a client happy? All the answers and a bill that gets lost in the mail. . . . You mentioned the Mafia. I don't get the connection, Hal."

Hal squeezed the last Lucky out of the pack and lit it, grinning, enjoying himself, innocent in a peculiar way, full of healthy malice. "This part of the story goes back to New York, and my details are sketchy. But the basics are guaranteed by yours truly. Somewhere along the line with one of his goddamn newspapers or magazines, maybe it was his scheme to do in-flight magazines for the small feeder lines—somewhere Donovan went in hock to the dude in his office today, Vittorio Laggiardi . . . a mick and a wop, they deserve each other. But guys like Laggiardi use guys like Donovan for batting practice, y'know? Vito's probably got the acetylene torch to Donovan's nuts this very minute, and loud screams are music to Vito's ears—ya get it, Bob? I don't know the details, but I know what I see, and Donovan is wedged between Maximus on one side, since they're putting up the money for *The Coast*, and Vito on the other, because Vito holds a ton of markers. And Laggiardi visits out here once a week and he's a New York hood, he hates to leave the Big Apple. . . . And there's something about a new kid moving into a big job at Maximus, some kid Vito knows or likes or owns, I'm not sure. It could be Maximus TV, but I'm fuzzy on this, so don't quote me.

"But Fast Jack's on the tightrope . . . so what does the bastard do? He fires Hal Buller. It's like having a lousy day and going home and kicking the shit out of the dog. So, Bob, old buddy, welcome to what I know. I hope your client can use it. Tell him to leave it sticking out of Donovan's back, okay? That'll be payment enough for Hal Buller, you better believe it."

Buller was growing weary, resting his deeply lined, shaggy-browed head in the palm of a hand, staring at the three gardenias on the shiny bar. He subsided into a silence laced with heavy, rasping inhalation, the breathing of an overage, out-of-shape, three-pack-a-day man. Challis nursed the melting ice in the bottom of the cheap, fancy mug, watched as Zoot Sims and his companions wandered away from the stage. He kept looking at Goldie and Donovan in his mind, trying to get them and their relationship straightened out. Goldie was on one track and Donovan on another, and at some point they met, interacted, and Goldie began making all those jabs at her datebook. It seemed to Challis that they were not simply friends, or lovers: those notations were something else, full of business and impatience and pressure.

Did Donovan know the truth she had planned to tell Toby that last night? And where, really, did Donovan fit into the larger picture—not simply with Goldie, but with whatever his Maximus connection actually was? And how many lives had Donovan actually led? As a gossip columnist/leg man he'd been instrumental in running Morgan Dyer's father. In New York he'd sold some part of his soul to Laggiardi, and once those guys had a piece of you, you never quite got it back. Was Donovan really a new satellite circling Maximus? Had he jumped the fence around Aaron Roth: had grief, as Buller had said, brought the two of them together? Challis sneaked a peek at Buller, whose heavy-lidded frog's eyes had drooped almost shut. It wasn't worth getting him started again, but the grief-stricken union of Donovan and Roth lacked the quality of verisimilitude which distinguished good work from hack: it was tough to throw such a wild improbability past an old screenwriter. . . . But how did Goldie and Donovan have Aaron Roth in common? That would take some answering.

Watching Buller slowly fall asleep in the dark quiet
118

of the bar, Toby Challis wondered what came next. There was no reason Donovan would see him. What good was access to anyone else going to do him? It wasn't a movie and he wasn't a detective and he was confused, awash in details he couldn't quite connect, and scared to death that someone would come running at him from behind a bush, screaming his name and asking for a reward.

He paid for all the drinks, stood up feeling stiff and rumpled, and left.

He went back outside into the encompassing grayness, where the wind was still trapped in the patio courtyard, thrashing the awnings and snuffling at his trouser legs. He went inside the hotel's lower level. A man coming out of the liquor store had a fresh copy of the *Herald-Examiner* and the front page leaped at Challis: "WHERE IS THIS MAN?" Beneath the headline, a full-page photograph of his face, thankfully bearded, stared at the world. "Storm Coverage Inside" ran along beneath his picture. He went into the drugstore and bought a copy, folded it over, fished out a dime, and went to the bank of telephones across the hallway. He found the piece of paper in his shirt pocket and dialed. She answered the telephone crisply.

"Morgan, it's me, Toby you-know-who. I don't know what the hell I'm doing, you get the picture?" He swallowed dryly. "I need help."

[13]

MORGAN DYER'S HOUSE clung like a misplaced New England saltbox to one of the hillsides rising wetly above the Sunset Strip. Gaping, deep wounds had been gouged from the muddy hills by the virtually unceasing rain, giving the mountain range the look of something very old and decomposing. Somewhere underneath it all the great plates tying the planet together were shifting microscopically, building up to the one mighty, inevitable shove which could make her fine little house a traffic hazard on Sunset. The palms waved good-bye, slowly and without energy in the wind drifting lazily in the canyons, as he rounded the last sharp curve and pulled into her narrow driveway, stopped beneath the latticework weighed down with curling bougainvillea. Challis sagged in the driver's seat for a moment, feeling the tiredness, the letdown that comes with the notion that you're home safe.

She came outside to greet him, smiling, her mouth wide and a gap showing between her front teeth. She was wearing faded Levi's, a green tanktop, and no shoes, and she hugged his arm, watching his eyes. "Come on in, I've got a pitcher of tea—I'm mainly an iced-tea person, year round. Coffee gives me the willies. How are you? Are you all right?" She took his hand and pulled him inside, through the wide living room and onto the patio with Los Angeles stretching out below. "Just a second—and help yourself to the tea." He poured a glassful with ice cubes clinking and followed her out into the backyard. The wind was picking up, smelled of rain. The fringe of awning over the patio, faded canvas that had once been bright green and orange, flapped in warning. She was standing by the small oblong swimming pool fishing for leaves with a net. Waves lapped at the sides, leaves eddying along the gutters. A tiny faded brown bikini bathing suit lay in two pieces beside a chaise longue. She squatted at the pool's edge and snared the last clump of brown leaves. Watching her, Challis felt a strong sexual urge, the first in a long time. Worry, fear, jail—they had laid his sex drive to rest, but he wanted to touch her.

"There," she said, dropping the net on the lawn, which was long and silky, needed mowing. "Come here, look at this." He followed her back to the chainlink fence at the back of her property, all but obscured by vines. "I've been taking crud out of that damn pool for two days, and the crud is gaining on me!" As she spoke, a gust of wind whipped leaves across the grass. "Look," she said, pointing. Beyond her fence the hill was disintegrating. Several hundred feet below, a swimming pool was full of collapsed hillside. Several men stood around looking at the mess. "If we survive the rain, the fire danger will be all the worse next year— the weeds and grasses will grow all the faster and get just as dry. Dante would have understood." She looked at the ridges of houses and streets layered one atop the next on the canyon wall opposite. "All the circles, ready-made, waiting for the fire." She laughed. "Sorry. This is no place to be philosophical. Let's go inside, the rain's going to start any minute."

It was a small house with only one large room surrounded by a couple of bedrooms and a kitchen. The comfortable jumble of furniture looked like it had been accumulated over a long time. He dropped into a soft couch and took a long drink of iced tea, felt the breeze from the patio. She sat on a hassock and asked him what he'd done since she left him under the marquee at the Beverly Hills Hotel.

He told her about Ollie Kreisler and Pete Schaeffer advising him to get out, once, for all, and for good. He told her about the link between Maximus, or at least Aaron Roth, and Donovan, which both men had mentioned. He told her about the visit to the beach house, the notations in the datebook, and the fight with the man on the deck. He told her about the futile visit to Donovan's office and Hal Buller's thoughts

121

about Donovan and Vittorio Laggiardi. He told her that he didn't know what the hell to do next.

"Today, after I walked out of the Hong Kong Bar," he said, "I felt spooked, afraid of being alone in the world with newspaper stories about me everywhere I looked, completely stymied about how the hell I was ever going to connect with Donovan . . . everybody's ass-deep in their own problems, I guess, and not all that interested in me. You know how it is here—you'd think people would come apart with amazement at my showing up, but Ollie and Pete just sort of nodded, gave me their advice, and got back to work. I'm not blaming them, I don't mean that, but my situation—which seems pretty damn remarkable to me—was just an incident in their days."

"But you're only involved in murder and escape from plane crashes," she said. "That's not the *business,* it has nothing to do with what really interests anybody here, and they both think that what is happening to you is only an inconvenience, something that can be fixed, like a hernia. They think nothing of offering to help you escape, but the moral question, who killed Goldie and why, strikes them as irrelevant."

"I wouldn't be surprised if they both still think I killed her. They don't seem to think it's particularly important whether I did or didn't, they don't seem to care what Goldie had gotten into that would get her killed." He shook his head. "I just don't get it." The wind came up stronger, the awning's fringe flapped noisily. "And all I keep thinking is, once we figure out what's going on, we'll be able to see what Goldie wanted to tell me . . . and then we'll see it all clearly. I've got to find out what she was on to. I owe her, for Chrissakes."

Morgan nodded soberly, looking at the piece of paper on which Challis had written the notations.

"I can help you," she said. "I can help you with Jack, for one thing. But, first, Vito Laggiardi—now, he's something new to the occasion. How much do you know about him?"

"Only what Buller told me."

"Well, you remember my former husband, Charlie Sharpe? Charlie had to do some checking on Vito for

122

one of the studios a couple of years ago. Vito wanted to finance a movie and he owned a piece of a Broadway musical the studio was also in on. The studio was one of the few without a major mob connection, and they sort of wanted it to stay that way . . . for as long as possible, anyway. So Charlie Sharpe took a pretty close look at Vito. Tying him into the mob was tough, at least in terms of hard evidence, but the studio wasn't interested in hard evidence. They just wanted the truth, they didn't have to prove it in court. And there were plenty of connections which looked more than merely probable. And Vito had been trying to buy up something for a long time—something glamorous, something kind of high-profile-ish. Vito wanted some fun, was the impression I got. He owned a big auto dealership in Chicago, one in Philadelphia, and one in Los Angeles. He owned a shoe company in St. Louis. A chain of drugstores in Detroit. Real estate in New Jersey and San Diego. An interstate-trucking company. A restaurant in Palm Springs, a couple of apartment complexes in Phoenix and Scottsdale—that wasn't fun, that was business. So he got into the Broadway thing, backed a couple of shows that went belly-up on the road. He tried to crack Vegas with a bid on a hotel and casino and came up short. Then he went back to what he knew and acquired one of the largest storefront loan companies in America . . . and tried to buy control of a chain of suburban newspapers, failed. Then a publishing company, failed. The fun things kept getting away. A team in the National Hockey League, no dice. Then he went after the studio Charlie Sharpe was retained by . . . and the decision there was that the only way he could accomplish that was if the studio management and the stockholders asked him in—I mean, this guy was being watched up close by the SEC and the IRS and a bunch of other regulatory agencies. And the studio said no, thank you, and he couldn't really run the risk of pushing it . . . so Charlie Sharpe said that the only way Vito could get more than he already had was to either keep acquisitions small or go way underground with money that would be hard to connect to him personally. Charlie Sharpe's conclusion was that Vito was

123

a very, very big crook, the kind that is relatively safe from prosecution *now* but had better be awfully damned careful because Big Brother is watching."

Challis said, "And now he owns Donovan."

"Maybe," she said.

"And Donovan and Roth have become chums."

"Maybe," she said. "But we don't really know. Remember what Ollie Kreisler told you about Donovan and my father? Well, Ollie was right—Jack Donovan is not exactly a day at the beach. . . . Well, Vito Laggiardi is like stepping on a broken beer bottle. You said Pete Schaeffer thought maybe somebody killed Goldie to make a point? Look at these notations. *V.L.*" She made a face at him. "Vito Laggiardi lives in that kind of world. Where you sometimes have to make a point the hard way."

"Good God."

"I'm not saying he did it, Toby. Just that he's the kind of man who might order it done as a matter of business policy. Maybe *V.L.* means something else altogether. But Goldie seemed to know some odd people, as Schaeffer reminded you. Donovan's no prize."

"So how can you help me with Donovan?"

"Stroke of luck," she said. She was throwing herself into his predicament, and he felt himself drawing strength from her. She wasn't part of the business; she had the touch of real life. She squirmed with anticipation, enthused with the idea of constructing their plot. "I'm launching a new mystery novel at the store tonight. Arch Crosby, it's his fiftieth novel, and I've set up a cocktail party, he'll say a few words and we'll all look uncomfortably at trays of slowly drying canapés . . . he'll sign a hundred books, he's always been popular out here, writes about the Los Angeles mystique. He knows everybody in the business, and among those he knows is Jack Donovan, who will definitely be there tonight. Jack always likes it when I pay attention to him—I think it's because of what he did to my father, he gets a kick out of talking a little risqué with the daughter. God, he's a real prize! So, I can get you and Jack into my office. Alone. And, God willing, you take it from there. I'll even have a tape recorder going if you want. . . . You read enough mysteries, you learn about these things."

Challis wandered back outside onto the patio while Morgan went to bathe and dress. Sirens drifted up from Sunset, and the wind was colder. The afternoon had gone quickly. He felt some raindrops riding on the wind, and finally, when it had turned to a spray, he went back inside and turned on the television.

Jerry Dunphy's familiar rugged face appeared, pink and topped with all the curly white hair. "From the mountains to the sea, to all of Southern California— here's what's happening. Late this afternoon a mysterious development in the Toby Challis case . . . we've got Joanne Ishimine live from St. Christopher's School to tell us all about it. . . . Joanne, what's happening out there in Santa Monica?"

The screen filled with the face of a pretty Oriental girl-woman who was as well known in Los Angeles as most movie stars. She was trying to keep from blowing away, wore a raincoat, and stood outside a high wrought-iron gate with a Spanish-mission-style school building behind her. A plaque beside her face was in focus enough to give the name of the school, a motto in Latin, and the inscription "Founded 1926."

"It's raining cats and dogs right now, but the situation is this. You may recall that at the same time the plane carrying Toby Challis was down on the mountainside, we were also concerned about a group of children who had wandered away from a campsite in the same area, within just a few miles. Well, the children were found safe and sound at the lodge belonging to a woman . . . ah, Morgan Dyer. Now, at the time there seemed to be no connection between the children and Mr. Challis—this afternoon all this changed. One of the smaller boys mentioned to a teacher that something previously unreported had happened up there, and I've got the teacher, Eileen Wheeler, right here. . . . Mrs. Wheeler, what did the boy tell you?" Mrs. Wheeler moved into the picture, looking earnest, stocky, with lots of dark curls framing her face. A crew member was holding an umbrella over the two women now, but the teacher's glasses were glistening with raindrops.

"Stevie Faber mentioned to me—I guess I should say he blurted it out like it had been building up in him—he told me that a man covered in blood had found them, or maybe been found by them on the mountain, and that this man had led them to safety . . . he said that the man's name was . . . Bandersnatch. That's what he said, Bandersnatch." She looked alertly at Joanne. "I thought I'd better call the police, and I guess that's what brought you here. . . ."

"How much credence do you put in what Stevie said? I mean, he wasn't alone up there, what do all the other campers say?"

"Well, this is very hard to tell—the others say they don't remember . . ." She sighed like a woman who realized the difficulties in dealing with groups of children, who knew the kinds of peer pressure and intimidation and shame. "Of course, you talked with Ralphie . . ."

"That's the other thing, Jerry, we did speak with one of the members of the camping expedition, the oldest boy, Ralph Halliday, who's nearly fourteen, and we've got that piece of film . . ."

The screen was now occupied by the reporter and the large, tubby figure of Ralph Halliday. They were standing in a corridor, brightly lit for the cameras, with children milling about behind them, curious to see what was going on. Tired out and emotionally unwound by the rest on the couch, Challis felt tears filling his eyes at the sight of Ralph, who wore a Dodgers warm-up jacket over a slipover shirt that was tight around his ample waist. Ralph frowned intently at the microphone as he listened to the question.

"You're the oldest of the campers, all the others seem to look to you as the leader—you've heard what Stevie Faber has said about the blood-covered man on the mountain, the man whose name he says was Bandersnatch. Now, did you see this man Bandersnatch, too?"

"It'll be the Abominable Snowman next," Ralph growled like Edward G. Robinson. "We're up on the mountain, see? The littlest kids are cold and hungry, but I'm not worried. I find us a nice cave, build a fire, make some coffee, divvy up some candy bars, turn on the radio—it's no big deal, see? I had the whole thing under control. I had a compass, I knew where we were . . . more or less, anyway. But kids like Stevie—well, Stevie's a nice little kid, but he's not playing with a full deck, y'know what I mean?"

"But Bandersnatch—if he didn't see a man covered in blood, what did he see?"

"That's his imagination, see? I had all the kids marching along reciting Lewis Carroll's poem, the 'Jabberwocky' poem—you know that poem? Okay, there's that part about the frumious Bandersnatch, and Stevie wanted to know about what one was, and everybody was telling him, making up this terrible stuff— well, then, I suppose Stevie got to dreaming about it, see? And here we are—me on television!" He suddenly grinned broadly into the camera and said in a perfectly normal voice: "Here I am—cast me!"

The film ended, and Dunphy and his co-anchor, Christine Lund, who was not only as well known as the movie stars but substantially better looking than almost all of them, were laughing and shaking their heads. Christine Lund, her mouth moist and tantalizing, her blond hair in the trademark shag, said: "Joanne, we realize the story isn't funny, but that, boy, he's really—"

"He's on his way," Dunphy said. "What's going to happen next, Joanne?"

"To be honest, I don't know. At this point, Ralph Halliday—who'll probably have his own series by the time this is over—and Stevie Faber are at odds and the other kids aren't talking. But the police were here most of the afternoon talking to Mrs. Wheeler and the boys who were up on the mountain, and I was assured that they'll be following up on all the leads they get. And I'll be in touch and keep you posted. For KABC News, this is Joanne Ishimine at St. Christopher's School in Santa Monica."

Christine Lund reappeared, the smile wiped off the glistening lips. "In a moment . . . more storm damage last night in Malibu and an interview with the man in charge of the Hillside Strangler Task Force." A commercial clicked into place, and Challis realized that Morgan had come back, was standing behind the couch.

"Damn," she said. "They're not going to just forget about what Stevie said, regardless of how many stops old Ralph pulls out—what an amazing kid!"

Challis wiped at his eye, nodded. The hanging ferns swayed in the wind. Thunder rolled somewhere up above Mulholland Drive, and rain pattered in the trees outside. The sky had gone completely dark. Morgan went to the sliding screen door, flipped a switch, and a couple of floodlights came on, casting huge ominous shadows across the lawn. She was wearing a khaki gabardine pantsuit with a pale orange scarf. The pants rode high and tight, made her legs look even longer, and the jacket was fitted at the waist, flared across the firm, round swell of her hips. Challis got up, went to her, stood behind her, and put his hands on her shoulders. She leaned back against him, her thick hair against his cheek. His hands were shaking.

"I should never have gotten you into this," he said. "Jesus, it's getting worse and worse . . . now this Bandersnatch thing . . ." The smell of the rain and her perfume mingled, gave him a lightheaded feeling.

"Don't be silly, don't talk like this," she whispered. "If you start to give in now, you're a dead duck. Look at my position if you want to see something idiotic. I've got to keep from letting myself go with you, I can't give in to the normal urges I feel. I've never been able to just let myself be serviced, like an animal, because I need it, because it would feel good and calm me down . . . no, not me. I have to care about a man, and even I can look at you and see I ought to be careful, you're not a really great bet, not yet. Still, still . . . I want to be with you. I want to go to bed with you. But what if they catch you, what if you can't find your way out of the mess—I don't know what I'd do. I'm not tough. I try to take charge, stay busy, but I'm not tough, Challis, I'm just not tough."

"Maybe I'm like you," he said after a moment, feeling the weight of her body against him. Her hips pressed against him, and finally, calling on an effort of will he wasn't sure he possessed, he pushed her gently away, turned her around to face him. Her wide pouty

128

lips parted, and he heard her breathing. She looked at him levelly, her eyes enormous and open wide, pale green jewels.

"I will, though," she said softly. "I will right now . . . I can't convince myself I'm not alive, I *am* alive, I'm ready for you."

"But I'm like you," he said. "I can't let go and forget about it. I'd care, really care, and if they do catch me, then I'd go crazy. . . . Let's just try to get through it the best way we can, then we can see . . . I've had a dream for as long as I can remember, a man in a white suit looking out across the water . . ."

She nodded, sniffed. "I don't know what's the matter with me." She tried to laugh, looked up at him. Then she pulled away. "My God, Challis, I'm behaving like a frustrated spinster. The truth is out. I'm not a seventies girl, I guess. Now, let's straighten up and behave ourselves and go to my party—"

The doorbell made an erratic, malfunctioning buzz.

Challis remained by the sliding door as Morgan went to answer it. He could see over her shoulder when she opened it. There were two men in damp raincoats, and Challis never doubted for a moment who they were.

Cops.

Morgan led them in, her face expressionless as she walked toward Challis. "Darling," she said in a voice he'd never heard before, "these two gentlemen are from the police."

A tall man who looked like a leathery, thin-faced cowboy pushing sixty came first and extended a large bony hand with his buzzer in it. "Otto Narleski," he said, and nodding toward the stocky, younger man who looked around as if he hated to intrude, "and Sergeant Overmeyer."

"Ed Streeter," Challis said, for some reason remembering the car parked outside and the chance that it could be checked on from the license plate. "Miss Dyer and I were just leaving . . ."

"It doesn't matter," Morgan said. "We just saw the television news—it wouldn't take a genius to realize you fellows were going to be stopping by." Detective Narleski stood quietly in front of the fireplace letting her talk. "I'm assuming this is about the—what was it? —the Bandersnatch man?"

"Yes, ma'am," Narleski said. "The Bandersnatch man—where are you going, Sergeant?" Overmeyer had slid the screen onto the patio and was going outside.

"I just wanted to see the view, Otto. Anything wrong with that?" Overmeyer sounded innocent rather than naive, but Narleski looked at Challis, closed his eyes, and shook his head.

"Sit down, Detective," Morgan said. "Can I get you something? Coffee? Iced tea?"

"No, nothing, thanks. I just wanted to ask you about this Bandersnatch thing—the little boy, Stevie, is adamant about seeing this guy covered in blood." He cleared his throat. He was still standing. Challis saw Overmeyer moving in the dark and rain out past the pool, out of the glow of the floodlamps. "You said nothing about any man accompanying the children when they arrived at your lodge. I would like you to look back, Miss Dyer, and take another crack at that, ma'am?"

"There's really nothing to go back to," she said. She sat down on the couch, calmly shaking her head, the blond hair swaying, leaning back, the picture of relaxation. "I either saw a man with the children or I didn't, it's not something I could have been mistaken about, is it? The children got into my house by the back door. I was drying my hair after a shower. By the time I was aware they were inside, they'd found the living room and were just sort of standing there being very dear and unsure of what to do next—there was no blood-drenched man, just the kids . . . a sort of fat one, older, called Ralph, was the natural leader . . . they just interviewed him on TV."

"But no man," Narleski said quietly.

"I'm sorry," she said. "But no man."

Narleski put his hands in his raincoat pocket and looked glum. "We haven't found a trace of this Challis fellow, the murderer. No leads, and the weather's so bad on the mountain we can't do any tracking up there . . . we've tried to throw a cordon around the mountain, but it's a waste of time now. It was probably a waste of time by the time the storm that brought the plane down subsided. He's either dead in the snow or off the mountain." He sighed and looked from Morgan to Challis. "What the devil is Overmeyer doing out there?"

Challis looked, said, "He's back by the hedge, looking at the view."

"It would have been nice if Bandersnatch had been real—he'd have been our man."

"Well, he wouldn't have had to make it all the way to my house," Morgan said. "Maybe they saw him, then separated from him before they got to my place . . ."

"Doesn't make any sense," Narleski said. "Nope, there's a flaw there. Ralph, this bigger kid, says there was *no* man, period. Stevie says there was. Nobody else is saying nothin'. So it looks to me like you'd have seen the man, if there was a man. And Stevie . . . well, he says the bloody man was with them at your house."

"I didn't realize that," she said.

"No, how could you? But he does."

"Excuse me," Challis said, "but if Ralph and Miss Dyer say there was no man, what's the problem?"

"Well, Mr. Streeter, the problem is that I wasn't there, I didn't see who was there . . . so somebody's lying to me."

"Not necessarily. Miss Dyer and Ralph concur, little Stevie has his own story . . . it seems to me that Ralph's explanation is pretty logical. An overworked imagination."

Narleski stopped pacing when he reached the sliding screen. "I suppose that's the answer," he mused. "There was no man, little Stevie's not playing with a full deck. To quote Ralph." But his voice said a lot beyond the words. "Overmeyer, get in here. You're all wet, man." He turned and looked at Challis. "Tell me, Mr. Streeter, have you ever been up to Miss Dyer's lodge?"

"Why, yes, I have. Just once. Last fall."

"Just once, you're quite sure?"

"Yes, last fall."

"You couldn't possibly have been up there when the children arrived? That might explain things . . . say, Stevie got up to use the john in the middle of the night and saw you . . . say, he was the only one who saw you—*that* would be an answer, an entirely innocent, plausible answer that would put my mind at ease."

"I'm sorry," Challis said. "I wasn't there."

"Of course not, of course not. Just looking for the easy way out." Overmeyer pushed into the room, stood blinking. "How was the view?"

"Fine, sir. A fine view . . . helluva view. But the hillside's giving away." He wiped his face. "God, I'm dripping on your carpet!" He hurried across the tiled entryway.

"We'll be going now, Miss Dyer," Narleski said. He looked sad. "We'll be in touch if anything else comes up. Stevie's story is the only one that constitutes a lead on Challis." He shrugged. "What we're going to do with it, I just don't know." Stopping at the door, he looked out at Overmeyer, who had reached the plain car and was sitting behind the wheel speaking into a two-way. "Thank you for your time, Miss Dyer, Mr. Streeter. Overmeyer thanks you, too. Good night."

Morgan and Toby watched him hurry through the rain and get in on the passenger side. Overmeyer was peering at the Mustang's rear end and talking into the black mike. Rain streaked the windows, blurred their faces. Morgan waved and closed the door.

"I feel like throwing up," she said. "They believe Stevie."

"That's fear talking. But if the rest of the kids blow, well, it might get pretty sticky . . . it's up to Ralph, if he can keep them in line. I really mean it, I'm sorry you're in on this and you're getting deeper—"

"Where did you get Eddie Streeter, anyway?"

"It's his car. He parks cars at the Beverly Hills Hotel. It's a damn good thing I thought of it, too. Overmeyer was checking the plates just now. I don't think I'm cut out for this sort of thing."

She frowned. "Who is?"

[14]

MORGAN LED THE WAY over the hump of the mountains and down into the valley, with Challis in the Mustang behind her. The rain couldn't quite make up its mind, and the spray was just enough to keep the wipers going. The bookstore was on Ventura, and the activity inside lit up the street in front, threatened to spill out onto the sidewalk. Morgan drove slowly past, then around the corner and into the alley, where she pulled into a place next to a trash barrel behind the store. Challis sidled the Mustang up close and got out. They stood under the eaves beside the back door. They could hear the hubbub of the party inside.

"My partner, Marjorie, has got everything going nicely, thank God. All you have to do is go in, eat some pâté and little doodads, drink some Mumm's, and be inconspicuous. I'll do some maneuvering and get Jack ready in my office—just don't worry." She touched his arm and smiled reassuringly. "Okay. Let's go."

Morgan was swept up in the greetings, and Challis did as he'd been told. The champagne was good, made him realize how hungry he was. He loaded pâté, which was topped with walnuts and tasted lightly of cognac, from a thick dish with a traditional rabbit-head cover onto a quick succession of crackers, wolfing them down. Terrifyingly, he knew half the people crowded into the store. Ray Bradbury was beaming expansively while a short man with wavy gray hair told him how wonderful the stage production of *The Martian Chronicles* was . . . Richard Anderson, tall and tanned, was shaking hands with a television writer who'd done several scripts for his two shows, *The Six Million Dollar Man* and *The Bionic Woman*. "Good to see you, pal," Anderson said softly, and the man turned

133

to his wife: "Honey, meet the only man ever to star on two networks at the same time." Challis knew them all, walked away.

"Look, Harry, I saw that blond's test—you know the one—and lemme tell you, she's table-grade stuff. I wouldn't push hamburger at you, Harry."

"Listen, Begelman's the top of the iceberg, kid. I hear there's a cool million missing at Twentieth and nobody wants to go to court."

"Charlie, how many times I gotta tell you, mystery pictures are dead. Too much talk . . . people get ants in their pants, they want to watch a nine-point-two hit LA, hospitals coming apart, big fish eating kids, we're dealing with an audience with a twelve-second attention span and you're gonna have to face it."

Irv Letofsky of the *Times* looked deadpan at a man laboriously drawing toward the end of a story. "It's not funny, Marvin. Don't you see that? It wasn't funny when the Captain and Tenille did it, and it's not funny now. It's like my root-canal work, one of the least amusing things that's ever happened to me. Sorry." He smiled to himself as the man walked away.

Where the hell was Morgan? The crowd seemed to be inflating as if it were required to completely fill the room. The walls, top to bottom, were lined with shelves of mystery novels, volumes of true crime and memoirs, books about mystery movies, busts of Sherlock Holmes and Edgar Allan Poe and Nero Wolfe, hardbacks, paperbacks, spiral-bound collections of film scripts. A display of pretend murder weapons filled a glass-fronted case: a pistol, several daggers, a syringe, a length of silk stocking, a heavy chipped ashtray stained with very real-looking blood. A slipper full of tobacco, reminiscent of Holmes, rested on the mantelpiece, nearby a London bobby's domed hat. The space above the fireplace was dominated by a large movie poster of *The Big Sleep*.

"About a week ago I heard my house begin to kind of moan," a woman said. "Death throes, I said to myself, moaning that came and went each day. Well, what was I to do? I couldn't get a cottage at the Beverly Hills, so I wound up on top of the Beverly Wilshire . . . guess who's my neighbor? Warren Beatty.

I see him every day—my God, talk about the years being kind!" She cackled. "The house went yesterday, slid down the hill."

He was thinking about another crack at the pâté when Morgan joined him. "Enjoying the party?"

"I still haven't seen the novelist."

"He's sitting down at the table signing books, little white-haired chap . . . maybe you should sign some more of your books for me, remind me, will you? It's time. I left Jack in my office, he's waiting. I just said there's someone who wanted to see him on an urgent matter. Alone. He took my word that it was important."

"Oh, God," Challis said.

"Come on, I'll leave you at the door. Just go in."

Challis opened the door leading from a quiet passage at the back of the shop into Morgan's office. The room was simultaneously neat and messy. There was a large framed portrait of Sherlock Holmes by Paget, a replica of the black, stocky statuette of the Maltese falcon as it appeared in the movie, a statue of Inspector Maigret serving as a paperweight atop a stack of foolscap beside an old typewriter.

Donovan was waiting, even more massive in the small crowded office than he'd been in his own more spacious quarters. He stood behind the desk, half-turned toward the door as if he'd been inspecting the bookshelves while waiting for the mystery guest. His face was still the same shade of pink, a large head with the features glued onto the front, like a Magritte man. His expression was a compound of Irish wit, anxiety, charm, impatience. He picked up the Maltese falcon in a huge hand with almost no hair on the back of it, waved it toward Challis, almost like a weapon, but there was the grin in the pink face behind it.

"Well, well, me boy," he said with a highwayman's forced bonhomie, "Jack Donovan at your service. And who might you be, may I ask?" What was he thinking? Challis wondered. Why did he give off that slight aura of fear? Was it simply that he had things to fear?

"We had someone in common," Challis said, closing the door behind him. The rain was drumming on a metal trash can outside the window. Donovan raised his faint

135

eyebrows, tapping the black bird from hand to palm. "Goldie Challis," he said, "you remember the late Mrs. Challis."

"I'm afraid I don't understand." His breath whistled between his teeth. "I was acquainted with her, yes—"

"I'm Toby Challis." He held up his hand, palm toward Donovan like a traffic cop. "Don't say a word. I am Toby Challis. I'm alive and well and I've undergone a change in appearance, but it's me."

"What the hell is this?" He moved toward the door. "If this is Morgan's idea of a—"

"Stay where you are. I want to talk, that's all."

"Mother o' mercy," he muttered. The pinkness was sliding down out of his face: he looked like somebody had pulled the plug and he was emptying. He seemed to be shrinking inside his suit. He was clinging to the black bird as if it might keep him from falling down. "Look, I don't . . . I don't get the point of this. I've seen you somewhere, haven't I?" His composure was struggling to stay alive. "Look, maybe you are Toby Challis, maybe I'm Eamon de Valera, but . . ." He cleared his throat. ". . . but you killed your wife—your ex-wife, that is. I was a close friend of hers, you see, I was . . . shit, I want out of here!" He made another move, and Challis stepped between him and the door.

"Listen," Challis growled, feeling the kind of anger which had bubbled over in the struggle with the man at the beach house, "I'm prepared to take that bird away from you and stick it up your nose. Now, goddammit, sit down and talk to me and stop acting like an idiot—what are you scared of? Why should you be scared of me? I want to talk . . ." He waited, hoping.

"All right," Donovan huffed. "I'm not scared, get that straight, Challis. If you are Challis. I'm surprised. Christ, that's putting it mildly . . . but I loved Goldie, don't you see? And you killed her." He leaned back against the bookshelf and put the falcon down on the desk.

"You're wrong both times. I didn't kill Goldie and you weren't in love with her. Let's be honest—I know far more about you and Goldie than you can imagine. And my only hope of clearing myself begins with finding out what Goldie was doing. For instance, finding out what Goldie was bugging you about."

Donovan tried to laugh. "Bugging me? Goldie? What the hell are you talking about, man?" He shook a Gauloise out of its blue pack and ceremoniously lit it from a book of matches. He blew the smoke across the desk at Challis. He was getting bigger again, returning to his normal size, and the color was coming back. Pale eyes watched Challis through the smoke.

"She was bugging you, I know that she was, and I've got it in her own handwriting . . . she was pissed off and badgering you almost daily right up to the day she died. *'Call Jack—no damned mercy! What's going on? Whose side are you on? Why no action? Why no action? Give J.D. swift kick!'* Now, in my circles that's bugging. Knowing Goldie, it could have gotten pretty well intolerable, so don't con me, don't bullshit me—not a word of it. Just tell me what—"

"Holy Mother!" Donovan exploded, eyes wide, thick forefinger jabbing at Challis. "I *have* seen you before—you were skulking around in my office today, spying on me, no doubt! My God, what have I done to deserve this? What?"

"Skulking? I was waiting to see you, but you were busy with the Mafia."

"Insane. Insane to even think such a thing, let alone say it. Jail has made you crazy, it can do that to a man, he gets crazy and doesn't even know it, and it's happened to you, my man." But he wasn't moving toward the door this time. He was talking, babbling, trying to clear his thoughts.

"Why not just make it easy on both of us, tell me what Goldie's little notes really mean? Why not tell me what brought you and Aaron Roth together? We both know Aaron and Goldie were on lousy terms, and if Goldie had really had the hots for you—I know Aaron well enough to be damned sure he'd look down that bony nose and tell one of his grunt-and-groaners to squash you like something icky crawling across his patio. Now, the fact is, I'm in a position to be relatively unpleasant about this—so why not just help me? Unless you killed Goldie yourself, of course. She could be an irritating woman, I grant you. *But,* if you know what she meant when she called me the day she died and told me she had something to tell me, that she really had the goods on Aaron at long last—then tell me, and I'll take my business elsewhere. If you won't tell me, I'll have to keep poking a stick into your life. Think of it—what if I poked in the wrong place and got Vito Laggiardi in the eye? Why, my God, Vito might blame you and have some muscle-bound nitwit put you in Cedars Sinai with a tube in your nose . . . and what do I have to lose? They've already convicted me—"

"The best thing for me to do," Donovan said, "is to call the cops."

"You really want to do that? Think about what's really happening here. I'm not in this alone anymore. I've got a big-name reporter at the *Times* on my side, I've got a hotshot Beverly Hills lawyer wanting to get the case reopened."

"On what grounds, may I ask?"

"Suppression of evidence, for a start. Nobody on my side found Goldie's datebook, which shows in her own handwriting that I did have a reason to be at the beach house that night, that she was going to tell me something. The point is, I was set up . . . there was someone who wanted Goldie dead, who called the cops, who found me standing there in shock holding the gory fucking Oscar. . . . Go ahead, Jack, call the cops. Let's shake it out. Ask for Detective Captain Otto Narleski, he'll love it. We'll open this thing up and let the guts run out, Goldie's date-book, the frame somebody hung on me, you and Aaron and Vito—hell, we'll all get our names in the trades, the *Times,* Jim Bacon's column . . . and something will finally shake out, and it might be you. You've got fall guy written all over you, a big dumb Irishman with a shamrock behind your ear."

Donovan sat heavily behind the desk, massaged his chin with a huge hand. He rested his eyes on Challis' face for a long moment. "Look, my friend, you're not being realistic. You're on the wrong track with me and Aaron and . . . and Mr. Laggiardi is just an

138

old friend from New York days, we've done some deals together, kissed the Blarney stone, ey? Heard the chimes at midnight, don't y'know?" He smiled with the heavy falseness: he was misinterpreting the moment and his role in it. "I assure you, I wish you no ill," he said confidently. "On the contrary, you sound like you mean what you say, maybe you didn't kill Goldie and maybe you were framed, as you say . . . but, dammit, boy-o, it's got nothing to do with Jack Donovan, and that's the point so far as himself is concerned. How could it? Here, have a cigar . . ." He offered a pigskin case, and Challis held the cigar, rolled it between his fingertips. "Seriously . . . what could it all have to do with me?"

"I don't know," Challis said. The wind was getting in at the window, moving the curtain and belling it out around the air conditioner. "That's the point— I'm trying to build something on what I *have* got . . . and you're what I've got. Goldie's datebook, your buddy-buddy routine with Roth, and a big-time thug with his hooks in you—"

"Bullshit! You're trying my patience. I've been very tolerant—"

"We've been through this. Laggiardi owns you, right? No point in looking like a dead fish—I *know* about you. Laggiardi owns you. And Aaron Roth has, for some unimaginable reason, bet the farm on your magazine. The very idea stuns the unwary mind."

"What are you talking about now?"

"Roth's money is behind the magazine. You haven't got a pisspot to call your own. Without an angel, you'd have been out of business months ago."

"Rubbish! Aaron is one of many public-spirited men who have made nominal investments—"

"You kill me." Challis laughed. "The fact is, the Aaron Roths of this world do not go around putting money into magazines. Or into shysters like you. Don't forget, however close to Aaron you are now, I was there before you. So what's so bad about telling me what you and Goldie were onto, what made her so impatient with you? It's so simple . . ."

Donovan sat watching him, weighing the situation. Finally he sighed, with a look of pugnacity. "I have nothing to tell you, Challis. And let me offer some advice. Were I you, I'd get the hell away from here. There are ways, you must know that, you've been around for a long time—there's always a way. You can't change the past, and that's also something you should know. The jury says you're guilty. You've got your newspaperman and your lawyer and your date-book, but if they catch you again, that stuff's gonna be just so much garbage. I'm not gonna call the cops, you've got me in a somewhat sensitive position—I admit it—but I probably wouldn't call them anyway. I've gotten away with this and that all my life, I like to see guys get away with it, whatever it is. But you're gonna run out of luck before the cops run out of guys looking for you. You've got an edge now, you're halfway to freedom . . . take the edge. And you'll be free—South America, maybe? That wouldn't be so bad, would it? Why stay here and get your ass chopped up by Vito and Aaron Roth? What's happened has happened. Just put paid to it, me bucko, and thank God for a weird second chance."

"I know, I know," Challis said, "and may the sun always be at my back, so on and so forth."

"Trust me," Donovan said with massive pink-faced sincerity.

"Trust you? If all I knew about you was what you did to Morgan Dyer's father, I wouldn't trust you as far as I could drop-kick you."

"You can't be serious—you're that thick with Morgan? Well, well, well. She just can't let the past die." He stood up with an air of the conversation being closed and tapped the cigar ash into the wastebasket. "Women have blind spots, more than men." He came around the corner of the desk. "Morgan is a particularly unforgiving, dishonest, stupid little cunt. Now, get out of my way—do whatever you want. I've given you good advice, take it. You're no responsibility of mine." He put his hand on Challis' chest to push him aside. Without thinking, working in a sudden red anger, Challis stepped back, set himself, and slammed his fist into Donovan's face. Blood spattered immediately, on his hand, across Donovan's upper lip. The look of surprise faded almost as it appeared, and

140

Donovan threw his weight forward, smashing Challis back against the thin office door. The cigar, glowing, fell to the floor. Donovan's knee came up, driving at Challis' crotch; his fist pumped into Challis' sides and chest, knocking his breath out. Challis saw an empty blackness, fought to breathe, tried to move sideways to avoid the probing knee. Donovan outweighed him by thirty pounds, swarmed over him, panting and punching. The massive pink head was down, ramming at his breastbone, pinning him against the wall. Challis made a last attempt to fling himself away from the wall and door, and Donovan snapped his head up quickly, catching Challis' jaw. Feeling his knees turning wobbly, he sagged forward and fell against the front edge of the desk. He grabbed the statuette of the Maltese falcon, turned, and swung it weakly in an arc and caught the side of the pink head, slicing the top of a thick pink ear. Donovan groaned and went to his knees, shaking his head as Challis pulled himself to a standing position. Donovan stared at the floor. "Beat it," he muttered thickly. "Beat it . . . or you'll think Goldie was lucky." He looked up at Challis. His mouth was smeared with blood from his nose, and a river of blood dripped from his ear.

The door swept open. Morgan stood watching them. "Oh, for God's sake," she said. She stepped into the room, closed the door on the noise filtering down the hallway. "And I thought reason might prevail. Ah, well . . ."

"They catch this asshole," Donovan muttered, "and you're gonna be one lady in big fuckin' trouble."

"Look at him," Challis said. "Put the squeeze on him, and his Irish runs down his leg . . . and he's just a sleazy New York punk."

"Now, now," Morgan said. She was shaking her head in disbelief. "I grant you that Jack is a slimy creep—"

"Get him outta here, Morgan," Donovan said. He was cupping his injured ear with one hand, the other gripping the edge of the desk as he got up. "Get him out or I'll kill him with my bare hands."

"Put a sock in it, lard." Challis looked at Morgan.

"I'm going from here to see Aaron Roth and hear what he's got to say about our bloody leprechaun here. And you ought to take him off your guest list for good."

"Stay away from Roth," Donovan said, his fists clenching. But there was a sudden pleading quality in the tenor voice. "Stay away. For your own good. Morgan, tell him—tell him to get out while he can."

Morgan flared at him, as if she had just remembered who he was: "To save your neck? Don't be ridiculous, Jack—really. If Toby had just killed you in here, I'd help him bury the body . . . you know that. What do I care what happens to you? My God, now you're bleeding on my desk—get out! Now, get out of my office, my store!" She grabbed the large man's arm and yanked his hand away from the ear, pulling him toward the door, pushing him into the hallway toward the rear. Challis heard him yell in pain. In a moment she was back.

"Now I really am going to see Aaron," Challis said.

"When will I see you again?"

"I don't know. But I'll be in touch. . . . The thing is, I just feel time running out, and who knows what Donovan's going to do? I have to press on this whole thing, across the board."

"I know what Jack will do—he'll go hide on that yacht and wait until it's safe to come out. He lives for days at a time on the boat." She looked him over. "You'd better straighten yourself up in the powder room. You're rumpled and there's blood on your hand." Her eyes settled on his, and she smiled a trifle sadly. "I wonder what's going to become of you?"

"I've stopped wondering," he said. In the quiet the rain beat heavily and a distant siren wailed in sorrow. Somebody else's life was sliding down a canyon wall nearby.

[15]

THE RAIN was pattering like clumsy insects trapped in the thick suffocating vegetation that flanked the high stone columns and the black iron gates to Seraglio, the Roth estate in Bel Air. Huge thick leaves like pods groped toward the Mustang. Squat palms, fat and with an alligator's rough hide, loomed behind the gates, which stood open, and as the driveway of finely crushed pink rock snaked its way through the darkness, Challis saw the elongated shapes of the high palms marching onward toward the fountain in the turnaround in front of the house. The headlamps parted the night as the small car squeezed between the trees and the moist, hungry vegetation.

The house beyond the fountain was pink to match the gravel, gray-shuttered, three stories, gray columns, white wrought-iron furniture along beneath the windows, an old Bentley saloon, and a Mark V littered the turnaround. He pulled the Mustang up in front of the door and left the keys in the ignition. Wall sconces glowed on either side of the double white doors, and a child's tricycle lay on its side directly in his path. He heard the chimes ring deeply, softly somewhere inside the house. In one of the thirty rooms someone moved a chair, scraping it on the wooden floor. When the door opened, he saw the familiar square, heavy-jowled face of Herbert, who wore a black alpaca coat, gray wool trousers, a white shirt, and black tie. His eyes were the same gray as the house trim and had just as much feeling, which was deceiving, because Herbert wasn't a bad guy.

"Good evening, Herbert," Challis said, not knowing quite what to expect.

"Good evening, Mr. Challis. We've been expecting you." He stood back for Challis to enter past him.

To hear him, you'd have thought Challis was getting home from dinner at the Bel Air Country Club.

"Well, Herbert," he said. "Well, well. How are you?"

"Never better, sir, except for a touch of pleurisy now and then. The night air in winter has always been my nemesis, as you may recall. Your coat, sir?"

"You've been expecting me, you say . . ." He felt the raincoat slip off into Herbert's hands.

"Mr. Donovan called with the most welcome news of your survival, sir."

"Doesn't sound like him."

"The news was welcome to us, though Mr. Donovan, I admit, did not seem particularly gratified by your resilience. You gave him quite a fright, to hear him tell it." Herbert put the raincoat on a hanger and looked at the Mustang through leaded glass windows. The rain had almost stopped again. "While you're with us, it might be best for your car to be out of sight . . . we don't want anyone finding you, do we, sir? I'll have Weed put it in the garage, if you don't mind."

"By all means," Challis said, watching Herbert pick up the house telephone and dial for the chauffeur. The large foyer was quiet and polished: black-and-white parquet floor, a double stairway curving around and framing the archway leading into the huge reception room with its grand piano lost down at one end, the two walk-in fireplaces, the tapestries on the walls, the Renoirs and Matisses and the one large Breughel, the smallish Frans Hals—he couldn't see any of that from where he stood, but he knew it was there. What he could see was the glass which ran the entire length of the room and gave the impression that Los Angeles was an elaborate family possession.

Herbert finished with Weed, dialed again and informed Aaron that Challis was in the house. Herbert had once been an actor, a resourceful supporting man, a long time ago. If you couldn't get Eric Blore, you got Herbert Graydon, who had come over from London with a touring company doing *Ruggles of Red Gap* and a drawing-room mystery and *Macbeth*. He liked the California climate, discovered that there was

144

always room in the movies for someone with the right accent and a pompous, heavy-lidded, down-the-nose appearance. He played so many snotty butlers and headwaiters that he mastered the trade. During World War II, between pictures, he'd worked parties and restaurants. In the end, he'd gone into private service with the Roth family and left the business entirely. He made a guest appearance on Jack Benny's television show, one last Bob Hope picture, and that had been that. Once, in an unlikely moment of camaraderie, he'd told Challis that he'd gotten out the day he had a million dollars in the Wells Fargo savings account.

Herbert was watching Weed starting the car. "Quite a peculiar vehicle, sir," he said.

"Well, it was the best I could do in a pinch." Herbert always made him smile.

"Undoubtedly. Mr. Aaron is down in the hot tub. Hacker is on his way—he'll escort you."

"I need an escort?"

"Mr. Aaron asked if you were armed. I told him that I had not inquired as to personal weaponry but, to my knowledge, you had not shot your way out of prison. Are you armed, sir? Merely my personal curiosity." Herbert rarely smiled, but when he was amused, something happened in the pale irises of his eyes. It was happening now.

"It's a secret, Herbert."

"Aha, of course. It would have been enjoyable to hold a rod again . . . yes, let me see, the last time was in 1943. *Commandos Never Say Die.* I played Cuthbert, a retired army man from Shropshire, lured into guerrilla warfare by Mr. Donlevy. As I recall, he won the war but I unfortunately died a hero's death at the end. Such a long time ago. . . . Ah, I hear Master Anson . . ."

The boy's shouts preceded him like Cyrano's nose, imploring his mother to see something from his point of view. Daffodil Roth appeared on the landing over the archway and stared down at Herbert and Challis, brushing loose strands of blond hair away from her face. She was of medium height, slender, wore French

145

jeans and a tennis sweater. She was in her mid-thirties, twenty years Aaron's junior, but she didn't seem to mind. She had been a starlet once, moved over into real-estate sales, then into the agency business; but what she had always wanted was a big house, a well-to-do husband, and the power to run the establishment as she saw fit. She'd got it all with Aaron, whom she had married only a year after Kay Roth's death. Very quickly she'd cemented the relationship by bearing a son, Aaron's only male issue, who was at this moment standing beside her in his Los Angeles Dodgers pajamas, hands on hips, looking worried.

"But I've never seen *Key Largo,*" he said. "It's important and it starts in five minutes. Come on, Mom, I'll tape it, too, okay? Then we can watch it whenever we want."

"It's too late," she said, turning back to him. "Now, not—"

"But, Mom! It's *Key Largo*. Dad said I should be sure to see it. Bogart shoots Robinson at the end—"

"See, you already know the ending."

"Daffy, for Chrissakes," Challis said, "let the kid see the movie."

She looked down again. "Oh, all right. But be sure to tape it, and don't let the commercials take you by surprise."

"I won't, I won't. Watch for the white dots and use the remote pause button. Great, t'riffic, Mom. Thanks, mister!" He was in heaven, pounding off down the hallway.

Daffy leaned on the balcony railing. "I wish someone would tell me what's going on around here. I really do." She came down the stairway in bare feet. Somewhere a telephone rang, muffled by distance and closed doors. She walked up to Challis, stood on tiptoe, and kissed him on the mouth. Herbert went in search of the telephone. Daffy pressed her whole body against him for a long moment, then stepped back looking cross and confused. "I'd recognize you, I think. But maybe not. It's amazing. Goddammit, what is going on, Toby? Why aren't you dead? I had a bad time when the news of the plane crash came out. You

146

know me, a serious indiscretion makes a friend forever, something like that." She took a cigarette out of a box on the mirror table and lit it with a square crystal lighter that looked like it weighed ten pounds. "While I've a lucifer to light my fag . . ." she sang, and went across the foyer and through the arch. The room was dim, lit only by the wood fires burning at each end. On the floor in front of one of the fireplaces, Daffy Roth had gotten down on her hands and knees, wearing nothing but Frye boots, and told Toby Challis to fuck her. Go ahead, she'd said, take out your frustrations . . . my frustrations, and we'll both feel better. And she'd been right, of course, and the anger at Goldie had deadened. The affair had continued for some time, had never really ended: was not ended at the moment, for all Challis knew, but events had had a way of intervening. Aaron traveled a lot, as Daffy pointed out, and he probably couldn't have cared less anyway. So far as she knew, he was screwing Phil Dorfman's wife, Anita, anyway, ever since Phil came out of the closet and into the record business. Sometimes it was all rather confusing.

She stood looking out at the fog, smoking furiously, arms folded beneath her breasts. The overhead cables stretching from the trellised dock by the frog pond wandered off into space and fog and disappeared like lifelines that had been severed long ago. "Aaron's a wreck," she said in a halfway accusatory tone. "Just a wreck—you know how he gets, all the more controlled and crappy. What's the matter? Is it Laggiardi? Or that creepy all-American nephew of his—Howard? One generation of money and all the Vitos and Sals and Dominics are Howards and Bills and Toms all of a sudden. God, what a crock! And then you come back from the dead like something from a bad movie and scare the shit out of Paddy the Irishman . . . so what the hell am I supposed to make of it?"

"I just want to see Aaron, have a little chat, be on my way." Challis hoped he was smiling reassuringly. "Just relax, Daffy, and let it pass you by."

"My God, the crash made you crazy!" She lit another cigarette impatiently. "What are you going to

147

do, Toby? You can't just give yourself up, you've got to get away—"

"Do you think I killed Goldie?"

"I haven't the vaguest idea . . . what difference does it make? You're free and you've got to escape, let them believe you're dead, and start a . . . a new life—"

Challis laughed. "That's a movie, dear."

"Bullshit! Not anymore, kiddo. The guys who make the movies can make the movies come true . . . Aaron or Sol can figure something out, you're one of the family, Toby."

"So was Goldie."

"You know about where Goldie stood with everybody around here. Sol didn't even like her, and he's cracked on the family, which includes you." She came toward him. She wore a little pout and her mind was casting about in the future, transparent as crystal. There was almost nothing that could make Daffy Roth unattractive, but the transparency worked against her in the long run. "They'll get you out of this, Toby."

"I'm sure you're right. The crippled newsie on Vine Street could get me safely away to Belize City, the way things are going."

The telephone was ringing again. She cocked her head. "Talk to Aaron about it . . . if he's got his attention span under control. You can tell how serious it is, he called Bernie and Lena Berkowitz before he went down to the tub. Can you believe it?"

"Listen, I can believe anything," Challis said.

Herbert appeared in the archway, his face blocked out by the light of the foyer behind him.

"It's Mr. Laggiardi on the telephone again, madam. For Mr. Aaron."

"Which Mr. Laggiardi, Herbert?"

"Vito Laggiardi. *Not* Howard, madam."

Daffy sighed and made a screaming face. "Tell him you're sorry but Mr. Roth cannot possibly be disturbed the remainder of this evening."

"He may not be receptive to accepting no for an answer."

"Then tell him to shove it up his ass and hang up

148

on him. God, he's no better than a murderer . . . sorry, Toby, absolutely nothing personal . . . oh, what am I saying? I'm sorry. Go, Herbert, go. Oh, Toby! Yeecch. Hold me or I'll fall down."

He put his arms around her lightly and pretended she meant nothing to him.

"Who is this Howard?"

"A chip off the old block, I guess. Laggiardi's nephew. He wants a job at the studio, or so it seems. But I only know what I overhear by accident." She tugged at his jacket almost wistfully.

"What do you know about Donovan?"

"In the first place, I don't want to know anything about him. In the second place, I've only been aware of him since . . . well, since a couple months before Goldie died. Donovan's the kind of guy . . . Okay, I've got it. He had us out on that old fifty-foot Chris Craft of his, it's a beautiful boat, lots of wood and polish and pre–World War Two, he keeps it up in Castle Moon Bay, just past that big gay beach—aha, yet another clue to Mr. Donovan's relationship with Goldie—and he actually wore a blazer with a Tuna Club patch on the breast pocket, white flannels, white shoes, white shirt, a club tie from a club he never saw the inside of . . . and a brand new peaked yachtsman's cap. Gatsby lives! And is a cornball. That's what I know about Jack Donovan." She was out of breath and tightening her grip on his coat. Suddenly she sucked in. "Listen carefully, my love, and you'll hear the measured tread of the Hulk himself scuttling down the hall."

Turning, he saw a tall, stooped, familiar figure in the archway.

"How are you, Hack?"

"Not bad, Toby. I reckon you're glad to be up and around yourself." The voice coming from the high wide shape was soft, a little gravelly, and devoid of any inflection beyond just a hint of the rural boyhood Tully Hacker had spent in Kansas during the late twenties and thirties. You could look at Tully Hacker and see much of the warfare of an era: Anzio, Italy, France, Germany with two wounds and a pocketful

149

of medals, then the LAPD for twenty-five years. Tully Hacker was what they used to call a "hat" in Los Angeles, one of the plainclothes police detectives who made up the rules as they went along. The Miranda law had completely loused up Tully Hacker's career. But when a confused little hubcap man named Mendoza got scared and put a bullet through Tully's knee one night in the Coliseum parking lot during a Rams exhibition, Tully had blown bits and pieces of Mendoza from the fender of the 450SL all the way to the Orange County line. It was his last shootout and left him with a leg which wasn't going to do much more bending. But once you were on the outside, you didn't worry about Miranda and reading people their rights. In a private army, a man was free to be a man, and once in a while you could drop a body into a drainage ditch like in the old days. The way it turned out, Tully Hacker didn't join Roth's army. He *was* Roth's army, which wasn't bad for a guy almost sixty with a bum leg and sometimes a touch of angina.

"Is the master ready to see me?" Challis began extricating himself from Daffy's grasp.

"Always enjoy seeing you, Toby. Just follow me . . . that is, if you've finished with him, Mrs. Roth."

"How about fucking yourself, Tully?" She had turned away and was looking at all three of them reflected in the window.

"What kind of talk is that for such a pretty lady?" Hacker asked kindly. There was a distant chuckle in the back of his throat that helped define the place where lovely ladies were placed in his universe.

"Daffy," Challis said. "I'll stop in before I leave—"

"Don't bother." She wouldn't look at him. "Just get away from here. We'll let the rest of it take care of itself . . . just get safe somewhere."

He followed Hacker.

"How's the leg, Hack?"

"Leg? What leg, Toby?" He put the brown felt Borsalino on and snapped the brim. He smiled at Toby from behind heavy horn rimmed glasses. "After you," he said. They crossed the patio toward the dock. The rain on the grass smelled good. Daffy was standing in the same place, cigarette glowing, watching them through the glass. A blue light from an upstairs room where Bogey had just arrived in Key Largo looking for Lionel Barrymore and finding Lauren Bacall.

Hacker pressed the button which started the cable car on its way back up from the distant lower shelf of lawn where Aaron Roth went to soak in his hot tub and meditate on his life. The engine whirred. Hacker got a cigar case from his pocket and lit a Monte Cristo. He always smoked Monte Cristos. Challis knew the aroma. "Well, well," Hacker said as he puffed. "You're a lucky man. You just may be a survivor, Toby. You never know. I always thought it was the hard men who survived, but you never know. I wouldn't call you hard. You've got that soft civilized quality, if you don't mind my saying so."

"Why, I don't mind. You're right." Challis waited, said, "Been to the bridge lately, Hack?"

It was a long-standing joke between them. In the old days Hack had used his own colorful interrogation techniques. He'd stake out a corner or a bar or a drugstore, anywhere his quarry was known to hang out. When the guy he was looking for wandered by, Hack would get him like a moray eel coming out of his hole. Snap. Hack would climb into the backseat of the unmarked car. His partner drove. "Never handcuffed them," Hack had told Challis. "You don't handcuff him, and the fella knows what's going on. He knows we're going to kill him, and we don't want those marks on his wrists . . . those cuff marks, you see, mean cops, and if you are going to kill a fella, you don't want those marks pointing at the cops. So, we'd drive him out to, say, the North Broadway Street bridge. We don't say anything to him. Just let him do the shaking there on the seat beside you. Then we get him out of the car and hustle him over to the bridge railing, hoist him up, and get him hanging out over the bridge . . . you hold him by the heels. Yeah, sure, once in a while you wind up holding an empty pair of shoes, bound to happen every now and then. But usually the guy is dangling upside down with the blood running to his head and he's watching the quarters and dimes falling out of his pockets, falling

151

past his head . . . well, a fella in a position of that type doesn't stay hard very long. They'll tell you pretty much anything you want to know . . . funny thing, they're usually real grateful when you pull 'em back up. They don't remember you as the guy who hung 'em over the bridge in the first place. To them you're the guy who saved their lives. Part of the psychology of being a hat, I guess." He'd told Challis the story a long time ago, at a bar in Marina del Rey where they were looking for Goldie. Aaron had sent him to help Challis, who'd been distraught. They hadn't found Goldie, but Hacker had gotten him drunk and taken him back to the house in Malibu to sleep it off. When he'd wakened Hacker had been sitting on the deck reading Alan Moorehead's *The March to Tunisia* with a jug of Bloody Marys ready for the recovery. Goldie hadn't come back for a week.

"No, I haven't been to the bridge in quite some time," he was saying. "But I'm ready, should the need arise, Toby. You never know. I've got a couple of bridges left in me." He puffed deeply, looking off into the middle distance.

"Nostalgia got you, Hack?"

"You're quite a kidder, ain't you? Well, that's okay, Toby. You're okay. Yeah, Toby, I hope you get away with it. Come on, here's the train."

The cable car clanged into its mooring and jolted to a stop. Hacker swung the door open, pivoted on his bad leg, waiting. Challis climbed up the steps and settled into the wobbly carriage. Hacker sat across from him and pressed the button to activate the contraption. "Leave the driving to us," he said. They began to descend. The swimming pool glowed turquoise with the underwater lights on. The shrubs lurked menacingly in the background. Mist filtered in on them. The car creaked. Below them the swimming pool receded and they passed over the barbecue area and the changing rooms, still heading into fog. Challis shivered in the cold and damp. They creaked onward, passing through a heavy cloud bank, unable to see either the house and pool at one end or the lights of the city at the other. Then slowly they slid beneath the fog and saw Aaron Roth fifty yards farther on at the cliff edge of the property. He was submerged shoulder deep in the hot tub, steam rising around him like fire smoke. He was looking out at the blurred lights of the city, winking through the fog like stars a million years dead.

[16]

AS THE RIDE ENDED, Hacker leaned across to unlatch the gate and whispered to Challis, "About Mrs. Roth, I'd be very careful with the hugging and kissing. She and Aaron aren't getting along all that great just now . . . she's caught the fever that's going around these days, this female discontent, wondering what her life's about—you've heard about all that, I suppose? Well, the boss is on edge about her . . . a word to the wise." He got the latch pulled back and swung the gate wide. "Watch your step, there," he said as Challis climbed out. "If you get my point? If he asks me, well, he's the man who pays me." He raised his voice as they walked away from the shelter of the dock toward the rising clouds of steam. The rain was starting again. Hacker stopped at the edge of the patio, took a black umbrella out of a brick stand which held croquet mallets, several putters, and some ancient tennis rackets. He opened the umbrella, held it over Challis' head. "Mr. Roth," he said, "Mr. Challis is here."

"I know, Hacker, I know who he is, whatever he may look like. Graydon announced him some time ago . . . what took you so long, Toby? Or should I call you Bandersnatch?" He had his hand over the telephone mouthpiece; somebody must have been talking at the other end, because he shifted his attention back to the previous conversation. "Now, you listen to me," he said in his quiet, precise voice, his small oval face composed and smooth, like a very old child's. His shoulders, back, and chest were covered with black hair, matted by the hot water. Perspiration beaded neatly on his forehead. "There are certain things I will allow, others I will not. I have been exceedingly generous, but you must realize that every prudent man sets limits. You have reached the limits I have set—

if you persist with such vulgarity I shall replace the telephone on its cradle and you can carry on to your heart's content." He covered the mouthpiece. "Hacker, I want ten more degrees of heat in here, please." Hacker turned the dial set into the brick wall. "Excuse me," he said to the mouthpiece, "but you know nothing about this business. Your man confines himself to making deals—then he shoots the deal. He is an ignorant young man. I make the deal, but I shoot a picture . . . a very large difference, as you will learn to your regret, should you be so foolhardy . . . I suggest you think it over long and hard. And when you come to your senses, we'll have the man from Bank of America interface with the Boston bankers and sweep up the details. Probably with the Hamburg and Munich people. Good-bye." He hung up the phone. "And good riddance," he added. "Now, Toby . . ." He smiled curiously. "That feels fine, Hacker. You may leave us. Tell Mrs. Roth that the Berkowitzes may arrive at any moment. And tell Graydon I'm taking only a call from Toronto or Germany, nothing else. And don't let your ash fall in my water, please." Hacker nodded and went back to the carriage dock. "Toby, my son . . . what in the name of God did you do to Mr. Donovan? I am all ears." He looked up benignly, his short curly hair mostly gray, his face brushed with only a hint of tan; his eyes behind the silver-dollar spectacles were small and bright like something looking at you from a dark place. His nose was aquiline in the true meaning of the word, hooked but not long, and his mouth had a well-formed sensuality which added a nice contrast to what was otherwise the face of a slightly tarted-up accountant. Challis forgot momentarily that he was staring at a face which he hadn't seen for several months, remembering the various circumstances in which he'd seen it. He hadn't thought of his relationship with Daffy for a long time, until he'd seen her a few minutes ago; now he was surprised by all the memories seeing Aaron Roth was bringing back. "Well, Toby, say something."

"Donovan," Challis repeated, shifting under the umbrella. The rain tapped lightly. The trees whispered in the breeze. "I wanted to know what was going on

155

between him and Goldie, between him and you . . . I was looking for a connection, Aaron. I know Goldie was up to something and I want to know what it was. She said she finally had something on you . . . something that was going to fix you for good."

"And instead, some unknown person, assuming you didn't do it, fixed *her* for good." He sighed at the vagaries of human nature. "Toby, you know that Goldie was always sure she had something that was going to ruin me. Wish fulfillment, of course. She was rabid on the subject of her father, and there was nothing I could do about it except pretend she was a headstrong eccentric who was going through a rebellious phase. My friends went along with my excuses for my daughter, but neither they nor anyone else was fooled. Goldie was crazy. Crackers. Who should know that better than you?" He put his arms up along the rim of the tub and kicked his feet quietly out in front of him. A plastic shark, a remnant of the *Jaws* summer, floated toward him, appeared to begin nibbling at his chest.

"Okay, leave that aside," Challis said. "Donovan went crazy when I brought you into the conversation—"

"Come, come. You didn't simply bring me in. You surely made accusations, drew your own conclusions, buried him in unfounded assumptions. Let's be frank, Toby. Donovan is undoubtedly a man with many things to be frightened of . . . not my kind of man, you must have noticed. But still . . . let me be absolutely open with you. My relationship with Jack Donovan is a very uncomplicated one. I have invested some money in his magazine. He is an enterprising man, a good salesman—an emotional man. He was crushed by Goldie's death, at which time I had met him on only a couple of occasions. After her death, brought together by our shared grief, we got to know each other rather well—"

Shared grief came like an echo. Everybody had the same script. Challis interrupted. "Aaron, Aaron, Aaron . . . you forget how long we've known each other! You can't make me swallow that shared-grief crap, you wouldn't know grief from tuna salad."

156

"How thoughtless, Toby. And we've always been such good friends—"

"I don't believe a word of what you say." Challis switched the umbrella to his other hand. "For all I know, Goldie really had you by the nuts and you killed her—"

"Toby! Really, how unorthodox you are!" He almost smiled. He was, as Challis had often reflected, beyond insult, beyond persuasion, beyond normal temptations. "One would have thought a man in your delicate position would be a shade more diplomatic."

"One would have been wrong. What was Goldie into with Donovan?"

"Excuse me, Toby. In any case, how can you possibly be taking up your getaway time asking silly questions about something that doesn't concern you? Your behavior baffles me—or did you merely come to say good-bye to Daffy?" He cocked his head at that, the dim light reflecting on the round disks of the steel-rimmed spectacles. The water in the tub was like the pool, lit from below, a pale turquoise green. The shadows played across Roth's face, emphasized his remoteness.

"I want to know why Goldie wanted to see me the night she died. I want to know what she was bugging Donovan about—what was it he was doing for her, but too slowly. I'm betting what she had on you and what she was badgering Donovan about were the same thing—it's all wrapped up together, but Donovan wasn't doing what she wanted him to do . . . and where does Vito Laggiardi fit into it? Why does it all seem to be connected?"

"Only in your troubled mind, I'm afraid." Roth's voice was soothing. His calm seductive. "Don't be offended by what I'm about to say, Toby . . . but you're a fool. Or, let me be less harsh, you're behaving in a foolish manner. I don't blame you—goodness, no, not with what you've been through. I refuse to be uncharitable . . . why, you're nearly out of your head, aren't you? But you are foolish to be here, you're a fool to be wasting even one valuable minute and to be concerning yourself with other people's lives." His manner was so cool, so dispassionate. He was shielding his

157

nerves. It was hard to see it, but it was there: a high-strung man, precision his watchword, under control and facing the untidiness of a peculiar situation. "Sit down, Toby. You must be exhausted . . . you look like someone at a funeral with that black umbrella. Sit down. How do you feel? Are you all right?"

Challis sat. "Stop being such an asshole, Aaron. You're acting like I don't know you. But I do know you."

"Of course you do, Toby. Now, listen to me and try to think clearly, and remember that I have always been your friend. Isn't that true? If you didn't kill Goldie, and I have an open mind on that, I'm prepared to believe whatever you have to say about that."

"You've heard what I have to say." Challis suddenly felt very tired. Being alone with Aaron Roth was an utterly exhausting experience. His mind wandered away, and he wondered what the cops were doing, where they were looking for him.

"Then what difference does it make who killed her? She was a confused, unhappy, amoral woman. The fact of the matter is, her life was a cesspool. She was not a normal, decent person . . . loyalty was left out of her personality, do you understand that? No loyalty to me, to her grandfather, to you." He picked up the plastic shark and pointed its gory red mouth, gaping and full of little plastic teeth, at Challis. "You want to know who killed her? Right? Well, I know who killed Goldie . . . it's no great job figuring it out. Do you seriously think you're the only man she ever drove crazy, the only poor bastard she ever drove to a murderous rage? Good heavens, Toby, it was a way of life for her. She set men's lives on fire just to see them burn. Who killed her? A beach bum she picked up . . . an out-of-work actor from a party at the marina . . . a biker who said to hell with her act and wasted her with the handiest blunt object . . . some poor nameless slob she tried to throw away after a night's hard usage. Some guy they'll never catch. Now, you've got to start being sensible and beat a retreat—"

"Goddammit, Aaron!" Challis was on his feet, shouting, glaring down at the man in the hot swirling water. "Why don't you *care*? What did she do to you that

158

was so horrible that now you don't care? She was your daughter."

"Calm yourself, calm down. You're under a great deal of pressure. The answer is, because she's dead. She and I are not going to have a tender reconciliation this side of eternity. Because I didn't like her and she hated me." He reached for a goblet of Perrier water. Ice cubes clinked as he sipped. Over the rim his eyes regarded Challis calmly, unblinking.

"Was she blackmailing you? Is that it?" Challis felt his pulse quicken. "Were she and Donovan blackmailing you? Jesus, Aaron, is that it?" He smiled down at Roth, who carefully replaced his goblet on the tray. Was there a tremor in his hand? Or was it Challis' imagination?

Suddenly he was aware of the whirring of the cable car, the faint grinding of the gears. Someone was coming.

"And where does your Laggiardi fit in? If Donovan isn't quite your type, what is Laggiardi? What's he got to do with Maximus? Is the mob muscling in on you? Maybe it was a threesome—Goldie, Donovan, and Vito Laggiardi? Where's your little smirk now? Ah, Aaron, you're so full of shit—"

"Shut up," Roth snapped. "There's somebody—"

"And who is Howard Laggiardi? Are they moving in on you, moving you out?"

"There's somebody coming, you imbecile."

The cable car drifted out of the fog. Like something from a Fellini film, there were two clowns in white face with bulbous red noses, black diamonds painted over their eyes, conical red hats perched atop orange fringes of fright wigs; they leaned out of the cars, mouths gaping in terrible smiles, hands waving.

Aaron Roth regarded them with a mildly apprehensive stare, reached slowly for another sip of Perrier and lime. "Lena . . . Bernie," he said as they clambered down the steps. Lena was fat with double chins wobbling beneath the whiteface; there were several diamond rings on her pudgy fingers, and she carried a large Vuitton shopping bag. Bernie was lean, and even behind the makeup you could sense the solemn, sepulchral face of a Giacometti martyr. He wore French jeans and Gucci loafers and thirty or forty dainty gold bracelets on his thin, hairy wrist. Her jeans were too tight and a terrible mistake. They were the current hot therapists, shrinks to the stars. Whatever the stars did this season, whatever the outrage they were into, for a fee, Bernie and Lena would assure them that their behavior was, after all, okay. Clowns were in. Clown therapy was the answer.

"Aaron, darling," Lena cried as she waddled toward the hot tub. "You call, we come. You'll never know how much it means to Lena and Bernie that you don't hesitate, that you call us when the hat is dropping . . . how are you, Aaron? You look tired, overworked, of course you're all wet, and it's not easy to see through all this smoke—"

"That's steam, Lena," Aaron said. "Hi, Bernie, hi, hi, hi . . ." He looked at Challis out of the corner of his eye, but no one was paying any attention to the man with the umbrella.

"Steam, smoke, borscht, I can't see you." She plopped down on a cedar bench and put the Vuitton bag between her feet. She blinked at Challis. "You," she said. "What's new?"

Challis shrugged.

"Well, I don't see you around much anymore."

"I guess not," he said.

Bernie sat on the edge of the hot tub and lit a Dunhill pipe with a gold band. He sucked contentedly, not saying a word while Lena rummaged in her bag.

"Pressures," Aaron Roth said. The tremor had traveled from his hand to his voice, making it sound thin, reedy. "I've been feeling a little pressure lately. Not enough sleep . . ."

"Remember, you're a very important man, Aaron. Forget your humility for just a minute, stop trying to be so good, so caring, you should think about what's good for Aaron Roth once in a while, start caring about Aaron Roth. Tell him, Bernie, he's got to use the joy deep inside himself, bring it out, make people see that joy . . . the gift of happiness and joy, your greatest quality, you've got to let it shine through the troubles and cares of such an important man as Aaron

160

Roth. Tell him, Bernie." She rummaged on like a great fat scavenger.

"She's right," Bernie said, looking into the bowl of his pipe. "Lena's right." He cocked his head, blinked his protuberant round eyes, looked at Challis. "Do we know you? I have the feeling . . ."

"No, you don't know me."

"I've seen your face, but it was different. Somehow. I'm quite a physiognomist . . ."

"You don't say."

"*Au contraire,* I do say." He frowned and looked away.

"Clowns don't smoke pipes," Challis said.

"This clown does," he said sourly, refusing to look back at Challis. He looked at Aaron. "Did you buy your clown suit yet?"

"I haven't had time—"

"Naughty boy," Lena said. She shook her sausage-like index finger at Roth. "What's more important? Movies or happiness? Weekend grosses in Mobile or clowning? You need to improve your perspective . . . but you're a lucky boy tonight. Lucky, lucky!" With a squat flourish she pulled a clown suit, a shiny, silky-looking garment in white with ballooning trousers and sleeves, red pompon buttons down the front, from the shopping bag. "Your own tailor-made clown suit! Your very own . . ." She kept pulling bits and pieces out of the bag. Challis couldn't quite believe what he was seeing. "Your own red nose . . . your own orange fright wig . . . your own makeup case . . . and . . . your own floppy shoes!"

"How much is all this costing?"

The outer husk of a clown lay all about the circular tub. Somewhere out there Challis knew there was a naked clown.

"Cost? How much does happiness cost? Joy? The life force . . . can you put a price tag on it? I don't think so."

"Try Lena . . ." Roth said. "Put a price tag on it for me."

Roth's fingers were drumming on the tub's rim.

"Now, remember our key words, Aaron." Lena was ignoring the price, babbling on. "Nonviolent. Cheery.

Feeling good behavior mode. Life-giver. Life-enhancer. Repeat them . . ."

"I've read the book, Lena." Roth looked markedly more tired than he had when the clowns arrived.

"You're okay. The next step, you wear your clown suit to a meeting—all your executives should wear the clown suits. It's the synthesis of all we know, the symbol of everything we've ever learned."

Hacker stepped out of the shadows. Unheard, he'd come back, a kind of protective specter.

"It's time to go now," he said quietly, moving toward the Berkowitzes.

"Thank you, Lena, Bernie," Roth said. "Thank you for coming. I feel much better." He didn't look it.

"Remember how we helped you after Goldie . . ." Lena began to shuffle backward, away from the cloud of steam, away from Tully Hacker. "We'll always be here when you need us."

"Thank you," Roth said. His head floated on the water.

"Mr. Roth thanks you," Hacker said calmly. "I'll see you out. So very nice of you to come like this. Mr. Roth is tired . . ."

"You see that he wears his clown suit."

"Of course, of course." Somehow, as if he'd ensnared them in a vast net, Hacker was herding them away toward the cable car. Soon they were enveloped in the fog, the machinery was clanking.

Roth's eyes blinked like a clockwork doll's behind his steamy round spectacles. His arms floated before him, pale, with black tendrils of hair waving in the water. He seemed suddenly vulnerable, smaller and thinner than he'd been a few minutes before. The steel and irony had gone out of him. Rather than helping him, pumping him up with their idiotic bullshit, Lena and Bernie had drained him like a couple of vampires. The clown attire lay in a clump on a bench.

"If I didn't know you better, I'd say you'd become a real wimp. What in the name of God was that all about?"

"Clown therapy. You saw it . . ." Aaron cleared his throat.

162

"Seeing is not necessarily believing. Why doesn't someone murder them? The wrong people always—"

"I'm rather surprised someone hasn't. They know all the secrets."

"Don't be despondent. You look terrible."

"I haven't been well. You wouldn't understand, Toby—"

"Donovan and Laggiardi would make anyone sick. I don't see why you can't ease your conscience with me, get it off your chest."

"Just drop that line entirely." His voice came weakly from the pale face. "Why don't you just escape—that's what I can't see."

"I want to know about Goldie before I go . . . hell, if I do it right, Aaron, I won't *have* to go. I'll clear myself . . . and you don't care enough to help me out. I come to you, I expose myself to capture and God knows what else, I trust you, and you won't get me off square one." Challis had moved all the way back to the sunken tub and was looking down at Roth, who seemed particularly fragile at just that moment.

"You sound crazy to me," Aaron said. "Do you realize you've practically accused me of killing my own daughter?"

"Well, why not? Why else would you be so intent on covering up? I like the blackmailing theory, it makes a weird kind of sense to me . . . Goldie would have appreciated it as a technique, blackmailing her father, with Donovan and Laggiardi playing the enforcers." Aaron was waving his hand at Challis, trying to make him stop. "But what could she have had on you? That's what confuses me—what would you ever have let her get on you?"

"For God's sake"—Roth's voice came in a strangled monotone—"be quiet. We're not alone . . . we're not alone. . . ." His small bulbous eyes wavered across the deck toward a fog bank. He was right. Something was coming, and it was on all fours.

[17]

THE HUGE DOG strained forward, sniffing: a Doberman the size of a Subaru, tongue askew, big paws slipping on the wet grass. He gurgled a trifle ominously when he saw Challis, let a bark roll about in his throat and cavernous chest before producing it as a silly Yorkshire-terrier yap. He looked a little silly, suddenly demure as he approached the hot tub like a professional wrestler afraid of smashing the china in an English tearoom. Standing stolidly in front of Challis, he began to lick the hand which reached out to pet his magnificent bony head.

"Towser," Challis said, feeling the slippery tongue on his skin. "Good boy, Towser, good boy. . . ."

Behind the dog, emerging from the fog, was Solomon Roth, his wide mouth with its jagged coastline of old teeth drawn back in the familiar crocodile smile. His eyes were long and slightly slanted; his dark dyed hair was combed straight back from his forehead and hung loosely at the end of its journey, curling over the shawl collar of his white, initialed bathrobe. His eyebrows were black and bushy, like caterpillars, and there was a thicket of bristles in each ear. He padded along, bare feet pink and babylike, legs hairless from age. And always the predator's grin which was anything but that: Solomon Roth was a great man.

"Why, Toby, it is you, isn't it? It is Toby, Towser . . . you see, Towser knew you right off. It's the smell, you can't get rid of that like a beard, can you? You can't fool Towser . . . Graydon told me you were here and I thought to myself, has old Graydon finally gone gaga? But he's not the type, our Graydon, I'll be gaga long before Graydon. Toby, I can't believe it . . . let me look at you. Amazing. I would have passed you by on the street."

164

He took Challis' wet hand and gave it a firm, congratulatory shake, steered himself into a redwood deck chair, and seated himself slowly a few feet away. He saw the clown things and looked at his son. "Aaron, I've told you about those people. I don't want them coming here . . ."

"It was all a mistake, Father," Aaron said. He poured more Perrier into his goblet.

"That has been apparent for quite some time," Solomon Roth said. Towser lowered himself in sections, got settled at his master's feet. "I'm sorry I wasn't here when you arrived, Toby." He took a Dunhill cigarette from the pocket of his robe, fitted it into a plain black holder, and lit it with a kitchen match he scraped on his thumbnail. It was a neat trick. "I'm going to have to ask you to tell your story all over again. I'm sure something can be done . . . absolutely sure."

While he ran through it again, Challis tried to take Solomon Roth's measure, tried to figure out what his position was likely to be. He'd never been quite sure of where Sol stood on certain kinds of issues—personal issues primarily, since his public attitudes were well documented. Solomon Roth was one of the pillars which had kept the film industry from falling to pieces during its various crises. When Sol arrived, you always had the feeling he was accompanied by the shades of D. W. Griffith and De Mille and Lasky and Goldwyn, all the great ones. But there was a difference, too. Sol Roth wasn't going to wind up living out the years pinching floozies and starlets in a rundown hotel room like everybody says Griffith did. Sol Roth seemed not to carry the seeds of his own diminution, nor was he the brigand or killer that seemed to inhabit Hollywood's Hall of Fame. He wasn't a great moviemaker, either. What he was best at, better than anyone else had ever been, was keeping the idea of the movie business—his idea of the movie business—from disappearing altogether into the crud and crap the schlock merchants were always, always shilling. He had spent a lifetime playing fair and keeping his word. He made responsible pictures and funny pictures and American pictures. They may not always have reflected what America was like at a given moment, but they did reflect what Solomon Roth wanted America to be. And when television just about put paid to the movie business, Solomon Roth had refused to give up on Hollywood. He didn't get into runaway productions, he didn't piss and moan about the unions, and somehow he made both movies that were profitable and peace with television. The Maximus television wing was instantaneously profitable and the movie operation never left the black ink.

He had fought scandal and corruption in the movie business. He had kept Maximus clean. He had a Presidential Medal of Freedom and if he ever actually died, the Academy was sure to inaugurate a Solomon Roth Memorial Ward for something or other. He played a lot of golf with presidents, ex-presidents, and Arnold Palmer; he raised money for Israel and spastics and waifs. Solomon Roth was a moral imperative and his effect had never been accurately measured, except by the fact that the three interlocked Roman columns in the gladiator's shield which had been the studio's symbol from the very first day of its existence were as creamy white and spotless now as ever they had been. But Solomon Roth was seventy-nine years old, and as John Garfield used to say, "Everybody dies."

Aaron Roth kept his mouth tightly shut while Toby told Solomon Roth the story of the past few days, beginning with the plane crash. His eyes flickered behind his spectacles. He was thinking. His fingertips tapped on the edge of the tub.

Solomon Roth sat staring at Toby when the story was over. Finally he shook his head, stroked Towser's jowls. "Never heard such a story, never! What a picture it would make. Thank God you're alive, thank him for what a man must never expect—a second chance. But now, what is your plan? Indeed, do you have a plan?" He pulled the robe closer around his neck, where a tuft of gray hair showed on his chest.

"Just what I said, Sol. I want to find out what Goldie was doing at the end . . . with Donovan. I just can't see heading off into the bush without ever knowing what was going on. And don't tell me I'm being stupid, don't ask me who cares, what difference does any of it make—"

166

"You know me better than that, Toby. You know I am the man who will understand your situation." He fit another cigarette into the holder and did the match trick again. "Who knows you're alive and well?" Toby told him, and Roth's eyebrows pulled together, the long eyes narrowing. "That seems like a lot of people . . . the more people who know—well, you see my point. What about the clown people, Aaron? Do they know?"

"Certainly not," Aaron said without looking at his father. "Do you think I just introduced them all?"

"Aaron, if those crazy people are invited here again, I'll have Mr. Hacker and Towser here run them out of town. Do you understand me?"

"Isn't that a little harsh, Father? All they preach is happiness."

"There is no room for charlatan's fakery and japery and what-not here. They give our community and our work a bad name."

"I won't ask them here again, Father. It was my mistake—"

"You should develop a hobby, Aaron." The old man had developed a tendency to cling to an idea, to keep refining it until it had been reduced to a nameless silt and everybody else was climbing the walls. "You should develop a hobby like my Stainforths . . . the paintings of horses are more expensive than maintaining a stable, perhaps, but the upkeep is so much less— Toby, there you are! Forgive me, late at night my mind sometimes wanders, I forget what I should be attending to—now, why is it you're here? What exactly is going on?" Towser unexpectedly let out a yelp and Aaron threw the shark at him. Towser gave him a hurt look and pulled the shark's head off, spit it out.

"I came here to pick on Aaron . . . about Donovan and Laggiardi. I was doing a pretty damned good job of it, too." Toby smiled at the old man. The mist was lowering upon them. Los Angeles was only a faint yellow blur of light behind the fog. There were no sounds anymore. It was always strange, listening to Sol flicker in and out of a conversation.

"You know, I've never thought you killed my granddaughter," Sol said. "You're aware of that . . ." For a moment he was conducting a conversation all his own.

Toby went on. "I asked Aaron what the hell Goldie was doing to him. I ran into a stone wall . . . your son won't be candid with me, Sol. So what can I do?"

"I've never thought you were guilty. It was a circumstantial case . . . I got you the very best lawyers I could find. You must believe that."

"I know that, Sol, and I appreciate it. But it didn't do me any good in the end, so here I am. I've got to dig it all out myself, and the digging isn't easy. My guess is that Goldie was blackmailing poor Aaron here . . . real hard-edged blackmail could drive anybody to the clowns."

"For God's sake, Toby," Aaron said softly, almost imploring him, "shut it off, you're on the wrong track entirely."

"What do you say, Sol? Am I on the wrong track? Aaron says you've just taken to investing in magazines as a hardheaded business venture. With a little shared grief thrown in . . . and I say that particular piece of hamburger has been in the sun too long, smells like shit."

Solomon Roth held up his big soft hand, his mouth set in the crocodile grin. It was an involuntary configuration, the way his mouth worked. It didn't mean he saw anything funny in the situation. "Please, please," he said. "Much too graphic, but as usual, you're very close to the bone, very acute. You're a sly one, clever. . . . Aaron, I think you owe our Tobias an apology. I think we'd better tell Tobias the truth."

"No apology from me," Aaron said. His shark was in ribbons.

Solomon Roth stared at Toby.

"What did she have on him, Sol? It comes down to that." It crossed Challis' mind at just that instant: have I gone too far? Do I really want to know? But the questions were gone as quickly as they'd come.

Aaron said, "You amaze me, Toby. You really amaze me."

Solomon Roth said, "Be still! We're talking to a member of the family now. We owe him the truth . . . then we can see what comes next."

"I won't be a party to this," Aaron said. He hoisted himself up out of the steaming water, looking frail in the dim light, the black hair matted on his white body. He grabbed a robe and crawled quickly inside its folds. "Tell him whatever you like . . . I'm tempted to call the cops. No, no, I won't." He was polishing his glasses on the robe's belt. "But you're making a mistake. That's my opinion, and I will stick to it. Goodbye, Toby. You're on your own, as far as I'm concerned." His voice was shaking. He clutched his robe, and struck off into the fog.

Challis said, "The truth . . ." A wave of tiredness swept across him. "I wouldn't recognize the truth if I found it in my underpants." He sighed.

Solomon Roth laughed, his lower jaw jutting out beyond the upper, and a big jagged incisor drooping over his lip.

"The truth is frequently a letdown, Toby. But it's always better to stick to it. It keeps things simple. You must be selfless to cope with it, though. Suppress the ego. Which is why truth is such a rare commodity in our business. Too much ego, and the truth can always be shaped to our ends."

"So what is the truth, Sol? What did Goldie have on Aaron? How did Donovan get into it?"

"You amaze me with your reluctance to ask the one logical question—and you a writer!" His eyes were the narrowest of slits, as if he were peering out from inside a cage. "You should keep asking about the identity of the murderer. You're trying to clear yourself, am I right? Then act the part, Toby, or people will think you already know."

"Sometimes I think I do know," Challis said softly. "The killer?"

"Yes, I think I know it, the name, but then it's not there. I feel like I actually saw him, saw it happen. . . . I don't know how to explain it, but maybe it frightened me, maybe I don't want to accept the identity of the murderer—maybe I'm just punchy, who knows?" He stared at the flat surface of turquoise water, glowing. "I heard a noise that night. I see Goldie lying there, and I hear a noise outside . . . someone watching me as I stand there holding the bloody Oscar. I get that far, and my memory gets wiped away—fear, I suppose, I remember I was dripping with cold sweat when the cops got there. I dream about it, and the same thing happens, I get just so far, knowing there's somebody outside watching me, then I wake up shaking and wet." He shrugged, turned back to Sol. "Who the hell was outside watching me? Maybe I actually saw him and can't handle the knowledge. Anyway, I can't seem to force it." He shook his head, getting straight again. "So what's the story about Goldie and Aaron?"

"It's a cheap story," Solomon Roth said. "You'll see why it couldn't come out at the trial. There was no way it could have affected the trial, anyway." He rubbed his pulpy white foot along Towser's spine, and the dog yawned. There was a piece of shark stuck between two long, sharp teeth. "It all comes down to the unhappy part women have played in Aaron's life, first Kay, then Goldie. Digging into the psychopathology of their lives is hardly my place. Aaron is the one with the education in the family, but for all his education, he came into Maximus a complete innocent, fresh-faced idealist, eager to learn, willing to work his way up. But for all his willingness and determination, he had a terrible blind spot. Women . . . can you believe, little Aaron was a virgin when he left New Haven and came home to go to work! And here he was, Solomon Roth's son, surrounded by some of the most beautiful, alluring women in the world, women who saw him not simply as a young man trying to make his way in an incredibly complex and sophisticated business, but as my son . . . a quick ticket to the top. Not exactly a new story . . . no, not exactly."

"The last tycoon," Challis muttered. "What has this got to do with—"

"Kay Flanders was a star at this point, twenty years old in 1941. She'd been a star for Maximus since she was, what? Fourteen? Her first big picture was that Civil War musical . . . 1935, it was. She was too big too young. An unspoiled girl at fourteen when I saw the potential in her . . ." The old man drifted for a moment in a reverie of swaying magnolias and smiling black folks on the old plantation and cotton fields and dashing fellows with mustaches and gray uniforms with braid. And the little girl with long soft curls and puffy sleeves and the bell of a voice and the sloe eyes with the heavy dark fringe of lashes. "She grew up fast. She was sexually mature very early, and I'll go to my grave believing that Terry Downes—sixty if he was a day—who directed her in that first big one, was her first man. I'm positive, but I could never prove it, it's neither here nor there, I suppose. But she liked it . . . you know, Toby, the way some women really like it? It's fun, it doesn't mean anything, it's just fun?"

"You mean Kay looked at sex the same way as the men she was screwing? Sure, I get the idea."

"Terry when she was fourteen, Tony Ashton at fifteen, Cedric Darwin at sixteen, Paul Irving at seventeen, Lydia Duncan—yes, a woman, a great star, Lydia Duncan—at eighteen, and Lydia's husband, Sylvester, too, he was a cameraman . . . Kay was rapacious, but she was so beautiful, so angelic, so fetching—and I didn't know what she was up to then. No, no, it all came to my attention later on, what sort of creature she was. But in 1941 she was still Maximus' top star and I believed our own publicity on her . . . blame me if you wish, I was as innocent as poor Aaron, I didn't know there were women like Kay Flanders—was I naive? Hell yes. Oh, yes, I knew there were such women, yes, but not in my family—that's the way I looked at Maximus . . . *my family*. There was nothing I wouldn't do for that family, everybody knows that, but I felt I could trust them all. I *did* trust them all. And when Aaron graduated from Yale in 1939 and came home, he met Kay . . . and it came on slowly, slowly, but it seemed like such a sweet thing to me. My son and Kay Flanders, falling in love . . . it was a wonderful movie, Toby, it really was. They were married in 1941. There were a thousand people at the reception, everybody in our world who mattered, who made the industry a great force in the world . . . they were celebrating the marriage of my son and America's sweetheart. The happiest day of my life? I think so. Maybe the last time I knew such happiness." He shivered like a man discovering leeches sucking at his belly. "How many of my guests knew the truth? How many were drinking my Veuve Clicquot and Mumm's and looking at me and Aaron and snickering? How many, Toby? How many were saying Aaron Roth had just married the easiest fuck in the business? Terry, Tony, Cedric, the Duncans—hell, they were all there at the reception. And I was smiling and Aaron was adoring her and we danced with the bride . . . well, that's when it all began, Toby—1941, about six weeks before Pearl Harbor."

"How did you ever find out the truth about her?"

"Aaron came to me, admitted it . . . but by then I knew they were not happy. I knew there was something wrong and Aaron had to tell me about the drugs and the drinking first, had to because I was continually seeing evidence with my own eyes. I'm not a fool, whatever else may be said about me—naive, innocent, unobservant, trusting. But not a stupid man." The crocodile's grin was still there, masking the old man's feelings. "Aaron went into the service, the Navy, first in the Pacific, then in Washington as a liaison with Hollywood, and in 1942 while he was on a battleship, Goldie was born. America was happy for us. Daddy fighting the war, Mommy still making movies and having time to bear a beautiful blond daughter—Goldie was on the cover of *Life,* but you know that of course. Little Goldie, eight weeks old, smiling up at her mother. The picture went all over the world. . . . The pride I felt! They had an interview with Aaron and a picture of him taken somewhere with Admiral Halsey. . . . God, what days they were!"

"So when did it all begin to go wrong?"

"Aaron came back to us in 1945 and Kay made two more big musicals in 1946 and 1948 and was spending time being a mother. But there was something wrong with Aaron—he was thirty, he'd come out of the war in fine shape, he was taking hold nicely at the studio, he had a beautiful daughter, his wife was a great star . . . you'd think, here's a man who has it all."

"That's what I'd think, all right," Toby said.

"But Aaron was a badly troubled man. He wouldn't talk to me about his problems, he was distant, terribly nervous, he wouldn't seek help or comfort from anyone. Well, it was years before I knew what was going on . . . but it was all to do with Kay. She'd begun to drink heavily, at home, on the sly. She didn't make a picture for . . . what, five years . . . 1953. And it was a comedy she seemed to walk through, no spirit, no verve, and the rumors began. Tantrums on the set, firing secretaries and hairdressers and stand-ins, but everybody at Maximus was trying to shield me, they knew how I worshiped her and Goldie, who was eleven then. No one wanted me to know the truth, but when the 1953 picture came out it was such a flop, well, things began to come to a head. Aaron finally told me what was going on. And it was a nightmare story —drugs, drinking, abuse of Aaron and Goldie . . . and he told me how she'd disappear for days at a time, and he hired private detectives to find her . . . the head of publicity at Maximus had his hands full half of the time keeping it all quiet. And he kept it quiet, all right—I didn't even know, and I was involved in everything at the studio in those days. Everything.

"We did all we could to get Kay back on the track. It was distasteful to me, but what could I do? Throw her to the wolves? She'd have been ripped to pieces . . . and I believed there was still hope for her. My God, Toby, she was only thirty-three, thirty-four years old. We put her in a very private clinic in Switzerland, got the dope and the liquor out of her system, but . . ." The old man swallowed hard, as if the memories and the effort of talking such a long time were working on him. "But she'd had hard usage, Toby. She was getting old long before her time, she had the shakes, and there was nothing she could do about them. She was terrified of a thousand little things . . . people, crowds, being seen, having to talk, any kind of noise, even Goldie—she didn't want to see her own daughter, or be seen by her. She lost a lot of hair, got gray, lost weight, couldn't remember things, she'd wander around the grounds of the sanatorium in Switzerland quite naked, like some pathetic survivor of a death camp. It was tragic. But at least no one knew about it, we kept it all in the family. Aaron was a monk, worked like a madman, was always flying to Paris and then going to see her incognito . . . a couple of times a year they'd go out, to a premiere in London or to Cannes or visiting dear friends at Cap Ferrat or in New York. The world would see her and she'd look fine. But it was all camouflage. Then back to Switzerland. Slowly she seemed to improve. Seven years went by, and in 1960 she was determined to make a comeback . . . but not a picture. She wanted to do a concert. She worked hard, her voice was different now, ragged and strange, but she worked hard, she saw to every part of the show, and she did it at the Olympia in Paris. Well, it made history, as you know. She was utterly different from America's sweetheart, she wasn't yet forty, but she looked fifty, frail, used, and the French went crazy. She played two weeks and she didn't come apart, she held up. Aaron was so happy. Arrangements were made for her to play the Palace in New York, Aaron set the whole thing up—he was a man possessed. And the show at the Palace was a triumph . . . people still buy the recording today. But it was then that Aaron discovered how she was holding herself together—more drugs, new drugs, and an endless succession of men. Preying on her. . . . At one time I feared for Aaron's sanity. I thought he might kill himself. But he's strong. What was he to do? Commit her to another sanatorium? Send her back to Switzerland? She was famous again, maybe bigger than she'd ever been before . . . there was no tasteful way to get her out of the spotlight, not anymore. So he let it go on, tried to keep up appearances, covered for her in every way he could . . . and in 1967 you married Goldie, so you know what she was like at the end. Barely human, barely alive, totally dependent on drugs. You saw her, Toby, you saw what was left of Kay Roth by the time you met her in 1966, 1967. And then, when she went back to Paris to play the Olympia again, she died . . . she killed herself, of course, one way or another. Too much pills and liquor, the wrong man, and that was it. The French loved it, a grand finale." Solomon Roth got another cigarette into his holder after several tries: his hands wouldn't work quite right. He did the match thing, flung the match into the hot tub.

It wasn't quite the story Challis had expected, but

Solomon surely knew the truth. To Challis, Kay had seemed frail, unwell, but composed, friendly, little seen.

"I still don't get it," Toby said. "What has it got to do with Goldie ten years later?"

"Oh," Solomon Roth said. "The diary . . . Kay had kept a diary. Meticulously detailed. No matter how terrible her condition, she kept a diary. Everything was in the diary, all the men, all the drugs she tried, all the sewer stuff scraped out of her diseased mind. You see, nobody knew she'd kept this detailed record, nobody at all . . . until Goldie . . .

"When Kay died in Paris, she had trunks of stuff with her. It was eventually all shipped back here, and we just stored it, no one ever opened the trunks, until Goldie did a year, eighteen months ago, and she didn't even tell anybody she was going to do it. But she'd become very interested in Kay's life in recent years—maybe it had struck her that she was just about the age when her mother went round the bend. I don't know. What matters is that she got into the trunks and found the diary . . . diaries, I suppose, to be accurate. And it was all there, the whole story." He puffed smoke before him, pushed his hand slowly through it.

"Jesus," Challis said. "I was right, then. Blackmail."

"Goldie hated her father that much," Roth said sadly, each word pulled forth at the cost of considerable psychic agony. "She had met Jack Donovan, and in her mind she made the connection, Donovan and the diaries. He had a magazine, he knew the publishing business. I doubt if she even thought of the kind of killing she could make through the book rights, the paperback rights, world rights. What she wanted was to get back at her father, at all of us I suppose, but mainly at Aaron. She knew she finally had him." His old face sagged like his body somewhere deep inside the robe, but the grin remained.

"My God," Challis breathed softly. "Aaron had a hell of a motive for—"

"Don't even think it, Toby. In the first place, killing Goldie wouldn't have done any good. Donovan was already in on it . . . and he's alive, don't you see? No, Goldie had no interest in blackmail, none whatsoever.

She wanted the diaries published. She wanted Donovan to run them in his magazine. In installments. She saw it as a circulation builder for Donovan and revenge on Aaron for herself.

"It was Jack Donovan who saw the blackmail potential. He came to us and told us that Goldie had offered the diaries to him, free and clear, for the purpose of running them in his magazine. Mr. Donovan just let that hang there between him and Aaron . . . then he told Aaron what was in the diaries. Aaron was suddenly faced with the whole cesspool, just dumped in his lap. Well, he had no choice but to come to me for guidance. What to do? By coming to us, Donovan had signaled that there was a way out of our dilemma. After all, he hadn't just gone off to the printer and let us simply read it all in the magazine. He came to us . . . and Aaron. And let Aaron know that he needed a million dollars to prop up the magazine, to get it where he wanted it. He wasn't asking for a gift. He was asking for an investment of one million dollars. Aaron couldn't do that by himself, he had to come to me. It didn't take me long to say yes. The man had us by the short hairs . . . he told us he had the diaries, we gave him the money on his assurance that he could control Goldie. It was indescribably sloppy on our part, we were panic-stricken, we had to stop publication."

"And the diaries?" Challis asked.

"I leave that to Aaron—"

"You mean to tell me you don't know?"

"I don't know. I'm an old man, I've tried not to think about it." Towser looked up, sniffed the wet night air. "It was pay up or Kay's filth would go out to the world . . . can you imagine that? Kay Roth?" He shuddered. "So I don't think Aaron did anything to Goldie, and I don't think her death was involved in any way with all this—"

"Solomon, you're crazy."

"And why is that?"

"What if Donovan didn't have the diaries? What if he'd only read them? And he finds a couple of quaking imbeciles who'll fork over a million bucks for nothing but his assurances. But then Goldie gets fed

176

up with Donovan's stalling around and not publishing them, she gets pissed off and says she's going to some-one else. But Donovan's got the million she doesn't know about, and he keeps seeing Tully Hacker pull-ing his head off and spitting in the hole—you get the picture? And Aaron and you might be angry over a million dollars just thrown away . . . Goldie won't listen to reason. So Jack beats her to death just before I wander in looking for my dinner! Christ, and you sit here telling me there was no point in bringing it up at the trial?"

"Now, now, Toby. Bringing it up at the trial would have wasted our million, too. And Goldie would have had her revenge. From the grave. No, we couldn't allow that, I'm afraid."

"Sol, I don't know what to say. I guess good night will have to do." Challis stood up, watched Towser prick his ears and growl.

"Good night, Toby." Challis was walking away. "Come see me tomorrow, Toby. We'll get you out of this." His voice faded away in the fog.

[18]

HALFWAY UP the long, slow rising terraces, a yellow
light blurred through the fog, soft light, like something
growing on a milky culture. Challis walked toward the
edge of the jungle growth which Manuel and Pepe
spent their waking hours day after day, year after
year, trimming back, holding at bay. He reached the
barrier of huge, thick leaves and creeping, winding
vines and stood with his hands in his pockets, smelling
the jungle. In the halo of light they stood watching
him. Illuminated from below, the shadows giving them
an unusually expressive look, were the two dinosaurs.
Raindrops dripped from their tiny heads. They watched
him as if they were shy, ready only to keep their
distance and wait for him to go. Tons of concrete, their
huge abbreviated legs sunk in the black jungle floor,
they watched. A long time ago Solomon Roth had
wished for them, snapped his magic fingers, and they
had appeared. Elves from the studio had come in the
night, and by morning Solomon Roth had had his
dinosaurs, the first dinosaurs in Bel Air in millions of
years.

Daffodil Roth was pacing the hallways. She was
smoking a cigarette, and when she turned to see Challis, she batted both arms at the blue clouds. "My God,
I wish I knew what's going on around here." Her
small blue eyes darted from Challis to the door to the
sound of a log crackling in the other room. Her feet
pattered on the parquetry. "Sol goes wandering off
into the night, he won't take the goddamn cable car,
and he's going to slip on the wet grass some night and
break his neck, and nobody's going to hear him . . .
Toby, please, what's going on?"

"You're asking me? I'm the one who just escaped
from jail."

"Well, I'm going crazy, Aaron tearing around here like a madman—doesn't anybody ever go to sleep in this house? Now, where are you going? You haven't told me anything."

"Daffy, you've got to calm down . . ."

She jerked away from him and headed back down the hallway. "You're no help, you never were. For Christ's sake, Toby, stay and have a drink with me. Please?"

"I've got things to do . . ." A longing flared in his throat, a desire.

"He's right, Mrs. Roth." Hacker stepped out of the shadows in the foyer. He didn't make much noise, not for so large a man.

"Someday!" Daffodil Roth shook a tiny fist at Tully Hacker. "Soon. God . . ." She marched off toward the kitchen. Hacker watched her go, his arms folded, his hat square on his big head.

"She resents me," he said matter-of-factly. "I guess I don't blame her. But if she had any sense, she'd come to terms with having me around." He shook his head at the silliness of it. "Weed is bringing your car, Toby. You'd better make tracks, get done whatever you've got to do." He sighed, walked beside Challis toward the front door. They went outside. "She's right. Nobody ever seems to go to bed around here."

"Where's your room, Hack?"

"Upstairs. I'm wired to the closed-circuit TV system, about a dozen different alarm systems, room like an armory. Pity the poor bugger who picks this place to break in. He'll just go out with the garbage in the morning." He laughed abruptly. Weed arrived with the cancerous Mustang and melted away, nodding. Challis got in, and Tully closed the door for him. "Listen, Toby, I got a couple of messages for you. Aaron says I'm supposed to run you out of town. Or shoot you if you turn up here again. But he's nervous, and I have to guess what he really means, you know how he is. Menopause, maybe. But Solomon says he's got a passport man . . . you can be gone in twelve hours and nobody'll ever find you. All you've got to do is give us the word. It's not a bad offer, you gotta admit that. You do what you think best, but the old man, he's real fond of you, Toby . . . he means what he says, you know that. Okay, amigo?" He stepped back from the car. "Take care of yourself, you hear?" He smiled and went back into the house. Challis didn't envy him. Not with Daffy to deal with.

By the time he'd reached the Bel Air gate, the leak in the roof had begun again like a metronome and the windshield had fogged up. Hunched over the steering wheel, he maneuvered onto Sunset, where the traffic was thin and cautious, hooked around to the left, and headed into the darkness of Beverly Glen Canyon. A muddy film was running downhill, but the mudslide and fallen trees had been cleared away, and ten minutes later he'd crested Mulholland and slid down the other side into the valley. It was midnight, and Ventura Boulevard was a wet, uninspiring sight. He pulled to the curb in front of the Murder, He Says, Bookshop.

From the street the main room where the party had been located was dark, but behind it there was a light shining in the hallway and a shadow moved. Maybe she was still there. He stood under the eaves, out of the rain, and knocked several times. A police car passed slowly, the driver staring at him. The shadow appeared in the hallway and came hesitantly across the darkened room. The door opened on a chain lock.

"Oh, hello." It was Morgan's partner. "You came back." She was thinking out loud. "The party's over."

"I wondered if Morgan might still be here . . ."

"Gosh, I'm just cleaning up. Morgan left me to do it all alone, wouldn't you know." She made a face. "She said she wasn't feeling well."

"When did she go? Maybe I could catch her before she goes to bed."

"Say, you're the man who came with her, aren't you? And then you and Mr. Donovan had an . . . altercation? That's a civilized word. What was going on?" She took the chain off, opened the door. "Would you like to come in? Eat the last of the canapés? Anchor Steam Beer?"

"Thanks, but I have some business to do."

She looked at her watch. "Pretty late for business, isn't it?"

"Night work," he said. He smiled at her. She had

180

pigtails and freckles and bangs over bright, curious eyes.

"Well, far be it from me to keep you from your appointed rounds," she said. "Morgan left about an hour after you slugged Mr. Donovan. She really looked white and faint, to be fair to her."

"Did she say where she was going?"

"I don't think so. I had the party to keep going, and the author got drunk and that was a trial. He started signing other writers' names to his book . . . Raymond Chandler, Earl Derr Biggers, it was a problem. But it was understood that she was going home. I mean, she felt crummy."

"What did Donovan do?"

"He left, too. Before she did. Stormed out, practically at a run, after he talked with Morgan a bit."

Challis thanked her, and with a wistful, middle-of-the-night smile she said it was a shame he didn't have time for a frolic among the canapés.

It was late, and there was no point in getting Morgan out of bed. He could do this alone. It was better to do it alone, anyway. He headed the Mustang out toward the Pacific Coast Highway. The night was dark. Anybody with a brain was home in bed.

Was Donovan the murderer?

He went back through the story Solomon Roth had told him, checking it out against what few facts he knew, what he'd been able to learn about Kay Roth from Goldie. It was the oldest of Hollywood stories, and there was no point in challenging it. Kay's eccentricities, the disappearances, the comeback, her death. It all fit. And Goldie's willingness to use it against her father fit, too. Everything Sol said rang true, and anyway, why would he lie? Insofar as Toby went, Sol still felt a loyalty and friendship; but the fact was, preserving the family's dignity was more important. It wasn't anything to argue about, it simply was. If Toby got caught in a squeeze, the family came first. Solomon Roth had his priorities.

So that was a blind alley. But Donovan . . . Donovan fit perfectly into the pattern Sol had revealed. His greed had backed him into a corner: he'd taken the million dollars, yet Goldie expected him to carry out her plan to run the diaries. The million had been paid to stop that happening, but the million was no good if it didn't stop Goldie. The whole thing had been so crazily thought out. The Roths had just panicked and run scared, buying their way out of it and making it Jack Donovan's problem. Then Donovan had panicked: how to stop Goldie? He must have been aware that the Roths were counting on him . . . maybe he even thought the million was a payoff for shutting Goldie up for good. Why hadn't Aaron or Solomon gone to Goldie themselves? Wouldn't it have been worth one last try? But even as the thought crossed Challis' mind, he knew it wouldn't have done any good, wouldn't have deflected Goldie from her target. And they all must have known that—Aaron, Solomon, Donovan. But Donovan had the million, and with it the responsibility to talk Goldie out of it. To keep the diaries from being published. And if he failed, Tully Hacker would be waiting to take him to the bridge.

He took the Mustang up a winding canyon road and down the ocean side with the wind off the water turning the soft rain to spray against the windshield. Piles of mud encroached on the twisty road from time to time, and if he hadn't been tired and anxious he'd have gone another, safer route. But he was tired and he was anxious, and he finally felt as if he was getting close to something like the truth. At the Pacific Coast Highway, his vision blurred and he sat for a moment with his eyes closed. Borrowed time. He was on borrowed time, and the events of the past two days were draped across his mind like clothes on furniture in a deserted room. Behind, beneath each cloth lurked a shape, unidentified and inevitably ominous. He waited for a pickup truck to pass, and turned into the rain-slick empty highway. The surf roared off to his left, and the wind was pushing the car around.

But there was something wrong about it, something he couldn't quite remember . . . the shred of memory flapping, drawing attention to itself, but always ducking away as you took a step toward it, a mug's game. Gregory Peck in *Spellbound*—he couldn't quite remember why herringbone patterns drove him nuts, why

182

the marks of a fork's tines made on a tablecloth would set him off. Well, this was like that . . . he kept thinking he saw who killed Goldie, saw the figure on the porch.

He pushed himself back into the past as the Mustang hurtled along beside the ocean exploding against the beach. He'd done it so many times before, yet he never seemed to increase the sum total of his memory. It was always the same, indelible: seeing the dark blood matted in her hair, the smeared base of the Oscar with some kind of matter clotted in the blood, the smell of the salty ocean coming from the beach . . . How long had he stood there? What had he been waiting for? Why would he simply stand still over her body, frozen? Waiting . . . the waiting had made him guilty, had cost him his freedom. He'd been waiting like a fool, and the police had found him, the Oscar in his hand. But why?

There was something funny going on, something wrong with the time frame, a distortion for which he had no explanation. In the beginning, he hadn't realized how long he'd stood there; that came later. At first he'd thought the police had arrived only minutes behind him, but that was an illusion: at least that much became clear without his having to be told. He knew he'd waited.

The sand. There had been sand on the floor, dry sand, wet sand. How had it gotten there? He hadn't walked through any sand. But he stood watching the sand, footprints, bare feet down the hallway, a trail of sand, Goldie dead . . . a noise on the porch, a figure moving . . . Had there been a scream? Had he heard someone scream? Or had the scream been his own voice? He could still feel the weight of the Oscar in his hand, the heavy marble base he'd had it set upon, heavy enough to crack a skull. . . .

Suddenly he found himself plummeting into a dense fog bank, fear gnawing at his chest, remembering the plane going down through the veil of snow. He stepped on the brakes, slowed to a crawl with great solid gouts or fog nestling against the car, clinging. He'd lost the view of the highway entirely, seemed to float in the clouds. Somebody had called him a man in the fog— was it Ollie Kreisler? Only yesterday. It seemed ages ago. Nobody would miss a man in the fog, he could be killed and no one would miss him because no one knew where he was. What would his life have meant? Would anyone be changed by his not being there anymore? He couldn't imagine whom. Morgan Dyer? They'd barely made contact. For her, surely, he was nothing more than a peculiar adventure. She had no stake in him. If he never came back from this night's work, it would be nothing more than an odd dream for her. He was an unnecessary man, no ties, no place in anyone else's life, and there really wasn't any other side to it.

What if Donovan was the murderer?

What might he do with Challis sweeping down on him by night, pursuing him, threatening him? Killing Challis could conceivably be construed as a public service . . . at the least, justifiable homicide, self-defense.

So why wasn't he afraid?

Because there didn't seem to be anything to lose: perhaps that was it. Everybody just wanted him to go away. No one cared if he'd killed Goldie in the first place. That was last year's show, gone and forgotten, canceled. Just go away, Toby, stop bothering us, don't become a bore who hangs around when the party's over. Goldie's dead, so beat it, whether you killed her or not. Just have the common decency and grace to go away, we've got problems of our own.

Hell, they had all just let him go to prison, had forgotten about him. And then he was back, the man who fell from the sky . . . the man in the fog who had no business being anywhere. Tired, running on empty, or on nervous energy: curiosity pushing him along, time running out, more and more people knowing he's loose. Ahead of him the billowing fog seemed to become a thick scum trying to suck him under. There was nobody there to say good-bye.

He checked a map at an all-night service station.

"You're about half an hour away," the attendant said. He was drinking coffee from a dirty plastic cup and smoking a cigarette. Dave Brubeck's "Take Five" was coming from a transistor radio. "Half an hour

184

in this fog, anyway. Watch close for the turnoff, or you'll miss it." He took a drag on the butt. "Ain't gonna be nothin' open at this hour." The thought seemed to sadden him.

"That's all right," Challis said. "Makes no difference to me."

"Just thought I'd tell you." He looked off into the middle distance, didn't seem to notice Challis' departure.

He found the turnoff, and as the narrow road dipped toward the ocean, he burrowed in under the fog, where the rain blew lightly, and below him a scattering of yachts lay tethered to half a dozen old piers pointing out toward the center of Castle Moon Bay. The harbor curved like a horseshoe, with abrupt hills sheltering in on the north and south. The slope eastward was gentler, and at the bottom on the flats there was a small gathering of plain buildings forming a community whose sole purpose was to serve the yacht people. It wasn't a marina in the Los Angeles sense: no English pubs, discos, high-rise condo towers; just eight or nine large, old-fashioned pleasure craft sidling up to weather-beaten docks with thick pilings and ropes the size of your arm. All but one were dark, wrapped in cocoons of canvas, tied down. Challis had been there once before a long time ago, and someone had told him: "Nobody ever goes to Castle Moon Bay by mistake. If you're not headed there, you don't go. Which is why people who like it, like it. Privacy."

Challis parked the car under an immense Morton Bay fig tree and looked out at the yachts. He sat opposite the one with the light coming from somewhere inside: it was the only one with any sign of life. There were several cars parked along the street. They looked as if they hadn't been moved in days. An Olympia beer sign burned in the window of a shut-down tavern. Nothing moved but the streetlights and the rain whispering in the branches overhead. There was no point in just sitting there, so he pulled the raincoat close around him, turned up the collar, and hurried across the wide street. The wind caught him full in the face, whistled off the water. Hulls bumped solidly against the wet wood of the docks. Windswept waves lapped sibilantly at the pilings. He saw the mailbox as he reached the dock. *Donovan.* And the light was still there, yellow through the rain. The night smelled salty, the way it had when he stood still watching the blood seeping from Goldie's head. . . .

He blinked his eyes, shook his head to clear the memory away, and held onto the handrail as he crossed the narrow walkway, stepped down onto the wet afterdeck. He put the yacht at eighty feet or so, lots of shining brass under cover, much polished wood, and probably dating from before World War II. The rain tapped overhead. A charcoal grill gave off warmth. Beneath ash, red embers glowed. The doorway to the cabin was closed, but the light came through the small window at eye level. Through the window he saw only the narrow corridor paneled like a lawyer's office, leading past a couple of the doorways, the galley, to a dark wooden door at the end. Light in the hallway came from a couple of sconces high enough on the walls so you wouldn't bump your head. The wind whipped at the canvas flaps guarding the afterdeck; a linen napkin fell to the floor from the table where someone had eaten a steak and left the dishes.

Challis opened the doorway and stepped into the corridor, leaning against the wall, feeling the boat roll in its moorings. He listened, heard nothing but the odd creak, the lapping waves, the wind. Christ, what was he doing on Donovan's boat in the middle of the night? But that was the question, the anxiety of a normal man prowling around in someone else's private life. He was no longer a normal man with a place to go. A man in his position was an intruder anywhere, and he might as well get used to it. He went on down the corridor and rapped softly on the dark door, waited. He tried the knob, which turned. He swallowed hard and opened it.

Donovan was sitting at his desk, one eye open, fixed on the doorway. The desk chair was turned slightly, and Donovan had assumed a somewhat sprawled position, as if he'd been thrown into the chair and had chosen to remain as he landed. The eye was unfocused. The other eye, indeed the other side of his face and skull, was gone altogether, exposing edges of

186

bone and gristle and runny matter which had until recently been held in place by skin. Challis felt his stomach turn over, smelled something acrid which must have lingered from the gunshot, smelling spoiling meat and blood. His body quaked with a fit of shivering which ran from his jaw, down his spine, to his legs, which were going weak. He made himself cross the open space to the desk. Papers were smeared across the desk, a cup of coffee had been overturned, leaving damp brown splotches, and two drawers of the desk lay on the floor beside the desk, empty. A set of Indian clubs stood against the wall, a touch of the 1920s. A small Sony transistor radio was playing Brubeck, the same station he'd heard less than an hour before. The boat moved against the dock, and the leather chair swiveled. Challis heard himself shout wordlessly as Jack Donovan seemed to lurch toward him, alive. But it was only the rocking of the waves, and Donovan hung more to one side. Challis looked away from the insides of the man's head. Blood and refuse speckled the wall behind Donovan's chair. Blood had stained the sailing shirt of broad blue and white stripes. He went gingerly around the desk: there was no gun on the floor or dangling from the dead hand. Back he went to the front of the desk, unable to stop watching Donovan, the distortion of the downward-drooping mouth, the hair clotted in the wound. It was hot in the room, and he felt lightheaded. He was going to a porthole when he knew there was someone behind him. Maybe it was a footfall or the rustle of clothing or a stifled breath, but he wasn't alone, and as he turned the tall figure fled at him, coat billowing, one arm extended over its head, a huge club whistling down at him.

He tried to move sideways, but he seemed stuck in slow motion, was able only to twist and bump into the desk as the club bounced off his shoulder. He grabbed the arm and threw his weight against the figure, both of them careening off balance and falling to the floor. His face was buried in the raincoat, but he hoisted himself atop his assailant, pinning the arms down. "Goddammit," he shouted, adrenaline overloading, "god damn you!" The words meant nothing, came out of the red fury in his head, the fear, the frustration: suddenly there was somebody to take it out on. His eyes were clenched tight, afraid, not wanting to identify but only to hurt, to get rid of it all on whoever had killed Donovan. He reached for the face, the throat, as he straddled the body, felt his fingers digging into the flesh . . . soft flesh . . . a woman . . .

And then he looked, loosening his grip.

Gasping, choking, she turned her head away and lay still. Her cheeks were wet with tears. She coughed, slowly looked up at him.

"You killed him," she said, whispered, her blond hair plastered in points across her forehead. "Why did you have to kill him . . . and you were going to kill me."

"Morgan . . ." he said.

[19]

DONOVAN'S SIGHTLESS, Cyclopean eye stared at them. With the shifting of the water his chair creaked, complementing the moaning of the wind. Side by side, Challis and Morgan Dyer sat on the quilted leather sofa, waiting to catch their breath, staring before them like zombies in an Antonioni movie. Challis was fighting to calm his mind, fighting to stifle the frustration building in the path of her two accusations. It was as if he were reliving the frustration of the night in Malibu. *Why did you kill her? What do you mean . . . what's going on? Why did you kill her, why, why, why?* His mind had tripped then, slid off the wire. It couldn't be happening again, not with Morgan. His hands worked at one another, sweaty. His eyes burned and he tried not to look at what was left of Jack Donovan. Beside him she was shaking, clearing her throat, wiping tears from her face with a tight white knuckle.

"I didn't kill him," he said slowly. "And I figured you were the murderer. I turned around and there was this thing coming at me with a club or a knife . . ."

She looked at him from the corners of her eyes. Somehow she had made her long body small, had drawn in around herself like a bird folding its wings protectively. Her white face nestled down in her scarf and trench-coat collar. She was shivering, and it was hot in the cabin. The quality of trust was noticeably absent from the flat plane of her face. She looked at him from behind a shield.

"Christ, you're the one with the motive to kill Donovan," he said. "I come out here in the middle of the night to talk with Donovan, find him dead, and you come around the corner with your goddamn club . . .

189

and he's the man who ruined your father—and you think I killed him. My God, where's the logic in that?"

She spoke. "I'd have killed him a long time ago if I'd wanted to revenge my father . . . and I've never killed anyone for misbehaving at one of my parties. But you . . . well, I've never been convicted of murder, either." But her face softened, and she spoke with a dying fall. "I'm sorry, I didn't mean that quite that way." She looked him in the eyes, no longer shivering. But the distance was still there.

"Well, I don't have *any* motive."

She was way ahead of him, made him blink. "If he killed Goldie, you do."

"What are you . . . ? Well, that's what the cops will say, I guess."

"No." She shook her head. "No, you're not thinking clearly. They'll say you killed Goldie because she was having an affair with Donovan. And that you killed Donovan when you got loose, and for the same reason. That's what they'll think, that's the way they think."

"Is it what *you* think?"

She looked at him long enough for him to become aware of all the small noises again. "Why are you here? Why did you come all this way, when you'd already spoken with him once tonight? God, look at it, Toby. You have a bloody fistfight with him at my bookstore, and a few hours later you follow him to his yacht and, bang, he's dead. . . . Why didn't you just come back to my house?"

"Oh, God." He sighed, squeezed his temples in a vise of fingers. "Look, I've had a very weird night. . . ." His eyes roved irresistibly, against his will, toward the thing in the chair behind the desk. "And I keep thinking he's gonna get up out of his chair, come right over here, and drip that runny stuff on me—"

"Stop it!" she cried past a clenched fist.

He stood up slowly, steadied himself on the back of the couch, and opened the porthole above their heads. The breeze and the mist seemed to cool his frustration and anger.

"Don't worry about how weird it's been." Her voice flexed with tension. "It makes a difference—just tell me why you came here."

"Look, shouldn't we leave? Aren't you in shock or something? I mean—"

"I'm tough, I'm not in shock, and this won't take long. I just want you to convince me you didn't come here and kill Jack Donovan."

"What if I did kill him? Would it make any difference, was he so wonderful?"

"To me?"

"To you, of course. Would it change anything, really?"

"Don't be ridiculous. Yes, it would make a difference to me. It has nothing to do with what kind of man Jack was . . . good Lord, what kind of reasoning is that?"

"Well, hallelujah! Somebody cares about this asshole even though he's only got half his head—this is something new for me, see. I've been getting the idea that once you're dead, it just doesn't matter who killed you."

"The point is, Toby, I don't want you to be the one who killed him. Now, come on, sit down, or stand, but stop clenching your fists and looking like you're about to burst a blood vessel." She almost smiled, looking up at him.

Watching her, he felt his breath regulating and his blood pressure doing a belly-flop back toward a semblance of normality. "Like I say, it's been a weird night that has just kept getting weirder. It's like I'm being asked to pass a series of crazy tests. You wouldn't believe it . . . people in clown makeup coming out of the fog like flying saucers, Sol Roth padding around in the dark with a dog the size of a horse, people lying to me, people telling me the truth—I went to see them, Aaron and Sol, when I left your party."

"Then we can add them to the list of people who know you're alive and well—"

"Oh, hell, Sol and Aaron and Daffy and Tully Hacker and the butler. I mean, they were ready and waiting, Donovan had called Aaron and told him to expect me. Old Graydon met me at the door and didn't bat an eye, seemed like old times."

"Donovan?" The reserve and fear were finally gone; her natural curiosity and whatever existed between her

191

and Challis had gotten the better of her. She had unfolded her legs, resumed her normal length, and was leaning forward anxiously, licking her lips, eyes darting, color back in her cheeks. "Donovan told them to expect you? Why, for heaven's sake?"

"You're not going to believe this, lady, but here goes." He took a deep breath. "I came to this goddamn boat because Solomon Roth told me that Donovan had blackmailed the Roths out of a million dollars, blackmail plain and simple." Her eyes widened, her face drew itself together in a look of concentration he was growing accustomed to—and welcomed—while he told her what had happened with Aaron and Solomon Roth. It all came tumbling out like a dog's breakfast: Aaron's evasions, Solomon's insistence on telling the truth about Kay's diaries, Goldie's threat to publish them, Donovan's double cross of Goldie . . . the cool million . . . and the motive it gave Donovan for wanting Goldie shut up for good.

Morgan raised her eyebrows and right hand simultaneously. "But money didn't mean anything to Goldie, right?"

"Right," Challis said. "There wasn't money enough anywhere to buy her out of her chance to stick it to Aaron."

"So Donovan was in big trouble with Goldie if the diaries didn't get published, with Sol and Aaron if they did." She nibbled a blunt, clear fingernail.

"So I came out to the boat on this rotten, wet, exhausted night to confront Donovan with all this, no big-deal plan—I'm too damn tired and scared to have a plan. I figured he'd had quite a night himself and was scared, too, maybe not as scared as old Toby, but he had a helluva lot more to lose than old Toby. Maybe if I came on strong enough, I could crack him—well, I had to get him to admit the blackmail, then he might go all the way and admit killing her. I think maybe I was hoping that breaking him down might make my own memory of the night come back— maybe I saw him, Donovan, the murderer . . . somebody on the porch, a noise in the hallway . . ." He was drifting, almost too tired to fight it off. "All that sand on the floor . . . I need to remember all that . . ."

She put her hand on his arm, spoke quietly. "Are you all right?"

"Yeah, I'm okay, tired . . . but why were you here? You convince me you didn't come out here and kill Citizen Kane." He sneezed and his eyes watered. "If I get a cold, I'm gonna kill myself."

"I went home from the party early, not long after you and Jack left. Everything just went sour . . . the author got drunk and made a clumsy, stupid pass at me, grabbed my breast and hurt me, the little jerk . . . I mean, he's not a jerk, but, Christ, I wasn't in the mood, I wasn't feeling well—I've been more upset about this whole thing, the more I've come to grips with the facts of your situation. It had had sort of a larky quality up in the mountains, and when I was turning you into somebody new and buying clothes for you . . . but I was fooling myself, pretending it was all going to be all right, like an old movie. When you and Jack had the fight, the reality got to me and I felt lousy. When I got back to the house, it wasn't any better. I didn't know what had gone on between you and Jack. I didn't know where you had gone. But I was sure of where Jack would go—the boat. So I called him here and tried to ask him about your conversation, but he sounded strange, sort of drunk and depressed and crazy and terrified, it was all he could do to talk, he kept babbling about you and my father, none of it made any sense. It was stupid of me, but I decided to drive out and see him. I certainly wasn't going to be able to sleep. I kept hearing the mountain collapsing, anyway, the damn rain dripping on the patio . . . dumb, dumb, dumb. The truth is, I was worried about you, dammit, *you*. I didn't know what the hell was going on, what to expect . . . Well"—she wiped at a tear in the corner of her eye, sniffled—"I got here and I could smell what turned out to be the gunshot, I guess, all the way out on the deck. I don't know what I was thinking—I came running down the corridor, and there he was in the chair and I just stood there trying to take it all in, so scared and confused I couldn't move, then somebody hit me a funny glancing blow on the head and grabbed me around the face from behind and sort of smothered me or something.

Anyway, like an idiot I blacked out and woke up in a closet . . . I must have interrupted the killer . . . I kept fading in and out in that fucking little closet, I thought I'd suffocate, but I finally broke the lock with that club I found on the floor in the closet—and that was when I heard you on the deck. I thought the killer had come back to finish me off, that he'd decided I might have seen him . . . Well, I heard you go into the cabin, and I was so goddamn mad I was gonna get the son of a bitch—"

"But it was me," Challis said.

"And you tried to kill me." She pouted.

"You're doing a lousy Mary Tyler Moore—"

"Bullshit!"

He kissed her. He couldn't help himself. She laughed.

But Jack Donovan wasn't smelling any better.

Whoever had killed him had been conducting a search when Morgan had burst in on him. One drawer had been emptied on the desktop and then flung into a corner, where it lay with one wooden side split. Another drawer had been pulled out a few inches and left there. A bookcase stood empty, the books heaped beside it. As Challis inspected the scene, he was amazed he hadn't noticed it all before.

They'd been rummaging for ten minutes when Challis yanked the bottom-left-hand drawer open and sighed.

"Don't despair," she said. "I found *The Magic Lantern,* by Robert Cafson. Maybe Jack wasn't so bad after all."

"No, not despair. But at this very moment a dead man's Topsider shoe is touching my foot, I can smell the part of him that's on the wall, and I'm looking into yet another drawer full of astrology garbage."

"What sign are you?" She was working hard at not throwing up in the rocking, overheated, awful room.

"Slippery when wet. No kidding, look at all this— my God, is everybody crazy out here?"

"Everybody's looking for an answer, that's all."

"Well," he said, shuffling the astrological charts through his hands, trying to keep his fingertips off them, "what the hell is this?" He poked his hand toward the bottom of the drawer built deep for filing. "Goldie never read these goddamned charts," he muttered, "and it doesn't look like old dead Jack did either. . . . My God, I'm getting my second wind— lookie here!" He stood up too quickly, half-blacked-out. He was holding a stack of four leather-and-cloth bound books, light green cloth with black leather corners and spines, the word "RECORD" stamped on each cover. "Eureka! Kay Roth lives." He flipped open the book on top. Page after page of spidery penmanship in faded green ink, old-fashioned penmanship, disciplined and utterly out of joint with the 1970's. He thought: *God love her, she's better off dead. . . .*

Watching the blur of the Mercedes' red taillights, he felt like an astronaut left forever on the far side of a dark planet in the wrong galaxy. The rain fell steadily, the drip from the torn Mustang top drummed steadily, and the wind came in gusts from the Pacific, swirled in the muddy canyons where the night was dark, impenetrable, like the inside of a box. The smell of the earth rode on the wind. One windshield wiper was coming apart and beginning to clack against its mooring. He turned the radio on to keep himself awake, and it worked reasonably well, like propping his eyelids open with toothpicks.

It was tough enough to think, even harder to rethink the situation. A couple of hours before, he'd been certain, morally certain, that Jack Donovan had killed Goldie. Now, with Donovan murdered, had that conclusion changed? Not necessarily. Two murders in a tight group of people made you think of a single killer! Somebody who killed somebody else, then had to go on killing to protect himself. But this was all different; the tidiness was absent . . . the reality was such a catch-all of motives, of egocentricity, of callousness, of dissimilar people with their own very personal and, as it happened, unique concerns. Remember, Toby old son, remember all those potential murderers.

Who might have killed her?

Donovan could have killed her to stop publication of the diaries, to keep from having to face the prospect of Tully Hacker shooting his eyes out to teach him a lesson.

Okay, Challis, dive into the pit. Aaron Roth could —repeat, *could*—have killed his daughter to keep his diaries private. He wanted it all forgotten, as if Kay had never lived. But, Jesus, murdering your daughter because you had trouble with a crazy wife? That one just won't hang together.

A beach bum, one of her pickups, as Aaron had suggested . . . come on, youse guys, get in line here, step right up. . . .

So who might have killed Donovan? Aaron? But Aaron didn't have the balls to kill a mean, aggressive heel like Donovan. Did he? And why would he kill Donovan, anyway? As long as Goldie was dead, she wasn't going to go to another publisher—and Donovan had his million, so he wasn't going to back out on the deal, not with Tully there, waiting to do the Roths' dirty work. So who else? There it was, the untidiness of reality.

Morgan, even with her apparent motive, hadn't killed him: he couldn't believe that, though her explanation of why she'd gone to the boat didn't make a hell of a lot of sense. Good Christ, what was the matter with him? Morgan had saved him, she was the only friend he had, she'd even believed him when he told her that he hadn't done it . . . and she'd been helpless with his hands tightening around her throat. . . . But why had she befriended him on the mountain? What was in it for her? The worm of unreason gnawed determinedly on one hemisphere or the other.

So who else could have slipped the big sleep to the Irishman? Vito Laggiardi? You couldn't have a pile of steaming shit without drawing flies and guys like Vito Laggiardi. . . .

He watched Morgan pull into her driveway, and he went on past, around the curve of the canyon road, parked under a dripping eucalyptus. He walked through the rain back to her house. He could smell the mud and thought he heard the hillside trying to break loose.

[20]

CHALLIS WAS beginning to think the night would never end.

Morgan brewed strong coffee, lit a couple of half-burned logs in the fireplace, and they settled down on the floor with a low table between them, the fire popping like a minor Central American rebellion. She put some Nate 'n' Al's cheesecake on a platter with forks. Challis picked up the first volume of diaries and began to read.

After an hour's reading he finished his second cup of coffee, licked the crumbs from his lower lip, and stared at Morgan Dyer. She sat looking into the fire, which was burning low. Rain ran down the chimney walls, hissed in the embers. Dark circles were growing beneath her eyes, and the lines and dimples at the corners of her mouth were cut deeper, her age showing through. She had the kind of long, lean face and regular features, the high eyebrows and cheekbones, the long nose and wide mouth that looked even better, more defined when she was tired or underweight or without makeup.

Watching her, his tired mind reeling, he listened to a few phrases of Ella Fitzgerald singing "It Had To Be You." His body ached and his eyes burned from tiredness, from reading page after page of the faint green script.

Challis said, "Somebody was lying to somebody." He sneezed into a paper napkin that bore a gilt inscription, "Welcome Home."

"Aaron is the villain of these diaries," she said slowly, carefully laying out the architecture of her thoughts. "Not Kay. Accepting the fact that these are her diaries, her view of events, even with that you get the feeling that this is a record of the truth . . . she

197

wasn't writing it as a defense, it wasn't for anyone else to read, there's nothing we've read that sounds like she's making a case for herself. She's unsparing of herself, in fact . . . but it's Aaron who . . . Oh, shit, I feel like crying, I'm that close . . . it's such a sad story . . . these people, they had everything, I mean everything, Toby. How did they get so fucked up?" She brushed a shaking fingertip beneath her eye, looked intently at the fire.

"Kay was doomed from the beginning, or so it seems to me at four o'clock in the morning of what has become a very bizarre lifetime."

"Still, when she married Aaron, there must have been a feeling of hope, a new life. She was only twenty years old . . . then the baby, Aaron coming out of the war all right . . ."

"She'd have been better off if Aaron had gotten killed," Challis said with a sudden rush of feeling. "Kay would have been better off, Goldie wouldn't have had a father to spend her life hating . . . all of our lives would have gone a different way. I'd never have met Goldie if her father hadn't been Aaron Roth of Maximus. Yeah, why didn't some Jap kill the son of a bitch? Would have made the war worthwhile—so, what have we got on Aaron at this point?"

Morgan pulled a legal pad toward her and started jotting down the indictment.

"The customary movie-mogul infidelities," she said. "No big deal, but he flaunted them, hurt her . . . women who worked for him on the one hand, women Kay knew on the other."

"Check."

"Then the business end of things—she saw what he did and she couldn't believe it."

"How much did he take?"

"She says he embezzled half a million dollars from Maximus . . . from his *father*."

"And apparently kept it quiet," Challis said. "Can you imagine, stealing that kind of money from Solomon Roth and having to keep him from finding out."

Morgan picked up one of the diaries and opened it to a shred of legal-pad paper used as a bookmark. She read:

A. and I had another terrible slugfest last night at Draycott's. Arthur D. actually held him back or I think he'd have done an honestogod Joe Louis on me. Penny took me out by the pool house and asked me if A. had started drinking—would that he had! I had a good cry and then P. & I went for a midnight horseback ride—when we got back I was calmed down and A. had taken the Rolls and left, apparently sputtering to Arthur that if he, Art, wanted me for a loan-out he could have me, but only on a permanent live-in basis. Etc. Lots of obscene suggestions about what I'm best at. Charming. I stayed the night and tried to think it out, listening to the horses snorting in the stable. Read some Robert Benchley but couldn't keep my mind on it. Why did Aaron tell me about taking the money? I'll never understand that—if he'd wanted aid and comfort, I'd have supplied it gladly. But no, not him! He told me, then acts as if it's my fault. Sometimes I think he could kill me because he told me about the money. *Life* called us and wants to come to our next party! Quel joke!

Morgan pushed her reading glasses down her nose and blinked, looked at Challis. "She was twenty-six when she wrote that. Now, we move ahead just a few months . . ." She flipped to the next bookmark, adjusted her glasses, and began reading again:

A. got hysterical again last night—typical for the day he gets home from New York. When he's hysterical and sobbing, he always tells me the things he later hates me for knowing. I finally know why he took the money from Maximus—gambling. I suppose I should be glad it wasn't for presents for his girlfriends, but I'm not sure I really care anymore. Anyway, he owed some shady character in New York a lot of money, and I'd swear it had something to do with basketball games. Hard to believe. I know more about basketball than Aaron does, but when I told him that, he said you don't have to know anything about basketball if the game is fixed! Suppose he's right about that. He wants me to make another picture *soon*. We need the money, he says. How can that be?

Morgan put the diary down and closed it. "So, the refrain repeats itself like an infinity of mirrors. Money, women, insults, hysteria, threats of violence . . . she keeps talking about trouble at the studio, how worried Aaron is about the mess, the scandal, but she never says what the hell it is . . . this still in 1947. She went ahead and did the big musical in 1948, but she tells it like it was, talks about how she started hitting the bottle, how her nerve was gone, how Aaron kept taunting her with his women, how he spent the money she'd made. God, why didn't she leave him? Did she need him, Toby? In some weird way?" She munched a piece of cheesecake, reached over and poked the coals.

"I very much doubt if we'll ever know. Long time ago, one side of the story, and who the hell knows what kind of kicks they gave each other? But the point is, somebody was lying. Aaron certainly lied to Sol when he told him about Donovan and Goldie having the diaries. Aaron told Sol that the nasty truth about Kay was going to wind up in *Cosmopolitan* or some-place, what was going to get noised around was the awful truth about poor hysterical, sobbing, gambling, womanizing, embezzling Aaron! Well, shit, that would never do . . . and it would sure never do for Sol to know what was in the diaries. Aaron is still scared half to death of the old man, you can see it in his eyes and the way his hands shake when the old man arrives. Hell, Donovan probably offered to show the diaries to Sol and sent Aaron back into a 1947-style frenzy. You gotta believe that Donovan let Aaron know what was in them . . . and you can imagine what those diaries meant to Goldie—I really get the point of her excite-ment, for the first time. She was really about to nail Aaron head-on, not obliquely by dragging Kay through the mud. It was Aaron himself who was going into the toilet." He shook his head, grinned philosophically. "You have to give Goldie credit. She'd hated Aaron all these years—now, I assume because of what she'd seen him do to Kay—and she wasn't about to forgive and forget. She was taking Aaron apart for Kay, at least as much as for herself."

Morgan said, "Aaron must have wanted the diaries destroyed more than anything—"

"Look, he could've burned them himself and it wouldn't have done any good. Photocopies . . . but, you're right, I suppose he would have felt better, logic be damned."

"But with Donovan and Goldie both dead, the diaries burned, well . . . that sounds a lot safer to me."

"Then you think Aaron killed Donovan? And Goldie?"

"He looks like a better bet all the time."

"Except for one thing. No guts."

Morgan sipped cold coffee, tiredly brushed a strand of blond hair from the corner of her eye. "He may not have lots of guts, Toby, but think of it this way. What would he be more frightened of—killing people or facing one Solomon Roth who knew about the actual contents of the diaries?"

They sat silently, listening to the rain outside.

Challis said, "What's that envelope?"

"Oh, that . . . it was stuck inside the back cover of the last diary. Bent the cover all out of shape." She fingered the envelope, plucked weakly at a red rubber band.

"Well," he said, trying to work up some kind of impatience, "what is it?"

"Can't we call it a night?" She tried to cover a yawn and missed. "No, silly, we can't call it a night when Toby is still awake." She handed him the envelope. "I haven't got the strength."

He rolled the rubber band back. "Checks." He shrugged, dumped them onto the coffee table. "Lots of checks."

Working together, they sorted the checks into piles by dates, beginning in 1954. Through 1968, the checks were all signed by Kay Roth, dated at irregular intervals, fifty-six checks totaling $16,800. From the death of Kay Roth in 1968 until early 1970, there were no checks at all. Then they began again on a monthly basis, eighty-seven more checks totaling $39,150, all signed by Goldie Challis. There were seven checks signed by Jack Donovan, up through December 1977, again on a monthly basis, adding up to $3,500. They were all made out to the same person. One hundred and fifty checks. $59,450. Almost twenty-four years. One recipient.

"So who the hell is Priscilla Morpeth?" Challis sagged back and massaged his calf, moaning.

Morgan, eyes closed, leaned against the couch, shook her head. "Is she in the diaries?"

"No," Morgan said.

"All three of them, Kay and Goldie and Donovan —they're all writing checks to Priscilla Morpeth. A quarter of a century, for God's sake."

"And they're all dead, Toby."

"Blackmail?"

"Somehow Priscilla Morpeth doesn't strike me as the name of a blackmailer. Pay up, Sluggo, or Priscilla will stop round and beat the shit out of you. No, it doesn't play."

Morgan stretched her long arms over her head, pulling her sweater tight across her small breasts. Challis was almost too tired to notice, almost. "Y'know," she said, "that name is familiar . . . Morpeth . . ."

"It's a street in Westminster, by the cathedral, a couple of blocks from Victoria Station—"

"I mean a person," she interrupted. "I can remember somebody . . . no, I guess I can't, but I think I should be able to . . . something Hollywood, somebody in the business. My father, I remember something he was talking about, and Morpeth came up in what he said. But it's gone, I can't get it. Dammit!" She rubbed her eyes. "I've had it, Toby. Bed."

She made up the couch in her library, kissed him good night, and staggered off to her bedroom.

His exhaustion was complete. He lay on his back with a dim light casting blurred shadows. Morpeth . . . The walls were covered with photographs Morgan had of movie people, a gallery. They looked down at him. Maria Montez. Turhan Bey. Buddy Ebsen. Donald O'Connor. Charles Coburn. Phyllis Thaxter. Charles Laughton. Bill Demarest. Veronica Lake. Mary

Murphy. John Kerr. Bruce Bennett. Richard Denning. Christ, it scared him . . . he knew them all, didn't miss a one. Nobody in the world should be able to identify all those people. Two murders . . . Hitchcock looked down from the wall above his head, eyes bulging from gray pouches of fleshy tissue, a fisheye lens. Goldie and Donovan . . . How many people knew two murder victims? One in a million, maybe . . . no, longer odds than that. . . . Priscilla Morpeth sure hadn't been lucky for Kay and Goldie and Donovan. Vernon might know. That was a thought—Vernon Purcell. He wished he were holding Morgan . . . the little breasts, the long body flexing. But his last thoughts were of Vernon Purcell.

[21]

SHE WAS WAITING at the breakfast table on the patio, dressed in gray Jax slacks and a turtleneck in forest green, reading the Los Angeles *Times,* absentmindedly pushing a buttery piece of toast into her mouth. She waved without looking up. "Bring your own coffee," she called. The fog seemed not to have moved, and the city continued to recede behind it, as if ashamed of an awful secret, looking for somewhere to hide. He brought his coffee and sat down. The cold wet air felt good. He burned his tongue on the first sip. "I don't think Aaron killed anybody," he said. "That was middle-of-the-night talk. I mean, what the hell can Sol do to him now for embezzling a little money thirty years ago? Treat him with scorn? So be it. Aaron would need more of a prod than that."

"Look at *The Hollywood Reporter*. Page one, lower right . . ." She went after another piece of toast while he read:

LAGGIARDI NEW TV
HEAD AT MAXIMUS

Howard Laggiardi, a New York lawyer-accountant, has been named new chief of Maximus TV, it was announced by longtime CEO Solomon Roth. "We have chosen this outstanding young man from outside our industry," Roth said, "because it is increasingly obvious that a fresh objectivity is required in an era of change and new challenges which weren't dreamed of as recently as a decade ago." Laggiardi is already officed on the Maximus lot. At 31, he is one of the youngest men ever to hold a position of such power within a major video production studio. In a brief statement, Laggiardi noted that he intended "to maintain a low profile, keep my nose out of the creative end, and attend to the numbers and learning something about the business/art mutant that television is."

Challis looked up and frowned. "He's a Trojan horse for Vito. Right? Vito's inside the gates. Next he'll try to put a skateboard under Aaron, send him off with a knife in his back, and wait for Sol to keel over of natural causes. And if that takes too long, well, you can always fiddle with Mother Nature."

Morgan finally looked up from the *Times*. She smelled like a garden in the rain. She licked butter from her upper lip. "It makes you wonder, doesn't it? What did Vito have to do to get this Howard the job? Is it tied in with Aaron and Donovan romancing all over town? What a dance card those three make—Aaron, Jack, and Vito. Ouch. Whattya think?"

"I don't know. I've spent twenty years trying to figure this kind of Hollywood doodah, and I don't think I've ever come close. Maybe Howard went to the Maximus personnel office, filled out an application, took the Minnesota Multi-Phasic, and got the job. No, you don't think so . . . well, I suppose not. Am I in the papers somewhere this side of the funnies?"

The fog carried rain. The wind shifted, and he felt the spray.

"You've been demoted to the Metro section," she said, "but you have a wee headline of your own, which is something. You're still missing, as you have doubtless surmised, and the search of the mountain has been called off. Fellow in charge says there's maybe a ten-percent chance you got down off the mountain, and they are pursuing the Bandersnatch lead and interviewing 'the wanted man's former associates.' Do you think anybody will tell on you? Your agent? Anybody?"

"I doubt it. They're all too busy planning my getaway. No, I haven't met a solitary soul who wants me back in jail . . . they just want me gone. I'm not complaining, just confused. The rich, the powerful, they pay late—"

"They don't pay at all. You know that."

Sirens were going again as more houses slid down more canyon walls.

"Did you remember who Morpeth was?"

"No," she said.

"Well, I know a man. He'll tell us."

Vernon Purcell was the rarest of the rare, a man who had turned his back on Hollywood success and found his own kind of happiness by letting himself go, submerging into a haywire world uniquely his own. Almost everybody who had known him in the old days, when he had held court from his own perfectly central table at Romanoff's, when he had been the architect of a dozen hugely successful careers and responsible for scores of the most publicized pictures ever made, almost all of those old friends had lost track of him and figured he was dead. As far as the business went, he was dead. But he was only living in Santa Monica.

The little bastard-Spanish stucco was so worn and chipped that it blurred into the thick furry fog. A scruffy palm that needed trimming listed until it had finally come to rest like a bleary old wino against the cracked red tile roof. A bus stopped in front of the house, picked up a woman wearing a snood, wheezed blackness out of its backside, and ground down the wide, empty street. Challis parked the Mustang behind a mailbox. He was sweating in the thick humidity.

"I called Vernon early this morning," he said. "I told him that it was indeed me, and Vernon just laughed. Vernon looks at life's passing parade and just doesn't give a shit. So relax . . . dammit, I forgot to tell you to wear a gas mask. If you can't take it after a while, just step outside. It's not fatal."

Vernon Purcell, five-foot-eight and three hundred pounds, met them at the door wearing clothes he hadn't changed in a month. He had lived in them, eaten in and on them, bathed his seventeen black cats while wearing them, and slept in them. His thin gray hair was plastered straight back from his pale, fleshy face, giving him a youthful, innocent quality, though he was pushing seventy. There was a brown crust at the neckline of his heavy T-shirt which seemed at first glance to be an extra chin crease. He smiled at Challis, his eyes floated sleepily, and the first shock wave of his peculiar scent hit them. Morgan turned her head and coughed into her fist. Kitty litter? Sweat? Cooking smells?

"Tobias," he said, his voice a still-strong tenor, "I never thought I'd see you again. How long has it been? Ten years? Twelve? Come in, both of you . . . you're just in time to see me put the finishing touches on an oddity." He parted the sea of black cats. To the left the kitchen rotted, dozens of plates speckled with fossilized pork chops and scrambled eggs and tacos, all developing a growth of mold. Dishes of cat food; one small ragged-looking animal bathed in the water dish. "Over here, an original four-color poster from *The Sun Also Rises* . . . Ty Power, Miss Gardner, Eddie Albert, Flynn at his best, and young Robert Evans." Purcell stood back and viewed the poster, which was framed under glass, hooking his thumbs in his pockets, rocking on his heels. "Found this in a junk shop in Petaluma. Mounted it on white linen, painstaking work, and I have to keep the cats from walking all over it, but now it's worth eight-hundred and fifty dollars to a collector in Santa Barbara." He stood back admiring the poster, which was garish and appealing. "And so it goes. The years pass, Tobias, and now they're all pretty much the same. Which is just the way I wanted it."

"I finally wore out my soundtrack from that picture," Morgan said.

"Tobias? A fellow collector?"

"The lady I mentioned on the phone."

"Of course, Dyer's daughter." He smiled at her and creased his bulk ever so slightly in the hint of a bow. "Your father's picture *Man in the Fog* had a wonderful poster. Quite a demand for it. I sold one in mint condition to a Japanese collector about a year ago. Two thousand simoleons—my way of getting back at them for Pearl Harbor." He wheezed like a man with ground glass and Elmer's glue clogging his throat. "Miss Dyer, I have become a human archive, a repository—or refuse dump, maybe—of movie history,

207

paraphernalia, trivia, a resource, if you will. Perhaps Tobias has recounted to you my bizarre story. I was once somebody in this town, but I suppose the industry, the profligacy of it, the waste and the sorrow of the reality of it, I suppose it wore me down . . . too many years in the sun, you finally go crazy—that is, if you have any brains at all. Instead of wandering off to a mountaintop and howling at the moon, instead of going religious, I finally discovered that the movies themselves are what matters about the business—not the poor jerks and fools and greedmongers and ruined idealists and outright criminals who make them. Not even the good, decent people who somehow survive and succeed—they aren't what matters. They aren't important to anyone but themselves . . . it's the movies that matter. And I know more about them than I should. For instance, I've got six soundtracks of *The Sun Also Rises* in the original wrappers, never played, and one is for you. . . . Coffee? Tea?"

The mustiness of the room seemed to suck the breath from their lungs. Both Challis and Morgan declined, sat down carefully on a cat-hair sofa, and waited while Purcell waddled off to the kitchen and added the smell of steaming tea to the overall miasma.

"Are you okay?" Challis whispered.

"Mmm." She kept her mouth tightly closed, rolled her eyes.

A large black cat with green eyes like pumpkin seeds wormed its way out from under a stack of ancient, dusty *Hollywood Reporters*. The animal's face was festooned with dust and cobwebs. There were two Mickey Mouse lamps at the end of a leatherette couch which belonged in a rundown bus depot. A perfect framed poster of *Mr. Blandings Builds His Dream House* was propped against a six-foot-high stack of forties press kits; the poster was a masterpiece, all the copy and art laid over a blueprint.

Purcell wedged his way back through a wide archway stacked tight with newspapers, file folders, books about movies, and the dented fender of an old Thunderbird. He sipped tea from a Porky Pig mug and handed Morgan the soundtrack recording. "In fond memory of your father, my dear. One of the industry's very good, very decent men, and you may quote me on that." He wheezed mightily and lowered himself into a wicker porch chair that had once been apple-green. Over the years the apple had spoiled, gone bad. Creamy tea dribbled over the rim, ran down Porky Pig, and added several more splotches to his grim plaid shirt. "Now, Tobias, you mentioned that you had a question for me." He rubbed the stubble on his face. The only life in his face came from his tiny eyes, waiting for the question, the challenge.

"Morpeth," Challis said.

"Ah, poor Morpeth . . ." Purcell slurped his tea, wiped his mouth with the long sleeve of his undershirt, which projected from beneath the rolled back cuff of his plaid shirt. "Morton Alexander Morpeth, born 1920, died 1947, a man of little consequence and therefore largely unnoticed in our little community. His demise created a very minor stir, mentioned in passing for a day or two at Romanoff's, the Brown Derby, Schwab's. Then he slipped into the unimportant past."

"What happened to him, Vernon?"

"Well, it's a strange story, if you have a moment?" He raised his eyebrows, which appeared to have been both greased and plucked. Challis nodded, motioned him onward. "Morty Morpeth was a member of the postwar English community, which stuck together fairly closely in those days. I only met him once, as I recollect, he was a lean, tallish gent, one of those *sandy* Englishmen. Bit of an adventurer, something of a hero in North Africa with Montgomery . . . he'd seen a lot and he gave the impression that there were things going on under the surface that you might not want to know about—there were a lot of men who came back from the war who gave off that sort of aura. A bright, literate young man. I remember asking him what he thought about Southern California, and he surprised me by quoting my own favorite novelist —that of course, would be J. B. Priestley. He said he agreed with Priestley, who had summed it up, 'We've more nutty people to the square mile here than anywhere on God's green earth. . . . It's just one big loony bin.' Well, you had to like a fellow who could come up with that on the spur of the moment."

One of the cats sidled across Purcell's mountainous chest and abdomen, stretched his long black neck, licked some tea from the mug. The cat looked up, fur on his head spiky and greasy like a punk-rocker, and ran his tongue along his whiskers.

"But you couldn't ignore this somewhat shady quality about him. Are you sure you wouldn't like a cookie? There must be some English muffin somewhere . . ."

"No, really, Vernon, it's all right. Go on."

"Well, Morty had a minor position as a studio accountant, which seemed somewhat amusing, because he looked like such an active, rascally fellow, glint in his eyes, kind of a handsome smirk . . . but he'd been in training in the Korda organization as a teenager before the war, had shown an ability to work with figures. Then, one day in the late spring or summer of 1947, Morty Morpeth disappeared. Who would have cared? People run off all the time, go home, float off into the Pacific. But one very hot dry day there was a serious brushfire in one of the canyons above Beverly Hills, lots of wind swirling around, movie stars' homes endangered, sirens going off all day, the same old story. The authorities had to make a thorough sweep through the burned hillsides looking for any bodies, any human remains of any kind. They found two, a child of about five, and a man who, as you can predict, turned out to be Morty Morpeth. At first they couldn't identify him . . . he was naked, but he was only a little singed at the edges, not burned to blackened bones. And the police discovered that he hadn't died of anything related to the fire . . . he had died of a bullet fired at close range into his skull." Another cat clambered clumsily toward the tea, and Purcell gently pushed him away, muttering, "Now, now, Horace, you know you don't like tea. . . . Naturally the discovery of the body, which had been stuffed down into a natural rocky depression and partially covered with rocks— well, this was news. Who the dickens was he? Well, the police began to comb their missing-persons files, began to call relatives and friends of missing persons to come down to the morgue and have a gander at the remains of Mr. X.

"Inevitably the wheel turned round and round, and it was Mrs. Morpeth's turn—"

Morgan swallowed a gasp, asked through clenched teeth, "Do you know Mrs. Morpeth's first name?" She coughed behind her hand.

"Prudence, I seem to recall . . . Penelope . . . I'm not quite sure. It's all in my newspaper-cutting file. Y'know, Tobias, I'm rather surprised you don't know all this. I mean, after all . . ."

"What are you talking about, Vernon? I'm no movieland wax historian."

"No, no. The Maximus connection!" He sighed, pursed the tiny lips in the vast gray reaches of his face, clasped his fat hands across his tummy, and slowly ripened. "Morpeth was a Maximus employee . . . I'd have thought you'd know the lore there."

"No, Vernon, I don't recall it ever coming up." He felt his breath shortening, his adrenaline giving an extra squirt.

"Well, no matter. Simon Karr did a better job than I'd thought. Simon was a public-relations specialist, a free-lance, who specialized in keeping things out of the paper, and Maximus—I suppose Solomon Roth—hired him to put the lid on the Morpeth murder. You know how Solomon is, wants nothing bad to speckle the Maximus shield, and a murder—a particularly mysterious and publicized murder—is bad, a ton of mud about to slop all over the shield. So Simon Karr went to work with his contacts, and they included everybody, people at the *Times,* the morgue, the LAPD, everybody. Greased a half-dozen palms, I suppose, and the whole thing went to the dead-letter office."

"What did I tell you about Vernon?" Challis said to Morgan. "He was bound to know . . . but one thing, could you check your file for Morty Morpeth's wife's name? It's important."

"Get down, my little kitties." He pushed himself forward, to the edge of the couch, and gritted his teeth deep within his suet face. He waddled to a corner of the room where the cardboard boxes, tattered and torn, bulged with soiled manila folders, covered unfinished wooden shelving, the top of an ancient Philco radio-phonograph; piles of the cartons tilted precariously toward the ceiling, completely blocking one window. He turned on a table lamp, and the grass skirt on the hips of a hula dancer began to rotate slowly. He took a fringed, motheaten pillow with the silk lettering "Honolulu 1941" from the top of one box and dropped it on a nosy cat. "Here it is," he wheezed. "Very incomplete." He thumbed through the slim file. "But the woman . . . the woman . . . aha, I was close, by gum. Priscilla, that was her name, Priscilla Morpeth." He offered the file to Challis, who took it, began to read. Morgan got up and stood looking over his shoulder.

"Say, I've just thought of something else," Purcell interrupted. "The story that got out and went the rounds, strictly word of mouth, was that Morpeth had embezzled a million bucks from Maximus. Sure, it comes back to me." A cat shrieked as Purcell trod on its tail, but he took no notice. "Morpeth embezzled the million—and it struck me as not unlikely, given the charming-scoundrel impression he'd made on me —and that his colleagues in rascality had shot him and taken the money for themselves." He shrugged. "Sounded good when I heard it in one studio commissary after another. Hung together beautifully. And Roth certainly wouldn't have wanted that to get into the papers. Make Maximus look like damned fools . . . a million was a hell of a lot of money in 1947. The only problem with the story was that it was too good, do you see? Perfect. And I knew that Simon Karr had been working on it day and night for a week or two. Two and two always make four in Karr's world. . . . In the real world"—he chuckled—"it's usually five or nine or seventeen. Get it? I think the whole thing was Simon's exercise in creative writing. That's all we did then anyway, make up stories. Do you see my point, miss? The one cardinal rule about movie people—all of them, the best and the worst, the kind and the cruel, the decent and the plain criminals —you must realize that they always lie. Not often, not

212

merely almost always, but *invariably*. It's part of the business. They lie from good motives and bad. They lie to convince you . . . or themselves . . . or somebody who just happened to walk into the room. It's their nature. They're like children, and as often as not you shouldn't even hold it against them. You know they're lying. They know they're lying. The truth never occurs to them. So Simon Karr took his job seriously, was paid a great deal of money for muddying the waters, and made up this wonderful tidy lie." He sneezed, stuck out his tongue, and tweezed some hair out of his mouth. "Fur balls. That's the problem with cats. They get fur balls all the time . . . they're like cows with their cuds, they've all got big wads of fur in their tummies. Live with them, you're going to get fur balls, too. It's in the air." He slid his sneakered foot under a medium-sized cat, slowly lifted it off the floor while steadying himself on the arm of a broken chair, and flipped the cat through the air. It passed Challis' head, looked around with only a hint of mild concern, and landed calmly on a pile of books and newspapers. Purcell looked at Morgan and Challis apologetically. "It's the only exercise I get. I have phlebitis in my other leg."

Challis thanked him for all the help.

"It's been a pleasure, Tobias. Anytime. And I'm delighted that you're alive and well after the plane crash. I'm building quite a nice murder file on you. Did you kill her, by the way? None of my business, I realize . . ."

"Justice is blind," Challis said.

"Ah, that good lady. She's not at home hereabouts, I'm afraid." He wheezed happily.

"Is Simon Karr still alive, Vernon?"

"Aha, I thought you'd never ask. Yes, he's still alive. More or less. Sequestered in a very fancy hostelry for the old, the infirm, and—I'm told—gangsters on the lam. That last bit may be apocryphal. And may not. Do you know where Marineland is? Well, you get out that way, south of there, its Rancho Mafioso something. No, no, merely an attempt at levity . . . it's not far from San Clemente, not too far from La Costa

213

. . . Pacifica House, I believe. Not to be confused with Mr. Nixon's home." He wheezed another laugh and saw them to the door. "Good-bye, Miss Dyer. Take good care of my old friend Tobias Challis. Don't let Hollywood do him any great harm."

[22]

THE OCEAN EXPLODED like blue-green crystal on the reddish-brown rocks at the base of the cliffs. The breeze blew cool, moist fog from the direction of Catalina, and the pots of flowers hanging from the awning braces swayed like colorful dancers in an old movie. Behind the fog the sun burned yellow and cast a Renoir softness across the long flagstone walkway and the lazy expanse of Pacific. Turning back toward the long, elegant white hacienda crowning the slope of green perfectly trimmed grass, Challis saw the old people in bathrobes, nightgowns, leotards, bathing suits, and wheelchairs promenading on the veranda. One old codger wore an ice-cream suit, a broad-brimmed white hat, white shoes, smoked a long greenish panatella. A male attendant separated from the slow-moving crowd of Fellini extras and set off down the path of finely crushed pink stone. He was pushing a wheelchair which contained an old man, or what was left of one. There were no legs. There was an eyepatch. There was a mane of white hair, a hearing aid, and knuckles broken and rearranged by arthritis. Morgan was breathing the fresh air, humming under her breath.

The attendant slid the wheelchair to a stop. He was a tanned beach-and-surf type, healthy and eager to please. " 'Morning," he said with a smile like ivory in the klieg lights. "This is Mr. Simon Karr. Mr. Streeter, Miss Dyer . . . have a nice chat. I'll just go along and have a chair over on the lawn. Call me when you're all through. Enjoy yourselves and let me know if you'd like any iced tea, just anything—"

"Go, for Chrissakes, Duke, we get the idea." Simon Karr's voice was larger than the remnant of his physical self.

"Yessir—"

"You're a nice boy but you talk too much." He cocked his small, shrunken head beneath the waving white pompadour, and looked at Challis. "Whoever the hell you are, pal, you got here in the nick of time. I could do my last buck and wing at any moment. And don't sing no sad songs for me, as the man said. I am ready . . . how are you, miss? May I say that you are one foxy lady? Is that the proper colloquialism? I must rely on *Baretta* and *Starsky and Hutch* to keep up with the outside world, so you can appreciate how much trouble I'm in . . . but, what can I do for you? You mentioned crazy old Vernon Purcell—does he still smell so bad? I've never visited his cage, but word gets around."

"It's pretty fragrant," Morgan said.

"Not so loud, sister. You've learned about hearing aids from Marjorie Main and Percy Kilbride pictures. This little bastard is like a CIA bug, picks up everything . . . Duke over there farts, pardon my French, and I'll hear it over here. There's no escape unless I unhook, some big temptation with the kinda bullshit, you should pardon me again, they talk around this joint . . . unhook, unplug, and shove off, that's my motto. So what can I do for you?"

"Vernon told me back that you did a special job for Maximus Pictures back in forty-seven, a little reverse PR, keep something out of the papers . . . ring any bells?"

"Solly Roth, is he dead yet?"

"No, not by quite a hell of a long way."

"Too bad. I never particularly liked Sol. He was such a sanctimonious old turd, even when he was younger. Miss, you're just going to have to excuse my French. Seems I can't get through a fucking sentence —see there, that's what I mean—without resorting to illiterate vulgarity. Ah, yes, Solly Roth and his wimp of a son. Christ in heaven, what a wet bunch that family was. Except for Kay. Now, there was a girl with spunk. Until the Wimp wore her down. Am I telling tales out of school? Well, so what, eh? Who cares? In a week I'll be dead! With any luck, let me add. Did I do anything for Solly in forty-seven! Hell, yes, I held him up is what I did. Fifty grand to put the lid on a murder and an embezzlement . . . guy's name was lemme see, Morton? Was that it?"

"Morpeth," Challis said.

"You know why I couldn't stand Solly? I'll tell you. He never worked on the holidays, always went to temple, did the whole shtick, which is fine, but you know how you get a feeling about a guy? Well, I always had the idea that Solly did that just for show, y'know? That he didn't really give a fuck one way or the other . . . which just boils down to I didn't like the putz, don't tell me." His one eye blinked, momentarily confused. His head swiveled from side to side like a ventriloquist's dummy and a fist knotted against the arm of the wheelchair. "You know, miss, I look at you, you know what I think of? Nooky, I think of nooky . . . I remember nooky surprisingly well for a man as far gone as I am. Does she remind you of nooky, young man? Eh?"

"Incessantly, Mr. Karr . . . but about you and Solomon Roth and Morpeth . . . what was the story?"

"Story? No story . . . the little schmuck, some kinda English war hero, stole a million or so from Solly . . . we figured his accomplices knocked him off and took all the money."

"Who filled in the blanks?"

"Solly and I, we worked on it together. We just tried to figure it out . . . funny thing how it was all sort of in the family, though that helped, to be perfectly frank."

"All in the family," Challis said. "What does that mean?"

"Well, it was a friend of Morpeth's who identified the body. His wife . . . well, Priscilla—say, is she still alive? What a crazy bunch they were . . . is she? Still alive, eh?"

"I don't know, Mr. Karr. Go on."

"Well, Priscilla was weird, told fortunes and read tea leaves, always wearing a sheet with stars painted on it . . . had a little storefront place on Sunset, the part down by Elysian Park, Dodger Stadium. God, what a zoo. Anyway, this crazy Priscilla was acting like an idiot, fainting spells, the fucking vapors, so Morpeth's old chum, been his teacher or something, or knew him at Rank . . . anyway, this friend of Morpeth's wound up working for Solly, the guy who identified Morpeth's body for Priscilla—"

"Who went to work for Solomon Roth?"

"Everybody involved, actually . . . Morpeth's pal was what's-his-name, that stuffy majordomo type from central casting . . ." He shrugged jerkily as if the movement hurt him.

"Graydon," Challis said. "Herbert Graydon."

"He's the one, went into the morgue and told 'em sure, that's old Morpeth . . . Herbert Graydon. A class act, Herbert. Pompous stuffy old cunt." He hawked and spit onto the pink path.

"How did you keep it quiet, Mr. Karr?" Morgan's voice had a soothing effect on the old man. He lifted one runny eye and twisted his bleached lips into a smile.

"The way I always kept things quiet. They always thought I was this magician type who could fix anything . . . that's why my price was so high, eh? Shit, I just paid everybody off . . . cops mainly. It didn't take much, either. A grand here and there, a man could buy a new car for a grand in the old days . . . or take his family on a nice vacation. I suppose I used three, four grand of Solly's fifty getting mouths shut, a reasonable business expense. Now, that particular case, Morpeth, was another man who went to work for Solly . . . we always had our little chats up in Griffith Park or down in Chinatown or out by the water, we'd eat little cardboard containers of shrimp and walk along the Santa Monica pier and I'd tell him what I was trying to keep quiet and why, he was an honorable man but he was open to this kind of whatchamacallit, *blandishment*. I'd tell him my side of it, what kind of money was involved, and he'd tell me if it was the kind of investigation he could soft pedal. He was homicide, of course, and the funny thing was, he said homicides were the easiest ones to quash, said nobody really gave a good goddamn about most homicides . . . he worked on the Black Dahlia thing, did some technical advisory work on some pictures, was a hell of a cop, and in his spare time fixed a thing

218

or two here and there for Simon Karr . . . like Morpeth." The old man, his memory and appetite whetted, slumped back exhausted, lips working against one another as if chewing an invisible string, knuckles fluttering on the arms of the wheelchair.

"Tully Hacker," Challis said.

The old head nodded spasmodically. "Tully Hacker," he whispered. "Tell me, young man, is he still alive? He . . . seemed like a man . . . who knew how . . . to stay alive but . . . he was in a dangerous . . . line of work." The fronds of a Boston fern blew near the old man's face, trying to caress him. A nice gesture. "But people get old . . . and die." He sighed. "Most everybody dead, of course . . . pussy, I close this eye . . . dream about pussy. They better have . . . pussy . . . where I'm going . . ." He gasped softly. Morgan strolled along the railing to the cliff's edge, motioned unobtrusively to Duke, who nodded, got up at once. "The real article," Simon Karr concluded, fell silent, his one eyelid drooping like a crumpled tissue. He was asleep, and Duke rolled him away.

Heading back through the fog sweeping the freeway, Morgan asked him what came next.

"The only thing I'm sure I can't do is stop," Challis said. "We've got the diaries that show Aaron to have been a shit, we've got a ton of checks written to Priscilla Morpeth by Kay Roth, Goldie, and Jack Donovan over a period of nearly a quarter of a century. And we know that Priscilla's husband, Morty, was murdered in 1947 . . . that *he* embezzled Maximus money . . ." Challis cranked the Mustang's side window down, sniffed. "I think this heap has got an exhaust leak coming into the car. God, what have I come to?" He sighed, took a deep breath.

"What do you make of all the supporting players getting into it? The butler, for God's sake—maybe he did it, Toby!"

"You never know. Anything can happen in Hollywood."

"And Tully Hacker . . . I mean, he's the one who actually covered up, or stifled or whatever, the murder

219

of Morpeth. And now he's Solomon Roth's security man. More than that, Toby—you made it sound like he's practically a member of the family."

"He is. Almost. The Roths are like a family from another century. Tully plays a lot of roles, carries the burden of their lives. He's the bodyguard, sure, but he's also like an adviser, even a priest who's always at hand. To hear their confessions, to accept their guilt and fear . . . he wears it all so easily."

Morgan said, "It's because he knows how unimportant their guilt and fear are. Don't you see? He's a man of action, living in a world where . . . where . . . well, you told me about hanging people upside down over bridges. He just gets to the point, doesn't worry about things—the perfect priest, Toby. Everybody else is scared and weak. Not Tully. He fixes things."

"You have, I think, grasped the essentials of his mission in life." He grinned at her.

"Do I really make you think about nooky?" She stared straight ahead into the blowing fog, her face composed and solemn.

"Absolutely," he said.

She began to smile at the fog.

They stopped for lunch at a franchised diner stamped out of Styrofoam and plastic, much like the food itself. You were faceless there at the end of Wilshire Boulevard, the palm trees watching for the Japanese fleet to materialize out of the fog, the smell of salt and fishiness on the wind, the hamburgers hiding under the goo that was supposed to give them a flavor.

Challis fished a nickel and a dime from his pocket and got the first *Herald-Examiner* from a sidewalk box. He lost his appetite on page three.

PUBLISHER FOUND SHOT
FOUL PLAY INDICATED

Jack Donovan's picture was a little grainy, taken from a sideways angle that thinned the fleshiness from his heavy face. The news had obviously broken too late for any details of the murder beyond the simple fact that his body had been found by his housekeeper, who had arrived on the yacht in Castle Moon Bay shortly after seven o'clock in the morning. There followed a brief recapitulation of Donovan's recent career, clearly drawn from the material which would make up the full-length obit bound to appear in later editions.

Morgan read it, chewed suspiciously on her cheeseburger. "It'll put you back in their minds, Toby. They'll start making connections and go back at old Ralph with the Bandersnatch stuff and come hounding me again. They'll go to the Roths and your agent and they'll eventually figure out something about this strange, unidentified man . . . they'll find out you had a punch-up with Donovan at my party and they'll remember that the description tallies with the guy standing in my living room for the first time they came to see me . . . and they're going to discover that Eddie Streeter is some kid parking cars at the Beverly Hills Hotel. The thing is, Toby, it's not going to take them very long. God help us if they find any fingerprints on Jack's boat. Open-and-shut. Both of us."

They looked at the food, at the imitation leather upholstery, the people eating in apparent trances. They looked out at the fog and the traffic on Wilshire and the first of the day's rain budding on the plate glass.

"Not much time, then," he said finally. "And no place safe."

She nodded.

"And I still don't know what I'm really looking for."

"If you just keep at it, maybe it'll find you."

"How long would you say I've got?"

"Not long, Toby, not long. Look, what about getting out now? Couldn't you go back to Ollie Kreisler? Or that Pete, the newspaperman? Or—there's no point in kidding ourselves—the Roths . . . and Mr. Hacker. They could do it, they could help you get away."

"No."

"You know they could, Toby. You don't want to get caught for another murder you didn't commit . . . go back to prison for good, for the rest of your life. I don't want them to catch you, Toby. Don't you understand?"

221

"But the point is, I've got to find out what happened to Goldie."

"Oh, Christ, who cares, Toby? Who the hell cares?"

When he got her back to her house on the slipping mountainside above Sunset, they were waiting for him.

[23]

THE THREE MEN weren't Californians. They waited calmly in Morgan Dyer's driveway, sheltered by three black umbrellas, one smoking a pipeful of Cherry Blend Challis could smell the moment he got out of the car. They wore conservative gray suits, a plaid and a pinstripe and a plain flannel, white shirts, and ties. One wore a hat with a plastic rain cover. A block-long Lincoln limo, in black, stood sedately on the sharply canted street. Challis parked behind it. The men watched them but did not move. They looked as if they had come from a galaxy long ago and far away.

"Don't stop," Morgan said anxiously. "They're waiting for us."

"Well, they're not cops."

"They don't even look human. Let's go."

"Where? What is it I'm supposed to do? Where should I go? No, I'm going to see who these guys are." He opened the door and smelled the tobacco. "Come on. Look at those umbrellas . . ." Rain slanted down from the hillside. The foliage dripped and he got his shoes muddy in the street.

The man with the pipe spoke with his teeth clamped on the stem. "Miss Dyer, good afternoon. My name is Carl Phillips, these two gentlemen are my associates." He nodded to the other men, who came forward, flanked him. Youngish men all of them, clean-cut, fair skin, like overage college boys. "And you are Mr. . . . ah?" He smiled tightly and the pipe wobbled for an instant.

"Mr. Streeter," Challis said.

"Of course, Mr. Streeter."

"What is it, Mr. Phillips?" Morgan asked.

"Nothing to concern yourself with, miss. We have some business with Mr. Streeter." He smiled engagingly from Morgan to Challis. "We'll be going now, if you don't mind, Mr. Streeter." He reached for Challis' arm.

"Touch me and I'll scream, you bully. I don't believe I know you, Mr. Phillips." He didn't know whether to laugh or cry.

"Very amusing." Phillips chuckled.

"You're dribbling ashes," Challis said.

"Well, well, well," Phillips said, rubbing his hands together. "Shall we go, then? Ted . . . John, would you see Mr. Streeter to the car?"

"Of course, Carl." Ted and John came forward.

"Where am I going?" Challis asked. "Carl? Ted? John? Or is it a fun kind of surprise?" He thought: Be flip, be tough, don't let them smell fear.

"Are you kidnapping Mr. Streeter?" Morgan frowned.

"Good heavens, what a thought!" Carl was clearly shocked.

"Well, where are you taking him? When is he coming back?" Morgan's frown deepened to a scowl.

"Not to worry, not to worry. He'll be fine. If you'll just excuse us, the sooner we go, the sooner we'll be back." Ted and John were trundling Challis toward the limo, the umbrellas moving like june bugs in lockstep.

"Remember," Challis said over the roof of the car. "My last thoughts were of you." Then he disappeared into the darkness behind the impenetrable black windows.

"Quite a kidder, isn't he?" Carl smiled at her, his teeth even and white, the pipe still in place. "We'll be gentle with him, miss. No reason he shouldn't be back for dinner."

"You don't sound like you mean it."

Carl Phillips just flashed his Colgate smile and went away. Standing alone in the driveway, the rain falling softly, she watched the limo move off. She felt like the party had ended. Then she went inside and began reading Kay Roth's diaries again.

Nobody said anything in the cavelike interior of the Lincoln. The aroma of the tobacco hung like taffy,

224

sickening in the closeness. Down the hill, across Sunset, right on Santa Monica, left into Century City, right into the crowded driveway of the Century Plaza Hotel. An attendant in a funny outfit opened the rear door and Carl and Ted escorted Challis into the football field of a lobby with the sunken cocktail lounge and the waitresses in short skirts and mesh stockings. Rain blew across the broad patio beyond the glass walls. Palm trees bent in the wind, overlooking the parking lot, where the heroes of Twentieth Century-Fox had acted out their fantasies, the fantasies of the world's moviegoers, in the long ago.

Challis felt a slight pressure on his elbow which tilted him toward the elevators on the left. "We'll go right up, Mr. Streeter. You're expected." They waited in a crowd of Japanese vacationers. Challis had never before seen so many cameras dangling from so few people. Everyone smiled.

By the time they disembarked, they were the last passengers. It was the top floor. Carl led the way, knocked on a door, and went in. The suite stretched into the fog and rain, dull green carpet only slightly larger than a polo field. There was a fully stocked bar with bamboo stools, three groupings of Italian-modern couches and chairs, a dining table laid with china, silver, and crystal for eight, and a variety of oils in frames worth more than the paintings.

"Why don't I ever get a room like this, Carl?" Challis said.

The reply came from the one dim corner of the room. There was a tall figure behind the gigantic, ornately carved pool table.

"Because you can't afford five hundred dollars a day," the man said. He stepped out of the shadow, laid his pool cue on the green. He was wearing a pearl-gray pinstripe suit. His tie against the pale blue shirt matched the shred of handkerchief peeking out of his breast pocket. He looked like a page from *Gentlemen's Quarterly*.

"Vito Laggiardi, as I live and breathe."

"Well, you have the advantage of me there, haven't you? Carl, would you fetch Mr. Woodruff, please? I

225

hope I haven't spoiled your afternoon, but this is a necessity."

"Not for me, it's not."

"A point well-taken." He moved across to a tufted leather couch that gave onto a view of what was left of the Twentieth backlot: a street from *Hello, Dolly!* and the lions resting in front of the New York Public Library, Santa Monica Boulevard and Olympic heading out toward the ocean but disappearing in the fog long before that, to the left a smudge of wet green from the Rancho Park golf course. "Lovely weather you have here in California. This I can get in New York."

"Like hell. New York is offering six inches of snow and high winds today."

"Try not to be so contentious. Please, sit down, relax." Laggiardi flickered two percent of his Palm Beach tan smile. The smile meant nothing. The scimitar nose looked sharp enough to cut a silk thread. He gave the impression, as he had that day in Donovan's office, of a Borgia prince taking time from his busy round of murder and conspiracy to interview candidates for the papacy. Something about him reminded Challis of Aaron Roth. "Always remember that no one ever truly enjoys the company of an asshole."

Challis sat down on the couch. "I'll try to remember that, I will sincerely try, but I have trouble with social abstractions."

"There's nothing abstract about an asshole and something very palpable about the cure. . . . Ah, Bruce. Over here, please join us. Would you like Bruce to get you some coffee? A drink? Some Perrier?"

"I had my heart set on Famous Amos and Ovaltine."

"It would only give you pimples. Bruce, this gentleman is some sort of comedian apparently. Do we know who he is yet?"

"Why don't you just ask me, Vito?"

"Ask him, Bruce."

Bruce Woodruff was the young man who had attended his master in Donovan's office. He was still the color of typing bond and still wore the unfortunate mouselike mustache. He had changed to a dark blue suit and he was sweating into his collar. Looking at him, you felt sure that under his clothing he was floating in perspiration and his armpits were caked with talcum. He was breathing a little hard.

"Well"—he fidgeted as he sat down in a chair so low as to make escape impossible—"uh, what is your name?"

"My name is Eddie Streeter."

"That's the point, Mr. Laggiardi," he said, turning moistly in his chair, struggling with the thirty extra pounds stuffed under his vest. "He's not Eddie Streeter. That, uh, wreck of a car he drives is registered to an Eddie Streeter, but this is not Eddie Streeter. Uh, Streeter is a . . . a little creep who parks cars at the Beverly Hills Hotel."

"Big deal," Challis said. "Big detective work. He may not work for a hot ticket like your Vito, but he's not about to drown in his own sweat *like some people*. Vito, you didn't bring me here to insult your hired hand . . . what the hell do you want?"

Woodruff's chubby fingers tightened in his lap. Turning to check Laggiardi's reaction, he exposed the boil on his neck. It was an angry red and the tight collar exacerbated it. He was grinding his teeth and sweating like a man who'd like to mount a machine gun on the balcony and go to work on the populace below.

"The matter of your identity aside for the moment," Laggiardi said, looking like a man sitting calmly in the path of a gently blowing air conditioner, "there is another matter. Or two, even. Ah, Bruce. A Perrier and lime, please. Too much lobster and egg mayonnaise for lunch."

"You don't have to explain to me." Challis sighed.

"Of course, you're quite right there. I think I was making conversation, trying to relieve you of your apprehension."

"Forget it. Apprehension gives me the will to live. You know how it is . . . you must always be apprehensive, afraid the cops'll finally nail you, or some poor bastard you goosed with a rusty crowbar—now, that's an apprehension inducer."

227

"No, I never feel it. I pay people to feel it, recognize it, fix it. Take Bruce . . ."

"No, thanks."

"Bruce is, for all his sweat, an apprehension fixer." Bruce arrived with the Perrier. "Thank you, Bruce."

"What has he got against me, anyway?" Bruce asked. "There's no need to be insulting."

"You heard him. Be nice. He may not look it, but Bruce can break your face in no time at all."

"Bruce? This Bruce? Come on, Vito . . ."

"Enough of the bullshit," Bruce muttered menacingly.

"Christ, he's lowering the tone of the whole afternoon."

"Well, it is time," Laggiardi said. Bruce went a few feet away to flex his muscles. He suddenly seemed to have more muscle than Challis had assumed. "Time to lower the tone . . ." He smiled his little nonsmile, a trifle sadly. He took a swallow of Perrier and looked out the window. "Last night you murdered a business associate of mine. You were also hanging around his office the other day. Yesterday? Well, you were there. Jack Donovan was a business associate and a friend from the old days, way back when he was starting out—was that in Jersey, Carl? Well, wherever it was—"

"I can see you two were very close."

"Excuse me, but a word to the wise . . . don't keep interrupting me with this cheap private-eye garbage. I'm trying to talk to you. Now, before I go on, I'd like to know why you iced my friend Jack. Save yourself a truckload of trouble and answer me." He waited. Woodruff was looking out the window, trying to burst the seams of his suit.

"I don't know this Donovan, I've never spoken with him, and I certainly didn't kill him. That's about that, I guess."

"Not really, not yet. No, because I've already caught you in a little white lie. You may not have spoken to Mr. Donovan in his office, but you spoke with him last night at that nutty bookstore your girlfriend runs. Then you tried to kill him with your bare hands."

"Who told you that? It's crazy."

"Jack called me himself to tell me about it."

"Did he habitually call you when someone took a poke at him? Phone lines must have been humming."

"No, he didn't. Only in your case he made an exception. He said he knew who you were."

"Bullshit, Donovan wouldn't know—"

"You're digging a very deep hole. But let me conclude my thought. Jack said that you had told him who you are. He was very confused, very much afraid, because among other things, you were involved with Goldie Challis, who was also an associate of ours. As you can see, a web of complicated relationships. Jack told me that you claim to be Toby Challis, Goldie's murderer. And the whole world knows Challis is loose somewhere. If you are in fact Mr. Challis, then you are twice a murderer."

"And your kind of guy, right?"

"We know damn well you killed him, Mr. Challis."

"You don't know I'm Challis. Did you ever see the picture in the papers? Then you can see I'm—"

"Why did you kill him?"

"I didn't kill him."

Laggiardi drank some more Perrier and softly cleared his throat. "But you were there, on his boat?" Challis nodded. "All right, now we're getting somewhere. Listen carefully . . . why did you go to the boat?"

"Because I had pretty much decided that he had killed my wife. I thought we could discuss it."

"Maybe he'd want to give himself up, clear you? That kind of thing? You've been under a good deal of pressure, Mr. Challis. I appreciate that, I assure you. But why am I to believe that you didn't cancel Mr. Donovan's ticket?"

"I don't know. My own bet is that you had one of your pink and wholesome homicidal maniacs kill him because he was of no more use to you. He'd succeeded in prying open the gates of Maximus for you—the way I see it, you exchanged a fistful of Donovan's balls for poor Aaron's . . . and little Howard, the CPA, gets to pretend he's a big-time TV executive."

"I don't quite follow this. Do you follow this train of thought, Bruce? I don't quite follow this."

"No, Mr. Laggiardi, I don't follow it at all."

"It must be comforting to know that no matter where you are, Vito, somewhere Bruce is sweating in your service."

"Make him stop that, Mr.—"

"Aw, fuck yourself, you goddamn miserable sweating steaming pile of shit!" Challis felt himself bubbling over, saw red. He lunged up off the couch, reaching toward Woodruff. "Laggiardi, I hate your suit, your tie, your stupid matching hankie, and your moronic attempt to impersonate a human being . . . now I'm leaving your padded cell!" He stormed around the edge of the couch. Laggiardi was smiling imperceptibly.

Carl stepped forward, hands out. "Now, come on, Mr. Challis. This isn't going to take much longer, so calm down. We really do appreciate what you've been through . . . if you'll just bear with us, Mr. Laggiardi is trying to make this all as easy as he possibly can . . ." His arms closed around Challis. It felt like an injection of Novocain. Challis knew his strength was dribbling away. "Just come back and sit down, that's the way, just hear us out, Mr. Challis, and then you'll be on your way safe and sound." He was almost crooning as he led Challis back to the couch. The words were immaterial, it was the sound, hypnotic and soothing. Challis slumped, sighed, and leaned back.

Laggiardi clinked ice in his glass, held it up to Bruce, who took it to the bar for a refill. Laggiardi said, "You see, if my homicidal maniacs had killed Jack Donovan, then I'd have the diaries . . . Kay Roth's diaries, the ones Goldie Challis found . . . but I don't have the diaries. So . . . my conclusion is that some other homicidal maniacs or single maniac, if that is the case, left old Jack with only half as much head as he needed. Deep down inside, I still pick you, young man, which means you've got the diaries. It simply stands to reason, the killer got the diaries. Thank you, Bruce, thank you." He had some more Perrier, bumping ice cubes against his nose. "Have I made clear my position regarding the morality in question here? You kill Donovan, that's your business. You take the diaries, that's *my* business. I'm not going to turn you in to the cops . . . but I might have somebody

230

chew your ear off over the diaries. I need those diaries as a kind of hole card—do you see what I mean? It's entirely possible that Aaron Roth is going to see things my way, that our interests will be entirely congruent, and nobody will have to get angry . . . but what if he acts up? Where am I then? Do I want to tell him that if he doesn't do things my way I'll have one of my homicidal maniacs pay a visit on his adorable little Daffodil or that fine son? Would I want to threaten him that way? Of course not. If I actually have the diaries, other threats become irrelevant. With the diaries I *own* Aaron Roth . . . I *own* Maximus."

"Out of idle curiosity," Challis said, "why would you, with all your other holdings and interests, want to own Maximus? I don't see it."

Laggiardi stood up, put his hands in his jacket pockets, and assumed a philosophical pose. "Two reasons. First, have you any idea what *Star Wars* meant to Twentieth? *Jaws* to Universal? *The Godfather* to Paramount? To a businessman, a gambler, the lure is more than obsessive. Second . . . second, Mr. Challis, is that it's fun. It's within my reach and it is fun. More fun than I find in my other businesses. Got it? That's the sum total, all the explanation you are about to get from me." He paced across the gray light of the high windows, penumbras of grayness moving with his outline like a visible aura.

"One other question," Challis said. "What is in the diaries that gives you ownership of so dubious a property as Aaron Roth?"

"You have the diaries—is this a purely rhetorical question?"

"I don't have them and it isn't."

Laggiardi turned to face him head-on, the dark eyes piercing him like a hypnotist's. He squinted slightly, as if confronted by a particularly irritating riddle.

"I don't know, Mr. Challis."

"Pardon me, but I don't understand—"

"I don't know. I took it on faith. Jack told me that it showed Aaron Roth for what he is . . . Jack was doing this for me, the whole blackmailing number, for me, because, shall we say, he owed me? From the old days. He said we owned Aaron . . . that we would own

231

Aaron so long as we alone had the diaries. Goldie was his problem. Keeping her quiet, I mean. Maybe you're right, maybe Jack did kill her—I don't know. But I'm *positive* he was right about the diaries. Aaron came up with a million dollars. Proof, at least in my circles. But what's in the diaries? You're in a better position to know than I. I've known Aaron Roth a long time, too, see? Back to the same old days when I knew Jack . . . young men, all of us. And I've got a lot of bad stuff on Aaron . . . you wanna know like what I've got maybe?"

Before Challis' eyes, Laggiardi began to transform himself, become a protean shape, tensing, arching, posturing almost like a street punk. The shallow patina of restraint and observed manner cracked, chipped, slid away like cheap plaster. "He's a welcher and he's a crook. He's owed me money for a hundred years, but I play him along . . . I've always played him because of who he was, his connections, because he's Solomon Roth's son. Creeps like that, a smart man knows they're gonna do you some good one day, right? He has me to his house, I go to his parties, I do business with his movie friends, the years go by." A fine dew had broken out on his bronze forehead. His gold signet ring flashed as he gestured. "You wanna know what kind of a porker Aaron Roth is? I'll tell you what kind. He was desperate and I was squeezing just a little bit . . . you know what this guy did? He gave me his wife! That's right, he said to me, here's Kay Roth, Vito, she's yours, you can have her for as long as you want her. Can you believe that? And she went along with it . . . and that's show biz, right? Jeez, Challis, you oughta see your face, man! Poor woman was on the edge by then, drinking and pill-popping . . ." He wiped at one eye with a fist. Challis wondered: was it a performance? If so, why? "And so help me God, I'll have to live with the guilt for the rest of my life . . . I couldn't resist the offer! The shame of it. Screwing this woman, this poor creature, but she was still Kay Roth. I'd fly to Paris to screw this woman. I don't know, Challis, maybe I fell in love with her. Or what she had been once." Abruptly he turned his back on Challis, stalked to the windows, folded his arms, and stared at the weather. Challis heard a sniffle, saw the paisley handkerchief flourished across the face. Woodruff stood nervously looking into the middle distance, rubbing his hand against the boil. One of the homicidal maniacs whistled under his breath. Rain blew against the window. Finally Laggiardi turned back, the swarthy face composed and impersonal. "Kay Roth's famous comeback? I paid for that, financed the whole thing. I did it for Kay. This was a woman headed for death as fast as her legs would carry her, but the talent, my God, the talent was still there, and I made sure she got to use it, she died having done that . . . so Aaron kept on stealing her money, even from those last years, very successful years, and I let him do it. Sooner or later I'd call everything back in . . . it wasn't a bad feeling for a guy like me." He smiled bleakly, just the corners of his tight mouth. "And now it's time for Aaron to pay up. Get it? The markers are coming in . . . Vito is collecting. But you've got to have the edge when you're picking up the paper on heavy people. Aaron? Not so heavy, but Aaron and Solomon and Maximus? Lotta heavy there. Which is why I want the diaries. I don't give a shit, y'know, about what's in 'em—no matter what it is. It gave Donovan a million-dollar edge, it gave Goldie the hold she wanted, so it comes down to that—whoever's got the diaries has got the edge he needs, has got Maximus. I stand here looking at you starting to shake and look like you're going to puke, I say to myself this guy's got the diaries. Or knows where they are. I'm never wrong about stuff like this, see? So, where are they?" He looked at a gold watch the thickness of a dime. "Whattaya say, Mr. Challis? And let me assure you, you don't talk to us, Mr. Woodruff is going to use your girlfriend's eyeballs for martini olives."

"I had the diaries," Challis said, taken aback by the pathetic weakness of his own voice. "And . . ."

"And?"

"This morning after we glanced through them—and honest to God, I didn't see anything like what you're talking about . . . I swear it, nothing but the kind of stuff you've been telling me . . ." The fight was gone:

233

he felt like a pig wallowing in a slop trough. Where had bravery and frustration and anger gone?

"Where are they, Mr. Challis?"

A helicopter hovered beyond the window like a monster gnat. The fog was coming closer, the day darkening too soon.

"I mailed them to my agent. This morning. Put them in a couple of Jiffy bags, sent them third class to my agent. Christ, I haven't got a home."

"Who is your agent?"

"It's the Kreisler office on Sunset. Ollie Kreisler. You'd like him, you wouldn't want to hurt him. He never goes to the mail room. Never."

"They were actually sent to Mr. Kreisler? Personally?"

"Yes."

"All right. Can you get something straight now? Are you listening to me, Mr. Challis?"

"Attentively. All ears."

"You've got troubles of your own. I realize that. You don't want to go back to jail . . . you want to clear yourself. That's fine. Good luck to you, in fact. You say that you came by these diaries in the course of discovering Jack Donovan's corpse. Maybe you did, maybe you didn't. There's a lot about you I don't know. I don't want to know. I don't want to know if you were even looking for the diaries . . . maybe they leaped off a table into your hands. It doesn't make any difference to me. I have no business with or interest in you, aside from getting those diaries. Am I making myself clear?"

"Abundantly."

"But I do want to impress one thing on you. Carl, Ted, would you assist Mr. Challis to his feet? It's a matter of a quick look into your future."

Carl and Ted stood beside Challis. Then they were holding his arms tightly, pinning them against his body. It was like being in the little airplane again, feeling it dropping down through the snowstorm . . . maybe this was worse.

"Now, Bruce, would you come over here? I want you to help Mr. Challis to see what the future could hold." Bruce came toward him, took something from his pocket. "While Bruce is one of my many attorneys, he is also one of my many homicidal maniacs." Laggiardi almost grinned. "Show him your Swiss army knife, will you please, Bruce?" The bright redness gleamed in the pudgy hand. "You've seen these, of course. Lots of blades, scissors, corkscrews, awls, leather punch, maybe." The fat fingers slipped several times, the red plastic moistened from the hands holding it, finally the punch was separated from the thick bulk of the knife. Bruce held it unsteadily before Challis' face, maybe six inches away. Bruce's eyes began to cross watching the silvery punch. "Forty-eight hours, Mr. Challis," Laggiardi said. "You know what would be worse than going back to prison? I'll tell you. Going back to prison blind. Even blind in one eye would be no fun, would it? Forty-eight hours. Imagine what the experience would be like—acute pain, maybe? Beats me. Lots of nerve-tissue damage. Blood vessels rupturing . . . I've heard of heart attacks at such moments of stress. Then—one of your eyes looking back at you from an ashtray. I want you to think about that. You've got forty-eight hours to get the diaries to me. Fuck me over on this one, and first some guy in Brentwood gets up for his morning swim and finds some pet food that used to be Miss Dyer in his pool . . . and then Woodruff starts playing mumblety-peg with your eyeball. Does that frighten you, Mr. Challis?"

Challis nodded.

"Well, that's fine, then. Go now and do your best. And more likely than not we'll be watching you."

Carl and Ted loosened his arms, and Laggiardi walked beside him to the door.

Laggiardi slapped him on the shoulder, said, "You'd better put your prayers on the U.S. mail, my friend."

[24]

"A BOY-SCOUT KNIFE?" She looked at him in mock horror, handed him a cup of coffee. The diaries were open on the kitchen table. The coffee tasted of orange peel.

"A Swiss army knife, actually." He was cold and the coffee was building a bridge between him and real life, warmth. He poked around in his guts for a smile, couldn't find one. "Listen, it's no joke. That is one scary bunch of guys. The trick with the threatening business is to make the poor guy you're threatening believe it."

"And you believe it?"

"Oh, how I believe it. You should see Bruce, watch him sweat . . . you don't believe he's capable of anything, you're crazy and they're all so polite . . . everybody's a Mr."

"But we've *got* the diaries, Toby. Why not just give Laggiardi the diaries . . . we've read them, we're not going to blackmail anybody. And in the end they could hurt us, they could prove we were on Donovan's boat." She was wearing a heavy blue fisherman's sweater against the cold, a cotton turtleneck underneath, French jeans. She was leaning back in the kitchen chair and had draped her legs over the corner of the table. She looked about six-three. She brushed blond hair away from her eyes.

"Contrariness maybe. I was so damned scared . . . I can't explain it. I almost made a mess on the floor when Carl and Ted had me stand up. I resent it, I've gone through enough, and now this sweaty creep was running a knife up my nose. So I told them a lie they'd believe and now we've got forty-eight hours *and* the diaries. The thing is, Laggiardi convinced me of their worth—whether *we* know what makes them so

236

important or not. Let's just say he's right . . . let's say they confer this crazy power on whoever holds them. Then we've got the power, the magic—it doesn't make any difference if we understand why . . . we've got them, we might just as well use them." He smelled the coffee as he drained the cup, watched her legs, let his eyes roam the length of her body. He didn't want to think of her that way. He needed his concentration, the tunnel vision that might get him the hell out of the hole he'd been in so long.

"I'm just hoping that we've got the forty-eight hours," she said. "The news of Donovan's murder is all over the radio, they've got promos for the evening news on TV—'Murder of publishing tycoon in Castle Moon Bay, film at five,' blah-blah-blah. I'm really worried about the cops, Toby, they're not dumb and they'll start seeing the patterns—"

"We've only got about forty-six hours as it is," Challis said. He set the cup down and stood up. The wind shook the plate-glass sliding door, whipped the shrubbery edging on the patio. Rain still slanted. The fog had closed in, erased Los Angeles, sealed them off on the canyon wall. "Where can we hide the diaries, just in case Carl and Ted decide to do some checking up?"

"See the little shed back at the edge of my property? Right where the fog starts? Pump for the pool, lawn tools, croquet set. We can put them in there, under the leftover swimming suits."

The lock had gotten rusty, but a little patience and Three-in-One oil did the job. The swimming suits were growing mold, and a variety of spiders had set up housekeeping. It was the perfect spot. He worked quickly with Morgan standing guard on the patio, keeping an eye out for the enemy, whoever it might be. Through the fog he glimpsed a team of men trying to shore up the hillside beneath a white villa. The owner looked down at them from the remains of his terrace.

Challis locked the door again and went back to the house, through the wet leaves and grass. Morgan had put her glasses on, as if they helped her think through difficult problems. "Are you still scared?" she said, touching his arm.

237

He shrugged. "I think I'm scared for good. Let's get going."

"Where? I've been thinking and . . . well, I don't know what to do."

"Think about the diaries—it's all we've got to think about anymore. I'm terribly confused and my brain is damn well going on strike if I try to tie this all together one more time. But we have got a time limit, two time limits actually—Vito's and the cops'. And we've got the diaries. The only thing about the diaries that makes no sense to us is all those checks—Priscilla Morpeth, God love her. We know her husband got killed, but why the checks? Were they just charity? But if they were, why would Goldie have felt responsible for keeping up the charity? And even if she did it for the memory of her mother, something to keep the continuity . . . why the hell should Jack Donovan keep paying? That's what I can't figure out." She nodded; Challis went on: "So there's nothing left for us to do but keep pushing against what we don't know —Priscilla Morpeth. And Herbert Graydon is the fellow who befriended her, identified Morty Morpeth's body—"

"And Tully Hacker," she said, "covered the whole thing up. Okay, let's go." She hugged his arm. That was all.

The Mustang nosed fearlessly into the narrow corridor between the grasping leaves and green, sinewy arms of the vegetation, negotiated the turnaround without slamming into one of the Rolls convertibles and a white Stutz that had put down an anchor in a widening puddle. Behind the pink walls and gray shutters, lamps blurred in the late-afternoon fog shroud but you didn't get the feeling that there was life in there. In the stillness their feet crunched loudly on the wet gravel. No one had picked up the tricycle. Herbert Graydon answered the door, his impassive face adjusting to accommodate what was for him a warm smile.

"Come in, come in, Mr. Challis," he whispered, his head turning quickly to check the foyer. "You just missed them . . . they left not more than ten minutes ago."

238

"Who, Herbert?"

"The police, I'm afraid. They were here to talk with Mrs. Roth. From what I gathered, it was concerning the possibility that you might show up . . . they were circumspect but I got the impression that they had some kind of new lead. But nothing specific."

"The Donovan thing," Morgan said softly. Challis introduced her, and Herbert's face brightened again.

"I worked with your father, Miss Dyer. A fine man . . . and a great pleasure to meet you." He shook her hand. "Mrs. Roth is soaking in a hot tub. What, may I ask, are you doing here? I don't think this is altogether a safe place for you to be, sir."

"We've got to talk."

"But not here in the foyer," Herbert said. "Follow me."

At the end of a dim corridor, not far from the kitchen, he ushered them into a comfortable, book-lined room overlooking the terraces that led down toward the turquoise glow that was the pool. "My private quarters," he said softly, closing the door. "Not a bad life for a broken-down old actor. All the books I want, color TV, good antiques—sit down. Sherry? Something stronger . . . a damned stiff shot?" His manner had changed, the performance of the faithful family retainer abruptly shed. He nodded, poured three stiff shots of Glenlivet, and sat down across from them in a shiny leather club chair with brass studs. He unbuttoned the black alpaca coat, lit a deeply colored meerschaum pipe, and leaned back as if he were moving on into the character of a kindly old professorial type. "Now, then, what's this all in aid of? How can I help out?" He sucked the pipe and tamped it down with a stubby index finger.

"Do you have a good memory, Mr. Graydon?"

"Why, yes, miss, I pride myself on my memory. Runs in the family—my father was a dustman in Wolverhampton, then London, and he never forgot a client, regulars on his route—and I'm the same way, if I do say so myself."

"All right," Challis said. "Tell us about Morty and Priscilla Morpeth."

"Love a duck!" he exclaimed, jowls quivering.

239

"That's a bit close to the bone, it is . . . you've heard about the man who befouled his own nest? Well, then, there you are!" He puffed intently. "That's all best forgotten, sir. Long, long time ago, it was. What's it signify for you, eh?" The eyes watched alertly from the massive face. The pipe stem clicked against his teeth.

"Herbert, listen to me. It's a long story and there just isn't time to go into it. But I've talked with Vernon Purcell and Simon Karr today—"

"Simon Karr—good Lord in heaven, surely he's dead! He must be dead."

"Not quite yet. But the point is, everything I need to know to get me out of this mess points back thirty years, to Priscilla Morpeth—I don't know how or why, I don't know what the connection is, but it has to do with Priscilla Morpeth and maybe her husband. Simon Karr told us that you were close to them, that you went with Priscilla and identified the body. Herbert, just tell us about it . . . I really haven't got anyone else to go to and I'm pretty well worn out. The cops are getting closer, Donovan's dead and they're gonna think I killed him, and I'm running in circles. Vito Laggiardi wants to cut my eyeballs out . . ."

"The man is a cur," Herbert said, "an irredeemable cur. You have my word on that."

"I don't need your word on that, Herbert, only on the Morpeth—"

"All right, then! You shall have it. After the war, we had something of an English community here in Hollywood, as you know. We would meet, talk over old times, mostly theater and film woolgathering, somebody would do up fish and chips, and we'd natter on about things in general. Morty Morpeth was a young fellow but he had a certain quality about him, he was like a fictional character, if you see what I mean. Some of the actors watched him, went to school on him, as we used to say . . . if he'd been a character in a film, Niven would have made a good Morpeth. Or Ray Milland . . . good-looking, dashing—he really was one of the Desert Rats, y'know, plenty of decorations, had been at El Alamein with Montgomery. But he was shady, which is what gave him so much charm, what?

Isn't that so often the way? He made no bones about having been in the black market in Cairo and Alexandria, for example. And the stories the chap could tell—curl your hair . . . said he'd become an accountant before the war because he liked playing with sums. You'll never get any of the money, he used to say, unless you get close enough to the money to smell its breath. Well, he was a charming, colorful bloke and the actors took to him . . . and Aaron Roth was quite amused by him—I think Aaron saw a kind of daring in Morty that he didn't have himself . . . that sort of sneaking admiration can draw men together. I saw the two of them out drinking together a few times, very odd thing for a man in Aaron's posish to do, out mucking about with Morty. Morty was always out on the town with men you'd have thought wouldn't have time for him. But they genuinely liked him. Errol Flynn, for instance, he was always buying Morty drinks and they'd gab on and on for hours. . . .

"He had this peculiar little wife who came along sometimes, she was English, too. I think he'd married her in Cairo or someplace like that right after the war. Anyway, she had curly red hair, like coils of copper wire, big floppy lips, a robust figger, a habit of wearing rather more jewelry than was good for her, strange blue eyes that could stop you cold and make a believer of you . . . an odd woman . . . those eyes, she claimed she could see the future and she enjoyed quite a vogue at various times, as a kind of seer—at regular intervals, y'know, Hollywood goes quietly mad over the latest seer. Used to, anyway. . . . God, the memories, please forgive me." The pipe smoke curled around his face, hung in the still dry air. A Meissen clock ticked on a bookshelf. He had touched a button on a small tape deck and Chopin waltzes tinkled softly, very softly in the background. "She was having one of her periods of success . . . and then Morty disappeared and the next thing we all knew he was dead. It was all very shocking because he'd been so extraordinarily alive, but when you got to thinking about it, it wasn't so surprising after all. Remember the black market? Remember wanting to be near the money? Well, you see how it all began to make a kind of sense . . . the story

241

made the rounds among the movie people that he'd embezzled a lot of money from Maximus, and Aaron was in a certain amount of hot water with Solomon Roth for having hired him in the first place. Admittedly, Morty was not the old man's kind of bloke. And then Simon Karr was hired to keep it all quiet—he came to see me because I'd identified the body, seen the bullet wound, heard them talking about it at the morgue—Simon asked me to please not discuss it with anyone, particularly the columnists and such."

"Did he offer you any money?"

"No, Toby, he didn't, though I think he would have if I'd hinted a bit. But I'd done some pictures at Maximus, always been well treated there, and I saw no reason to noise the story about . . . and the Roths never forgot my attitude, though they'd never spoken about the matter to me. When I let it be known that I was considering going into service if the arrangement was one I liked, Solomon Roth called me, said he would consider it an honor if I would even entertain the idea of coming here . . . well, I was flattered and I've never regretted it. There have been some difficult times, of course, particularly when Mrs. Roth—the first Mrs. Roth—was unwell, but every family has its unhappy moments, I'm sure." He cleared his throat, relit the meerschaum. "It was at the time of Morty's murder that I also met Tully for the first time . . . he was very helpful to the family, I understand. Certainly the story never made any headlines, and I'm sure Tully was right—Morty was greedy, got his hands on the money, and had a falling-out with his gangland chums . . . his reward, a bullet in the brain. Very sad."

"Did you still see Priscilla?" Morgan asked.

"Oh, my, yes, frequently for a time. She had another vogue a year or so after Morty's death, and, vogue or not, she was always there, on the fringe. Hollywood's full of those people, has been for as long as I can remember. She used to go to parties which, for one reason or another, I'd also attend. I remember she had a crystal ball, the complete paraphernalia, and was still in the fortune-telling business—I saw her once at Eddie Robinson's house, she was set up at a table with the crystal ball, wearing a kind of costume, and all of Eddie's incredible paintings on the walls . . . Manet, Monet, Degas, Utrillo—what a setting! I liked Priscilla, I liked the way she made a go of it on her own. I'd drop in at her shop on Sunset for a cuppa now and then, she always had the teapot on a little gas ring, and I'd tell her about my career, tell her if I was worried—oh, yes, I admit it, I asked her about the future—and she advised me a bit, told me finally that it was TV or nothing. I couldn't face that. I even took Treacher with me to see her once, but you know him, looking down from his great height and telling me I was an imbecile to put any faith in the word of someone who belonged in an asylum, but that was just the way he was, y'see. She'd go into a bit of a trance and maybe she was batty, but we were close friends for a few years . . . after Morty's death she turned to me, maybe because I wasn't a big star, I can't say. Very fond of her, I was. Another peculiar thing, for some years after Morty's death, she told me she was communicating with him from the great beyond, that's what she called it, as if it had capital letters, the Great Beyond, and she said he had terrible things to tell her about his death, awful things, but she never told me what they were. . . . Then, you know how it is, the years passed and made fools of us all, eh? What difference had any of it made, that we'd been here at all, eh? I lost touch with Priscilla, oh, I heard of her now and then, but once I was out of the business and my old friends began to die off, well, it's the old story, isn't it? Let's see, I last saw Priscilla about ten years ago. Ran into her on Hollywood Boulevard, she was coming out of Larry Edmunds' Cinema Bookstore—she had her arms full of a great number of books about the movie business, said she was thinking about writing her memoirs and wanted to read some, sort of get the hang of it—she sounded a little bit crazy, that high-pitched voice of hers, but those blue eyes were bright and clear. She was about fifty then, I expect, wearing an old fox fur around her throat, a flowered print dress, hair all curly and red but with a little gray in it . . . she looked just like a weird middle-aged woman who belongs on Hollywood Boulevard."

"Then she'd only be sixty now," Morgan said.

"Where is she, Herbert?"

"Well," he said, "it was ten years ago, and you know how people move around out here. But she said she'd just left a trailer park down in Orange County and headed up the coast past Malibu . . . she said she'd found a fine place." He paused and tugged at his pipe with a smooth, powerful fist.

"Come on, Herbert, goddammit."

"Coincidence always makes me nervous," he said. Fingers of rain tapped at the window. "She said her trailer park, the one she was newly settled in, was up in the hills above the coast, halfway between Esterville and . . . Castle Moon Bay."

Morgan said, "You don't know how little we have to go on, Mr. Graydon. Anything is . . . something. Now we've got two connections between Donovan and Priscilla, the checks and Castle Moon Bay."

"I'm at a loss, Miss Dyer," Graydon said. "And I wouldn't put much stock in where she lived that long ago."

A knock rattled on the door. Graydon got up, opened it a crack, then let Tully Hacker come in. He was in his stocking feet, wearing a loose-fitting suede jacket, a brown hat, and carrying a pair of ornately tooled cowboy boots. At the sight of Morgan and Challis he frowned.

"What the hell are you doing here, Toby? The coppers just—"

"Yes, yes," Graydon said. "I've told them."

"Well, pay attention," Hacker growled. "You're hot and getting hotter, Toby . . . and you, young lady, you're keeping bad company." The smell of leather filled the room. "I wanted to show Herbert my new boots . . . I've got a young fella in Tucson makes 'em for me, see the iguana hide here on the toe and heel. Best boots money can buy."

"They've come about Priscilla Morpeth, Tully." Graydon puffed deeply and sank back into his chair. He sipped Glenlivet while Chopin filled the silence; then Hacker sat down on the edge of the couch and whistled.

"Shit, Toby, what the hell do you think you're doing? Morpeth . . . for Christ's sake. You've got more urgent things to worry about. Morpeth . . ." He opened his jacket. He wore a specially fitted harness and the immense weapon that became the symbol of movie tough guys and private security men all over the world. Challis' knowledge of guns could have been engraved in triplicate on the head of a pin, but he was a screenwriter and every screenwriter knew about the Ingram M-10 LISP. Tully Hacker looked at the faces staring at him. "Excuse my gun, but I'm about to put these boots on and I can't lean that far down with this thing on." With a loud, solid clicking sound he ripped the gun from the harness and placed it, black and shining dully, on the couch beside him. "And where does Mrs. Morpeth fit into your worries, Toby? . . . Christ, I worry about you." He slid his foot into the soft, supple boot and hooked his fingers into the straps, tugged.

"All part of the big picture, Hack. I'm still trying to dig my way out of the hole, but I just keep getting in deeper."

"Morpeth is deep, all right," he said.

"I talked to Simon Karr this morning. He told me you were the one who covered up the Morpeth murder." Challis tasted his Scotch, rolled it on his tongue, waited. Hacker got the first boot on.

"More or less," Hacker said. "Kept the lid on. No big deal . . . just kept Maximus out of the papers. Over the years it all adds up, a favor here, a favor there. Then one day you've got enough tucked away to buy an avocado ranch." He started on the other boot. "Which is just what I did. But what it's got to do with you and Goldie and now Donovan . . . well, I'll be damned if I know." He gave a final tug and stood up, stomping his feet down into the boots. He picked up the machine pistol, hefted it as if calculating its weight to the ounce, and carefully fitted it back into the harness. "Toby, I can't make you do anything. I can't do anything but give you my opinion . . . and that's too bad, because you could still, just maybe, get out of this in one piece. Mr. Roth, Solomon Roth, is very worried about you, Toby . . . he has everything you need to get out of the country—passport, and transport ready when you are. He thinks of you as blood kin. You should already know that, Toby. He

245

wouldn't put it on the line for many people." He buttoned the loose jacket and the gun disappeared. "He felt this way all through the trial, too. He likes you, Toby, he doesn't want you to rot in a cell."

"Does he think I killed his granddaughter?"

"I've never heard him say. I guess that that doesn't really enter into it."

"Well, Hack, you're a real sport. But we've got to get moving. Come on, Morgan."

"Sir," Herbert Graydon said. "Why don't you put yourself in Mr. Hacker's hands?" His voice was soft, almost tentative, as if he feared he was overstepping the bounds of propriety.

"I'm beginning to forget, Herbert. Maybe I'd be lost without the search . . . I'll know when it's time. Thanks, Herbert. I mean it."

"Take care of him, miss," Graydon said, reaching for her hand.

"I'll see you out, Toby," Hacker said. Herbert watched from the doorway as they went, puffing billowing smoke, brows furrowed.

In the foyer they saw Daffy pacing against the gray glow of the windows overlooking the terraces. She looked up, stared at them for a few seconds, then resumed her pacing without speaking. "As Herbert would say," Hacker said, holding the front door open, "Mrs. Roth has the wind up. Aaron is wrapped up in the Laggiardi thing at the studio . . . big party this afternoon to introduce young Howard around . . . and Solomon is gone half the time and she doesn't know what to say to him anyway. God, these boots feel like I've worn 'em all my life—the kid's a genius." They reached the car. "You know, Toby, they're figuring it out, the coppers . . . they're closer than you think, they know damn well you didn't die on the mountain, they told us to be ready for you to contact us . . . so poor Mrs. Roth doesn't know what the hell to think. Toby, think about Sol's offer. You're never going to get a better one. Stop and think what you're doing, and tell me who cares what you find out, what good it's going to do. If they don't get you for Goldie, they're going to get you for Donovan. No way out." He held the Mustang's spotty door. "It isn't just Mrs. Roth.

I'm nervous myself. I don't get nervous much, but I'm nervous as a cat. It's like I can almost hear sounds coming at me from the future, from out there in the dark. It's funny, Toby. It's like something's building up out there in the future." He chuckled self-consciously. "Pretty soon everybody'll be able to hear it . . . or they'll come and pack me away somewhere. Remember what Sol says, Toby. Be smart. . . ."

[25]

THE HIGH TAN WALLS, the palm trees, the elaborate black iron—all you could see of Maximus Studios from the street was meant to look good in the sunshine, but in the rain the joint looked like hell. From Mulholland Drive you could look down and see the red-roofed soundstages looking like a bunch of Pinks' hot dogs waiting for chili and onions. Once you threaded your way down the canyon to the valley, you couldn't see the red anymore and there was nothing left but the tan concrete streaked with rain, the fancy gate, the palms drooping disconsolately. Maybe a factory, like any other. Then a glimpse of the parking lot with the acre or so of 450SL's, the Rolls-Royces, the limos and Mark V customized convertibles. And on the gate, fashioned in wrought iron, the original Maximus logo. The Roman warrior's shield strapped on the brawny arm, the word "MAXIMUS" in some forgotten studio designer's idea of Roman script spread across the shield, the massive clenched fist. Solomon Roth's idea: Challis had seen the original sketch framed on the wall in Sol's office. Why not? It was Sol Roth's studio. Somehow, from beyond the grave, it would always be Sol Roth's studio.

The guard gave the Mustang a faintly horror-stricken look, consulted his clipboard. "Come on, man," Challis yelled past the rain and wind. "Regis Philbin's in there doing Howard what's-his-name, your new TV honcho, and we've got all of Philbin's notes, background . . . Miss Dobson here is his secretary, she must be on your list—we gotta step on it, man."

"Okay, okay, it's the Executive Building—"

"Right, gotcha," Challis said, heading down past Sound Stage One toward the yellow painted parking stripes, the reserved spots, where as Aaron Roth's son-in-law he'd always parked with impunity. "Okay, now stick with me," he said to Morgan. "You're my witness."

"To what?"

"Damned if I know. I just know I want a witness. Let's go."

Everything about Maximus had been redone in the thirties, the interior design and decoration and furnishings. Then Sol Roth had seen to it that the clock stopped. Anywhere you looked there was Hollywood-modern blond wood, large rounded curves, the black and chrome and glass, the layered pastels and ornately trimmed archways of Art Deco classicism. Walking into the Executive Building was like entering a tomb, but the sounds coming from the reception room were somewhat livelier if every bit as ritualistic as what had gone on during an Egyptian entombment. The crowd meeting Howard Laggiardi was staying on following the one-o'clock luncheon. The press had been joined by the studio execs, the casts of movies and television productions, assorted managers, agents, publicity men, and starlets; lunch had been served from a buffet of Rangoon Racket Club chili and curry; an ice sculpture of a swan melted, champagne and caviar warmed as the afternoon wore on. A well-known television macho hero made a discreet play for one of the waiters and an agreement was struck. A blond actress with huge nipples bulging through a clinging silk shirt opened to her waist hung groggily on the producer, his identical shirt open almost as far, who had used her in an S/M porno film ten years before and had engineered her career ever since. A week hence, he was telling everyone, she would be on the cover of *People*. Her new contract called for $40,000 per week, which would keep her in cocaine and pay for the inevitable reconstruction of her nasal passages.

Challis and Morgan took champagne from a passing tray and looked for Aaron Roth. It took ten minutes in the glut of freeloaders. They finally saw him standing with Howard Laggiardi and one of the trade papers' columnists. Aaron smiled distantly in the role of Laggiardi's shepherd. Howard himself was pale, tall, and thin. He wore an expression of sincere interest which perfectly complemented his sincere gray flannel suit, a white button-down shirt, a red-and-blue-striped rep tie, black wingtips, a gold watch with a round face and a leather strap. He was an Eastern clone among Western clones, a product of money, good schools, and moderation in all things. His wife stood next to him, a large slightly horsey woman with a friendly face; she looked like she had a couple of kids and a master's in English from Smith.

They worked their way closer, approaching Aaron from the rear. He had been joined by a large man whose face looked like a bag of exploded veins. Aaron said, "Let me make my stance perfectly clear, Harvey. I'm interested only in the 1870 Château Lafites, nothing else. As many bottles as you can find, and you may go as high as one thousand dollars per bottle, not a penny more. And anyone getting that price for bottles in a single lot should thank his lucky stars and take it before I change my mind."

Challis stepped close, spoke into Aaron's ear: "Why not have Vito's assassins simply steal them . . . and you can spend the money to buy Kay's diaries from me." Aaron turned slowly, the silver-dollar spectacles momentarily opaque in the light. His soft, sensual mouth hung open for a moment. He said, "Harvey, will you excuse us, please?" He looked tentatively at the columnist, Howard, and Howard's wife. They were chatting quietly, and Aaron turned slowly away, back to Challis and Morgan. "You . . . you . . ." he murmured, swallowing. He was keeping his voice quiet, precise. He smelled of sandalwood. "Come to my office." They all moved slowly through the crowd, which itself was functioning in a kind of champagne slow motion. Across the room, down the hall, through the unmarked door which led directly to his office, missing the secretary. The venetian blinds were immaculate, the draperies a putty color with a faint mauve pattern. The room was as carefully faithful to the past as the rest of the building. The mauve pattern was repeated in the carpet. Art Deco glasses and decanters sat on a glass-and-chrome tray which decorated a sideboard. Two lamps in the shape of early propeller-driven airliners flanked the marble pen set on Aaron's desk. Challis half-expected William Powell and Myrna Loy to follow them into the office. The desk was a vast blond affair with swooping curves at the sides, which somehow became bookcases. You had to keep remembering who you were, what year it was. There was something terribly wrong with the scene. It ought to have been shot in black and white.

"Who is this woman?"

"Morgan Dyer. She's my witness."

"Toby, you aggravate me more than I can tell you. Now, what in God's name are you doing . . . what did that tasteless crack about poor Kay's diaries mean?" He took a cigarette from a chrome box on the desk, lit it with a matching lighter. It was almost gray in the office. The only light came from the strips of window and the glowing, plump airliner. "Surely they're going to catch you and tuck you back in prison at any moment . . ." He let the thought drift away on the cigarette smoke. "What do you want?"

"It's come-clean time, Aaron. Nobody's going to send in the clowns this time. I've got Laggiardi's torture masters and the police closing in on me. . . . You're a liar, Aaron. At the very least. You lied about the diaries, you lied to your father, and just for the hell of it, you lied to me, and my life is at stake. I've read the diaries, I know that Kay's not the disgrace in the family—it's you, the smudge on the old Maximus shield."

Suddenly Aaron seemed to choke, his face turning red. The coughing jerked his body like electric shocks. Behind the glass circles his eyes bugged, watered. His hands clawed for a water pitcher. He poured a fat glass of water, hands shaking, water dribbling onto the desktop. From his pocket he pulled a pillbox, levered it open, and washed two small white pills down with water. Several pills spilled, rolled across the desktop. Aaron sank back in the chair, slipped the spectacles off, and held a white handkerchief to his eyes. Challis applauded.

"I've never seen it done better," he said. "Cut. Print it."

"Toby . . ." Morgan gave him an appealing look. "Are you all right?"

"Yes," Aaron croaked, trying to clear his throat. Challis turned away, looked at the framed movie posters. They were all old, growing brittle behind the glass. "You wretch," Aaron said to Challis. "You are a swine . . . you'd have let me choke to death."

"It's better than you deserve."

"Oh, God," Morgan said, standing between them.

"So I'm the disgrace, am I?" Aaron's small, finely manicured hands were flat on the desk before him, as if he needed to hold on. The color was leaving his face. His sloping forehead was covered with sweat. "Well, what does that mean? And what makes you think so?" His voice was dry, his tongue sticking. He sipped water.

"The diaries. You stole from Kay, you drove her off the edge, you misused her in every way imaginable . . . and in the end you put her in Vito Laggiardi's bed to save your own neck. You leave a trail of slime, Aaron. You stink of fear and corruption. You were afraid of Goldie because she had the diaries, and the diaries told the truth about you and Kay, they made it clear which one was the monster—no wonder she hated you, always hated you. She knew the truth, and finally she had the proof—"

"Stop shouting, Toby." His voice was barely a whisper. His face was like the putty color of the draperies and carpet. Without his glasses his eyes swam, the irises seemed murky, unfocused. "Why are you doing this? I don't understand you at all . . . my God, I could *help* you, and you choose to be unkind to me . . ." He swallowed with enormous effort, slid his glasses back over his ears, settled them in the red depressions along the bridge of his hooked nose. "Miss Dyer, reason with him—why is he doing this to me? Why shouldn't I simply call the police now? I don't have to listen to all this raving, I'm a sensitive man, I've got high blood pressure, and he has no evidence . . ." His voice had a faraway sound, disembodied, smaller than life. The words came out but didn't seem connected to one another, unrelated to thought processes. A mechanical man, running down, running on empty. "No proof, no proof . . ."

Morgan said, "You haven't been listening, Mr.

Roth. He does have proof . . . we *have* the diaries. Do you hear me?"

"Oh, yes, the . . . diaries." Aaron's eyes moved slowly up to Challis' face, as if the news had slipped his mind. "Kay's diaries . . . but Donovan had the diaries, Donovan told me he had the diaries." He sounded like a child trying to deal in abstract concepts for the first time. "My God, you took them from Donovan, from the boat . . . you killed him, Toby, you actually killed him!" The zombie was gone; his voice was coming back, and his hands were flexing on the desk, filling themselves with blood and life. "You are . . . are—"

"So call the cops, Aaron. Call them now. I've got the diaries. I've got the checks." Whatever the hell they were worth. Challis took a deep breath, wondered what he was doing. Wielding the power, the magic, was all well and good, but what did it *mean?* "I know about the Morpeth cover-up, and I know about Priscilla Morpeth . . . we've got three dead people and they've all written checks to Priscilla Morpeth . . ." There was no place to go from there because he didn't know any more. "Now, it's up to you, Aaron. Call the cops. Fine, they can have the diaries and the checks, and everything in your life hits the fan. Now, I don't *want* to do all these bad things to you, I just want to know what's been going on and how the hell I get off the hook. I want to know who's been killing people . . . who killed Goldie. Did Donovan kill her? To shut her up about the diaries, so he'd have his million safe and sound?"

With a ghastly moaning gurgle Aaron Roth began to cry. He snuffled, and the tears washed down his face, and the recovery he seemed to have been making began to collapse. Aaron Roth, as Challis had known him, had disappeared: the precision and discipline and style were gone, as if a devastating wand had passed over him, slain his dignity. The infection in the man was suppurating.

Challis said, "Stop blubbering, you miserable shit! All right . . . so who killed Donovan? Did you kill him yourself?" He felt the red rage and fear and disgust boiling in himself. "Tell me!" He watched from inside

253

his head, saw his own hand grab one of the airplane lamps and smash it to bits on the edge of the desk. Then he was around the desk, had Aaron's head in his hands, wrapped his fingers in the tight gray curls, saw and felt and heard as he slammed the head, face-down, into the desk. He heard the glasses break. He yanked the head up, blood bubbling from the nose, the cheekbones lacerated by slivers of glass. He heard Morgan's voice shrieking his name.

Without warning he felt the heavy, hard slap, felt the bones in his jaw grinding and pain shooting in knife points into his ear. He turned to face her and she slapped the other side of his face. He cut the lining of his cheek on a tooth, tasted blood. Morgan was staring into his eyes. She was strong and angry and she drew back her open hand to hit him again. Challis shook his head, backed away, let Aaron Roth's skull drop heavily to the desk. At rest, Aaron blew bubbles in his own blood, one eye open and watching Challis like a fish about to die, about to feel the knife sliding through its guts.

Morgan grabbed Challis' shoulders and shook him. "Are you crazy? Are you? You've gotten so far without killing anybody, do you want to start now? Don't be an idiot!" Her voice hit him like a sledge. The heat in his head, behind his eyes, turned cold as he looked at her. "Now, behave like a human being."

"It's hard," he said. He felt her cool hand on his face. "All right, you're right . . ."

Aaron moaned, smeared blood across his face. Challis watched, fists clenched. The bent, broken airplane lay on the carpet. Glass and pills littered the desk. "Get back, just stand and take some deep breaths and try to remember how the hell human beings behave." She grabbed a handful of Kleenex from a desk drawer, wet it from the pitcher, and began dabbing at Aaron's face. She held his head up, gently leaned him against the leather back of his chair. She wiped blood away from his eyes, murmuring, "Keep your eyes closed, we don't want any glass to get in there, that's right, the cuts are actually very small . . . most of the blood is from your nosebleed, you're going to be all right . . . do you have another pair of glasses? I'm afraid these are done for." Her voice droned on, calming him. Challis leaned against the sideboard, getting his breath, forcing his pulse rate downward.

One glass disk remained in the frame, and Aaron fumbled with the spectacles, tried to bend them back to what they'd been. Morgan watched protectively, ignoring Challis, helped hook the wire over Aaron's small, perfect ear.

"Thank you," he whispered. "You're very kind . . . very kind." Miraculously, with her hands, Morgan had undone the damage Challis had done with his. Aside from a smudge of blood on his collar, redness around his eyes, and the off-center glasses, Aaron had returned to normal. He took a sip of water, began sweepnig pills and broken glass into a pile before him. There was a smear of blood on the desk; slowly he wiped it away, crumpled the Kleenex.

"Did you kill Donovan?" Challis waited, hands in pockets.

"No, I didn't kill Donovan." There was a croak still stuck in his throat, and he coughed, smoothing his mouth into his cupped hand. "You must be insane, Toby. *Me?* Kill somebody? You know me, you must have noticed that in addition to my other failings, I am also a coward. He told me he had the diaries, he told me he'd go public with them if I didn't let Laggiardi into Maximus. Well, what could I do? So I told my father that half-baked story about the diaries, making Kay the villain—she wasn't the Virgin Mary, you know, a lot of it was true . . . I told him how Kay even from the grave could bring disgrace to the studio and the family, I told him that Goldie wanted to ruin us but that Donovan could save us. My only hope rested on the crucial assumption that Solomon Roth is crazy—he must be the last man on earth who could be blackmailed by a dead woman's nutty diary. But he fell for it . . . when he could have just said the hell with it, let Donovan do whatever he wants with the silly damn diaries, all we have to do is cluck sympathetically about poor deranged, besotted, drugged Kay and nobody would have given a tinker's damn a week after it was published . . . but"—Aaron sighed tiredly—"but he didn't . . . he stayed true to form.

My God, if he'd said no to the million, I can't say what I'd have done. I was the one who *needed* the diaries suppressed, my father only *thought* he did. I'd have lost my father, I can't imagine what he'd have done to me . . . but I gambled, won, and we paid Donovan the million."

"So, who killed Donovan?" Challis asked patiently. "And why? For the diaries? Who wants the diaries now? Laggiardi's into Maximus, Donovan had his million, Goldie was dead . . . you were safe. So, who the hell killed him?"

"I don't know," Aaron whispered. "Vito didn't need him anymore, maybe he killed him, just tidying up . . . that Bruce creature of his. Then Vito would have simplified everything, one less complication. And with Donovan dead I think Vito owns the magazine, too . . . and Vito may have wanted to get his hands on the diaries, just as insurance." Aaron sniffled, touched his nose tentatively. "My nose feels odd . . ." He looked at Morgan for sympathy. "But you've got the diaries . . . it looks to me like you must have killed him, Toby. You've tried to kill me—didn't he, Miss Dyer?" He sniffled again, winced. He looked at her for help.

"But Donovan was dead when we got there," Morgan said. "Whoever killed him knocked me out and ran off, then Toby got there and we found the diaries."

"Tell me about Morpeth," Challis said.

"I don't even remember Morpeth, he's dead, thirty years ago." He sucked breath desperately, eyes flickering wildly. "My nose, I've got to do something about my nose. . . . He was a criminal, a crook, he died like a crook."

"Priscilla Morpeth, then—what about her?"

"What do you mean? What about her? I never knew her—she's stuck away up there in that trailer camp."

"Kay, Goldie, and Donovan have been paying her off for years—why?"

"I don't know what you're talking about, Toby. Please believe me." Aaron was babbling. "They killed Morty, they found him after the fire was out, there was Morty under the rocks . . . he was always talking

256

about how hot it was in Africa during the war . . . think how hot it was under the rocks . . . never knew what hit him, bang, poor Morty the war hero, dead and buried under the rocks."

Morgan said, "Who killed Morpeth?"

"Don't know, none of my business . . . hush it up . . ."

"Maybe Priscilla knows who killed Morty," Challis said.

Aaron shook his head. "No, no, she didn't come forward, she'd have come forward if she knew."

"Not if she was being paid off."

"But the checks didn't start until later," Morgan said. "Morty had been dead for years before the checks began."

Aaron moaned, hung his head, shaking.

"Are you going to live, Aaron?" Challis said.

Aaron looked up, blinking. "They're going to get you, too, Toby. No more friends for Toby, not in this town. Vito's going to get you, the cops . . . you should have gotten out when you could."

"All that matters to you is that I've got the diaries. You'd better hope nobody gets me . . . I'm a holy man as far as you're concerned."

Aaron laughed, the sound almost unidentifiable. "Holy men die, too."

[26]

CHALLIS WAS moving fast when he left the back door of the Executive Building; he heard Morgan behind him, she was calling to him angrily, but he didn't slacken the pace. She would have to keep up, she could jump ship anytime she wanted to. His heart was beating too fast, his brain turning over as he moved. The images of the day flickered before him as he filed through them, heard the voices feeding him impressions, memories, reflections: Vernon Purcell and Simon Karr and Vito Laggiardi and Herbert Graydon and Tully Hacker and Aaron Roth . . . Somewhere in that thicket lay the answers. But where? Where else could he go? How many sources were left? He heard Morgan but he wasn't waiting. If she didn't like the way he was handling the matter of his own fate, that was her business. Maybe it was a mistake, having trusted her. He was heading for the far end of the street, the little cottage in the cul-de-sac with the gingerbread bandstand in the grassy park which closed off the street. But that was crazy, Challis. Don't turn against her, get control of yourself, she's on your side . . . listen to me, Challis, the voice in his head said. He turned. "Come on, you don't want to miss the heavy stuff."

She was out of breath. "Bastard! Violence freak!"

"So this is love," he said.

The old man was wearing a powder-blue jumpsuit, striped running shoes, and a powder-blue rain hat. He was getting wet, standing before the long window box where he was digging among the wintry roots and remains with an old wooden-handled trowel. He looked older than Challis had ever seen him, poking in the dirt, the black-dyed hair scraggly over the collar of the jumpsuit. He looked up briefly, smiled slightly like the sleeping crocodile. "Don't worry, Towser," he said, "it's only our friend Tobias." Towser was sheltering from the rain under the flower boxes. "I'm glad you've come to your sense, Tobias." The old voice came slowly, scraping like a bow drawn across badly tuned strings.

"Sol," Challis said, "you're getting wet, you'll get pneumonia."

"Listen, Towser. Tobias is worried about me . . . don't worry, I'll be all right. Resilient old bird. I have my ups and downs, if anybody really cares . . . I feel a little foggy today, but there's been so much happening with Messrs. Laggiardi—it's all very tiring, but I'll hold my own. I'm very glad you're here . . . with . . . with this very brave young lady, ah, Miss . . ."

"Morgan Dyer," Challis said.

"How do you do, Mr. Roth?"

"As well as can be expected, I suppose." Suddenly his attention seemed to wander. He regarded the trowel in his hand with a mixture of curiosity and suspicion, then stabbed it into the dirt. He took a handkerchief from his pocket and blew his nose. "Marty Ritt got me onto these jumpsuits, he always wears 'em, always. One of the greats, Marty Ritt . . . well, well, I'm glad you've come, yes." He looked around, stared up the Western street. "They've all come down that street, Tobias. Guns blazing . . . Coop, Stewart, Fonda, Duke, all the greats, guns blazing." He looked at Challis. "Well, you're doing the right thing, I can get the machinery going right away and you can hole up right here in my little cottage . . . just like the movies, eh, Tobias? Yes, you're doing the right thing." His voice wandered off. He dropped the trowel, which hit Towser's large, muddy foot. The huge dog gave one of his absurd tiny yelps, and Sol muttered, "Who cares who killed the rotten bitch? She'd have covered us all with her filth, her mother's filth, just for the amusement it afforded her . . . my own granddaughter—ach, you're well out of it."

"Sol, please—"

"Now, this is your route, listen closely. You'll go from Los Angeles to Buenos Aires, then to the

259

Canaries, then to Cairo, and finally by ship to Marseilles, two passports with a change of identity in Buenos Aires. There'll be a villa rented for you near Cannes, you've got money coming from us, those deferred payments Mr. Kreisler so cleverly arranged for you . . . hell, Tobias, I could name a dozen men, a hundred, who would pay millions for the chance I'm offering you as a favor, as a member of the family."

"No, Solomon, stop, for Christ's sake! You've got it all wrong—I'm not going anywhere. I can't go now, I'm too close to knowing the answers . . . I'm getting closer all the time, Sol, and then I won't have to run away." Solomon Roth looked bewildered again, his mouth working, trying to respond. Finally the crocodile jaws clamped down softly, like forgotten machinery coming to rest, with that one big incisor showing. But the eyes were alive in their red-rimmed white saucers, moving restlessly, watching. "I feel it, Sol, I'm getting close to what happened the night Goldie died. I can almost remember it sometimes, like I saw it all happen and it's beginning to come back to me. Believe me, somebody's going to be damn sorry when I get it clear. The thing is, Sol, it's all tied together, everybody in the family is mixed up in it, you and me and Aaron and Kay, all of us, and it goes back a long way. Hear me out, Sol, just listen and be patient with me."

"You're a fool, Toby," the old man said, his voice unexpectedly harsh and strong. Towser's ears pricked at the derisive sound. "A stupid and silly man, bent on bringing tragedy. Forget Goldie, forget Malibu!"

"Don't try to order me, Sol. Just listen." Solomon Roth was poking aimlessly in the flower box. "I'm going to give you something to remember for me, a name . . . Morty Morpeth." Sol made a face. "What do you remember about the Morpeth case? Was anyone else ever caught? What really happened . . . how did it all turn out?"

"Listen to him, Towser, time is running out, he should be thinking about Buenos Aires, and here he is babbling about that little pervert. You know, if it hadn't been for Aaron, Morpeth's villainy might never have been discovered. Aaron was learning the business, spending several months in each department, and he'd shown a real aptitude for accounting, cost control, keeping track of budgets. We didn't have computers then, of course, we had *people* in there, accountants who kept books, *honest* books, not like the rest of this industry—Maximus stood for things, principles, Toby, and it still does!" He thrust his jaw forward pugnaciously, waiting to deal with any contradictions. "When I think—why, if it hadn't been for Aaron snooping around, God only knows how much a vermin like Morpeth could have stolen, but"—he beamed triumphantly—"Aaron caught on to it . . . of course, by then Morpeth had bolted, he must have had the thief's sense of being closed in on. We saw the situation, the money was gone for good, we did what we could to keep it quiet—we couldn't let it get out that we'd been looted, confidence would have been shaken . . . then the man's corpse was found and we were able to prevail on some of our friends to hush that up. We didn't want that kind of muck clinging to Maximus, eh? Did we?"

"So none of the money was ever recovered," Challis said. "Who killed Morpeth?"

"His foul accomplices, I presume. Who else? They took the money—"

"But the murderers were never found?"

"The man, this nobody, was dead," he said imperiously, the slant eyes narrowing, lids slipping down like shades. "Who really cared who killed him? We were interested in our money, but it was hopeless, it wasn't worth pursuing."

"But you can't keep playing God every time somebody dies!" Challis felt the anger, alive, throbbing.

"And why not, Toby?" he said soothingly. "Do you think that I don't know what is best for Maximus? Maximus comes first. Ours is a closed society, that's always been in my view . . . people come and go, even I will be gone someday . . . even I, but this industry is much like a nation within our great country, and our nation is divided into our own states, duchies, principalities—the great studios—"

"You should hear yourself," Challis said. "You really should."

"Now, now, you're getting all worked up over something that doesn't concern you. Come on, let's go sit in the bandstand." He took Challis by the arm, Towser following, and led the way to the white bandstand with the naked trellises and blistered, scabrous paint. Morgan with her long strides got there first. The rain tapped on the wooden roof.

"Sol, it was your damned closed society that decided I could take the fall for Goldie's murder, nothing personal Toby-old-chum-old-kid, but it's awfully convenient to stick you in the bin for this one—shit!" He slammed the side of his fist against a white pillar. The whole edifice shook.

"Toby . . ." Morgan whispered.

"And now we're taking you out of the bin and giving you back your life in a very nice wrapping . . . who can say, maybe better than it was before. My advice, take the new life . . ."

Challis leaned on the wooden pillar, stared up the desolate street, shook his head. He brushed Morgan's hand away.

"Sol," he said, "I can't even tell if you're all there anymore. I mean, you just rattle this stuff off like a grocery list, and you're crazy. Anywhere else in the world, they'd put you away."

"But we're here," he said. He smiled.

"You're one of a kind. You're crazy and arrogant and moralistic, you're an old bastard. You've been playing with my life as if it just didn't matter what happened."

Solomon Roth smiled, nodded, as if to reassure the man who was yelling at him. Indulgent.

"Okay, now it's your turn, old man. I'm gonna lay some very nasty facts on you, and we'll see how well you can take it."

"Please, Toby . . ." he said. He sat down on a freestanding porch swing that some anonymous property man thought went well with the bandstand, the village square, the tall elms and maples that cast shade on sunny days.

"You remember the diaries you never saw but paid a million dollars to suppress?"

"Of course."

"Well, see if you can play God with this. It was all a put-up job, Sol. Aaron got you to pay the million to save his own ass, not the studio's, not Kay's, but his own. Oh, the diaries could have soaked Maximus with plenty of dirt, that was true enough, but not for the reason you were told. Aaron was the villain of the diaries. Oh, Christ, was he!"

Solomon Roth's recovery began to dissipate at once. His hand groped for the armrest and his eyes began to float and jerk, from Challis to Morgan. He looked like a man who had deep in his heart expected the worst, and on hearing it, found it even worse than he'd feared.

"This bandstand," Sol said. "This pretty little bandstand, all white with bunting on the railing . . . forty-some years ago, Kay wore a gingham dress, little puffy sleeves . . . she got the townspeople together to celebrate the Fourth of July even though it was the Depression and the banker was a mean old man . . . do you remember that picture, Miss Dyer? Your father was the cameraman on that picture . . . hmmmm, yes, and the banker turned out to have a heart of gold . . . he didn't foreclose on Kay's father, the lumberyard, and he played the tuba in the town band and Kay led the parade down this street to the bandstand for the finale . . . it was a better world . . . back then, a better place."

"I've got the diaries, Sol," Challis said. *"I've got them."*

"What? I don't understand." The old man covered his eyes with a wrinkled hand. "Oh, no, Toby. You . . ."

"I got them from Donovan's boat last night."

"You've killed again? Oh, no . . . oh, no."

"We didn't kill anyone, Mr. Roth," Morgan said. Thunder rasped above the mountains. It was raining harder. "I was there, too, Jack was already dead."

"Listen to me, Sol. The diaries, Kay's diaries, they told the truth about Aaron . . . the kind of man Aaron

263

is, what he did to Kay, driving her to booze and dope and stealing from her . . . Listen, dammit, it's my life at stake, Aaron couldn't let the diaries come out, he couldn't let you know what kind of man he was and is. Who killed Goldie, Sol? Is Aaron a murderer? Did he kill his daughter? Or did Donovan have to do it for him? She knew all about her father, she'd always known what a rotten bastard he was, that's why she always hated him. And when she found the diaries, she knew she had him at last. But she made the mistake of going to an unscrupulous opportunist like Donovan, who had his own uses for them, and then, once he had his million from you two suckers, somebody had to make sure Goldie didn't start talking. So who killed her, who should have been tried and convicted? Donovan or Aaron?"

Solomon Roth stared off into the slanting gray rain; his fingertips drummed erratically on the arm of the swing. Slowly, the old chain couplings creaking eerily in the stillness, he swung to and fro. Finally he got unsteadily to his feet, turned slowly toward the steps.

Challis said, "And where does Morpeth fit in? Somebody must know, *somebody* . . . and it'll fit, I'll make it fit if I have the time, it's part of the whole thing. Morpeth, Goldie, Donovan, and Maximus . . ." The old man was carefully descending the steps one at a time. "Maximus is going to get dirty now, Sol . . . you can walk away from me, but I've got the diaries."

Sol was several feet from the bottom step, moving toward his cottage. The rain was blowing, and water dripped from his face.

"You know how rotten Aaron really is, Sol? He paid a debt by putting Kay into Vito Laggiardi's bed. Sol, your whole bloody corrupt world is coming apart . . . why not help me? You know something, you *know,* you *must know.*"

He turned to face Challis. He was standing on the wet grass.

"I do know, Toby." His face seemed ineffably sad. "I know who killed Goldie . . . you can't hurt me, Toby. You can't hurt me anymore because I understand all of you, all of you." He walked haltingly on toward the cottage, his voice trailing away. "You and

Aaron and Goldie and Donovan and Kay, and . . . and . . ."

He reached the cottage and the door swung open. Towser looked up attentively.

Tully Hacker stood in the doorway, watching.

"Do you have to be quite so hard on this family?"

In other circumstances it might have been a bleakly funny line, but there was an emotionless distance in her voice, not so much an accusation as an observation. They were walking back along the Western street. It was deserted.

"Morgan, I'd appreciate it if you'd stop giving me this bullshit—do you think you could handle that? Try to remember that I'm the one they let take the fall . . . every cop in California is looking for me, New York hoodlums are telling me they want to cut my eyes out, and now he says he *knows* who killed my wife. And you ask me if I have to be so hard on the poor Roth family."

"You're right, of course," she said, "but it gets so violent . . . the violence scares me more than . . . than . . . the rest of it. The way things are going, Toby, are you sure you're right? Don't close me out just because you're angry with me—say we, yes, *we,* do find out who killed Goldie, what if we can't do anything to clear you? Why burn your bridges behind you? Sol wasn't kidding, he can get you out of the country . . . I know he can, Toby, that's the way it works here."

"Sure, sure, Sol can fix it, men like Sol can fix everything in this crazy damned world, because it's *their* world, who the hell cares who killed old so-and-so, he's dead now, heh-heh, what the hell difference does it make—it all makes me want to scream."

"Toby, I understand how you feel." She wiped rain from her face. She looked as if she'd been crying. They turned the corner by the Executive Building. The press party was breaking up. "It's fine to have principles, but can you afford them right now? You're talking about a long time in prison, Toby, and if they tack Donovan on, too . . . you might as well be dead." She bit the words off cleanly, analyzing his situation, but he saw it, the personal concern, in her eyes. "Why not just take Sol's offer—"

"Morgan, try to understand. I've got the Roths in a nutcracker and I'm closing it, nice and steady, and the crunch is coming, and I'm going to leave them in pieces . . . or die trying. Something has happened to me, Morgan, I want to put some blood in the scuppers . . . and I don't really care who gets hurt—do you get it? I want justice, sure, but I also want some revenge . . . a lot of revenge."

She swallowed hard, looking straight ahead. "Do I know you?"

"Not very well, I'm afraid. We've met under unusual circumstances, haven't we? But when this is over, then we'll have time—"

"God, Toby, will I want to know you?"

When they arrived at the Mustang, she leaned across the stick shift, and he felt the warmth of her breath. "Kiss me," she said. "The bad is beginning to outweigh the good . . . kiss me."

He kissed her. She opened her mouth desperately, pulling him in. He felt the rain on her face, touched his fingertips to the smooth skin, felt her eyelashes flickering. He leaned back and stared out into the parking lot. "I've got too much riding on this as it is."

"You don't have to tell me," she said.

Backing out, he saw Aaron's empty parking space. The Corniche had been there earlier, now it was gone. At the guard's station, he stopped. The door slid back. The same guard stayed inside out of the rain.

"Did Aaron Roth just leave? I had a message for him—"

"Like a bat outta hell, he left! You'll never catch im . . . look at that No Parking sign over there, all bent funny. He hit it with that Rolls' fender, gave it a hell of a whack, lost a hub cap." He jerked his head toward the corner. "I brought it in here. . . . Never seen him drive like that before—say, did you find Mr. Philbin?"

Challis gunned the Mustang down the driveway and

267

out into traffic. It was a pretty night, lights reflecting on the wet streets, wipers clicking, traffic lights looking like Christmas. It was a perfect night for a movie: he'd written lots of rainy-night scenes, seen a thousand more. Christ, it was raining in the Mustang.

"Where are we going? Aren't you hungry?"

He laughed, shook his head. "Nervous stomach. We're going to find Priscilla Morpeth, bless her old soul. There isn't anybody else left."

"Toby, I'm thinking an awful thought . . ."

"What else is new?"

"No, I mean *awful*. Aaron said he never knew Priscilla, right?"

"Right. Morty was his chum—"

"But, Toby, Aaron just said something about her being tucked away up in that trailer park . . . up there, that means north, so he's up-to-date on Priscilla, whether he's met her or not. Now, why should he know that, what business is it of Aaron's? I don't like that, Toby . . . it scares me."

"I think maybe that's it," he said quietly. "I think maybe you've just cracked Aaron's nuts, my love!"

"What do you mean?"

"Aaron has made a mistake. I don't know what it means, but Priscilla must know something to be getting paid off about. Aaron . . . Jesus, he's gone to get her, goddammit, I *know* he has. Morgan, I think he's going to kill her!" Suddenly he was dripping with sweat. "We've got to hurry," he said almost to himself.

When he turned off the highway and began to wind upward and inland, they were plunged into a deeper darkness. There were no other cars, no other lights, nothing but the blackness of the forested hillsides. The smell of the ocean faded, was replaced by earth and trees. There was a faded wooden sign painted Lucky Strike green back in the days before Lucky Strike green had patriotically gone to war. The paint was peeling in spots and the sign was wet beneath the two headlights in their black metal shades. "VARNER'S TRAILER PARK" in big white letters, and beneath it, very small but still legible, the inscription "Established in

1934 for folks like you and me." Challis pulled the Mustang into the gravel drive. Down the road, just over the rise of a hill, the lights of the town glowed dimly in the rain. There was a neatly painted office in a small wooden frame building which stood guarding the entrance. No Los Angeles razzmatazz, no neon lights, no gaudy bullshit. It might still have been 1934. Challis drove up even with the door of the office. A man came out beneath a black, very old umbrella: shiny button eyes, a grizzle of white hair on his bony head and chin, a pipestem shape, a baggy sweater, a cigarette butt stuck on his lower lip. He looked as old as the century, but spry, like he might have come west with the Joads themselves.

" 'Evening, folks," he said. "Sam Varner's the name, what can I do you for?" The cigarette bobbed frantically when he spoke. He'd never lost his Oklahoma twang.

"We're looking for someone," Challis said, "an old friend . . ."

"Well, I got lots of them here. Damn near everybody lives here is an old friend, don'tcha know." He smiled from beneath the umbrella. "Which old friend would you like?"

"Priscilla Morpeth—we heard she was here, haven't seen her in ages."

"Well, for heaven's sake, why didn't you say so? I'm not sure Prissy's in, but you can go check for yourself . . . number forty-one, that's down the second row to your right here . . . t'other fella left, though." He was turning around, going back inside.

"Oh, shit," Challis said.

He drove carefully through the puddles. The trailers were all old, from long before they started calling them mobile homes, and they lay quietly in rows, like coffins, a light over each door, the blue glow of television sets at the windows, little soggy flowerbeds flanking the two or three steps up to each dwelling. It was the Social Security life, but you sensed immediately this was a place of old-time Norman Rockwell values, that the lawn mowers were the kind you pushed, and Grandpa took little Junior fishing in the streams nearby, and if you went to a movie, that meant it was Saturday night in town, and if you really wanted to raise hell you could get a sundae at the drugstore later. In the morning the crews weren't going to come and strike the set.

There was a faint light inside number forty-one, which was plain white with green trim, in good repair, with two flowerbeds and a tiny white picket fence protecting them. A mailbox was impaled on top of a chain that rose from the ground in a straight line, frozen. Challis and Morgan maneuvered through the slippery, muddy approach, stood pounding on the door. Wind blustered in the thick growth of trees that encroached prettily on the camp and gave it a permanent look.

"She's not in there, mister." A small man in a bathrobe and pajamas stood on the roofed stoop of the next-door trailer. "She's not at home tonight. . . . Wouldn't you know," he said sadly, "she wouldn't be home the night she's so popular."

"We're old friends of Mrs. Morpeth," Challis said. "You say she had other visitors tonight—that may have been my uncle, we were hoping to surprise her."

"Well, your uncle wasn't in very good spirits, I'll say that. Fella in a Rolls-Royce, big dent in the fender, hubcap missing?"

"That's uncle, all right. Always in a hurry. Did he leave any message for us?"

"Can't say as he did—in fact, he didn't say a damn thing. Looked half-crazy, if you don't mind my saying so . . . had this handkerchief he kept up to his nose. He was swearing, got back in his car and slammed the door—I thought another hubcap was about to fly off! Then he took off."

Morgan said, "You don't happen to know where Priscilla might be, do you? This is really rather important."

"Well, there you are, young lady. Happens I do know . . . but your uncle, hell, he didn't have time to say hello, or I'd have told him too—Priscilla's at Griffith Park! How do you like that? All the way back to Los Angeles!" He thought that was hellishly amusing.

"I don't quite understand," Challis said. "Griffith Park, it's a huge place—"

"The observatory, of course."

"Tonight? In this rain?"

"Rain makes no difference to Priscilla, no sir! Griffith Park three nights a week, like clockwork . . . some people are like that, got to have their routine. If it's clear she looks at the stars—she's very big on the stars, does those charts for folks, tells them all about themselves. Mind you, I personally don't think you need the stars to tell you about yourself, but others do, which is what makes for horseraces—"

"You're sure she's there?"

"Young fella, when John McEndollar tells you it's the case, count on it. It's the case." He looked at his watch. "She'll be there all evening. Beat-up yellow Toyota, you'll see it."

The Mustang had just turned around and was headed back up between the row of trailers when the headlights came around the corner, flicked up to bright, and blinded him. A long black car blocked the way. "Goddammit," he said. "What the hell . . ." Then the doors on the passenger side flew open and two men were running toward them. They reached both Mustang doors simultaneously, their faces in shadow. Metal rapped on the windows, the doors were yanked open. "Out! Out, come on . . . out!" Challis saw the oily sheen of the gun barrel, felt the hands grab him roughly and pull him out into the rain. Another voice said, "Stay where you are, lady, and don't make a sound." As he got out, Challis slipped, grabbed the door to keep from falling. There, in the beam of his headlights, stood the squat, solemn figure of Bruce Woodruff, his eyes demonic red in the glare.

"Mr. Challis," a familiar voice said, "steady as you go." Hands moved expertly, frisking him.

"Carl," Challis said, recovering his breath. "I've got forty hours to go, pal."

"Mr. Laggiardi has changed the plans, sir. We're going to split you and Miss Dyer up now. Ted, John, you follow us in the Mustang with the lady . . . you come with Mr. Woodruff and me, Mr. Challis. Don't worry, we're all going to the same place." He prodded Challis gently.

"If I'm not supposed to worry, why are you carrying a gun?"

Challis realized how quiet it had been: all the noise and fear had been in his head. The trailer park was unchanged, no doors being flung open, no cries of alarm.

Carl laughed ingenuously. "What is it they say out here? It's just a prop . . . dressing the scene. Don't worry. Just climb in back with Mr. Woodruff." He held the door. Woodruff was already in the car. Challis got in, sat warily, as far from Bruce as possible. Carl backed the Lincoln around and drove out the gate. The Mustang was right behind. It was raining hard and the tightly closed windows made the windshield fog up.

"Where are we going?"

"Not far," Woodruff said.

"I don't understand. I said the diaries are going to show up in Kreisler's office—what more can I do?"

"You weren't very nice to Mr. Roth."

"Which Mr. Roth?"

"You take your pick. I was thinking of Aaron."

"Nobody told me I couldn't be mean to Aaron."

"Our mistake. We should have told you it was a bad idea."

"Look, are you trying to throw a scare into me, Bruce?"

"Not at all. Just be quiet."

Woodruff had nothing else to say. Challis turned, saw the Mustang close behind, Morgan's white face blurred by the rain. At the main highway, they turned left, back toward Los Angeles. A mile or so along the highway, Carl hit the turn signal and slowed down. He was whistling "I Could Have Danced All Night," looking for something. The rain made it difficult to see, but finally he found a path between two clumps of bushy gorse flourishing in the wet sand. The lights poked out into the black void, and the Lincoln tilted forward. They were headed down a narrow one-lane path toward the ocean. The wind blowing hard, driving the smell of the sand and the salt water ahead of it. The immense weight of the limo sank in the wetness. The car's undercarriage scraped. The shrubbery ended. They moved out onto the concrete-hard wet sand of the beach. Fog blew across the headlights. Carl turned the ignition off. The surf exploded not far away, sounded like a train wreck. Carl turned back toward them. "Well . . ." he said.

"Please get out of the car," Woodruff said. "Just for a moment." Challis got out. Ted and John and Morgan were already standing by the Mustang. The wind howled, ripped at his hair. Ted's hat was jerked off his head. Suddenly everybody seemed very serious, and there were a lot of guns. Everywhere Challis looked there was a gun in somebody's hand. Somebody was speaking, but the wind blew the words away.

"What the hell's going on?" he yelled.

Carl was looking away from him, out at the ocean. In the cones of light the fog rose. The beach looked like it was burning, smoking in the rain and wind.

"Bruce?" Challis called.

"Mr. Laggiardi . . ." Bruce was saying something, but Challis couldn't hear all of it. ". . . sorry about this . . . said you'd understand . . ."

"I can't hear you," Challis said. Bruce was motioning with the gun. Morgan suddenly ran toward him, pale, her face distorted. She clung to him, her arms around him, blond hair plastered down with the rain.

"Toby . . ." Her voice was husky and hoarse near his face. "They're going to kill us."

He looked at Bruce. "For God's sake . . ."

Bruce didn't look well. "Not my idea." His hand shook. "Carl," he screamed. "Ted . . . *do it!*"

It was a job nobody seemed to want.

Ted scowled. Unexpectedly, when he seemed on the verge of bringing the automatic up, he spun around, faced the darkness from which they'd come.

With unspeakable, perfect precision, without any sound overriding the wind and the surf, people began to die.

Ted was bowled over backward, dropped to the sand like a dead fish. John was hit in the back and bounced off the Mustang. By the time he slid to the ground, Carl was already dead, pitched daintily for-

273

ward in front of the limo, his fingers curling spasmodically in the sand.

Bruce had only those few seconds to grasp what was going on. He turned toward the darkness, mouth open in a silent scream, eyes wide and searching, when he was slammed against the car for a moment, eyes frozen wide, then bent forward as if he were hinged at the waist, and fell with his face in the sand.

Challis felt his legs go. Abruptly he sat down and began swallowing dry spit to keep from puking. Morgan sank with him, her face buried against his chest. She was shaking uncontrollably, sobbing, gasping for breath.

When he finally focused his eyes, looked away from the bodies, he saw a large man coming toward them. The ungainly gun was drooping from one huge hand, and he limped on a stiff leg.

"Jesus Christ," Challis croaked. "Don't shoot!"

The other hand was offered and drew them to their feet.

"My God, thanks, Tully," Challis said.

[28]

"No, THAT WASN'T too tough, miss. When they don't know you're there, you can plan your shots. It's something like a set-up billiard shot, and you've got to know your own capabilities. And your weapon. I had the advantage of surprise and a gun that will do just what you want it to do. The wind and the noise of the surf were negatives, distractions, as well as the fact that I had so many guys to hit while making sure I didn't nick you and Toby. I had maybe six seconds at the outside, and I wanted to move the gun barrel smoothly in one direction, not get it jerking back and forth. The gun has such killing power, they didn't suffer unduly, ma'am." Tully Hacker straightened both arms ahead of him, pushing against the steering wheel of the ordinary green station wagon. He was working the tension out of his arms. Challis leaned his face against the side window, felt the cold, moist glass. Morgan sat between them. The three cars sat as before, angled across the sand. Carl's body was obscured; the other three lay like humps of seaweed washed up by the storm.

"I don't understand how you followed us," Morgan said. She was back to normal already, unlike Challis, who felt sick and had a catch in his side.

"Again, it's not so hard once you know how. I tailed you from in front, doubled back when you weren't in the mirror anymore."

"But why were you there at all?"

"A lot of worries were coming together in my mind —you know, I'm just an old mercenary, paid for thinking as much as for doing, and I've been thinking about poor old Toby here. I like him, he never was much of a match for the Roths, he never thought like they think—for them, even for Solomon, life is a battlefield,

275

a war zone where you work every angle . . . not your average family, miss. Hell, look at the way they behave, right down the line, it's something in the blood, if you ask me. So, I was worried about Toby because I like him. I was worried about Solomon and Aaron because I work for them. . . . Sol isn't quite as confused as he sometimes appears—when he came into the cottage back at the studio he told me what you were going to do, told me about this Priscilla Morpeth thing and the diaries." He shrugged. "So I thought I'd better go along, too. Frankly, I wanted to know what Priscilla would have to tell you. I just turned off my headlights and stayed behind you."

Challis said weakly, "Tully, you just killed four men . . ."

"Look at it this way, I just saved two good lives and spent four bad ones. That's not a bad deal—personally, I figure we'd all be a lot better off if we could do this more often."

"What about the bodies?" Morgan asked practically.

"The police know these guys. No big-deal investigation. Don't worry. All we're doing is teaching Mr. Laggiardi a lesson about bringing New York muscle in here. But now you've got to pay me back—I think we'll all sleep a lot easier if you'd give me the diaries. I don't even want to read them. I just want to put a match to them." He looked over at Challis and waited.

"They're safe," Challis said. "They're hidden in a little toolshed at the back of Morgan's yard. Nobody's going to find them."

"That's good," Tully said. "Very good."

"Laggiardi's going to have a fit."

"Correction," Tully said with a faint smile in his voice. "He's going to be very glad I don't run him out of town on a meat hook in a refrigerated truck. Relax, Toby . . . what happens now?"

"Aaron's running around loose," Morgan said. "And—"

"And we're going to Griffith Park to meet Priscilla Morpeth. Aaron doesn't know where she is."

Tully Hacker nodded. "Okay. You two take the Mustang. If you don't mind, I'll follow you. I'd kind of like to sit in on that conversation. I've been involved

276

there for a long time, and y'know, I never did get it all figured out. No, I never did. It's about time I did. Would you mind?"

"No," Challis said. "We wouldn't mind."

"Why did Laggiardi send these men?" Morgan asked, systematically wanting it clear. "What was the point?"

"Nerves, I'd say," Tully mused, staring out at the rain slashing across the beach. "He doesn't feel at home out here, he's got the jitters, he doesn't know who he can trust and who he can't . . . he's trying to clear up loose ends, reduce the margin for error—so he must have decided you two know way too much, and there was one way to get you off his mind."

"What's to keep him from going into Ollie Kreisler's mail room—I told him I'd sent the diaries to Ollie— and shooting people until he gets them?"

"In the first place, he's just run out of shooters. In the second place, when I tell him I've got them, he'll go light a candle somewhere and brush up on his manners. Now, let's get going, Toby."

Morgan was running through the rain toward the Mustang when Challis leaned back into the station wagon.

"You made it back to the bridge, Tully."

"I guess I did. It's no place for an old man with a bad leg, though. Wind and rain and no damn time to spare . . . I just wanted it to sound easy for the lady."

"Your John Wayne image."

Tully Hacker just smiled. He took his hands off the wheel. They were shaking still.

The Griffith Park Observatory sat out on its promontory like a mysterious pagan temple, the prototype for all the Southern California loonies who pitched their tents on mountaintops and made plans for the Second Coming, who herded their disciples inside, ate pine nuts and roots and berries, and worshiped the sun and flying things, who wore razor-sharp talons on leather thongs around their necks. The rain had calmed to a mist, but the wind was blowing hard as they parked the cars and walked past the beaten-up old yellow Toyota. Behind them Challis glimpsed the ruin of the HOLLYWOOD sign looking like an archaeological find.

Water stood in puddles on the path. It was all so familiar: a place he'd loved to come to, the towering statues of Hipparchus, Copernicus, Galileo, Newton, Kepler . . . he remembered the names without looking . . . and the sundial you could set your watch by in sunny weather. Ahead of them was the building itself, white in the pale glow of the lamps with the three green domes in which the telescopes stood.

As they climbed the steps which clung to the edge of the building and seemed in fact to be hanging perilously from a cliff facing, he was struck by the silence of it all. The lights of Los Angeles glimmered far below, beyond the veil of mist and fog. A dog barked far away and the sound rode briefly on the wind.

She stood at the white edge of the turret, looking out at the city, the wind snapping at the cape and hood which made her shapeless, massive. She was leaning slightly into the wind, like a sentry on the castle's battlements, watching the night. She could not possibly have seen them approaching, but she turned, whirled dramatically, and spoke in a shrill voice as Challis approached.

"You," she cried, "you are not well . . . there is death, you bring death with you . . . are you ill?" Her face was in shadow, hidden by the cape's hood. She moved forward, and the yellow light of the lamps reflecting on the white building caught her face.

Challis had seen her before.

The jangling woman in Jack Donovan's office. She had come to warn Donovan, and he had brushed her aside, hadn't had time for her just then. She had called the receptionist Marguerite, hadn't she? Something like that . . . Challis had been that close to her, had watched her, and she was Priscilla Morpeth. . . .

"Mrs. Morpeth," he said. Tully was breathing hard, clumping along on his bad leg, and Morgan was beside him, holding on to his arm.

"You know me?" She cocked her head and the wind picked at the hood. He caught a glimpse of the pointed nose, the bright red mouth that clashed with the coppery, henna-rinsed coils of hair. There was a glint of madness in the shining iris, but kindness, too, a crafty, sly kindness.

"I saw you in Jack Donovan's office," Challis said.

"Poor Jack," she said, exaggerating the sorrow in her voice, drawing the two words out to an absurd length. Then she cocked her head again, smiled crookedly. "I was right to be worried, wasn't I? There was no doubt in my mind . . . I am always right, invariably . . . who are you, young man?"

Tully Hacker stepped forward. "Mrs. Morpeth, do you remember me?"

She peered forward, her head and neck thrusting at them.

"Why, it's you," she said. "Hooker, was it? Something like that—I'm bad with names, but faces are something else. You were very kind to me at the time of my husband's death, I'd know you anywhere, though you've gotten older. . . ."

"Hacker, ma'am."

"Of course. But what are you doing here, might I ask?" She seemed to be enjoying herself, as if weird encounters in the night were the rule.

"We've been looking for you," Hacker said. "It's a helluva long story . . . but it has to do with . . ." He stopped and looked at Challis, then at Morgan.

Morgan said, "Herbert Graydon told us you might be able to help us . . . we need to know about your relationship with Kay Roth, then her daughter, Goldie, and it really is a matter of life and death." She looked at Toby, said, "This man's life depends on what you have to tell us . . . or, it *may*."

"Death is all around him. Believe me . . . I have the power to know these things, ignore me at your peril." She flashed the cockeyed grin again and brushed windblown red and gray hair away from her face. Rings, gold and bright stones, flashed; bracelets clattered up her sleeve.

"You're quite right," Challis said. "If I put some rather blunt, impertinent questions to you, would you give us the benefit of the doubt and try to answer them?"

"You want to know about Morty, don't you?" She sighed dramatically, looked away from them toward the emptiness and darkness which lay between them and the city. "For thirty years I've been waiting for you to come, to ask about poor Morty. And now you're here at last." She looked back at Hacker. "You were kind, yes, but you didn't want to know the truth, did you? Admit it!"

"That's right, ma'am," he said. "We just wanted everything to get back to normal . . . your husband shouldn't have stolen that money. And what happened to him, well . . . he knew the chances he was taking."

"But why," Challis said, "why were you blackmailing Kay and Goldie?"

She cackled furiously, shaking her head. "Now, there you are, jumping to conclusions, just like the people who think I come up here to look at the stars, which isn't the case at all. I don't have to *look* at the stars—they move by immutable laws, I know where they are without looking . . . I come here to *commune*. But they must jump to their conclusions, that's always the case. They jumped to all sorts of conclusions about Morty, and they were wrong. Now you jump to conclusions about me."

"We have the canceled checks," Morgan said quietly. Her face was damp with mist. She towered over Priscilla Morpeth. She seemed to be getting taller, Challis thought, unless he was shrinking.

"And why do you leap to the conclusion that I was blackmailing them? They paid me for services rendered, I did their astrological charts, gave them advice . . . I *do* that, it's what I *do* . . . Mrs. Roth and her daughter were both very kind to me, they let me do their charts when I'd fallen on bad times. Morty's money ran out, I had to live, so I went to Mrs. Roth and told her everything . . . my, my, it certainly wasn't blackmail . . . she was a kind, decent woman, she heard my story, she did her duty, plain and simple." She sniffed and shook her head. "Blackmail! The idea!"

"But what about Goldie?" Challis said. "She didn't give a damn about astrology." He remembered the charts, how she'd always thrown them in a drawer unopened.

"When Mrs. Roth died, her daughter saw her obligation to me . . . she acted honorably. And I did what I was paid to do. Look at the checks, you call that blackmail? That money meant nothing to them—and the world to me. I told Goldie the truth, the whole truth." She took a few steps along the battlement. "She knew I had to live, and she felt an obligation—she was a decent person . . . but she died, too. Everybody who knew the truth about Morty seems to have died, everyone but Aaron Roth . . . and me. Mr. Donovan knew, and he's dead. The Roth women knew, they're dead . . . I used to worry about what might happen to me, but now it's been thirty years. . . . I've kept the letter, though. I never knew when I might need it . . . it's at Wells Fargo in my safe-deposit box."

"What letter?" Morgan asked.

Priscilla Morpeth gave her a gimlet eye, a crafty smile. "Why, the letter that tells the whole story. . . . Morty knew that he was in danger, that he might not come out of it alive, so he wrote a long letter that explained exactly what he was doing and why. . . . He gave the letter to Herbert Graydon, told Herbert that it was personal, husband and wife, and that Herbert should give it to me if anything happened to him. So when Morty's body was found, Herbert gave me the letter . . . and I knew I couldn't do anything with it. It was no good to me . . . it wasn't what anyone here would have wanted to hear . . . you heard Mr. Hacker, his job was to keep everything calm, not stir things up."

"The story," Challis prodded. "What was in the letter?"

"Oh, you won't believe it either," she said. "I know that, and I don't even know who you are—"

"Please," he said. "Please tell us."

She made no move to leave the parapet, leaning into its embrace. Her eyes darted about, not crazily, but from an almost boundless sense of energy.

"It all began when Morty and I came here after the war," she said, eyes alternately half-closed, summoning up the memory, and large, round, bulging as she watched for reactions. "He had met some movie actors in Cairo and Alexandria and Paris during the war, they'd hit it off, and it wasn't just that he'd worked for Korda and knew about the business . . . it was the kind of fellow he was. He was a jolly good hero in the flesh, the kind of fellow the actors had only played on the screen, and they admired him, told him he'd have to find his way to Hollywood once the war was over . . . they'd vouch for him. So, we came here and they saw he got to meet people, and one of the people he met was Aaron Roth, and they got on famously with their war stories and what-not . . . Morty told me he thought Aaron was a little sweet on him, a crush, but nothing ever happened between them, of course, but Morty was used to the attention —pansies were always making eyes at Morty because he was such a dashing fellow, and handsome in a very English way, thin little mustache : . ." She cocked her head and abruptly remarked, "Seems strange to be talking about him now, remembering him so clearly— he's been on the other side for thirty years and I haven't spoken with him for, oh, my, ten years I expect, it was about ten years ago he began to fade away, he told me that he was all right, that he had faith in my ability to go on with the rest of my life, that he'd keep watch over me . . . and he'd be waiting for me when my time came to cross over." She was almost whispering, as if she'd forgotten their presence, but then the white globe of an eye flew open and stared at them from the shadows of her hood, and she was back.

"Anyway, Aaron hired him at Maximus and set him to work in the accounting end of things. Aaron put him on the budgeting for certain pictures, and just the two of them had access to those books. They'd go over the books every night, moving figures here and there and back again, cost-accounting, analyzing, and they'd go out for drinks in the evening after work . . . then Aaron popped the question! Could Morty use a little extra money? Because Aaron knew how to make some. Well, you had to know Morty—he was always looking for the easy chance, the angle, he'd positively come alive at the chance to work a fiddle on the side, funny money was always better value, he'd say, than honest money, money you had to sweat for . . . well, Aaron really went at it with a spade and a trowel, laying it on, confiding, telling Morty how he needed some money himself and how he was scared to ask his father and his father would never give it to him anyway. What it boiled down to was, Aaron needed a lot of money to pay off New York gambling debts, betting on basketball games. There was an Italian, Vitorrio Laggiardi, and Aaron owed him something like a half a million dollars. Aaron told Morty that he'd taken as much as he could from his wife's accounts, that he was half a million short. He said he'd cut Morty in for twenty-five thousand dollars for a few evenings' work on the books. Well, Morty wouldn't hesitate a moment on a fiddle like that, that was his specialty, and what could be safer than having the boss's son in it with him, and behind the whole thing, too? Well, Morty did it, cooked the books in the finest old Hollywood tradition, got Aaron his half-million and his own twenty-five thousand in about three months. But Morty took one precaution, he left the letter with Herbert Graydon. Because he knew there was a chance things could go wrong, Murphy's Law . . . and sure enough, things went wrong in the very worst way, because Aaron Roth wasn't quite the coward Morty had him figured out to be. Aaron killed Morty." She flashed the huge eyes at them, gave them the gaga smile, watched their faces absorb the story.

"The letter tells the whole story, and it says if anything happened to him, it was Aaron who did it. The funny thing was, Morty wrote that if he let a punk like Aaron kill him, he deserved to die! And he told me about the twenty-five thousand in a safe-deposit box in Santa Monica. So I went and got it and lived on it for as long as I could, set myself up in my little shop, but eventually it began to run out . . . so I worked up my courage and went to Kay Roth.

"She was such an *artiste,* such a sensitive lady, she was calm and understanding. She heard me out and then took my hand in hers—Kay Roth!—and she asked me if she could help me in any way. There was never any hint of blackmail, not a hint." She brushed mist away from her face, rings gleaming. Challis put his arm around Morgan and held her back out of the rain, which was blowing harder again. Tully Hacker's face was streaming wet, but he couldn't seem to take his eyes off Priscilla Morpeth.

"I asked her if she could find me a job, I'd have done anything, domestic work—Herbert could have given

283

me lessons, you know—or maybe something at the studio, but she wouldn't hear of anything like that. She said I had my own calling . . . do you know what kind of woman Kay Roth was? She said she would rather invest in my little shop, as a sort of silent partner, and she explained some tax aspects, and . . . well, she decided to do that her own way, sending me checks, and, well, I insisted on at least doing her charts. And when Mrs. Roth died, I went to her daughter, Goldie, the one that got murdered, poor thing, by her husband it was, and she was a strange one . . . she was so interested in everything, was always asking me questions about Morty and the letter, and I never could understand it exactly, but she was like her mother, they both just sort of accepted what Aaron had done to Morty. I couldn't fathom it at first, but then I saw it the way Morty did, the way they did, it was just a part of *our* lives, it was all in our family and was nobody else's business." Her eyes flashed at them, head cocked, in a world of her own. But it was the world they all belonged in, and it all made sense. "But in the end, Goldie got murdered . . . and the thing was, she'd told me about Mr. Donovan and his magazine, she thought I could maybe write an astrology column for his magazine, and he said okay, I was doing some columns—that was why you saw me in his office—and I was doing his charts, too, and I told him he was surrounded by death and danger, I *saw* it, and now he's dead and I don't suppose I'll be writing the column now . . . but I'll survive, I have my regular clientele now, I'll be all right, I don't need a lot of money . . . I never have."

She turned away, leaning against the wall, staring out over the domain she had just been at such pains to describe. From the look of her head, the angle of the thick, caped form, it was obvious that they had been dismissed, that she was communing again as if they had never been there. Challis looked at Morgan, then at Tully. The story was registering, but the reactions were masked. Even his own reaction to the fact that Aaron had murdered Morty Morpeth was imprecise, confused. His brain was trying to tie up the connections, read the final report, but there was precious data missing. . . .

They began to descend the clinging stairway. The shelter ended and the rain was driving again. Then they heard her call, and when Challis looked back, she was pointing at him—an eerie, dramatic gesture from an old movie.

"You," she called, "whoever you are, be careful . . . I tell you what I told Jack Donovan—you heard what I said. Death, it's all around you, past, present, future, it's part of you."

Then she whirled away and moved out of sight around the curve of the white building.

[29]

CHALLIS HAD never seen Herbert Graydon flustered, but he was somewhat the worse for wear when he bustled into the foyer, drawn by the sound of Tully Hacker's key in the lock. Herbert slid his hand through the straight gray hair usually flattened against his huge skull and left it spiked off in all directions. He was pale, and the worry in his eyes was real. He wanted to know what was going on, and Tully suggested that he tell them what, indeed, was going on.

"Aaron got home a while ago, he'd had an accident out on the Pacific Coast Highway, ran the Corniche into a barricade at one of the mudslides—he said he skidded on the wet. Weed's attending to the car, but Aaron hit the steering wheel with his head . . . blood all over his forehead from a cut, a bloody nose, glasses all bent . . . he came in acting like a madman, crying and staggering—shock, I suppose it must be shock . . ." His voice trailed off.

"Where is he now, Herbert?" Tully said.

"He and Solomon are in the billiard room—no, there's no use trying to get in, they've locked the door and we have no keys." He looked at Challis and Morgan. "What's happening, what—"

"We've just seen Priscilla," Challis said. "We've had a very busy day."

"Herbert," Morgan said, "you didn't tell us about the letter."

"Letter? I don't understand, miss."

"The letter Morty gave you to give Priscilla."

"My goodness, the letter! I haven't thought about it . . . why, there was so much going on, identifying the body, taking care of Prissy . . . I completely forgot about the letter. But what difference does it make?"

"A big difference," Tully said, heading across the

foyer toward the hallway. "The television room," he said. "Come on."

They followed him to the door two past Herbert's. Tully unlocked it and they went in. The small room was windowless, filled with a faint blue glow and a console of five twelve-inch television screens mounted in the wall above the flatbed of controls. Tully bent over the switches and dials. Challis sank onto a small chair. Screen number one—all were black and white—showed the front door through which they had just come: the camera lens was shooting through a plate of glass that was rain-spattered. Nothing was happening at the front door. Screen number two: the hot tub at the bottom of the terraces, lifeless, with steam visibly rising like ghosts from the shifting surface of the water. Screen number three: the long room with the glass wall and the fire burning in the huge fireplace, casting the only light in the empty room. Screen number four: another outdoor camera, this one panning slowly along the edges of the property; as Challis watched, the dinosaurs, standing stock-still as if listening for a peculiar, unexpected sound to come again, came into view. Challis blinked the tension out of his eyes. Screen number five: the upstairs library, where Daffodil Roth lay sprawled on a couch reading a thick book and sipping what looked like straight bourbon from a tall glass. There was a bottle of Wild Turkey on the table at her side. She looked soft in a white robe, a little drunk, her bare foot tapping the arm of the couch. Challis couldn't look at her without feeling a pang, a note of desire, a wish to have it all go back the way it had been, however bad it had been.

"Sound," Tully muttered to himself. Suddenly they heard Tom Waits' recording of "Grapefruit Moon." "That's the library," he said. "Every night she listens to that guy, hour after hour." He punched another button, and the image of the front door disappeared, replaced by what was obviously the billiard room. "Okay," he said to himself, "now for some sound . . ."

The camera took in the entire room from one end, and there, in a sharp black-and-white picture, were Sol and Aaron. They were standing by the billiard table in the foreground. In the middle distance there

287

was a leather couch, a couple of leather club chairs, and beyond that yet another fireplace. Aaron was disheveled, dabbing at his nose. There was a streak of blood on his forehead, and his entire face looked like a piece of bruised fruit. His tie hung loose, like a dead animal, and his shirt was blotched. In contrast, Solomon Roth was wearing a dinner jacket, looked immaculate, as unlike the maundering old man at the studio that afternoon as possible.

"My God," Challis said. "Sol's a new man."

"Yeah," Tully said, "that's the work of Dr. Feelgood . . . when the old man starts to run down, really run down like you saw him this afternoon, the good doctor pumps him full of snake oil, and presto chango, what you see before you . . ."

Sol stroked the ball, and they heard the clicks as it made its rounds. Aaron sighed, head down. His shoulders quivered. The camera panning the perimeters of the property was on a time lock and had stopped at the dinosaurs, who stood, like the four people in the control room, for the next act to begin. Daffy sipped, turned the page. She was reading the Modern Library edition of *The Red and the Black*.

"Shame on you, Aaron," Sol said, carefully lining up his next shot. "You have lied to me, Aaron"—click-click-click—"and I am deeply unhappy that you would do that. But, but, but . . . I understand why you did it. And as for me, I was blind, or insensitive, or self-deceiving, or all three, and I avoided the truth with all my power . . ." Click-click. Aaron's dabbing had stopped, and one eye was watching his father from behind the crumpled, bloody handkerchief. "Yes, I refused to see what was going on around me, I couldn't believe I could be touched by all the rot and corruption I saw out there." Click-click.

"Father, what in the name of God are you talking about?" The round spectacles sat crookedly on the hooked nose. Aaron's face seemed to be working its way around the pain and the words in an attempt to hold itself together. It was a near thing. If the last bits of composure went, Challis had the feeling that Aaron would go too. "Look at me, look what's hap-

288

pened to me . . . what are you going on about? We've
got to do something about *me*."

"Now, now, calm yourself, that's just what we're
going to do. But I've got to get clear about this lying
business . . . you lied to me about your poor wife's
diaries, Kay's diaries. You told me that they told the
whole sordid truth about Kay . . . and now what do
I discover? That they tell the truth about you, what
you did to her, what you drove the poor woman to—"

"Oh, for the love of God, make sense! What difference do the diaries make to anybody now?" Aaron
was losing the struggle: he was squeezing the edge of
the ornately carved billiard table like a man hanging
from a twentieth-floor window ledge.

"To begin with, my son, a million dollars' worth
of difference . . . to save your neck, not to save us
from the publication of Kay's calamitous indiscre-
tions." He was surveying the table, looking from side
to side in search of the right shot, refusing to look at
Aaron, whose voice was growing increasingly strident.

"You're a crazy old man," Aaron shouted, his voice
catching helplessly in his collapsed nasal passages.

"Careful," Solomon Roth said. Sol stroked the ball
again and watched the result, which was out of camera
range.

He stood the cue on the floor before himself, and
leaned on it with a fraction of his weight. The crocodile
smile lay in wait for Aaron. Towser looked up from
the far end of the room, stared at the scene. "You
see, you convinced me that not only was Kay reaching from beyond the grave to dirty our lives, but that
your daughter was just like her . . . two of a kind,
filthy, depraved sluts, an insult to everything my life
has stood for, everything I wanted Maximus to be. Kay
was dead, and we could buy Donovan off for a million . . . but I knew we couldn't trust Goldie—she'd
never keep her part of the bargain, not for a million,
not for anything . . . she hated you that much . . . but
what you had me believing was a lie, Goldie didn't hate
you *blindly,* it wasn't in her blood . . . she *knew* what
you had done to her mother, she had *read* the diaries,
and unlike old Solomon Roth, she wasn't operating on
the basis of hearsay, of your lies. . . . What I'm trying

289

to make clear to you, Aaron, is this—if I'd known the truth you kept from me, I would have looked at Goldie differently . . . I would have gone to Malibu that night to talk with her . . . *not to kill her!"*

For an instant Challis thought he was going to faint; he held on to the metal flatbed, closed his eyes: he was standing in the beach house, Goldie was dead at his feet, there was sand on the floor . . . something moved somewhere, a shape . . . he heard footsteps outside, saw a shadow—Solomon Roth. Morgan stood beside him, he felt her, smelled her, and he pressed the side of his face against her. But he couldn't keep his eyes from the monitor.

Aaron's mouth was open, gulping like a fish. He staggered back as if he'd received a physical blow. He couldn't stop the blood running from his nose. The handkerchief was dark with it.

"You," Aaron croaked. "You . . . and all the time I thought it was Toby! Yes, I really did, and I didn't blame him for killing her." He was almost talking to himself. "One too many beach boys, and Toby got a bellyful and hit her with the Oscar." He looked at Sol, squinting. "You . . ."

Sol turned his broad back on him, and measured another shot, drew the cue back slowly, and slid it through. Click-click. Challis heard Tully's breathing. Herbert bit a fingernail. Nobody moved.

"Please, Father, stop that." Aaron moved forward jerkily, as if his physiology was coming undone. His voice slipped on the scale, wavered upward, like a drunken whore in high heels. "Don't you understand what's happening tonight? Listen to me, god damn you . . . *listen to me!"*

Sol sighted along the trajectory of another shot.

Aaron suddenly flew at his father, fingers curled in a pathetic birdlike attack, a high-pitched howl sounding tinny. The fingers were raking the black dinner jacket weakly and uselessly, when Sol turned slowly, raised the cue deliberately, impassively, and smashed it across Aaron's arm and chest. The shock cut his cry in midair, killed it, and the round spectacles smashed on the edge of the table. Aaron clutched his arm, weaved backward.

"Don't ever touch me again, or come near me, or speak my name." The words hit him like slugs, each one driving him away from the camera. Towser pricked his ears. Aaron groped behind him, reached the couch in the center of the room. "You made me go to Malibu that night . . . you have no respect for life, for decency, for anything that matters." He took a few heavy strides toward his son. Glass from Aaron's spectacles crackled underfoot. Aaron stumbled, slipped, fell backward onto the couch. The television console gave off a slight whirring sound, a dry claustrophobic warmth mingling with the heat of their bodies. Challis' face felt greasy with perspiration. His stomach turned as he watched Solomon Roth's broad back as he advanced toward what was left of his son.

"Listen to me," Aaron cried, his hands up to ward off any more blows. "You're not the only one who has killed, Father . . . listen to me, I've killed too, I'm a murderer—"

"You contemptible coward!" Solomon Roth seemed to be gathering strength as the ordeal went on. "What are you talking about? You drive people to their death, but you can't commit the act yourself." He had built up to the final charge, the accusation of impotence and cowardice, and he stood looking down at Aaron.

"But I did, I did . . . I killed . . ."

Oh, God, here it comes, old Morty dragged out again. But Challis' mind was swirling, Goldie falling gently downward, hair like taffy, falling in layers, again, again, blood in her hair. It had been Solomon Roth. Oh, God . . . what was Aaron saying? What was that. . . ?

"I killed Jack Donovan." Aaron was sobbing, talking from between clenched teeth. "I had to kill him, I had to get the diaries . . . everything depended on . . . the diaries. Ah, Father, my God, he didn't have them, he didn't have them. I killed him, though, I can still hear it, my God, the noise . . . ."

Morgan gasped, and Tully Hacker squeezed his temples, their eyes never leaving the small black-and-white images.

"You killed Jack Donovan?" Solomon's voice rumbled in the stillness. "You pulled the trigger?" Aaron

291

whimpered, struggled to right himself in the couch, a terrified child of almost sixty. "You must be insane."

"Are *you* insane?" Aaron said.

"But why? Why Donovan? You knew he knew what was in the diaries . . . what was really in the diaries, and not just what you told me."

"Oh, no, he knew more . . . he told me a million wasn't enough, he told me he knew about the checks, what they really meant . . . he said he was going to take it all to Vito—"

"You make no sense," Solomon Roth said.

Aaron struggled to sound calm, but he only sounded demented.

"Oh, but I do make sense. Goldie had told Jack all about the checks, about Priscilla's letter, the whole story." He looked at his watch, shook his head spastically. "I don't know what to do, I've got to find Priscilla." He wiped at the leftover tears, straightened up. But his voice was all wrong; he sounded as if he were a child talking to a child. It was grotesque. "You see, Father, Priscilla's got the letter that proves it . . . proves I killed Morty Morpeth . . . the letter, and all the checks paying off Priscilla, that adds up to enough to convict me—but I had to kill Morty, because he might have gone to you and told you about the money . . . you can see that. I had to have the money, I'd gotten in so deep with Vito back in New York, gambling, I didn't have a choice."

"Go on, Aaron," Solomon said slowly. "You're telling me that you're the one who stole the money from Maximus thirty years ago—it wasn't the little accountant, after all . . ."

"And I had to kill him—I mean, what else could I do? He was the only one who knew what we'd done, and I couldn't run the risk of your ever finding out . . . why, my God, you'd have run me out of town . . . or worse! So, I killed him. . . ."

"But now I have found out, Aaron. I've found out that you stole from me, lied to me, drove your first wife to her death . . . after using her to satisfy Laggiardi's sexual needs."

"What? How did you—"

292

"I've found out that you planted the seeds of my hatred for Goldie," Solomon Roth said, taking a cigar from a box and clipping the end with a gold cutter. He sniffed the cigar, rolled it on his tongue. "You made me believe that she had to die for being the kind of person she was." He was measuring his thoughts, building some sort of case in his own mind. He lit the cigar with a wooden match, taking his time. He waved the match out, left a string of smoke hanging in the air. "You made it necessary for me to accept vermin like Laggiardi into my studio . . . *my studio* . . . and you have pointlessly murdered the Irishman—pointlessly, since he didn't have the diaries and since I've found out the truth anyway." He put his hands in his jacket pockets, stepped back, and looked down at his son, who twitched nervously, dabbing at the blood, straightening his dirty tie. "And you have made the fatal mistake of misreading me, of reaching the irrational conclusion that I am somehow like you because I have faced the need to murder. Well, Aaron, I am not like you, I am not lost and desperate and weak. No, and I do not accept the responsibility for the ridiculous, grotesque creature you have somehow become."

"Father!" The cry of anguish seemed prehuman, elemental.

"Do you have the gun you killed Donovan with? The one you'd have used on Priscilla Morpeth? . . . Answer me!"

"Yes, yes . . ." He fumbled in his coat pocket.

"My God, you're such a hopeless imbecile. If you'd killed her, the letter you're so afraid of would undoubtedly have gone to the police. . . . Do you have the gun?"

"Yes, yes, here it is." He held up the black weapon, difficult to make out on the small screen.

"All right, Aaron. You alone have the power to end all this." He turned his back on Aaron, walked toward the locked door and passed just out of the camera's range. "Do it . . . and rest assured, I'll see your mess is cleaned up. . . . Come, Towser." The room was quiet. Towser got up wearily and ambled on toward Solomon Roth, out of the picture. The door locks rattled briefly, the door clicked shut.

Tully Hacker reached out, hit another button. The hallway outside the billiard room popped onto one screen. Solomon Roth stood in the shadowy darkness, stared at the door for a moment, then began walking slowly toward the camera with Towser in step beside him.

Aaron Roth sat quietly on the couch. He wiped his eyes with his handkerchief and gingerly tried to blow his nose, gave it up, threw the splotchy cloth on the floor. With his free hand he scratched his head. He sat up, gave a deep sigh, straightened his shoulders. His other hand came up quickly with the gun in it. Morgan screamed: *"Oh, no!"* Aaron pushed the gun barrel into his mouth, blew most of his head off, fell backward on the couch. Blood spattered backward, and the slug, having removed the back of Aaron's head, still had enough power to smash the aquarium behind the couch. The glass exploded, water rushed out over Aaron and the couch. Morgan was crying.

Tully and Herbert Graydon pushed past her and ran across the foyer and down the dimly lit hall toward the billiard room. Solomon Roth turned and watched them reach the door, go inside. Solomon strode calmly toward Challis and Morgan.

"You saw the performance?" Sol asked. The smell of cigar smoke filled the narrow corridor.

Challis nodded. Morgan sagged against him.

"The world is a better place without him," the old man said calmly. "Failing health, pressure of work, suicide . . . Don't waste your sorrow on my son. Toby, time really is running out for you—my offer stands, we can get you away and I can keep this under control here. With Tully's help. He'll see me through it, he always gets us through things. But I'm afraid you're still in the soup. Aside from the fact that no one could ever prove that I killed Goldie, I was being absolutely accurate in there with Aaron. I went to the beach house that night with the intention of killing Goldie . . . the gatekeeper let me in, but I got him the job, he used to be at Maximus, and there's nothing that could make him place me there—but the point is, I didn't kill her, she was already dead when I got there. I was a wee bit late."

Challis said, "Solomon, are you *human?* At all?"

"Don't be tiresome and philosophical, Tobias. Ask my doctor . . . I'm not altogether sure, some days I feel quite human, other days I'm much better. Now, if you'll excuse me, I must go inform Daffy of Aaron's suicide—oh, you look so shocked, Tobias. You think I have no feelings, is that it? Well, in Aaron's case you're wrong . . . I do have feelings. Now I feel an overwhelming sense of relief. He was a terrible man. Please excuse me." He bowed slightly, nodded, and went up the stairway from the foyer to the second floor. His step was almost jaunty.

Tully was coming back down the hall, Herbert Graydon in his wake. Tully's face was hard, impassive, but he gave a grim little grin. "Jesus," he said. "What a mess. Goddamn gasping little fish all over the floor. You two had better get out of here. Herbert and I were having a brandy in his room when we heard the shot, we ran down the hall, found him already dead . . . I've got to report it right now."

"All right," Challis said. "You know what you're doing."

"I surely do. Now, hit the road. Are you going—"

"He's coming back with me," Morgan said.

"You know you're just about out of time, Toby."

"I know. I don't know what to do—I thought Aaron killed Goldie, then Sol . . . now Sol tells me he meant to kill her, but she was already dead." Challis rubbed his tired eyes. Tully Hacker was blurred before him. "I don't know what to do."

"You know what Sol has said all along."

"But who killed Goldie?"

"You're the only man left on earth who cares."

Tully walked them across the foyer, out to the Mustang.

"I don't understand Sol," Challis said. "What I saw in there, it's not human, Tully." Morgan was in the car, head back, eyes closed.

"It's the good doctor, that's all. He's got Sol running on high octane. Go get some sleep. Tomorrow's your day, one way or the other."

In the rearview mirror Challis saw the lights going on in the house. Then the grasping shrubbery closed around the car. By the time they got down to the Bel Air gate, the police car was coming in.

[30]

TOGETHER, thinking almost as a single organism, operating on that simple, driven level, they sought sex as a way of proving to themselves that they were still alive, awake, hopeful. Too tired to speak: sex without words, a mutual need to engulf one another. The exhaustion, the tension, the shock, all they had been through together with time imploding, collapsing on them, everything worked changes in their personalities which had been held back, against their natures. They *were* glad to be alive, whatever the future held.

In Challis' mind, mingling with the touch and smell and sounds of her damp, freshly bathed body and soft, throaty moans, were the afterimages of the night . . . the jerking, dying men on the rainy beach, Tully Hacker coming toward him out of darkness, the sound-proofing of wind and surf and fear which made it all unreal, like a movie . . . Priscilla Morpeth in her cape, with her jewelry and pointy nose and clicking-bright eyes, clinging to the parapet like a miniature Orson Welles at Elsinore . . . the disintegration of Aaron Roth and the impassivity of Solomon Roth, the old man's science-fiction recovery from the senility of the afternoon, his emergence in the evening as something the likes of which Challis could only associate with the old movies offering a villain who fluttered through the window as a bat.

Morgan's passion was almost out of control, desperate and uninhibited and vulnerable, weeping, then urging him on with animal cries. She twisted her long solid body, turned and groped the air with hooked fingers; she ground her teeth, eyes closed, driving against him, working out all the frustration and built-up heat with the strength of her firm, long muscles and the weight of her body. Rain drummed on the roof, their mouths slid wetly across their bodies, fingertips stroked, penetrated, stroked, and he emptied himself into her once, then again . . . and finally, smeared with sweat and tears and semen and saliva and her wetness, they lay quiet and uncovered, the bedclothes tangled and kicked aside, and their naked flesh grew cold in the dark. She curled against him, half-asleep. "I love you," she murmured, pushing her hips against his thighs, making him stiffen again, spreading herself again with the long fingers, drawing him inside yet again. . . .

Was it a dream? Or was he awake, mind drifting in sexually induced hallucination? Was it still the sweat from her breast and belly clinging to him, or had he begun sweating again? He heard her breathing as he lay on his back staring at the ceiling of her bedroom, smelling the rich, dark aroma of her sex, tasting her on his tongue. One of her long legs, a pale, languid river, was flung across a rope of sheet, carelessly, elegantly, like a kinky ad in *Vogue,* and a small white breast was visible beneath her arm. He watched her, the tiny pink nipple erect, rising in a series of delicate terraces like a pyramid; he leaned across, moved his tongue across the pyramid, tasted the saltiness, smiled to himself at the thought of the things you could live for. But the woman in the cape, the lumpy figure on the parapet, watched him from the forefront of his memory, withdrew the passion from him like blood into a syringe . . . past, present, and future, she knew it all, or so she said, past and present and future . . . and he'd been surrounded by death, she'd seen that clearly enough, and she'd had no idea who he was . . . she'd seen all the death, with him moving through it. He lay back on the bed, his brain too busy to sleep but much too worn down to stay alert.

The rifle shots woke him.

It was dark, still raining, and somebody was shooting at something. It sounded like the crack of a .22, snapping at him from his childhood.

He got out of bed; it was nearly five o'clock, but dark as the dead of night outside. Morgan was stretched the length of the bed, lying naked on her belly. He stood beside her, rested his hand on the swell of her hip, listened: nothing. No more shots. He put on his pants, walked out into the living room, hearing the rain. He went across to the sliding glass door, stopped again. He felt something: maybe it was the wind hitting the huge pane of glass; he fancied he saw the ripple.

He opened the door, stepped barefoot onto the wet patio.

The next shot sounded closer, and he flinched.

He moved to the far end of the patio near the low shrubs and the squat pines, stepped out onto the wet grass, felt the rain soaking him.

At the edge of the property he stared out into the canyon void. A man was shouting not far away . . . lights suddenly flared in a house cantilevered on stilts out over the canyon . . . another shot exploded and he heard the man in the house yelling, a voice but no words came through the curtain of wind and rain . . . then a rumbling, tearing sound, the ripping out of deep roots . . . another shot . . . he watched the house on stilts begin to sag. One stilt swayed, broke loose from its concrete mooring, swung loose from the bottom of the house, slipped away . . . the corner of the house slowly twisted downward, the canyon wall beneath the house began to move in the shadows cast from the lights burning above . . . the side of the canyon was sliding, moving faster, with a rush of trees, shrubs, rocks . . . he heard it and saw it . . . a second stilt bent loose and the house tilted dramatically backward . . . suddenly it came loose, the lights went out, and in the glow from the other houses clinging to the canyon rim the house was launched downward, moving in an almost stately fashion like an ocean liner sliding down the runners . . . it came apart slowly, kindling, bricks, metal supports, red tiles, furniture bursting through glass walls . . . Challis heard another shot . . . this time it came from closer, off to the right on his side of the canyon . . . afraid, he ran back into the house.

Morgan was already up, standing naked in the living room, holding a pair of jeans, listening. She held up

her hand, motioning him not to speak. Her breasts were
high and small, the nipples pointing downward and
to the sides of her rib cage as she leaned forward,
slipped the jeans on. Finally, in the stillness, she went
to the sliding door, stopped at the sound of sudden
shouts that flared up, then faded away. Two more shots
cracked, seemed to come from next door.

"Jesus Christ," she said softly, and went outside.

The night had come alive.

One after another the houses strung along the rim
were lit up, and shouts mingled with the rain, wind,
and gunfire. Sirens screamed on Sunset Boulevard, red
lights were flashing on the twisting canyon road below
them.

"Who's doing the shooting?" He'd joined her outside, slipping and falling on the wet grass. He heard
the rumbling noise, felt a tremor deep in the earth.
Morgan was running toward the shed at the back of
the lawn beyond the pool. The shots came again,
and the house next to them on the right—it had no
lawn, rested in air on stilts—began to go. The same
awful tearing sounds he'd heard before came again . . .
the house went quickly and Morgan turned halfway
along the length of the pool, stopped. Ahead of her,
the large pine beside the shed began to lean toward
emptiness.

"Come back," he called, moving toward her. "Everything's going."

She saw the tree going and ran back toward Challis.

The tree went over like a twig, and the lawn began
to disappear. The shed slid away in a matter of
seconds, was gone. The gunman had reached them, and
Challis stifled a scream as two shots seemed to crack
at the edge of the pool.

"Somebody's shooting at us," he yelled again, grabbing her, pulling her toward the patio.

"No, no," she said. "It's the gas lines breaking as
the hills slide away . . . they explode."

"Good God . . ."

As they reached the patio, she stopped him. At the
far end of what was left of the lawn, the swimming
pool grew an enormous jagged crack and broke off,
the water rushing like a miniature cataract, a tidal

wave pouring down with the sliding mud . . . and then, as quickly as it had started, it moved on, wiping away what lay next door.

She turned and clung to him, shaking, her naked breasts wet and cold and hard, flattened against his chest.

Seven o'clock, a wet gray morning. The canyon, in the aftermath of its collapse, looked like a battlefield, fog and steam rising from the mounds of mud, broken water and sewage pipes, all the bricks and kindling and I-beams, concrete boulders and slabs that had been swimming pools only hours before, the odd pink plastic flamingo, bits and pieces of palm trees . . . somewhere down there, Morgan's shed reduced to rubble, buried.

There was no electricity in the house. Morgan sat at the kitchen table drinking yesterday's cold coffee. A sense of immediate, desolate loneliness in the house. A wet breeze lapped at the windows. Challis stared into her eyes for a while, went to the bedroom to get dressed. The sheets bore the evidence of their love-making. The room still smelled of sex. He cleaned up and went back to the kitchen. Morgan looked up and forced a tiny smile.

"I feel like I've been sliding down the canyon for a week," she said. "Crash . . . finally at rest, time to dig my way out." She shrugged. "Don't say anything about last night. It was good, no more to say for now. What are you going to do, Toby?"

"I've got some people to see, last-hurrah bullshit. I insist on saying something about last night, by the way." He sipped the cold coffee and made a face. "I was safer in jail than I've been since I escaped. Last night the whole world gave way—"

"That's what you have to say about last night?"

"No. Being with you . . . being together like that, did it mean anything to you?"

"What a question!"

"Well . . ."

"Yes, it meant a great deal to me, Toby."

"Well, it meant more to me than I can tell you—

301

or than you can imagine. You're part of my life now, Morgan, you always will be. But . . ."

"You have got to get away. There aren't going to be any answers, there never are any big answers—only questions. You just have to keep going . . . in your case, going far away. Goldie's dead and we're not going to find out who killed her. It just doesn't matter anymore . . . don't keep struggling, things only keep getting worse and worse, Toby."

"I know," he said, nodding slowly. "But it's hard to accept not finding out . . . all these lives have come apart because I had to find out. I could have just gotten away, taken any of those offers . . . my God. But I've felt so close to the answer, as if I had the key to it and didn't know how to use it."

"There's no time left, you know. Listen, Toby, I told you that I love you. I'm not even sure that it's true, I'm not sure of much of anything anymore, but I'm a victim of what you've gone through, we've shared the ordeal . . . and I'm closer to you than I've ever been to anyone, and love is part of it, maybe. I can't let you go back to prison—I've got to have the hope that there's something ahead of us, *for* us."

"I'm going now," he said. "I've got to go. You'll hear from me, one way or another."

At the door she couldn't look at him.

"Morgan, remember this. I love you."

"Good-bye, Tobias."

He kissed her forehead.

When he got into the Mustang, he didn't look back. Once again he was the invisible man.

The Pacific Coast Highway ran wet and clean once he had gotten past the mountains of mud. The sun hitting the paving made it look like gleaming metal. He squinted against the glare. Sunlight brought out the emerald green in the vegetation, the long grasses on his left, the thick grass moving up the hillsides. He heard the birds sing. For the moment, and for the first time in a long time, life seemed simple. The difference between winning and giving up had turned out to be minimal, at best.

He passed the road leading down to the beach where

Tully had wiped out Laggiardi's army: it was quiet, undisturbed, and he wasn't even mildly curious. Let it be, let it be . . . as far as he knew, there were stiffs all over the beach with gulls breakfasting on eyeballs. It didn't make any difference, not anymore. It was all over now. Aaron, Donovan, Goldie, Morty . . . He was still alive and he wasn't quite sure what mattered anymore, only what didn't.

The trailer court was bright and clean and shabby. The same old guy nodded hello, asked what the hell was going on last night. Nothing, Challis told him, just a family reunion, everybody looking for Aunt Priscilla. And now you're back, the old guy said. Right, now I'm back.

She was out weeding her flowerbeds, wearing a floppy old hat, a ragged sweater with leather buttons, a billowing plaid skirt. She didn't look dramatic or ominous. She looked up from beneath the floppy hat, winked, shook her head.

"Oh, it's you, young man. I knew you'd turn up—d'you believe me? Well, no matter. I knew."

"Sure," Challis said. "You know the past, present, future."

"Mmmm." She got up from her knees, dropped a trowel into the pocket of her skirt. "Cuppa tea?"

He followed her into the neat little trailer home and sat in a threadbare overstuffed chair. She brought him tea and settled down at her tiny kitchen table, watching him, smiling.

"Well, Priscilla"—he sighed—"do your stuff. . . ."

My dearest Morgan,

See, it's just like the movies. A letter in the mailbox, nervous fingers fumbling in a close-up, paper tearing, then the magical movie words we know and love: "by the time you read this, I'll be gone." I'm unsure of myself, not at all sure if I know how to tell you this, because I'm not at all sure I understand it myself—no, I'm bullshitting you there. I understand it all just fine, and I'm having trouble with this because I don't know what your reaction will be. Sorry. I'm a fainthearted, cowardly son of a bitch.

303

All I ever really wanted was the identity of Goldie's killer. Remember? That almost got lost in the scuffle. It seems a million years ago, but there you are. So you saw it through with me, coming at the question of Goldie from any angle at all—the family, business associates, gangsters. The oddities kept coming up. Well, I'm responsible for digging up a lot of trouble and I don't know that anything is better now, but what's worse is pretty fucking obvious. But then, I'm no moralist, not anymore.

But even through the horror of yesterday and last night, I never seemed to get any closer to Goldie's killer. I was the only one who really cared, who really wanted the answer, who thought it was important at all.

I couldn't leave it alone, of course. I was the one who'd been convicted of murdering her and gotten his ass thrown in jail. I was the one who'd known her best, had been through so much of life with her—I don't know what she meant to me, if much of anything anymore, but our lives were intertwined for better or worse. . . . Worse, as it turned out. I had to have the answer. I owed that to Goldie. Which was why I chose to follow up on what she seemed to have on Aaron. It was all of a piece, what Goldie was doing, what I was determined to finish for her. . . . Obligation. That's what I felt I had, what I owed her.

But when I analyzed the situation I always came back to the prime question: what could I do about it? I had been there the night she was murdered. They had found me standing over her body, for God's sake. Blood everywhere, her skull smashed in, blood on the heavy base I'd had the Oscar mounted on. I was the obvious candidate for the big fall, and they saw to it that I took it.

My own memory of the night was cloudy. Aaron had said a beach boy had killed her, one pickup too many, and that hit a nerve in me—there was something like that stuck in the back of my memory, a clue; then I began to see it in my sleep, the murder night, I began to see it in my sleep . . . sandy footprints, that's what began it . . . it sounds stupid, but I saw them in my sleep, there they were, sandy footprints in the hallway of the beach house. And I thought that I could see the man who made them . . . a Chicano beach boy, strong, perfectly muscled, just the kind of trinket Goldie was so devoted to collecting.

Maybe Aaron was right. A beach boy, a drifter, a male prostitute—they particularly turned her on. She used to say, "I'm going to buy myself a stiff young cock tonight, Toby," stuff like that, and she'd laugh deep in her throat. Aaron's theory made awfully good sense, it fit with those weird incomplete, patchy memories that kept visiting me by night—why shouldn't she have picked out the wrong boy and been killed by him?

But the memories kept jumping at me from the dark. I kept remembering sounds I'd heard on the porch that night, sounds of someone moving around out there, bumping into things, but it was all so confused. It was the time element that did me in—I couldn't remember how long I stood there looking at Goldie's dead body and hearing the sounds on the porch and seeing the sandy, wet footprints on the floor. . . .

Well, now we know the sounds were made by Sol. He saw the whole thing, he saw the murder committed, and he realized that his intention to kill Goldie had been carried out by a sort of deus ex machina . . . but why, I wondered, would the old bastard let me go to prison when he knew the truth? And why wouldn't he just tell me who killed her?

Yesterday—last night—I was very moved by that thunder-and-lightning meeting with Priscilla Morpeth. Maybe her unreality made me feel a bond with her . . . or maybe it was because she had such a strong reaction to me when she saw me at the observatory—she didn't know who the hell I was, but she seemed to know something about me, to see something about me. So, this morning, after your hillside had collapsed and buried those goddamn stupid diaries forever, I went to her, back to the trailer park.

The crazy thing was, she was expecting me! I told her who I was, and we spent the morning sitting in her trailer, drinking tea, talking. She fed me homemade doughnuts, mothered me in a weird way. And together we remembered what happened that night at the beach house. . . . I listened to her voice, Morgan, and it began to come clear to me.

Who killed Goldie?

Priscilla knew everything. Past, present, future. She cleared away the fog in my mind. I began to remember what happened that night. . . .

For a start, at least, Aaron had been right in his assumption. There had been a beach boy. He had been there when I arrived, though I didn't know it. Poor silly bastard, I arrived on time for my dinner with Goldie, full of hope and wondering if I should have brought flowers and a box of chocolates. She'd sounded good on the phone, warm and friendly and hyper, and I went to Malibu in a fine mood. She still had that effect on me: I always responded to her when she chose to treat me with anything approaching decency and civility, no matter how many times I'd been taught a lesson. I had the idea that I might not be leaving until morning. No excuses.

I knocked at the door, smelled the sea and a wood fire. No answer. So I went inside. There was music coming from somewhere, a bossa nova, the kind of music she'd always put on when we were spending an evening devoted to sex. I made the connection . . . Christ. I called her name. The wind was blowing the curtains. It was dim, lit mainly from the fireplace, but I could see wet sandy footprints in the hallway. Astrud Gilberto and Stan Getz on the record player. I called her name again. The hallway was dark. I heard a noise at the end of the hallway, and I stood waiting, listening. Then she came out of the darkness toward me, her shape curved and smelling like a good time . . . she had a long sweater on, baggy, down around her hips, and her legs were bare. She was humming the song, she didn't say anything, just kept coming toward me, and I knew I'd been right about the night, about her mood. She came into my arms.

I kissed her and there was something wrong. She began to laugh and shake, she leaned back away from me, laughing. I tasted a man in her mouth, there was no doubt about that, and I ran to the sink in the kitchen, gagging and spitting it out of my mouth, listening to her laugh. She turned the light on, and when I looked at her, I saw she had that crazy glazed look she'd have when the dope and the sex and the rest of it all got to her. Her legs were still sweaty and her hair was plastered down with sweat, and she couldn't stop laughing at me. Then I sensed something else, another sound, and the beach boy came down the hallway . . . he was kind of slow and tentative, he was naked, obviously groggy and confused at being interrupted in the middle of his performance.

The next thing I knew—and now I remember it with total clarity—the boy was running, stark naked, back down the hallway. I heard the door slam and I made a charge at Goldie, knocked her backward against my desk. She couldn't stop laughing, it was the laughing that did it, pushed me all the way. . . .

I took the Oscar and stopped the laughter for good. That was what Solomon Roth saw from the deck. That was what I couldn't bring myself to remember.

He folded the letter, put it into an envelope, and sat staring out at the Pacific breaking across the sand, slapping the pilings. The sun was working hard and the gulls slid like shadows over the surf. Behind him Sunset Boulevard began its winding ascent inland from the Pacific Coast Highway. He had been sitting on the windblown deck with the Boston ferns and the sunshine. The tall blond girl came to replenish

307

the wine. She looked up at the sun and took a deep breath. She was extraordinarily beautiful, a California girl, the current model.

"This kind of day," she said. "Wow! Makes you glad to be alive."

"Lots of damage out here. They're closed next door—"

"Right, yeah, but you know California." She smiled. Her teeth were so white in the tanned face it made him want to cry. Goldie's face had looked like that once. "People just keep coming back, y'know. You just gotta go for it . . . and then you get a day like this and what the heck, y'know?"

He finished his Chablis and went inside to the pay telephone, dialed. He heard the familiar voice at the other end.

"Herbert," he said. "This is Toby. Give Tully the word. I'm ready."

He left the restaurant and drove into Santa Monica. The schoolyard was empty. A girl of twenty or so in running shorts and a sweatshirt was shooting baskets. Challis stood under an oak tree and waited, smoked a cigarette, watched. She was a good shot, tall and lean. A gym teacher. He had been waiting for about twenty minutes when the kids came piling out for recess. He saw Ralph right away, surrounded by a group of his protégés. Challis hadn't planned to force any contact; he'd just wanted to see the boy again. In the sunlight and the balmy weather, on a playground full of kids, Ralph seemed younger. Challis was about to leave when Ralph detached himself from the kids trading baseball cards and strolled toward him.

"Hi, Ralph." He nodded. "It's me."

"Bandersnatch," the boy said softly, huge eyes widening, a grin pushing gently at the corners of his mouth. "I saw you but you looked different . . . the beard, I guess." He appraised the newly revealed face. "Man, I don't know how I knew it was you."

"Telepathy." Challis winked.

"So how's it going?" There were no traces of Edward G. Robinson. The dark face flashed a smile.

308

"I got a few things figured out. Finally. Now I'm going to hit the road. You're my last stop."

"Well, I tried to keep you covered." He shrugged. "I guess I did okay. You're not back in jail, anyway."

"I'd better go. I wanted to see you . . . say goodbye."

Ralph nodded. "I'm not too good at this. Take care of yourself. . . . You gonna be okay?"

"Sure. You?"

"Oh, don't worry about Ralph Halliday." He looked back at his friends, shook his head. "I take these crazy little bastards and teach them the ropes, take care of them. Hell, I'll be outta here in no time. Next year I'll be in a regular school, y'know? Then I'll pick my shots." He smiled up at Challis.

"Well, goddammit, give me a kiss . . ."

Ralph leaned forward, and their cheeks touched.

"Don't forget the mountain," Challis whispered.

"We were dynamite on the mountain." Ralph stood back. "I better go. Don't want them over here asking questions. . . . Hey, don't be a stranger."

Their eyes met and they laughed.

The wide-bodies slid down out of the eastern sky, glowing pink over the desert, caught the sunset on their cold silver wings, and settled into the bustle of Los Angeles International Airport. He watched from the hangar where Maximus kept the two company jets. He smelled the same oil and fuel that polluted every hangar. Twenty yards away was the place he'd stood a few days before, handcuffed, waiting to disappear inside. Everything had changed, but here he was, waiting to disappear again.

Tully Hacker was talking to a mechanic who'd been playing with the aircraft. Someone from Maximus catering was loading champagne and containers of specially prepared food aboard. Challis watched, felt lightheaded.

Out at the end of the runway a magenta sun was falling into the Pacific, layers of clouds at the horizon cutting it into slices like a fancy Japanese illustration. Hacker left the mechanic, walked stiffly across the oily concrete floor. He looked out at the sun.

309

"Pretty ain't it?" He sighed. He was carrying a Gucci briefcase. "Well, you're doing the right thing."

"What's it like back at the house?"

"Running smoothly. Oh, it's one of your typical Hollywood tragedies, front-page stuff for a day or two . . ." He grinned thinly. "Sol is in seclusion. The studio has issued a statement. Daffy's drunk, sedated —she'll be fine. The little boy—well, it's tough, but kids are resilient." He made a small expressive gesture with his large hands. "This too will pass away, Toby." He rocked back on his heels. "Herbert's going up to see Priscilla after the funeral. Happy ending, maybe. Good man in a pinch, Herbert." He handed the briefcase to Toby. "Everything's in here—you're now a man named Tom Chesswardine. Your whole life story's there, passport, you're even a screenwriter . . . a doctor, no credits, but a letter of introduction to some people you're going to need to know. Money, bank drafts . . . you're a lucky man, you're lucky Sol feels so guilty about everything. Oh, and you'll get a kick out of this—two screenplays in folders, with notes. They need polishes, the Challis touch. Sol told me to tell you the price is a hundred grand each—doesn't want you to think you're taking charity." He laughed roughly, shook his head. Anything I can do for you, Toby?"

"No. No loose ends."

"The woman?"

"No. I'm an invisible man. Old Tom Chesswardine . . . a shadow." He shook Tully's hand. "We'll be in touch."

The pilot and the copilot came through a door. Hacker beckoned to them. "Don, Phil, come here . . . I'd like you to meet your passenger, this is Mr. Chesswardine . . ."

Challis leaned back in the plush swivel chair. The stewardess handed him a card. She was long-legged, big-breasted, and had a face that was pretty in a robot, airbrushed way.

"Those are the films we can run for you in flight, Mr. Chesswardine. Just give us the word." She put his eye out with her smile. Teeth the size of thumbnails. I love you, he thought.

"Read them to me, please." He handed her back the card.

"*Mr. Deeds Goes to Town, Saboteur, Bringing Up Baby, The Bridge on the River Kwai, Topper, On the Town, Ride the Pink Horse—*"

"That's fine," he said. "I'll watch those." The engines were vibrating, they were moving slowly. Tully Hacker was waving. She handed him another card. "Read it to me, please."

"Boned pheasant or Peking duck, fresh sweet peas—"

"Okay, okay. Surprise me."

"And Perrier Jouet champagne." She smiled again. "Are you buckled in?"

"At the very least."

She reached down, patted the buckle to make sure. Then she went away.

"It's a tough life," Challis said aloud. A bad guy. In the movies the bad guys got it in the end. She brought the gorgeous green bottle of champagne with the white flowers cut into the glass, poured him a goblet of the pale gold bubbles.

"Happy days," he said, sipped.

The sky was the color of blood as they lifted off.

The killer was getting away.

A man wearing an immaculate white suit, a pale blue shirt, a white tie with a touch of cream in it, stood above a beach, leaning on a stone wall. The breakers frothed against the pale, smooth sand, and sunshine exploded like a rain of diamonds on the shifting surface of the water. Tanning bodies lay motionless on beach towels, and the soft wind kept the man dry, though the day was hot. He wore dark glasses. He leaned against the wall, watching the people on the beach, who never moved a muscle; then he walked away through the crowds surging along the pavement by the wall.

Bestsellers
from
BALLANTINE